Wicked Fate Lusty Mates

Astrid Vail

Rogue Queen Publishing

Wicked Fate Lusty Mates Omnibus

Cover Art :

Paperback by GetCovers

eBook & Hardcover by Artscandare Book Design

Edited by NiceGirlNaughtyEdits

First Edition: October 2024

ISBN

eBook : 978-1-958641-38-5

Paperback: 978-1-958641-36-1

Hardcover: 978-1-958641-39-2

Broad Content warning includes on page sex scenes, adult language, blood, and death.

This author does not use AI in their writing or cover art.

Blurb & Content Warning

Witches and Lycanthropes are supposed to be enemies, not mates.
Wicked Fate, Lusty Mates is a six part romance series following a pack of lycanthropes and a group of misfit witches as they find love in the most unexpected of ways.
The omnibus includes –
Carnal Moon: A Steamy Paranormal Romance
Wild Moon: A Smoldering Paranormal Romance
Enchanted Moon: A Second Chance Paranormal Romance
Arctic Moon: A Sultry Paranormal Romance
Feral Moon: A Seductive Paranormal Romance
Scarlet Moon: A Spicy Paranormal Romance

Blurbs specific to each story are included before each novella starts.

This book is intended for mature readers only.

Content Warnings for each book areas follows:

Carnal Moon: steamy on page sex scenes, primal chase, and language.

Wild Moon: spicy on page sex scenes, near-death experiences that involve water and fire, relocation, divorce over infertility, past family & relationship mental abuse, cheating (not done by the main characters), and language.

Enchanted Moon: spicy on page sex scenes, abduction, murder, death, past child abuse, and language.

Arctic Moon: spicy on page sex scenes, murder, death, past child & spousal abuse, and language.

Feral Moon: Graphic sex scenes, references to past abuse & animal experiments, blood, murder, and explicit language.

Scarlet Moon: on page sex scenes, rough sex, primal chase, blood, death, sibling fighting, mentioned past family abuse and trauma, unhealthy coping to trauma, losing a loved one, patricide, thoughts of suicide (not acted upon), and adult language.

Carnal Moon

WICKED FATE LUSTY MATES

ASTRID VAIL

Blurb & Content Warning

Enter a new world of desire with a coven of misfit witches and the steamy discovery of their lycanthrope mates in this brand-new series by Astrid Vail.

Standing in a room full of lycanthropes, on the night of an exclusive event, is the last place Lily ever thought she would find herself.

To make matters even more complicated, she finds herself in the arms of the extremely handsome pack alpha, just the man and wolf, she came to speak with on behalf of her coven.

Only he is seductively whispering that she is his mate and has no plans on letting her go.

The only problem...

Witches and Lycanthropes are supposed to be age-old enemies, not mates.

WICKED FATE, LUSTY MATES

This novella is intended for mature readers only. **Content warning** includes steamy on page sex scenes, primal chase, and language.

Chapter One

LILY

"LILY, I STILL THINK you should let me come with you. Or better yet, I can go in your place."

Lily shook her head and tucked her hands farther under her thighs. She didn't want to show her best friend and coven member how nervous she really was by picking at her nails. "Silina, you know why I volunteered. Out of everyone in our coven, I am the least witchy. You, on the other hand, would probably get mauled after one sniff."

Silina side-eyed her before glancing out her car window at the wrought-iron gates across the road. "I still don't like leaving you here without any means of leaving."

"It's called legs and feet. I can walk out of there at any time. Plus, I have my phone."

"But—"

"No, this is happening. It's an opportunity we can't pass up. Our head priestess has been trying to get into contact with the pack alpha for a while now. This party gets me in front of him, so I can plead our case."

Silina sighed and tapped her hand against the steering wheel of her little hatchback. "I know you are right; I just don't like you going in there without anyone to watch your back. You can't even..."

She trailed off and Lily finished her sentence for her. "I can't do magic. I'm powerless. I know. That is why I'm the best person to do this."

"Rely on your instincts, Lily. And you're not powerless, you have a banging body. Men think with their dick nine times out of ten, so use it to your advantage if you need to get out of trouble. It doesn't matter if they're human, lycanthropes, or mages. They are all the same."

Lily choked slightly at Silina's words but didn't say anything. There wasn't enough time tonight to unpack *that* baggage. Silina might be her best friend in the coven and outside of it, but Lily knew relatively nothing about her past.

She took a deep breath and glanced at the clock on the dashboard. It was nearing ten p.m., and if she was really going to go through with this plan, she had to get going. She reached out and hugged Silina. "I promise I'll trust my gut. And if anything happens, I know you will come to my rescue."

Silina hugged her back. "I'm off from the club tonight. So yes, please call me if you need anything."

"And you won't wait here all night in the car."

"No promises," Silina murmured.

Lily let her comment slide as she released the hug and opened the door. The night was quiet, the waxing moon hanging high in the starless sky. It was slightly pink. A good omen. And it soothed Lily's nerves a little bit. The moon called to her in a way Lily suspected it called to the Lycans, if only on a smaller scale.

Except she wasn't a Lycan.

She was a witch.

Lily took a deep breath and focused her gaze on the wrought-iron gate in front of her. She shoved her shaking hands into her coat pocket, her fingers grazing the ticket the coven had bought collectively for this moment. She closed her eyes, trying to calm her racing heart. This had been her idea, after all, and she couldn't back out now. She had to do it for her coven, to find a way to speak to the biggest supernatural community in the city and not be shut out. And this was the easiest way to meet with *him.*

The alpha of the biggest Lycan pack in their city.

Resolve steeled her spine as Lily strode across the road, putting one heeled boot in front of the other. Far too soon for her liking, she was front and center. Reaching out, she pushed the buzzer.

Crackling of the intercom connecting seemed too loud for the night, and a shiver ran down Lily's spine as a growl echoed forth. "Name?"

Gulping, mouth suddenly going dry, she coughed, "Lilian Page."

The intercom clicked, and the gates slid open, rustling the fallen leaves surrounding it. Lily hurried through, her boots clicking against the asphalt drive.

Fear pulled at her deep inside. *It wasn't too late*, her inner monologue screamed. She could leave. She could walk right back out that gate and Silina wouldn't say a word. She would back her claim to tell her coven the alpha wouldn't see her. Wouldn't speak to her about such nonsense of treaties and abolishing old traditions to usher forth new ones. A world where witches and Lycans held hands and skipped through fields of daisies.

Lily snorted, and her fear faded slightly.

Okay, those weren't exactly the words the high priestess used, but the image in her mind set her at ease. Quickly glancing behind her, she caught Silina still sitting there in the car. She had a phone out and her feet propped out of the window.

"Silina," she hissed and made a shooing motion with her hands.

Silina responded with her middle finger, and Lily shook her head. There was nothing she could do about her staying out here all night, so she turned and continued along the drive. She followed the sound of music and boisterous laughter, up toward the sprawling estate dead ahead.

By the time Lily made it to the front steps of the main house, she was sweating. Why on goddess's green earth did the invite specifically request all guests to be dropped off at the front gates? It just seemed cruel and unusual to make someone walk up the winding drive. And in heels, nonetheless. Then again, many of the guests were probably lycanthropes, which meant they were in way better shape than she was.

Lily winced and hobbled forward, almost tripping up the four steps to the open front door. She wanted to kick off her shoes and just sit. To take a quick breather before marching into a house full of Lycans. She bit her lip, almost contemplating it, but she was already late. The party would be in full swing by now and she had to grab the attention of the alpha before midnight fell. Because there was no way Lily planned to stay around for the second part of the evening.

She made it two steps inside the foyer before a stylishly clad woman in a suit and heels stepped into view. The woman in question bowed, and before Lily could stop herself, she bowed as well. A burning sensation of a flush engulfing her whole body hit Lily immediately, and the woman cocked her head. Fear bubbled below her breastbone as the woman's nostrils flared, scenting the air. Lily gulped and hoped she didn't smell too witchy. Which was one of the main reasons why she volunteered for this task. She was more likely to pass the sniff test than anyone else in her coven. The woman smiled and extended a hand. "Ticket, please?"

Lily's heart pounded away in her chest as she scrambled for the ticket shoved in her coat pocket. She thrust it out like a madwoman, visibly shaking. Goddess be, this really was a bad idea. But it was her bad idea, and she had to see it through. The woman's lips twitched, as if she were suppressing a smile, but Lily couldn't be sure.

"Follow me, please," the woman chirped and turned on her heel. Lily nodded, even though the woman was already striding away. She hurried after her, only to slide to a stop in front of two doors. Next to the doors was a rack of black garment bags.

She briefly wondered why it would just be sitting in the hallway when a party was clearly in full swing in the house. The woman faced her once more and extended a hand. "Jacket and purse."

Lily shrugged off her jacket and small purse, handing them over to the woman before pulling at the hem of her tight dark blue pencil skirt. Along with the silver silken blouse she wore, Lily knew the outfit accentuated her curves just right. The ticket had said the party was themed, Suits and Bunnies, but Lily had no idea what the bunny part was about, so she settled on semi-formal sexy. She had even left the blouse slightly undone so the sheer lacy top underneath could peek out. Silina had called the look "office sexy." Yet the look the woman was giving Lily right now made her realize she might be underdressed for the occasion. "Ummm..." Lily wiped her sweaty hands against her skirt. "Do I look okay?"

The woman grabbed one of the black clothing bags. "Doesn't matter what you came in wearing. We have a strict dress code for this event. And you are definitely not a suit." She thrust out the bag in Lily's direction and pointed toward one of the small doors. "You can change in there. Your articles of clothing will be out here when you leave."

To demonstrate her point, the woman opened the door and a closet full of attire and coats greeted her. She pulled out a hanger and attached Lily's coat and purse before placing them in the closet. She motioned to the other door again, and Lily glanced at the mysterious garment bag in her hands. The label on the outside sported the number fourteen, and Lily arched her eyebrow. "How did you know my dress size?"

The woman dazzled Lily with a smile. "It's a special talent of mine. Now, please change, while I find a set of appropriate heels for you." She motioned to the door again.

Lily glanced down at her knee-high black leather boots with their chunky heels and sighed. The woman was probably right, and the shoes she was wearing were not going to go well with whatever was in the garment bag. Lily gave the woman a shy smile and whispered, "I'm a size nine in shoes."

The woman nodded but didn't say anything, clearly waiting for Lily to go into the mysterious room to change. Seeing as this was going to be the only way of getting into the party and fulfilling the task she volunteered for, Lily turned quickly and opened the door, stepping inside. Her jaw dropped as she realized the room wasn't just a simple changing room, but a powder room. Decorated in an eggshell and light mint color scheme, Lily stifled her laugh of disbelief. There was even gold speckling around the sink and on the floor tiles. It was gaudy and rich and everything Lily loathed. She scanned the rest of the room and shook her head. "Unbelievable."

She turned around and draped her garment bag on the hook bolted to the door. Unzipping the bag quickly, she stared in equal amounts of shock and horror. Compared to this outfit, the powder room was relatively tame. Her hand reached out of its own accord, stroking the dark silk scrap of fabric in front of her. A flush overcoming her body encased her from head to toe. This was almost too much, but she steeled her spine and slowly extracted the corseted bodice and barely-there mini skirt she knew wouldn't fully cover her ass. A pair of silken white bunny ears, along with a fluffy white tail, fell from the bag onto the floor. Lily cursed. "You have got to be fucking kidding me."

Chapter Two

HUNTER

HUNTER DIDN'T WANT TO be here.

Except this was his house, his late family's estate, and tonight was his year to host this ridiculous Suits and Bunnies event. The first part of the event allowed those in attendance to sniff each other out and if they wanted to, move onto the second part of the evening. A nice little primal chase through the woods. Exactly the thing Hunter wanted on his property.

A nice forest sex party.

Not.

He groaned inside. Hunter liked to live a more secluded life. He kept his pack in line, was a leading force on the supernatural council, and enjoyed his solitude. Which was something he really wished he had right now. Instead, his senses were on high alert as he watched the party goers mill about, a mixing of Lycans from various packs and a spattering of humans brave enough to show up. There were no other supernatural's present and Hunter was relieved. His species was high-strung, dangerous, and very territorial. Lycans rarely got along with others besides humans. Maybe because they had more in common with their human half than with their wolfish brethren?

Hunter mused over his philosophical thoughts, barely paying attention to the Lycan speaking to him, when he smelled it. The biting scent of magic. It was faint, oh so faint, but he picked it up all the same. Sweet and tart and absolutely captivating. His eyes darted around the room until he spotted the culprit.

His mouth watered instantly as he eyed the witch, who dared to enter a den full of Lycans.

A voluptuous beauty with a waterfall of dark ruby-red hair and creamy skin stood awkwardly in the middle of the room. She wore a ridiculous rabbit costume designated for the bunnies at the party. Except it didn't look so ridiculous on *her*. The corseted black bodice with white stitching hugged her curves, barely containing her luscious breasts. She tugged at the silk mini skirt, trying to keep her round ass from falling out. Hunter couldn't stop staring, his eyes roaming from the silly bunny tail she was wearing all the way up to the equally silly ears. Fuck, he wanted to chase her down and rut with her right in the middle of the dining room. He wondered how she would sound with him behind her, driving his throbbing cock into her warm pussy. Or better yet, with his face buried between her legs. She could even keep the bunny ears on; they looked cute on her.

The Lycan he was speaking to tilted his head to the side, following his gaze. The man's intake of breath made Hunter want to rip him to shreds. Actually, he wanted to rip this entire room to shreds, killing all who dared.

Oh shit.

This was not good.

Hunter barely processed his heightened emotions and the meaning behind them before someone approached *his* redheaded beauty. He snarled as the person in question pointed right at her face, crowding her in. Her beautiful features scrunched in panic, and she took a step away from the man, hands held up in defense.

The redhead teetered on the stupid stiletto heels she was wearing and crashed into Hunter's chest. His breathing had turned ragged in the few seconds it had taken him to make his way over. Yet feeling the redhead pushed against him calmed his racing pulse.

She would be safe now. Now that he was here to protect her.

Hunter linked his arm around her ribcage, right under her breasts, and pulled her in closer. His movement made her tits jiggle in the most enticing way, and it was a struggle to pull his eyes away from them. Yet he managed, barely.

His gaze followed the dip of her collarbone and up her slender neck to her face. Her full, lush lips were parted in surprise, and when he finally met her eyes, his breath caught. Those pretty hazel eyes would be the death of him. He reached up to trail his fingers across his redhead's racing pulse before whispering, "You're safe now."

The redhead opened her mouth before shutting it quickly, her eyes darting across his face frantically. She finally glanced away and to the man standing in front of her.

Oh yes. The waste of space harassing her. He should probably get rid of him.

He tore his eyes away from his redhead and focused his stare on the Lycan in question. "Who are you?"

The Lycan tried to meet his gaze, but it was impossible unless he was an alpha like Hunter. In the end, he settled a loathing stare at Hunter's redheaded beauty. "Alpha Hunter, my name is Derek, and the woman you are claiming to protect is a witch."

The redhead in Hunter's arms visibly flinched from the malice in the Lycan's voice. Which only made him squeeze her tighter to his frame. Fuck, she could probably feel how hard he was right now. Shit... Her short skirt had slid up when he grabbed her. Dropping his hand to her thick, warm thigh, he pulled it back into place. She was his, and no one was going to see her assets but him.

The redhead squeaked as his hand snaked around her thigh, and Hunter buried his head in her neck and breathed in deeply. He chuckled softly and nipped her skin before lifting his head and gazing at the Lycan before them. "She is but a little witch with barely any power. She isn't causing any trouble, unlike you."

Derek's face turned red as he sputtered, "Alpha Hunter, you don't understand. She's a double-crossing cu—"

Hunter moved, hand wrapping around Derek's throat before he could finish his sentence. "Watch your tone while in my house, you useless excuse for a Lycan."

Derek struggled feebly before giving up and muttering, "Apologies, Alpha Hunter."

Hunter growled and jerked his head. "Don't apologize to me. Apologize to..."

He trailed off as the redhead wiggled and slipped from his embrace. She glanced between the two of them, cheeks stained a rosy pink. "I'm... I'm... I shouldn't have come here," she stuttered before spinning on her flimsy heels and running out of the room.

Hunter's low growl reverberated through his chest as he watched his little bunny run away from him. He wanted... no, *needed* to go after her, but a crowd was gathering around them. He glared at Derek and shoved him away. The useless waste of space fell to the ground, rubbing at his throat. A bruise was already forming on his neck, but he would be fine, unfortunately.

Lycans healed fast.

Derek coughed, clearing his throat. "Alpha Hunter. I know this witch, and she can't be—"

Hunter cut him off with a swipe of his hand. "Get out of my house."

"But... but I came here to pension—"

Hunter roared, "I don't care who you are or why you are here. Get. Out. Of. My. House."

Derek scrambled and ran toward the outer doors. Thankfully, not the ones the redheaded beauty had left through. The crowd whispered and departed, the clinking of glasses and awkward laughter filling the room once more.

Hunter stalked over to the bar and gulped down a glass of water. He was drinking his third glass when a presence made herself known by his right side.

"Well... that was interesting, Alpha Brother."

Hunter glanced over to the female Lycan, his twin sister, to be exact. She gave him a wolfish smile as she leaned back against the bar top. "Is she still here?"

His sister laughed and grabbed the glass of water out of his hand. She twirled the glass like it held a fine whiskey instead of water as she glanced over the room of people. "Yes, Brother. The witch is still here. I followed her. She is in the lady's room, probably calming down after that hedonistic display of power you just demonstrated."

Hunter growled and grabbed the water back from his twin and gulped it down. He glanced at the long mirror behind the wall before looking away quickly. His normal brown eyes glinted with amber flecks, the sight of his wolf peeking out from within. He needed to calm down before he went after his redheaded witch.

"I want you on her all night until I calm down my wolf."

The purr that came from Hunter's sister could have rivaled that of any cat shifter. "Gladly."

Hunter grabbed her by the arm, territorial rage almost blinding him. "Sister, please."

She scoffed and rolled her eyes before peeling his fingers off her arm. "I'm just playing. I won't make any moves on your pretty little witch."

Hunter sighed in relief, and his twin pushed away from the bar. He watched her go and took a deep breath before focusing his thoughts inward to tame his wayward wolf.

His Lycan half howled at him, and he reassured his beast that they would claim the witch soon enough. He just had to figure out a way to convince his bunny that she was his.

Because there was only one logical reason behind the way he and his wolf felt in this moment.

The little witch was his mate.

Chapter Three

LILY

"Breathe. Just breathe. Everything will be fine if you just breathe."

Lily gripped the edge of the porcelain sink so hard she thought it might crack. A mix of embarrassment, rage, and lust flowed through her. Lily really, really wanted to dismiss that last feeling. Goddess above, she cannot be lusting after the sexy Lycan, the alpha of the pack her high priestess wanted Lily to make negotiations with. And she really needed to stop thinking about the way his arms felt when he wrapped them around her. The way he put his face in her neck and growled...

Nope. Most definitely shouldn't be thinking about that.

She glanced into the mirror and gritted her teeth.

"Breathe in. One. Two. Three. Breathe out. One. Two. Three," Lily murmured to herself over and over until she could finally think. The flush covering her face and chest finally dissipated, just as the sound of heels coming closer registered. The doorknob rattled, and Lily called out. "Occupied."

"No shit. Let me in. We need to talk."

Lily blinked, the woman's honeyed growl filling the small bathroom she had locked herself in. "Ummmm... I think you have the wrong person."

The woman on the other side of the door snorted. "No, I most definitely have the right person, little witch."

Panic bubbled under her breastbone and Lily glanced around franticly. There was no way out besides the door in front of her, which looked flimsy now that an angry Lycan female stood on the other side.

"Little witch, my brother sent me to watch you. Now open the damn door before I huff and puff and blow it down."

Lily bit her lip, and with the last ounce of bravery swimming through her veins, she reached forward, and unlocked the door. It creaked open slowly and the female Lycan peered in with a look of surprise on her face. Like she was already planning on breaking down the door and was shocked her threat worked. Lily gave her a hesitant wave and an awkward smile. "Please don't kill me." The female scoffed before stepping inside and shutting the door behind her. She threw the lock and gave Lily a toothy grin.

Lily's grip on the sink tightened once more.

Shit. The Lycan female *was* totally going to kill her.

Hysterical laughter tried to escape as Lily thought about what a mess her death would make. Blood splattered all over the nice mint and eggshell bathroom. She really hated that the colors in the bathroom matched the powder room she was in earlier this evening. A hiccup forced its way out and Lily slapped her hand over her mouth.

The Lycan female gave Lily an odd look and tilted her head, almost as if she was listening. After a moment, she whispered, "Okay, good. No eavesdroppers are present. I'm Sasha, and my brother really, really likes you. Which means I like you. No murder, I promise." She reached out and pulled Lily's hand away from the sink and shook it.

"I'm Li... Li... Lily."

She managed to stammer her name, eyes going wide. The fear of dying dissipated and she glanced at her hand, still being shaken in an ecstatic manner. Now that Sasha mentioned it, she did look vaguely like the Lycan who had rescued her earlier. She sported the same light tan skin, golden brown hair, and caramel brown eyes. They even had the same bone structure, except Sasha had more feminine features. Though, she was taller than her brother.

Lily glanced down quickly. No, they were the same height. She was wearing stilettoes. Just like Lily's, except Sasha looked a lot better in them with her outfit. Lily extracted her hand, and the words tumbled unbidden from her mouth. "Why do you get to wear a sexy pantsuit while all the other ladies are wearing *this* in random colors?"

Lily gestured to herself, and Sasha chuckled before turning to the mirror. She pulled out a tube of liquid red lipstick and started touching up her lips. "Because," she murmured, and Sasha's reflection winked at Lily, "I'm a predator. Not the prey. And there were a few other women out there wearing similar outfits to mine. You just missed them while successfully seducing my brother."

Lily gulped and shook her head as Sasha put the finishing touches on her lips and fluffed her long, curly hair. "I wasn't... I wouldn't... I didn't come here to seduce anyone. I'm sorry I made trouble out there. I was just about to leave, anyway. This was an absolute failure."

Sasha turned slowly, her gaze racking Lily up and down. "You're leaving?"

Lily nodded and hugged herself. "I shouldn't have even shown up. It was a stupid plan."

"Plan?" Sasha echoed.

"Yes, plan. The high priestess has been trying, unsuccessfully, I might add, to speak with the Lycan council. We... I know that witches and Lycans have a tumultuous relationship, but my high priestess wants to... thinks that...." Lily trailed off and shook her head. "I swear I had a whole spiel memorized."

Sasha's lip curled slightly. "Why didn't your high priestess just come herself? Seems cowardly to send you. By yourself, I might add."

Lily gulped and looked down at her feet. "It was my idea. I don't have any power. I have no witchy abilities, so I came here thinking..."

"That you could seduce an alpha without him knowing you were a witch?"

"What! No!" Lily squeaked out and shook her head violently. "I just thought because I don't have power, it wouldn't be seen as invading his territory and I might be able to speak to Gabriel..."

"Hunter," Sasha murmured.

"Er... I mean, Hunter, about possibly speaking to the council on behalf of the coven. But your brother is very busy and is rarely seen in public. And when I saw this event was open to the public, I took a chance at possibly trying the catch his attention."

Lily was panting by the end of her little speech, sweat pooling in places she really didn't want to think about. Great, now she was stinky *and* embarrassed. Wait... Lily frowned. "I thought the alpha's name was Gabriel."

Sasha shook her head. "He prefers to go by his last name."

Lily felt her curiosity take over, but she pushed it down. She didn't need to know why; she just needed to get out of this place. She stared at the expensive gold-flecked tile on the bathroom floor, wishing she was at home vegging out on her comfy couch, eating popcorn, instead of here, stuffed into heels that hurt her feet.

Sasha cleared her throat, and Lily glanced at her. "Who was that Lycan my brother saved you from, anyway? He was a complete douche bag, and I really, really want to kick his ass."

Lily rasped out a laugh and shook her head. "He was someone from my past, from when I first moved here three years ago. We met at a café, and he wouldn't take no for an answer when he asked me out on a date. I finally just gave in and went out to coffee with him. I didn't know he was a Lycan at the time, but once I found out, I told him I was a witch. He was not pleased, to say the least."

Sasha's lip curled up, a growl reverberating from her chest. "That's it. I'm kicking his ass if I ever see him again. This thing between witches and Lycans is old and pointless. A feud that doesn't even make sense anymore."

Lily exhaled a sigh of relief. "I agree. I'm so glad you and your brother agree."

Sasha smirked. "Well, Lily, I think you accomplished your coven's plan. You will most definitely be seeing much more of Hunter again."

Lily frowned. "What do you mean?"

Sasha gave her an innocent look, yet what tumbled out of her mouth was anything but.

"The only time a Lycan acts the way my brother did earlier with a virtual stranger is when that stranger is their mate."

Lily's mouth dropped, and she stared at Sasha in disbelief. She tried to make words come out, but the only thing rattling around in her mind was the word *mate*.

Sasha reached out and unlocked the bathroom door. "Welcome to the family, Little Witch."

Lily was still reeling from the bombshell dropped on her. She flinched as the door closed behind Sasha and she was once again alone in the bathroom. "Mate?" Lily whispered, staring at the mirror. "How could I be a Lycan's mate?"

She stared at her shocked expression reflected in the mirror. Lifting both of her hands, she pressed them against her cheeks. Her skin, only moments before flushed, had become cold and clammy. She shook her head and kicked off her shoes quickly. Picking them up, she dashed out of the bathroom and down the side hall, avoiding the few questions gazes pointed her way. Once she skidded out into the large foyer, she made her way back to the woman who had greeted her barely an hour before. She shoved the heels in her direction. "I need to leave. Can I have my stuff, please?"

The woman nodded before her eyes went wide, looking over Lily's shoulder. She gulped, and Lily didn't need to turn around to know that Gabriel Hunter, Alpha of the Southern Moon pack, was standing right behind her.

Chapter Four

LILY

Lily turned in slow motion, her mind bouncing between one of two scenarios. This was either the start of a badly written horror movie or a porno. Her eyes grazed Hunter's face and her heart beat wildly as he prowled closer. Heat pooled low in her abdomen, her body betraying the feeling she was trying to hide. Fuck, he was sexy as sin.

Porno alert, her mind screamed, and Lily started sweating again. Her mind filtered through two words. Porno. Mate.

Porno.

Mate.

"Seriously, get a fucking grip," Lily muttered, and Hunter paused barely a foot away from her. The blush that was heating Lily's chest and face burned hotter. Shit, she had said that out loud. Well, at least it was better than saying *porno* or *mate* out loud. Lily was still gazing at Hunter's perfectly chiseled face, and it was an effort to avert her gaze. Hunter tilted his head, eyes grazing over Lily's shoulder. She turned her head to see the woman she had all but forgotten about. The head tilt must have been Lycan code to scamper away, because that was just what the woman did.

Hunter took a deep breath and held it for a moment. "Here, let me help you."

Lily shivered, even though she was burning up, as Hunter grabbed her long coat and placed it over her shoulders. He held on to it as she quickly placed her arms through the sleeves. She held her breath as his fingers moved quickly over the buttons. Grabbing her heeled boots, he knelt, his hands hot as a brand against her bare calf. Lily bit her lip to suppress a whimper as he lifted her foot and placed the boot on. She swayed slightly and grabbed his shoulders for support. Her mind splintered into a myriad of wicked thoughts as she felt his hard muscles move under her hands. He finished putting on her other boot and stood. Lily's hands slid from his shoulders to rest on his chest. She stared at him, mouth slightly agape. "Thank you."

Hunter reached out, his fingers slightly caressing her skin as he moved a lock of her hair away from her face and tucked it behind her ear. "Little Witch,

I had hoped you would stay a little longer. You brighten up this drab party."

"You... you can call me Li... Lily," she stammered out while staring at his perfect lips.

Hunter smiled and leaned closer. Lily gulped, torn between pushing away or clutching his shirt. Insanity on her part seemed to win out as her hands gripped him closer. Hunter's lips scrapped against her ear. "I wish you were staying, Lily. It would be a pleasure to see what would happen between the two of us once midnight strikes."

His words made Lily pull away, doubt and uncertainty making her commonsense return. This had to be an elaborate ruse to get into her panties. This couldn't be real. "I'm sure you say that to all the ladies."

Hunter blinked slowly, as if stunned, and Lily mentally chastised herself. Great. She just called the Alpha of a Lycan pack a floozie. She was supposed to be helping her coven, trying to get an Alpha to take a meeting with their High Priestess. And she was most definitely not supposed to walk away from this party with a Lycan as a mate. Lily gulped, her throat parched, as if she had just run a mile and she realized they were just staring at each other. Her eyes grew wide as Hunter grazed his fingertips down her neck, placing his hand on her rapidly beating pulse. She made a noise, somewhere between a whimper and a gasp, before quickly taking a step away.

Hunter let his hand fall and Lily took another step back. "I, ummm... I should, I need..." Holy shit, she was a mess. "I, uhhh..."

She took another step back, angling toward the door. Hunter's eyes glowed amber as he watched her walk away, his body tense. She had almost made it to the door when he finally spoke. "I've never participated in a primal chase. Never interested me until now. Not until I gazed upon you."

Her heart skittered in her chest, and she wanted to curse at him. Was he saying this wasn't a stupid prank? That she, a powerless witch, was somehow special?

It was just too hard to accept. He was a Lycan, and she was a witch.

The word mate came to the forefront of her mind, and she shook it away. Now that she had put a few feet of distance between them, she could think a little better. "Your... your sister said I was your mate. I can't be your mate. You don't really want me. I'm just a powerless witch, no one of any consequence."

Then again, maybe her brain was still mush. Why had she just blurted out her greatest shame to this relative stranger?

A growl reverberated through the foyer, and Hunter stalked forward, pinning her between the door and his arms. She should have been petrified, yet her body betrayed her, arousal running through her bloodstream instead. She titled her chin up so she could gaze into Hunter's eyes. "You're wrong," he whispered.

"What?"

"You're not of no consequence. You are mine, and I am yours."

She wet her lips, swallowing the words she wanted to say. She wanted to say witches and Lycans were timeless enemies. That he should be interested in one of the classier women milling around inside the party. Not her, a self-proclaimed couch potato. Plus, he was an Alpha. He needed a strong mate, not someone like her. The words jumbled in her mind as Hunter pushed in closer and dipped his head. His lips scrapped against her ear as he asked again, "Why can't I be your mate, Lily? Am I not good enough for you?"

She turned her head, breathing in his scent. He smelled of the change in the seasons, spring on the verge of summer. Lily lost her goddess-driven mind once more and her tongue darted out to lick his neck. He tasted like home. She felt it in her bones, down in her core, and within her bloodstream. Everything he was and what they could be together filled her mind, and she felt a shift within her.

A spark of something buried deep, a lingering taste of magic.

Hunter groaned and pushed her against the door, and she could feel his hard erection between them. "Little Witch..." he rumbled and trailed a hand up her spine and neck, grasping her hair. He tilted her head slightly, and Lily angled her lips against his.

She opened her mouth, the kiss deep and claiming from the second their lips touched. Her entire body hummed to life. Electricity shot through her, and the sounds of fireworks burst through her mind. Hunter's hands slid down her spine to grasp her bare thighs. He lifted her up and Lily wrapped her legs around his waist. Somewhere in the back of her mind, Lily knew she needed to come up for air. That anyone could walk by right now and catch them mouth fucking each other on the entryway door.

Instead, she wrapped her hands around Hunter's neck, gripping his hair. Her hips moved of their own accord in slow, agonizing circles, rubbing her core against Hunter's straining erection. He matched her pace and the electricity running through her veins cascaded outwards. She felt the shock wave ripple through her every nerve ending, searing her lips. It felt good, too good. Lily broke the kiss first, needing to think through her lust-filled mind. Hunter growled and Lily groaned in response. The growl tugged at some primal instinct deep inside of her, and she wondered if he would growl like that between her legs. Hunter leaned down, nipping along her neck to her collarbone. Her breath hitched and Lily tugged at Hunter's hair.

Lily muttered a curse and yanked harder until Hunter finally looked at her. The intensity of his eyes burned her all the way down to her toes. She was ready to give everything to this Lycan she barely knew, and that thought alone should have scared her. As she searched his eyes, Hunter did the same. She leaned in to kiss him again, to tell him he could chase her under the moon, when a very pointed cough broke into the moment between them.

Chapter Five

HUNTER

HUNTER COULDN'T THINK.

His entire body hummed with static electricity, and his skin felt too tight. The witch in his arms was all soft skin and breathless moans. He could smell her arousal, yet she resisted him, her mind trying to find the logic behind the mate bond fighting to tether them together. Then she licked his neck, and he became unhinged. He kissed her with as much ferocity as he could manage. Claiming her as his mate in the only way she would understand. She just had to trust him.

He heard the fireworks going off outside, signaling that the chase would be starting soon, but he couldn't think about that. All he could concentrate on was his little witch in his arms, with her thick thighs wrapped around his waist.

He had her pushed up against the main door, his thick erection grinding against her wet pussy. She moved her hips in tandem with his, and he had to physically restrain himself from unzipping his pants and plunging his cock inside of her.

Fuck. His little witch, his fate-given mate, already had him wrapped around her delicate fingers. He would follow her like a good fucking wolf to the ends of the world if that was what she wanted. He growled as she broke the kiss, and Hunter started kissing and nipping around her neck. She pulled at his hair, squirming in his grasp. Finally, his little witch yanked hard enough to pull his head up. Their gazes connected, and he fell even harder into the deep chasm of her enchanting eyes. Her gaze seared him down to his bones and into the entire fabric of his being.

And he saw it in her eyes.

His little witch was about to give in. She wanted this just as much as he did. She was going to say yes to him, to this, to their mating bond.

Hunter leaned in for another kiss, just as a very loud and very annoying cough interrupted the moment.

He was going to murder whoever had just interrupted them, very... *very* slowly, with lots and lots of torture. A growl reverberated from his chest, and he bared his teeth before glancing over his shoulder.

His sister coughed into her hand and shrugged. He wanted to wipe that stupid shit-eating grin off her face as Lily squirmed in his grip again. He loosened his hold, allowing her to slide down his body to the floor. "What do you want, Sasha?"

Hunter's sister clapped her hands together and pointed at him and his little witch. "This I like. You two look adorable together. Butttt..."

She trailed off, and Hunter whistled through clenched teeth. "It's about to start, and I need to give the fucking speech, don't I?"

Sasha nodded and glanced over his shoulder expectantly at Lily. Hunter followed her gaze to his panting witch. She gulped, her beautiful rose-pink blush covering her chest and face. Lily shook a curtain of ruby-red hair over her face and mumbled something about needing some air. Her hand clawed at the doorknob, and Hunter rested his hand over hers. He opened the door for her, showing his little witch she wasn't trapped.

Glancing up at him, her hazel eyes darkened as they roamed over his face. She had been so quick to get away from him after their kiss, yet the look in her eyes made it seem like he was rejecting her. He leaned down and rested his forehead against hers. "Get your air, my little witch. But please don't leave. At least not without saying goodbye first."

She blinked quickly and broke contact, taking a wobbling step outside before turning to look back at him. "I... I won't leave," she stammered before shutting the door in his face.

That simple act alone equally ripped out Hunter's heart and made his stomach flutter with happiness. She wasn't going to leave. His little witch was just right outside. She hadn't rejected him, even if she did just shut the door in his face.

Hunter cracked his neck before straightening his tie and shirt. His mate had managed to untuck it with her hold on him. He chuckled, knowing that if their make-out session had lasted even a moment longer, he would have lost control and rutted her right against the door. For some reason, Hunter thought his sexy little witch would like that. "Later," he murmured as he licked his lips, the taste of her sweet lips against his still lingering. He would fuck her good and long against the door later... and probably the stairs, the wall, on top of the table in the dining room after he thoroughly worshiped her voluptuous body with long licks and—

The annoying laughter of his guests pulled him out of his dirty thoughts, and he snapped his eyes up to his still-waiting sister. She was looking at the ceiling, humming lightly and rocking on her heels. "Go watch my mate," he growled and pointed out the door.

Sasha snapped her head down and growled right back, "Is there a *please* attached to that order, Brother?"

Her eyes flashed with fury as she met his gaze; the only other Lycan in this house who had the power to do so. He breathed deeply, but held her gaze. "Please, Sister. I am on the edge right now. You know I mean no disrespect."

The fury slipped from her eyes, and she glanced away, before sighing with much more drama than needed. "Fineeeee, but hurry up. There is a sexy little blonde inside that I have had my eyes on for a bit. I've been slowly working my wiles on her, and I think she will let me chase her instead of the brutish Lycan male she came with."

Hunter barked out a laugh as she stalked past him and dramatically opened the door. She yelled, "Lilyyyyy, wait for meeeeee."

He shook his head before stalking back into the party to deliver a speech and make sure everything was in order for the chase.

Then he would get back to his own personal chase and convince his beautiful mate that this thing between them was very much real and everlasting. And once he did, he was never going to let her go.

Chapter Six

LILY

LILY STARED AT THE slightly pinkish moon in the sky and sighed. She wanted to kick off her shoes, strip naked, and bathe in the gorgeous moonlight to calm her racing mind. She didn't know why, as she had never actually bathed in the moonlight, but she just knew it would calm her down. It was something she always wanted to do but never acted on. Like a lot of things in her life. She always made up some sort of excuse as to why she couldn't. But she knew deep down inside what the real reason was.

She was a fool, a scared fool. In all aspects of her life, even now, her self-proclaimed mate was inside, waiting for her return. And what did she do after almost giving in, after finally stilling her racing mind and seeing that the growing magical bond between them was actually real?

She ran away to sit on an uncomfortable cement step, thinking up lame excuses for why she couldn't be his mate. She didn't even want to think of the remains of magic swirling inside of her from the kiss they shared. Something she had all but given up on ever feeling.

A mate and magic waited for her inside, if only she had the nerve to take the first step. Lily's thoughts skittered back and forth until a feminine bellow echoed out into the night. "Lilyyyyy, wait for meeeeee."

The mad clacking of heels running down the steps interrupted her thoughts as Sasha plopped down next to her with a large grin plastered across her face. Lily shied away, not wanting Hunter's sister to see the doubt clouding her mind. "Did my m..., er, Hunter send you to watch me?"

Lily had almost slipped, calling Hunter her mate. It already felt so natural and good. So why was she fighting so hard against it? Sasha snorted at her almost slip but didn't call her out on it.

"My brother is inside making sure part two of this shindig starts rolling. Speaking of which, are you going to do it?"

Lily blinked. "Do what?"

"The chase and accept my brother as your mate."

Her eyes grew wide at the question, her mind already spitting out reasons why she couldn't, even as her body turned to mush just thinking about it. Sasha held up her hand before Lily was able to speak. "How about this... tell me what you are worried about. Ask *me* all your burning questions and maybe my answers can easy your mind."

Lily felt a bit of weight lift off her chest and nodded. She asked the one question that had been skittering across her mind from the start. "Do I have a choice?"

Sasha's face softened, her grin falling into a slight lip tilt. She reached out to grab Lily's hand. "Of course, you do. You can walk away right now. You don't have to accept the mate bond."

Lily felt the sweet rush of relief pass through her. She had a choice. She could walk away. That was, until she thought about Hunter going out and mating with another woman. Jealousy bloomed throughout her, and she had to push it down.

She needed to get a grip on her emotions. One minute, she wanted to run away and, the next minute, she was more than willing to throw hands at anyone who dared touch her mate.

She closed her eyes and took a deep breath. Fuck, it was getting harder and harder to not think about Hunter being her mate. "What is the mating bond, exactly?" she asked. "Is it just a breeding thing? Or is it something more?"

Sasha laughed. "No, it isn't some sort of breeding thing. The mate bond is something much more; it is the connection to your other half. A ying and yang of sorts. Stars that shine brighter when they are together."

Lily glanced at Sasha out of the corner of her eye as the Lycan female's voice softened and cracked. She was staring up at the stars, eyes glistening before shaking her head and caught Lily looking at her. She saw something flash behind Sasha's eyes, something broken and bruised. Reaching out, she grabbed her hand. "Are you okay?"

Sasha took a deep breath and smiled weakly. It was a stark contrast to the confident woman Lily had experienced earlier. "Don't worry about me. This is about you and my brother. What do you feel deep down inside of you? Focus on that."

Lily gulped and did as Sasha said. She focused on the burning feeling in her heart, the understanding flowing through her veins. She had to trust her intuition, and her intuition was screaming at her that everything would work out better than she could ever dream.

Sasha straightened and stood, her demanding presence back in full force, her metaphorical armor sliding back into place, and Lily focused her gaze back to the Lycan female. "A mate bond doesn't happen to everyone. It's rare enough to be special, but you still need to choose. Because when the mate bond snaps into place, there is no undoing it. Our Alpha, my brother, is a good person. And our pack is a lot more progressive than others.

You being a witch doesn't matter to us. Not like that dick face from before. We aren't like that. Even if you weren't my brother's mate, he would have intervened. Honestly, I was about to intervene before my brother all but tackled you."

Tears welled in Lily's eyes at her words. Everything about this was alien and strange, yet... it didn't feel that way. Sasha and Hunter already felt like coming home and sitting down in front of a toasty fire after walking miles through a snowstorm. She couldn't explain the feeling, just that it was right. She took a deep breath and nodded.

Sasha beamed down at her and extended her hand. "Is that a yes, then?"

Fear and doubt still tugged at Lily, trying to cloud the feelings in her heart, but she buried them and reached out. Sasha pulled her into a standing position and waited for Lily to answer her question.

"Yes."

Sasha's grin glinted against the moonlit as she tugged Lily back up the stairs and into the foyer. Yet instead of heading back into the main party room, she tugged her to the left and toward the stairs. "Let's get you into something much more suited to running through the woods."

"Wellllll, it's *technically* more comfortable," Lily muttered while looking this way and that in the long mirror. She was dressed in a ridiculously short, black, silky slip. She could clearly make out her hard nipples through the fabric, and her booty was a hairsbreadth away from being revealed. Sasha was still clambering around in the large closest of the bedroom she had dragged Lily into.

Lily frowned and adjusted the silly rabbit ears still on her head. Sasha had insisted on keeping them on. Something about looking like a tasty little snack...

"Fuck ya," Sasha yelled, and a pair of shoes flew across the room, hitting the floor with a thump. She emerged a second later with a cheeky smile on her face. "Let's go, let's go. Don't wanna be late."

Lily tugged at the slip and sat down on the bed, reaching for the shoes, whilst trying to keep the slip from riding up. Sasha snorted at her struggles before rushing over to help. "Are you sure there isn't anything longer in the closest I could wear?"

Sasha shrugged. "Well, you wouldn't go with my naked idea, so no."

"I'm not prancing around butt ass naked with all these people around. Oh..."

"Oh, what?"

Fear wrapped its way up her spine for a moment. "The other Lycan guy won't be there, do you think?"

Sasha snorted and shook her head. "Hell no. Hunter kicked him out of the house immediately. He is long gone, probably running home to his rich daddy with his tail quiet literally tucked between his legs."

Lily sighed in relief before panic gripped her heart and she lunged across the bed, snatching up her purse and pulling out her cell phone. Her hands shook violently, and Sasha grabbed her hands.

"Lily, what wrong? I can smell your terror suddenly. If you don't want—"

"No... no, it's Silina. She... she... she was waiting at the gates in a car. What if he attacked her because he was angry about..."

Tears hazed her vision and Sasha grabbed the phone from her hands. "Breath, Lily... Breath. We have security cameras pointed out that way. We would have been alerted if anything happened."

Lily gulped as Sasha put her phone back in her hand and scrolled through her contacts until Silina's name came up. She whispered a silent thank you as she pushed the call number.

Silina picked up on the third ring. "You okay, Lily? Need me to pick you up?"

Lily closed her eyes, and sighed heavily. "No, no, I just wanted to make sure you were safe. You aren't still waiting, right? You left?"

"Ya, I went to a coffee shop down the road. But I can be there in five minutes if you need me."

"No need, I'll be here... for a while still."

A long silence greeted Lily, and she pulled the phone away to make sure the call didn't drop. "Silina?"

A rough chuckle finally came over the line. "You are staying past midnight?"

Lily gulped. "Yes."

Silina laughed again. "You dirty little horn dog, I love you. Get some and stay safe. Call me in the morning."

With her parting words, the line went dead, and Lily bit her lip, doubt starting to keep in again. Sasha patted Lily's thigh before hauling her up to standing and grabbing her hand. "Okay, your friend is fine and seems approving of you staying here. So enough muttering and whining. If you keep it up, I'm going to throw you over my shoulder and chase you through those woods myself."

Lily gave Sasha the once-over and almost... *almost* said she would like to see her try. But she really only wanted one person to chase her through the woods, and that was Hunter. She took another deep and stabilizing breath, pushing the keeping doubt away. Lily knew if she didn't go through with this, she would regret it for the rest of her life. She motioned to the door, "Fine, Fine, let's go."

Sasha squealed and clapped her hands before herding Lily out the door and down the stairs.

Chapter Seven

LILY

"Everyone is already outside," Sasha muttered as she kicked off her high heels at the sliding glass door leading to the massive backyard. The woods beckoned silently, pushing up against the well-manicured lawn. A small group of guests stood on the lawn in various states of undress and Lily searched for Hunter among the group. Her heart squeezed, anxiety pooling through her body when she couldn't find him.

"Where is he?" she hissed before realizing Sasha wasn't next to her anymore.

A strong arm encircled her waist from behind, and Lily crashed into a hard chest with a squeak. She grabbed the man's bare forearm and looked up. Hunter's gaze caught hers and his eyes pierced her down to the depths of her soul. Lily whimpered and squeezed her thighs shut, her pussy already going slick from just his penetrating gaze.

Oh, goddess above, she should not have thought of the word penetrate. Her pussy clenched at the thought of something else of his penetrating her.

"Where is who?" he rumbled before dipping his head and nipping at her lips. He squeezed Lily even tighter when she nipped his lips back.

"You," she breathed out before turning in his grasp, burying her hands into his short hair and standing on her tiptoes. His eyes widened slightly at her boldness, then he chuckled.

"Little Witch, I have a feeling you will be forever surprising me."

Lily smiled at his words and kissed him. Hunter tucked her against his body, hand tangling in her hair as he deepened the kiss. Lily wasn't sure how long they stood there, exploring each other's mouths.

Suddenly, Hunter broke the kiss, and Lily gasped as his eyes flashed amber. He sucked in a deep breath and an involuntary shiver ran down Lily's spine as he rumbled. He loosened his hold on her and only then did Lily glance around. They were all alone on the lawn. Her ears picked up the sound of squeals of delight and groans from within the forest. She bit her lip as she watched Hunter begin to shed his clothes. He winked at her. "This is where you run, Little Witch, and I chase you. Unless you want me to fuck you right here on the damn lawn."

Lily froze, thinking it over until she grinned like an idiot. No, she wanted this Lycan, her mate, to chase her.

She took off running, avoiding the sounds coming from the other couples in the woods. She headed away from the sounds, feet pounding hard against the damp forest floor. There were small trails weaving this way and that. Some made by animals and others by people. Lily sprinted down one of the smaller paths before veering to the left. A pull deep in her gut had her weaving between the trees, abandoning the footpath she was on until she spilled out of the trees into a small meadow decorated with a myriad of wildflowers. She paused, breathing harshly, as the moonlight spilled over her. A low growl emanated from the woods, and Lily turned. A wolf prowled toward her, and Lily's heart pounded in her ears.

Moon beams glinted over its silver and white fur as it stalked closer, corralling Lily farther into the small meadow. She really hoped this was Hunter and not some other random wolf. Her breath caught as shimmering fog started at the wolf's feet, slowly swallowing its entire body. Between one breath and the next, Hunter emerged from the shimmering fog, shadows and moonlight playing over his rugged features.

Lily's gut clenched, arousal spreading through her entire body all the way down to her toes. He prowled closer and Lily's chest heaved, nipples already puckering through the thin fabric. She took a step back and stumbled. Lily shut her eyes on instinct, knowing she was about to hit the ground hard. Except the fall never came, as strong arms engulfed her body. She snapped her eyes open to stare into Hunter's glowing orbs. She felt his muscles tense against hers as he slowly lowered both their bodies to the ground. His jaw clenched, nostrils flaring. His movement was stiff as he pushed her stray hairs out of her face and behind Lily's ear. "Do you really want this? Because once we mate, there is no going back. It's for life. I promise it will be a good life, but you still have the choice to walk away."

The words seemed to rip from Hunter's throat, and Lily realized then why he was so tense. He was fighting himself and the bond, still trying to give her a chance to take things at a normal pace. Except Lily had discovered something between walking into the party hours earlier to this moment.

Lightning coursed through her veins, and she knew somehow finding her mate had unlocked her magic, and with it a newfound confidence in herself. She pushed her chest into his, arching her back. Hunter groaned and leaned into her, hands digging into the soft earth next to her hips.

Lily whispered, "I want you. Claim me as your mate."

Hunter's mouth was on hers in an instant, hands at her thighs, pushing the thin fabric farther up and her legs open wider. Lily gasped as calloused fingers glided gently over her throbbing pussy. She was already so wet and ready for him. Lily shifted, trying to get closer to his fingers, desperately wanting them inside of her. She shifted her grip on his shoulders, hands roaming down the muscles over his sides until she got to his erection. He had shed all his clothing to chase her through the woods, and they both groaned as Lily squeezed his thick cock.

"Fuck, Little Witch," Hunter murmured as he broke their kiss, and Lily continued to stroke his shaft. She had to admit it, she really liked it when he called her Little Witch.

"Say it again," she whispered, and rubbed her fingertips over the tip of his cock.

"Fuck, Little Witch, just like that."

She smirked and lifted her fingers to her mouth. They were covered in pre-cum, and she moaned as her tongue darted out to clean them. Hunter growled low and deep, watching her suck on her fingers before lunging forward and pressing her into the dirt. He pushed her hand away and captured her lips with his again. The sound of tearing fabric echoed through the small meadow. Lily shivered as Hunter laid his bare body against hers, fingers twining through hers and shoving her hands overhead. The tip of his cock nudged at her drenched entrance and Lily lifted her hips as Hunter pushed into her.

Lily gasped as Hunter's cock filled her to the brink, burying himself in one long thrust. His grip tightened on her hands as he slowly pulled out and slammed back into her once again. She arched her back, heels digging into the soft ground beneath her as Hunter continued his slow and deep rhythm. Breaking the kiss, she cried out. She was on the edge of an orgasm and her magic flared out around them. The ground crackled with electricity, nipping at her skin. Hunter released her hands to grip the back of her neck and hair. "Little Witch," he murmured against her skin. "Look at me."

She opened her eyes, locking her gaze with his as Hunter moved over her. His skin glowed with the light of the moon, his eyes like living flames. She gripped his shoulders hard as her orgasm started to roll through her. Lily cried out as Hunter continued his thrusts, her pussy pulsating around his cock. He trailed kisses down her neck until he got to her shoulder. She felt him open his mouth, teeth cold against her bare skin before he bit down. When her skin split beneath his bite, instead of pain, all Lily felt was overwhelming pleasure. As she bucked her hips against his, her orgasm crested to new heights. The ground became electrified, static prickling at her skin, and then she felt it. A bond growing tight between her body and his. She could feel it with her magic. A tether linking the two of them together.

Hunter groaned as her pussy continued to milk his cock. He lost his rhythm, and three thrusts later, she felt him coming inside of her. Lily shivered in his arms and wrapped her legs around Hunter's waist as he rested his warm body against hers. All she could hear was the rapid beating of their two hearts, so in sync, they sounded almost one. Hunter licked the bite he had given her before trailing light kisses across her jaw to her lips. Her pussy gave his softening cock one last squeeze before he slipped out of her. She sighed against his soft kisses. "That felt... that was..."

Lily trailed off, unsure of how to explain the feeling of the mate bond between them and how her newly found power felt coursing through her veins. Hunter rumbled against her skin. "Electrifying?"

Scoffing, she felt his lips quirk up in a smile against her skin. He rolled away, taking Lily with him until she rested half over his chest. She snuggled into the crook of his arm and glanced at the dark sky above them. The moon was unwavering in its glow, bathing them in silver moonlight. Lily could finally feel the power and magic flowing out of it, could feel it coursing through her. She lifted her hand, floating it through a moonbeam until Hunter reached up and grasped her fingers. When she glanced back at him with a smile, he trailed kisses over her fingertips. Sighing, she rolled over on top of him, and Hunter chuckled, his cock growing hard between them once more.

Chapter Eight

HUNTER

FUCK, HIS MATE WAS gorgeous.

Hunter grasped her hips as Lily rolled on top of him and placed her hand over his thumping heart. His cock hardened between her warm thighs as she bit her lip and glanced down at him with her beautiful hazel eyes. He could feel the mate bond settling between them and grunted in satisfaction. A sparkle of mischief flowed through the bond, and Hunter smirked as his mate reached up to remove the rabbit ears still somehow gracing her head. She placed them on him and giggled. "Looks like this little witch caught a big, bad rabbit."

A blush formed across his mate's cheekbones, and she shifted slightly across his hard cock. Embarrassment flowed down the bond after her words, and he growled when she went to remove the ears she had put on him. "Don't you dare touch the bunny ears. They are mine now."

His mate paused, conflicting emotions flowing down their new bond. In the end, it settled into playful suspicion. Lily placed her palms lightly on his chest and wiggled her well-proportioned ass over his hips. Her pussy lips glided over his cock, and Hunter groaned. "Little Witch, my mate, are you trying to tease me?"

Lily bit her lip and shrugged, causing her ruby-red hair to tumble over her shoulder. Hunter felt doubt slowly creep down the bond and he sat up, placing a finger under his mate's chin. She stilled, her beautiful eyes connecting with his. "Do you feel it? The bond between us?"

Lily nodded slightly, and Hunter smiled.

"Now tell me, what do you feel exactly?"

He pushed everything he was feeling down their bond and watched as Lily's eyes widened and her pupils dilated. He felt her pussy dampen against his cock as he pushed his lust for her down the bond. She took a shuddering breath as Hunter dropped his hand to her neck, fingers trailing over the mating bite mark binding them together at the height of their orgasms. His hand trailed lower until he got to her plump breasts. He pinched and rolled her nipples slightly, and she arched into his hand before he dropped it even lower.

Her hips jerked as he skimmed her clit, and her fingernails bit into his shoulders. Lily moaned and rolled her hips against his cock in an intoxicating rhythm. He continued his strokes on her clit as he leaned in to nip at her jaw. His mate angled her face down to capture his lips.

"That's it, Little Witch. Tease me just like that," he murmured against her mouth before deepening the kiss. He could feel her magic surrounding them, building like a wave in the air and nipping at his skin. The forest floor around them radiated with electricity and Hunter broke the kiss quickly as he felt the immense pleasure from his mate flow down the bond. She was about to come, and he wanted to be inside of her. She must have had the same idea as she broke their kiss and pushed his chest, laying him down. He willingly submitted to her, the only person in the world who would ever have that type of power over him.

Hunter moved his hands to her hips, pulling Lily up slightly so his cock could align with her dripping entrance. He eased her down slowly, despite her wanting to slam herself onto him. He grinned as his mate whimpered and begged for more.

"I need all of you," Lily moaned and scraped her fingernails along his chest. Hunter tightened his grip and lifted her up his shaft slightly. A growl worthy of any Lycan spilled out from his mate's throat. "Hunter, please!"

He felt her magic pulse around them, her pussy starting to grip around the tip of his cock, and loosened his hold on her hips. She slid down his shaft easily, her pussy tightening at the very end, and Hunter groaned as Lily screamed in pleasure. Her pussy milked his cock, shuddering and pulsating as he pulled out and slammed into her again. He wasn't going to last much longer, not with his goddess of a mate riding him through her orgasm. Her magic broke, exploding around them and lighting up the night.

Hunter came with a growl two thrusts later, holding himself deep within his mate. Lily sighed and stretched, holding her arms up toward the moon. Hunter's cock twitched inside of her and, in response, her pussy squeezed around him. As his mate glanced at him, pure bliss painted across her face. Her eyes seemed glazed over and Hunter reached up, placing a hand on her cheek. "So beautiful," he murmured, and his mate giggled.

She turned her head, kissing the palm of his hand before sliding forward to lay on his chest. He wrapped his arms around her, gliding his fingers up and down her spine as she kissed the side of his neck. They lay like that, aimlessly caressing each other, until Hunter's cock went soft and slipped out of her soft pussy. Her breathing had deepened, tranquility flowing down their bond, and Hunter thought her asleep until she murmured almost too low for him to hear.

"So, now what?"

Hunter tightened his hold on her. "What do you mean, Little Witch?"

Lily turned her head and wiggled her body to the side. She stared up at the slowly lightening sky instead of at him and he felt uncertainty twist down their mating bond. She rubbed absentmindedly at the mating mark on her neck. When she didn't say anything, Hunter tucked her in closer to his side. "I'm not going to..." He stopped. "No, let me restart."

She snuggled in closer as Hunter struggled with his words. "Well... I mean, being mated is like... it's like being..."

He glanced over at Lily's big hazel eyes staring at him, waiting patiently, and his mind went blank. "I'll be yours. Happily yours for as long as you will have me."

Lily smiled softly and rested her hand on his chest. "I get that. I was just wondering, like, what now? Do we... date? Instantly move in together. What about your pack? Will they accept me? And what about my powers?"

Her voice took on a higher pitch, panic filtering down their bond, and she sat up, flinging out her hands. "Oh, my Goddess! Look at what I did while we were having sex."

She pointed to the slightly charred earth surrounding them.

Hunter threw his head back in laughter and grabbed Lily to his chest. He couldn't stop laughing as she grumbled against him. "It's not funny. I could have electrocuted you to death."

He hiccupped, wiping at the tears building in his eyes, and managed to suck in a breath. "Lily, baby. Fuck. When I die, I pray it's from having sex with you. Please ride me to the gates of death."

She tried pushing away from him, annoyance running down their bond. She nipped at his neck hard enough to bruise, which only made Hunter start to laugh again. His mate wrestled against him until she started laughing with him. Soon their laughter died off naturally, and Hunter rubbed his mate's back gently. "Little Witch, we can do all those things if you want. We can go as slow as you want."

Lily sat up and scrunched her nose. "Really?"

Hunter sat up with her and tapped his mate's nose gently. "I will take you out on as many dates as you want. I can move in with you or the other way around. I will follow you anywhere you want to go. And my pack *will* love you, so don't you worry about that. And as far as your powers go, I will do everything I can to make sure you can control them. And when you want to go scorched earth again while having sex, or call down the biggest lightning storm anyone has ever seen, you better be riding me through it all."

Lily bit her bottom lip as tears pricked at the corners of her eyes. Warm emotions of love and acceptance rolled down their bond, and Hunter wanted to bask in the feeling. He reached out, cupping her face. "It's you and me forever. You never have to doubt that."

She sniffled before wiping her eyes and reaching out to grab the bunny ears that had fallen off during their last sexcapade. Putting them on her head, she gave him a shy smile. "You promise?"

"Always, my little witch."

His mate shifted, coming to her knees before standing. His hand slipped away from her, and Hunter smirked.

Lily took a small step back and winked at him. "Chase me home, then."

She took off in a run, words barely registering in Hunter's mind, and he leapt to his feet. His shift was seamless, human to wolf in the blink of an eye. His eyes glinted in happiness, the love of his mate radiating down their bond as she turned to see if he was following.

He sprinted after his little witch, through the woods, and back home.

And Hunter knew this would be one chase he would never get enough of.

Chapter Nine

SIX MONTHS LATER - LILY

LILY PEEKED INSIDE THE small office room and frowned. The light on the desk was barely enough to illuminate her mate and the papers scattered all over the place. She had been looking for him all over the house for the last hour. She should have known he would still be in his office, pouring over the proposal her coven and high priestess were going to present to the council of supernaturals in the next couple of weeks. Her heart almost burst at the seams with happiness as she stared at him.

Hunter. Her mate.

She quickly caught the feeling before it floated down their mate bond. She had been practicing along with her other magic and it seemed to work because Hunter didn't raise his head. Silently padding over the carpet, she came up behind him.

He was still staring at the proposal and highlighted a sentence before rubbing his eyes.

"Hey, Little Witch. I know it's late. I hope you didn't stay up..."

He trailed off as Lily let one simple, yet effective feeling roll down their bond.

Lust.

The chair squeaked as Hunter turned around slowly, and his eyes lit up as Lily let the robe she was wearing float to the ground.

"Lily," Hunter growled as she crawled into his lap and grabbed his hands to place on her ass.

He fisted the black and white silk slip she was wearing and pulled her closer. His eyes raked over the thin material covering her breasts all the way up to the bunny ears she had donned just for the occasion.

Leaning in, she kissed him. Her mate opened his mouth instantly and Lily deepened the kiss. She threaded a hand through his hair and gripped the back of his neck with her other. Hunter slid his hands under her ass and lifted, sitting her on the desk in one fluid motion without breaking the kiss. As his hands roamed her body, Lily arched into him as he cupped her breasts. He pinched her nipples through the thin material before one of his hands slid lower. Her legs were already wide, and Hunter growled into her mouth when he discovered nothing between his hand and her pussy.

She broke the kiss and smirked at her mate. Hunter's eyes gleamed, and he licked his lips. "You know I didn't forget; I just got a little sidetracked."

Lily faked a pout. "Oh really? Because here I thought you forgot our six-month anniversary. Thought I had to get creative for you to remember." She pointed to the bunny ears.

A rumble echoed from Hunter's chest as his fingers tickled at her entrance. "I would never forget the date my mate came barreling into my life."

Hunter pulled away, and Lily murmured in protest. Her mate winked at her before falling to his knees and throwing her thighs over his shoulders. She grabbed his hair, tilting his head up, and Hunter gave her a wolfish smirk. "Is my big, bad wolf gonna eat bunny for dinner?"

Hunter grinned and shoved his face between her legs, licking her pussy all the way from top to bottom before circling her clit. Lily moaned, eyes rolling back as her mate continued to lick her core. Her magic started to swell, electricity humming around them. As her mate lavished her pussy with his tongue, Lily relaxed into the feeling, pleasure and magic mixing into one.

Hunter's hands gripped her ass, pulling her closer onto his face, and she groaned. She started to pant, and Hunter growled, the vibrations making Lily arch her back. When he pulled back and nipped at her clit, Lily's grip on his hair tightened as lightning lit up the night sky outside the window. Her orgasm came swiftly, and she cried out, magic whipping the papers off the desk and onto the floor.

The electricity flickered, and Lily fell back, breathless, against the office desk. Hunter gave her pussy one last lick before standing up. He reached up and plucked the ears from her head and, with a smirk, put them on himself. Lily snorted in laughter, which quickly turned into a moan as Hunter hooked one over her legs over his shoulder. The angle lifted her ass off the desk slightly and she held her breath as he unzipped his jeans. His cock nudged at her entrance, and he teased her with his tip. She squirmed against him, needy pants filling the electrically charged air. Her magic nipped at him, and Hunter shivered, his eyes hooding from the feeling.

Lily knew he liked it when she used her magic on him; he had told her as much on their first night together. His cock grew even harder at her entrance when she let her magic flow across his skin again. He slowly pushed into her, and Lily squirmed, wanting him to go faster.

"Always so impatient, my little witch."

Lily moaned and tried to buck her hips against his, but he held her in place. When he started to pull out, Lily nipped at him hard with her magic. He stilled and shivered slightly as her magic rolled over him again, wrapping its way over Hunter's entire body.

She gripped his cock with her pussy, and he growled as she sent a tingling shock wave into his cock. He threw his head back, jaw grinding down, and Lily knew she had won. His control snapped and Hunter slammed his hips forward, burying his cock deeper inside of her. Continuing his onslaught, he drove deeper with every thrust. His moans grew louder, mixing with his wild growls. Soon her magic released with a loud crack and crashed over them at the same time as they orgasmed together. The popping sound of a light bulb breaking caught both their attention and Lily giggled.

Hunter snorted and shook his head before releasing one of his hands from her hip. He pulled open the top drawer of his desk and took out a new lightbulb. His eyes glowed in the dark as he tossed the broken bulb into the trash and spun the new one onto the desk lamp. "Hmmm... I need to work harder next time."

Lily tilted her head in confusion as her mate took a step back and slid out of her.

"I don't understand. Work harder at what?"

Hunter gave her a lust-filled look. "I'm obviously not working hard enough if I'm only replacing one light bulb. Next time, I'm not stopping until every damn bulb in this house burns up."

It took her a moment to catch up, but when she did, a blush instantly covered Lily's entire body. Her mate had a wicked mind. He winked at her, still wearing those damn bunny ears, and she felt a tug down their mate bond. He wanted to chase her, and she was more than happy to oblige.

She took a few swaying steps back, toward the open office door and the still lit hallway. They were all alone in the estate she now called home, and she knew that they could play their games all night long. Hunter followed her with his eyes, allowing Lily a bit of a head start. She made it to the door before he took his first step forward, and she picked up her pace, taking off down the hallway in a mad dash. She made it all the way to the stairs before strong arms encircled her waist and pulled her into her mate's hard chest. She giggled like a fool as he nipped at her earlobe. She felt him place the bunny ears back on her head, and he whispered, "Tag. Your it, Little Witch."

The weight of his arm around her waist disappeared as Hunter vaulted over the top of the stairs and landed in the entryway of their home. He glanced up at Lily's shocked face and laughed. She gaped at him before growling softly, "You best run, Wolfie, because this rabbit is coming for you."

Lily rushed down the stairs after her mate and followed his laughter through the estate and out to the backyard. She took a deep breath, twirling around in circles, trying to find him. The trees rustled in the suddenly silent night, and she held her breath, reaching down their mate bond. She felt laughter, love, and happiness flowing through it, but couldn't quite pinpoint where her mate was.

He was playing with her, and she smirked.

Fine.

If her wolf wanted to play, she could play too.

She reached deep inside of herself to stir up her newfound magic, and pushed the power down their bond. Normally they had to be touching for her to zap him, but she discovered about a month ago that was no longer the case. She felt surprised on the other end and zapped him lightly again.

Lily snorted when Hunter appeared suddenly from the tree line, leveling a lust-filled stare her way. She zapped him down the bond again and his eyes lit up with carnal fire. He started stalking his way toward her, and Lily met him halfway. His arms encircled her waist, and he was inside of her before they hit the ground. Lily groaned out in pleasure as he bit down over their mating mark on her neck. He slammed his cock over and over inside of her as she kept flowing her power down the bond. Hunter groaned and pulled out of her, only to turn her around. Slapping her ass slightly, he aligned his cock up to her soaked pussy again. "Fuck, Lily. I need to get deeper inside of you," he rumbled, before driving into her with one thrust.

The new angle did exactly that and her eyes rolled back in her head as he started to grind against her slowly, reaching new depths inside her aching pussy. She throbbed around him, coming fast and hard as he reached around to pinch her clit. At the peak of her orgasm, Hunter bit down once more over their mating mark on her neck and Lily's power exploded.

Two thrusts later, Hunter's cock pulsated inside of her, and he collapsed on top of her. She loved how his weight bore down over her like a warm blanket on a cold winter's eve, and she sighed in bliss. He licked at the shell of her ear before reaching a hand around to her chin and tilted her head to the side. She blinked away the fog in her pleasure-hazed mind and stared at the now dark house.

He chuckled and licked the shell of her ear again. Realization had her chuckling along with him. Her mate had fucked her so hard that she blew the entire power out throughout the house. "Maybe I worked a little too hard," he whispered, and Lily frowned.

"Why do you say that?"

"Can you hear it?" he whispered, and Lily strained her ears.

The sounds of dogs howling finally reached her ears, along with the faint sound of car alarms going off. Her eyes widened as she reached out with a spark of power, searching for any electricity in the near vicinity. Her eyes widened when she couldn't feel anything.

She had taken out the electricity within a five-mile radius. Lily started to laugh, and Hunter joined her. They lay there, laughing in each other's arms under the bright moonlight of the night and counted the stars until they slowly winked out of existence and the darkness faded into dawn.

"I love you, my little witch," Hunter whispered and pulled her closer as the sky began to lighten.

Lily snuggled closer in his embrace and gave him a soft kiss. "I love you too, my sexy mate."

The End

Wild Moon

WICKED FATE LUSTY MATES

ASTRID VAIL

Blurb & Content Warning

Enter the delicious and sensual world of Lycanthropes and Witches as they learn what fate has in store for them in this new series by Astrid Vail.

"Go out into nature, they said. It will be fun, they said."

Careening towards her death through white water rapids is the last place Mariel ever thought she would end up.

Unable to use her powers to save herself, fate intervenes in the form of the hunkiest lycanthrope she has ever seen.

Now he is tossing her over his shoulder and saying they are mates.

Except she is a witch, and he is supposed to be her enemy.

Fortunately for her, he isn't backing down, and Mariel is about to learn how good a witch and a wolf can fit together.

This novella is intended for mature readers only. **Content warning** includes spicy on page sex scenes, near-death experiences that involve water and fire, relocation, divorce over infertility, past family & relationship mental abuse, cheating (not done by the main characters) , and language.

Chapter One

MARIEL

"GO OUT INTO NATURE, they said. It will be fun, they said," Mariel grumbled under her breath, her legs already on fire as she trudged up the never-ending hill. To be fair, the hill probably did end at some point. It wasn't like she was climbing Mount Everest. No, she was out in the wilderness, trying to connect with her magic once more.

Her best friend had taken one look at Mariel and prescribed the good ol' outdoors. And after everything Mariel had gone through over the past few years, she was more than happy to try it. It wasn't like she had anything else to lose. Her husband, now ex, was off on some tropical island, sipping fruity drinks with a new fling. Her house... burnt to a crispy shell in a fit of rage, meaning she couldn't claim insurance. And her magic, the one thing that made her feel like someone worthy, was stripped from her.

As punishment for losing control, but really, how was someone supposed to react when you find your husband in bed with not one, but two, young interns?

At least Mariel had waited until the women left before losing it, and honestly, it wasn't the cheating that pushed her over the edge. She knew her husband wasn't faithful. No, what pushed her to rage was how her husband blamed her for his infidelity.

Mariel kicked at the ground. It had been two years and his phantom words still stung. But what crushed her the most was when her magic was given back to her, she couldn't use it.

It wouldn't come when she called. Instead, it laid dormant inside her, unwilling to flicker.

And oh, how Mariel tried to make it flicker.

Finally, after years of being the center of sad murmurs and rumors, she decided enough was enough. Enough of pretending her old coven cared about her. Enough of the pity party she was still throwing for herself.

So, Mariel left.

She left behind the ruins of her old life and restarted here.

A soft smile cut through her frown.

Here wasn't so bad.

Mariel had managed to snag a job running a coffee shop in a small little town on the outskirts of a much larger city. She even had a cute little apartment, and her best friend lived nearby.

Well, close enough to nearby. Her best friend, Breena, was a nature witch who lived at the base of the mountains she was currently hiking. She was more of a recluse than anything else, who only left her place to go to coven meetings. She had been the one to convince Mariel to come out to the Sierra Nevada's and join the new coven. A band of misfits just like her, and who pretty much stayed out of everyone's business except once a month when they convened. Mariel agreed to meet with the coven, but on one condition. She wanted to approach the coven with the ability to do magic again. She didn't want to come in as a dead weight.

Mariel snorted as she recalled Breena's face, a mix of disbelief and anger, when she called herself a dead weight. Disbelief that Mariel thought she had to be anything other than she was at this moment. Anger because she knew the shit Mariel had been through and wished she could help. In the end, Breena simmered down and listened to Mariel's reasoning. She wasn't happy about it, but her friend understood. Hence why she suggested going out into nature. Breena suggested something small, in the vicinity of where she lived, but Mariel was having none of that. She was always a go big or go

home type of gal. Which led to her to the here
and now.

Pain radiated up Mariel's calf, snapping her
out of her thoughts, and she grimaced. Reaching
down to rub out the cramp, she looked around.
The woods pushed in on all sides of the small
path she was following, the low breeze nipping at
Mariel's cheeks. It was the end of summer, on the
precipice of fall, and while Mariel had checked
the weather before heading out, she glanced up,
knowing the weather in the mountains could turn
at any moment. Blue skies and fluffy clouds met
her gaze, and Mariel sighed in relief. She checked
her watch before readjusting the large pack on
her back. The cramp in her calf was still lingering,
but Mariel decided to push through. Based on her
calculations, she still had a few hours at her slow
pace before she reached her destination.

She wasn't going to make it.

Why did she think this was a good idea? Breena
had said to take it easy and go on a short hike, but
no, Mariel had to do what she did all the time.
She took a small idea and blew it up into epic
proportions.

Go on a day hike...

No, no, no, Mariel had to make it a two-week long camping trip.

Fine, go some place easy then. With lots of people around.

No, no, no, Mariel had to find the most random place, in the middle of a wilderness area, that would take her a full day of hiking to reach.

She reached up and wiped the sweat from her face. All she succeeded in doing was smearing it around.

Which was fine, since it wasn't like she was already drenched from head to toe. Mariel contemplated just taking off her pack and sitting down right here. But she knew if she did that, she wouldn't get back up and she really, really wanted to make it to the spot she found while searching the web.

It was perfect and secluded and next to a beautiful, winding river.

Mariel pulled out her map and brand-new GPS from the side pocket of her pack and frowned. Shit... she had missed the turnoff somehow.

Closing her eyes, she took a deep breath. Okay, she could do this. The last time she read a map was in college, four plus years ago, but she was confident she could figure out a different way to her destination. Opening her eyes, she found where she currently was and followed the possible paths on the map. One in particular caught her attention and she cocked her head. It didn't necessarily take her to her desired location, but it was close enough. Folding up the map, Mariel continued the way she was going until an overgrown trail sprung out of the forest. It was going in the right direction per her GPS, so she turned and hoped for the best.

If anything, she could just make camp once dusk fell. She was in the middle of the wilderness, after all.

Mariel laid her hands on her knees as sweat soaked her from head to toe. Her lungs and thighs were burning, and she was ready to collapse, but she fucking did it. She finally made it. She dropped her bag on the ground, on a bare spot between two trees that would make a perfect spot for her tent. Sure, her first desired location destination had been a pretty meadow and a small river—more of a stream. But this place would work. There was no meadow, but there was a wide river with a sandy little inlet. She took a deep breath, the smell of fresh water and pine trees, sun-kissed earth and fresh flowers flowing over her, and Mariel smiled. She wasn't a nature witch like Breena, but she did have an appreciation for nature and the woods in general. Hell, she had been going to college for a forestry and fire management degree before her life took a huge disappointing detour.

Mariel ran her hands through her sweaty hair and pushed those thoughts aside. Her old life was the last thing she wanted to think about while trying to turn a new leaf, so to speak. She glanced down at her pack and the surrounding area, knowing she should probably set up her tent and gather some firewood, but the river was beckoning.

She was hot and tired and more than a bit sweaty. Her whole body ached and a dip in the river sounded like heaven at the moment. She could set up camp after she cooled down.

Decision made, Mariel reached down to untie her hiking boots. She chucked them to the side, along with her grimy pants, shirt, and tank top. Leaving her booty shorts and sports bra, she ambled over to the river.

The sand was cool against her feet as she carefully took a few steps into the river. Soothing water worked its way over her overtaxed muscles, and Mariel groaned. The cold water felt amazing as she took a few more steps forward, the sand turning into small river rocks as she went in as far as her knees. The undercurrent tugged at her, and she stopped. Mariel knew better than to go any deeper, as the current would only get stronger the farther she went. But this was fine. She could just sit down and...

Mariel's heart dropped to her stomach as she turned. She slapped a hand over her mouth, trying to stifle her scream, but the large brown bear rooting through her pack was already lifting its head, eyes focused in her direction. It shook its massive shaggy head and charged. This time, the scream ripped through her throat, and she threw herself back, the water splashing higher and higher. Mariel screamed again, flailing as her foot slipped and the river swallowed her whole. She floundered, not knowing which way was up as the undercurrent swept her away. Spinning, she reached out desperately, trying to catch the slippery rocks as they flashed by. Her head breached the surface, and Mariel sucked in a breath, only to be pulled under again.

Chapter Two

BLANE

BLANE TOSSED HIS HIKING pack into the old wooden cabin, one that had been passed down through the generations, and grandfathered into the wildness area it now sat in the middle of. It was surrounded by deep forests, and as part of the agreement between the government and his family, was still owned by his family under certain conditions. No vehicles, nor modern appliances except the small generator and composting toilet set up in the small outhouse next to the cabin.

Blane loved this place with a passion he could never explain. It was his home away from the pack and civilization and people. It was his place for his wolf to run free, to connect with nature, and for his mind to rest.

He flicked on the battery-operated lanterns right inside the doorway and checked every nook and cranny of the old cabin, making sure no unwanted critters had made a home inside in the past five months he had been away. The cabin was small, with one open room and a loft, and he was done within minutes. Stripping off his t-shirt and boots, Blane headed out to the front porch before shucking off his pants and throwing them inside. He didn't have to worry about anyone seeing him naked this far into the wilderness as he took a knee and let the mist engulf his body.

His form twisted and shifted, wild magic changing his DNA as he stepped into his second self. Shaking out his shaggy black fur, he stretched his large paws, digging into the soft dirt. His back popped and Blane lifted his head, letting a howl build in his chest, radiating out of his throat to fill the now silent forest.

Yes, a predator is here, he thought. *Run, little bunnies. Fly, little birdies. The big, bad wolf is back. Did you miss me?*

A wolfish grin plastered itself to his muzzle as he turned and trotted down a deer path, nose to the ground, taking in all the fresh scents of the forest. His ears twitched at the small sounds surrounding him, before skidding to a halt. Lifting his head, the fur on his back raised. He thought he just heard...

His blood ran cold, adrenaline fueling his body as he took off at a breakneck speed. There was no mistaking that sound as it came again.

A woman's scream. A plea for help.

Blane flew through the forest, dodging low-hanging branches and jumping over fallen trees. The trees around him thinned, the roaring river filling his ears as he slowed his run and glanced around wildly.

There... he saw her.

The woman screaming for help, paddling desperately against the rapidly moving current.

Blane growled low in his throat as he swiftly hopped onto the large boulders along the river and ran the length of it. The woman caught sight of him, her face twisting in surprise, and her screaming stopped for a moment before the current dragged her under. The river was picking up speed by the second, already having turned to white water miles back. Blane wasn't sure how long she had been in the river, but he knew one thing. There was a waterfall dead ahead, and he didn't want her to go over it.

Launching himself off the rock, there was no time to waste to shift back into his human form. He paddled furiously as the woman resurfaced, using the current to his advantage to get behind her before she went under again. Her eyes widened as she reached out, nails sinking into his wet fur, her grip surprisingly tight for how small she was. The current dragged them under, the cold-water suffocating. Blane kicked and paddled with all his might, his muscles straining to get them to resurface. They both gasped, air filling their lungs before the river took them under again. This time, the woman let go, pushing him away, as if she were trying to save him. As if she knew she was dragging him down.

Blane growled and resurfaced in time to see the woman pop up a few feet down river. He pushed forward, horror wrapping its way around his body as he shifted. Reaching out, his fingers grazed hers before they both free fell through the air.

The air blasted from his lungs as he hit the bottom of the falls moments later before sinking far below the surface, the thunderous waterfall above pushing him down deeper and deeper. He struggled to turn, wildly looking around until he saw her. She floated mere feet from him, eyes closed, face blissful against the rushing water surrounding her.

Blane launched forward, scooping her into his arms, before kicking to the surface. He gasped a deep lungful of air and slung the woman up, propping her head against his shoulder. He couldn't feel her chest rising, nor her breath against his neck.

"Fuck, fuck, fuck. Please don't be dead," he growled as he swam them toward the shore.

The moment his feet hit the sandy bottom, he launched them out of the water and laid the woman down on her back. Pressing his head to her chest, he listened for anything at all. "Fuck!"

Blane reached up, pinching her nose and tilting her chin back before locking his mouth onto hers, blowing air into her lungs. Once, twice.

He broke away and settled his hands over her sternum, wincing as he started chest compressions. He tried not to think about the statistics on broken ribs and surviving CPR as he started to count.

One, two, three...

The woman trembled under his hands, and he quickly pushed her to the side as she sputtered, water draining from her body in coughing lungfuls. She fell back onto his bare chest as Blane patted her back.

"You're safe now. I've got you. It's..."

He paused mid-sentence as her spicy magic-laden scent engulfed him, and she turned in his arms, her dark blue eyes piercing through to his soul.

There was no way. This couldn't be happening. He leaned in on impulse, brushing his nose against her cold cheek to get another sniff of her scent.

The woman squealed, rearing back. "Oh my god! Why are you naked?" She threw herself to the side, her eyes growing wider. "Explain yourself!"

Blane shook his head, in no mood to play any games after what he had just discovered. "I know you're a witch and you damn well know I'm a Lycan." He got to his feet and stretched out his hand. "Now come. It's going to take a few hours to get back."

She stared up at him in shock, jaw going slack before her eyes slid down his body. Quickly covering her face, she shook her head. "No, no, no, this isn't happening. I'm fucking dead. I fucking drowned and now my body is a floating, bloated corpse somewhere in the river, getting eaten by fish."

"That's quite the vivid imagination," Blane murmured as he took a step closer and reached down to peel the woman's hands away from her face. "But you're not dead. Let's go."

Narrowing her eyes, she glared at him with a fiery passion. "Don't tell me what to do, naked stranger."

He snorted before squatting down to her level. "Name's Blane. Now we aren't strangers."

The woman took a deep breath, scooting away slowly before mumbling, "I'm Mariel."

"Mariel," Blane rumbled, closing his eyes as he tasted the way her name sounded on his tongue.

When he opened his eyes, Mariel had scooted farther away, hugging her legs to her chest, and was staring at him with open curiosity.

"Why did you say my name like that?" she whispered.

"Like what?"

"Like it gave you pleasure saying it."

The moment the words left her mouth, a blush ran across her cheeks, and she glanced away.

Blane chuckled and slowly crept closer to her, cupping her chin to pull her gaze to his. His eyes roamed her face, a light dusting of freckles covering her small nose and high cheekbones. She was a petite thing, yet still curvy, and she was all but fucking perfect sitting there, staring up at him with her beautiful midnight-blue eyes.

"Because, witch," Blane whispered, inching closer to her cupid-bow lips. "You're my mate."

Mariel gasped as he leaned in, about to kiss his mate properly, when she suddenly went limp in his arms.

"Fuck," Blane muttered, holding his mate in his arms.

She had fucking fainted on him.

Chapter Three

MARIEL

MARIEL GROANED, BLINKING SLOWLY as her eyes adjusted to the dim light around her. Her whole body ached, her throat sore and scratchy, and her head was pounding to the beat of her pulse. She shifted on the mattress, snuggling deeper into the musky and woodsy smelling comforter, and turned to her side, closing her eyes again. They popped open a second later as Mariel sat up, glancing around frantically. Last thing she remembered was that man, Blane, saving her and...

Mariel pressed a shaking hand to her mouth. "Oh god."

She had almost died, and it was a Lycan who saved her. The grudge between witches and Lycans was as old as time. And while they lived in the twenty-first century, the hostility between the two species was still there. Old families still looked upon each other in disdain, as if to be in each other's mere presence was horror enough. Mariel never thought of herself to be anti-Lycan, even when her family had been, but she also never met a Lycan up close before. She definitely didn't think she would meet one alone in the woods either, and in such an intimate way. Blane's naked body flashed through her mind, and Mariel gulped, pushing the image away.

Speaking of the Lycan, Mariel glanced around again, hands fisting the blanket on the large bed she had awoken in, which was taking up about all the space available in what she assumed was a loft. She stumbled her way out of the bed and leaned against the thick wooden railing in front of her. Glancing around, Mariel's eyes roamed the very small cabin. The loft held only the bed, and as she looked to the ground floor, she could see a large antique-looking fireplace, a few pots and pans hanging from hooks, and cabinets. Below the cabinets was a small counter, with a makeshift sink cut into it, and some sort of water contraption underneath. An old wooden table with two chairs sat in the tiny kitchen, and the only other thing she could see was a large bearskin rug covering the other half of the floor and a threadbare reclining chair.

Jesus fuck, where the hell was she?

And could she escape without being seen?

As grateful as Mariel was to be alive, this entire vibe she had awoken too was screaming horror movie in the making. And she was fucking powerless. She would have to defend herself like a normal person, and Mariel had no doubt in her mind Blane could overpower her. He could do whatever he wanted to her out in these woods, and no one would hear her scream. The blood rushed from her head, and Mariel sat down, feeling faint as her legs dangled over the loft ladder.

After a minute of deep breathing, Mariel decided she wasn't going to go out as a whimpering mess. If this did turn into something out of a horror movie, she was going to take Blane down with her, come hell or high water. She wasn't sure how, but the thought gave her enough resolve to slowly make her way down the ladder. She had to admit, as her feet finally hit the floor, that the ladder was rather well made. She ran her hand over the smooth rungs and then took a closer, less panicked look around.

The cabin was extremely well built and cared for. It wasn't a ramshackle hut in the middle of the woods, like she first thought. She noticed that while old, the cabinets and the large wardrobe hidden below the loft were in excellent condition. The only thing to look new was the water contraption under the table. Everything else looked straight out of the 1800s, minus the recliner and the few battery-operated lanterns.

The sound of splitting wood coming from outside caught her attention as Mariel tiptoed over to the upright wardrobe. She was still in nothing but her booty shorts and sports bra. If she was going to make a run for it, she wanted to be at least covered up. She grabbed an older looking flannel shirt and shrugged it on. It hit her mid-thigh, and she shoved the sleeves up, haphazardly rolling them until her hands poked out. Another glance around told her she wasn't going to find anything to shove her bare feet into, meaning she would have to make her escape shoeless, which wasn't ideal, but at least she had a shirt.

Mariel sucked on her bottom lip, not liking her odds of survival as she cautiously made her way to the front door. She pulled up on the latch and pushed, thanking the goddess silently as the door didn't make a sound. Taking a step out onto the porch, she looked around and her hope plummeted.

The cabin sat in a small clearing surrounded by thick forest as far as she could see. There were no roads, no vehicles, nothing to blatantly say, 'come this way to freedom.' Squinting, she saw a small path cutting through the underbrush, but it looked more like an animal path than anything else. She needed to see what was on the other side of the cabin before blindly launching headfirst into the forest.

She glanced to the right, seeing a small shed of sorts, and her jaw went slack for a moment. He was facing away from her, the ax falling and rising in smooth movements. She knew it was Blane without him turning around. She had seen this beautiful specimen of a male naked, with his swimmer's physique and lean muscles. Her gaze started at his ass before trailing up, taking in the sheen of sweat glistening across his naturally tanned skin, his broad back, and ...

Mariel bit back a moan as her gaze reached his shoulders. She had a thing for strong, well-defined shoulders, and fuck, did Blane have them. She could imagine gripping them with her hands, her fingers playing along his collarbone and neck.

Gulping, she pushed the image to the side as Mariel contemplated her next move. She needed to escape, not have sexy fantasies about the Lycan who pulled her out of the damn river like a fish. As she glanced left, she saw nothing but trees.

Dammit, there had to be a way out of here.

She glanced back to the right, to Blane, with his back still to her. The ax buried itself into another thick piece of wood, the logs splitting under the force. In any other circumstance, Mariel would have loved to just sit on the porch, watching a sexy man splitting logs all day. But now was not the time for daydreaming. Now was the time to escape whatever reality this was.

Slowly tiptoeing off the porch, she made a mad dash around the side of the cabin. She frantically looked around for anything to help her get as far away from Blane and the cabin as she could. A car, an off-road vehicle, hell, she would even take a horse if there was one. But there was nothing, no way out, only thick forest as far as she could see.

The sound of the ax burying deep into another piece of wood ricocheted through the air, before a deep rich growl reached her ears. "Mate, the only path out of here is right behind me. So why don't you come back to the front of the cabin and don't do anything stupid."

Mariel bit her lip and winced.

Fuck.

Did he just call her *mate*? Somewhere in the back of her subconscious, she realized he had called her that at the river. But she had thought then it was just a hallucination.

She took a deep breath and called out, her voice cracking. "What if I don't? What if I do something stupid?"

Blane's chuckle twisted something low in Mariel's gut, and she had to press her thighs together to keep her legs from wobbling. Shit, she was not turned on by this situation. Nope, not at all. She wasn't this fucking stupid, was she?

This was something out of a crime documentary, not a romance story.

Blane's footsteps were silent as he rounded the corner and stopped, his gaze roaming over Mariel. Her eyes did the same thing, gliding over his rippling abs, his shoulders she would die to be touching right now, and she sucked in a breath as she finally got a good look at his face.

Maybe she did actually die, and this was the afterlife?

No man should look that good.

He could rival the statues of the Greek gods, with his chiseled jaw, full lips, and straight nose. His chocolate brown eyes met hers and she froze.

Mariel felt like a rabbit caught in the heat-laden gaze of a predator.

And this predator most definitely wanted to eat her.

Blane ran his hand through his shaggy black hair, and she clenched her thighs again, her body betraying how turned on she was right now.

Shit, she was in big trouble.

Cocking his head, he maintained the distance between them. He kept staring at her, his gaze intense.

"Mate?" he questioned her again.

"I can't be your mate."

Blane grimaced at her words. "Why not?"

"Because I'm a witch and you're a Lycan."

"Irrelevant."

Mariel snorted in disbelief. There was no way this Lycan was so hard on for a mate, that he would put aside a centuries' old grudge to have his way with her. Then again, he was a guy. "Sure thing, buddy. Completely irrelevant."

His eyes flashed, going amber for a moment when she called him *buddy*. She gulped and took a slow step back as he took one toward her.

"I'm not your buddy. I'm your mate."

"Sureeee, and I'm a docile little bunny rabbit that likes to frolic with unicorns that shit rainbows. You sound ridiculous."

Blane chuckled again, taking another step in her direction. "You are anything but docile. I can sense the fire inside of you, twisting its way through your veins, begging for release."

Mariel's face hardened, and she glanced at the ground. His comment was too close for comfort, and her heart clenched as she reached for her magic as an automatic response. And just as she expected, it lay dormant. A flame turned to coal, nothing left to stoke.

She wanted to sob, to fall to the ground and scream until there was nothing left inside of her. She wanted to beg to the moon goddess, and rage to the fire goddess. She paid her dues and still her magic lay dormant.

It wasn't fair.

Mariel shook her head, keeping her tears at bay, and held up a hand, still pretending she could do something against this man. "Come any closer, and I'll firebomb you."

Blane hesitated for a moment before narrowing his eyes. "Okay then, little flame. Do it."

Mariel blanched, her hand shaking, and she did the only thing she could think of as he called her bluff. She turned and ran.

Chapter Four

BLANE

BLANE CURSED AS HIS silly mate ran off, heels digging into the dirt like a cartoon character as she sped away from him. The predator raging inside of him rose to the surface as he pursued her. The last thing he wanted to do was hurt his mate as he easily overtook her, tackling her to the ground as gently as he could. She shrieked in pure terror and rage as his big body engulfed hers. Flipping her over easily, he yanked her hands over her head, trapping her withering body with his. She growled and hissed at him like a demented cat, and Blane growled back, letting his wolf bleed into his eyes. "Mariel, for fuck's sake, stop. I'm not going to hurt you."

She growled right back at him. "Then get the fuck off me, you animal!"

Blane softened his grip, but didn't dare move as she tried to squirm out from under him. "You're just going to run again. And I can't let you do that."

"Yes, you can."

"Where would you run, mate?"

At his words, she stilled. Tears threatened to spill from her beautiful eyes even as she craned her neck, looking around at the dense woods surrounding him. He could almost see the wheels in her head spinning, still trying to figure out how to escape him.

Blane took a deep breath, and Mariel glared at him. He was about to say something, but she beat him to it. "So, what's your plan, buddy? Bag and tag a helpless witch for your alpha? And would this be before or after having your way with me?"

Blane growled at her accusations. "First of all, you are far from helpless, witch, nor would I ever force myself on you or anyone, for that matter. And secondly, again, I am not your buddy. So cut it out with the nickname."

Something flickered behind her eyes, and she gave him the most deranged smile he had ever seen. "Buddy."

Blane tightened his grip on her wrists and hauled himself up, bringing her up with him. She tugged at his grip as he yanked her flush with him, wrapping his arm around her waist. "Insolent little brat."

Mariel's jaw dropped, and Blane couldn't help his grin. "I'm not a brat."

"Yes, you are. And I will continue calling you one until you calm the fuck down and listen to me."

She glared at him before leaning into his chest slightly. He wasn't sure if Mariel even realized what she had done as she mumbled, "Fine, hurry up and state your case."

He snorted. "Why, got someplace to go?"

He watched her ground her jaw before spitting out her next words. "Ya, someplace away from you and your creepy murder cabin in the woods."

Closing his eyes out of frustration, he rested his chin on his mate's head. He felt her stiffen slightly before resuming her more relaxed position against his chest. A shiver ran down her body as the wind picked up. Blane took another deep breath, inhaling her sweet scent and calming himself before releasing her hands and wrapping his arm around her shoulders. She melted into him even more, and Blane knew the mating bond was starting to weave its magic. The fragile threads would be weak until he could solidify the bond by marking his mate in the throes of passion, but Blane had to wait.

Wait until his mate accepted that fate brought them together. And in the meantime, he had to keep her from running away. She shivered again in his hold just as her stomach rumbled. "Hungry?" he whispered.

"A little, yes. Trying to escape the big, bad wolf left me a bit peckish."

Blane chuckled and took a step away, twining his fingers with hers. He needed to maintain physical contact as long as possible. It calmed his inner wolf, and it seemed to calm his witch for long enough to make her listen to him. He glanced down at her bare legs and feet, and she scrunched her dirty toes into the grass. Hungry and dirty. Things he never wanted his mate to be, unless it was in bed with him. He rubbed at his face with his free hand before catching her gaze. She was studying him through her thick lashes, a frown resting on her full lips. "How about I show you how to use the outdoor shower and composting toilet while I make you some food?"

She perked up to his suggestion. "That seems reasonable."

He turned and tugged his mate with him around the cabin to the small building that housed the outdoor shower and toilet. Glancing up at the slightly darkening sky, he inhaled deeply. The taste of ozone and heavy rain coated the back of his throat, and he grunted as Mariel slipped her hand from his and pushed the door open. She ducked inside, and Blane followed her with his eyes. She took a quick turn, and a faint smile graced her face. "This is... nicer than I expected."

Blane mimicked her faint smile. "I'll show you how to use it, then I'll make you food. There is an incoming storm, so can we halt your ill-advised escape plans until it at least passes?"

Mariel's scathing look made him want to smile before she sighed and held out her hand. "Truce, for now?"

Blane accepted her hand, giving it a small shake. "Agreed, for now."

He stood over the small electric griddle on the makeshift kitchen counter he had installed a few years ago. Normally, he didn't bother pulling the small generator out to cook food, but he knew cooking it over the fireplace would take longer. And his mate was hungry.

He groaned.

His mate.

His fucking gorgeous mate with her small, luscious body was standing naked in the outdoor shower right now and his hands weren't all over her. He wasn't bringing her pleasure. Hell, they hadn't even kissed yet.

Blane flipped the pancake he was making onto the only plate he had in the cabin and poured more batter onto the griddle. His ears perked up at the sound of soft footsteps making their way to the front door over the growing wind. He didn't turn as Mariel opened the door quietly and sneaked in. Blane smirked as the smell of his mate wafted around him, wrapping its way into the very fabric of his being. All his instincts were telling him to put his scent all over her, to put a claiming mark on her.

Gripping the spatula in his hand tighter, he kept telling himself to remain calm and not turn into a slobbering mess. He could scent the emotions coming off her. And she was confused as all hell. A little bit scared, mixed with anger, sadness, and...

Blane bit back a groan as he scented her lust. He glanced over his shoulder and had to physically restrain himself from taking two quick steps and laying his mate down on the bearskin rug in front of the fireplace.

She was just standing there, in his goddamn flannel shirt, sucking on her lower lip and looking innocent and doe eyed.

But Blane knew she was anything but innocent. He could feel the magic shifting around her, and it was hot and wild. Burning her up from the inside, and yet her scent was lacking in it. As if she didn't practice, even though her magic was screaming to be unleashed. He could feel it in the invisible mating bond that was weaving itself between them.

Mariel cleared her throat, a blush overtaking her cheeks, and Blane realized he was just standing there staring at her over his shoulder. He turned back around and finished the last pancakes and turned the griddle off. Motioning toward the table, he prayed his mate wouldn't look down to see he had a massive hard-on just by her entering the cabin. Then again, she might love what she saw, and they could skip breakfast altogether...

Blane frowned. No, his mate was hungry. And he needed to feed her. And then he needed to figure out how the hell she ended up half naked, fighting for her life in the river. Surely, his mate wasn't silly enough to think she could just go for a leisurely dip in that type of river.

Mariel sat at the table without a word, and Blane put the plate between them. "Quiet doesn't suit you. What's wrong?"

She glanced at him in surprise before narrowing her eyes.

Yes, Blane thought, *there's that fire surrounding her.*

"You comment on my nature like we know each other? News flash, we don't."

Blane snorted. "We are mates. And I wouldn't have been given such a docile one."

"Given?" Mariel growled, all the pretense of being a docile little lamb gone. In front of Blane sat a dangerous woman fully capable of holding her own against him, even if she didn't know it yet. And fuck, did Blane love it.

He reached for a pancake and ripped off a piece, smirking at his glaring mate. "You heard me."

Mariel snorted and crossed her arms, leaning back in the chair. "You're fucking with me right now, aren't you?"

He dropped his smirk. "Little flame, if I were fucking with you right now, you wouldn't have a spare breath to ask."

Mariel's pupils dilated slightly before shaking her head. "Why do you call me that?"

Sighing, he pushed the stack of pancakes closer to her. "Eat. I know you're hungry. Then maybe you can tell me why you are running around these mountains with no shoes and clothes and why I had to fish you out of the river."

She snatched a pancake from the plate and started taking huge bites. Blane watched her eat until the pancake disappeared and she reached for another one. This time, she took a smaller bite and leveled him with a stare. "Do you live here year-round?" she asked.

Blane leaned back in his chair, stretching his legs out under the table. He brushed up against her and stilled. When she didn't pull away, Blane relaxed a bit and shook his head. "No, I have a place on my alpha's estate."

Mariel took another bite of her pancake. "Who's your alpha?" she asked, her mouth still full.

With a smile, he tapped his leg against hers. "It's your turn to answer my question, then I'll answer your second one."

Mariel frowned and put the half-eaten pancake back on the stack. She rubbed her hands on her thighs and glanced everywhere but at Blane's face. He signed, and sat up straight, reaching out with his hands and placing them on the table in front of her, palms up. She glanced down at them with equal amounts of terror and fascination. He wiggled his fingers and, ever so slowly, she placed her hands in his. Encircling her wrists, he rubbed his thumbs on her skin in a soothing motion. "I'm not going to hurt you, Mariel. You can talk to me."

At the sound of her name, she finally glanced up at him. She took a deep breath and let it out in one go, words tumbling forth like the river he had saved her from. "My stupid ass decided to go on a camping trip, but I got lost-ish. Then I found a nice place to set up camp, but I was hot and tired, and the river looked so nice and refreshing. I wasn't going to go in too deep. But then, there was a bear and it kind of charged me. So, I fell, and next thing you know, I'm just struggling to keep my head above water. The current was so fast and... and... I don't know how long I was in the river before this wolf launches out of the woods and into the river to try to save me. But I also realized I was dragging it... *you* under, so

I tried to push you away. I... I..." She trailed off, her sadness coating the air around them.

Blane took a deep breath with her, his smile slipping off his face. "Why didn't you use your magic? On the bear... on me?"

She glanced up at him in shock before pulling away and tucking her arms around her in an embrace.

Fuck, those should be his arms embracing her, comforting her. Blane barely managed his relaxed composure as she glanced at the table and mumbled, "I did something a few years back. Lost control and my powers were ... the best way to describe it is saying my powers were put on hold. I still had them but couldn't access them. Then, after a year, the hold was lifted. But..."

Blane knew where this was going. "You can't use your powers anymore?"

She shook her head, her answer a silent plea for help. "No."

"And this camping trip? A way to help or end your life?"

Mariel lifted her head so suddenly, the shock etched into her face. "To help. A hail Mary of sorts, to try to kick-start them again."

The tension in Blane's body dissipated, and he inhaled a deep breath, letting his mate's scent coat his tongue. "So, how do we kick-start these powers, then?"

Mariel blinked slowly, her gaze locked onto his. "We?" she whispered and shifted in her seat.

Blane nodded. "Yes, little flame. We're in this together. I wasn't joking when I said we are mates. So, let's figure this out, together."

Chapter Five

MARIEL

MARIEL STARED AT BLANE, trying to fit the pieces together in her head. Just earlier, she was hiking through the woods, trying to re-find her magic, only to almost die not once but twice by bear then by a waterfall. Now she was sitting across from a lycanthrope telling her that he was her mate and hell bent on helping her.

There had to be a catch.

Mariel snorted, and Blane arched an eyebrow. Ya, the catch was that she was a witch, and he was a Lycan. Their ancestors were sworn enemies, and yet, Blane didn't seem to care. She shook her head and looked away. "I know about mating bonds, and I also know it isn't complete until you bite me. You don't have to throw your pack and life away for someone you don't even know. After this storm passes, I can leave, and we can go back to our own little lives."

Blane shook his head, shock evident on his face as if she had slapped him.

"Am I not good enough for you, then?"

She flinched at his whispered words. "What? No. I'm trying to be the reasonable one here. You seem like a nice guy, a little growly, but nice. I also know that once you fully mate with someone, there is no turning back. You still have a chance to meet someone else. Someone who would be worthy of you and fit in with your pack. Not a witch who can't access her powers."

Blane's face softened, and he folded his arms across his still bare chest. "How long are you supposed to be on your camping trip?"

Mariel blinked rapidly, gathering her thoughts at the shift in conversation and trying not to drool all over herself by staring at Blane's chest. She really needed him to put on a shirt. "I... I think I wrote down twelve days on the backcountry pass."

"How long did it take you to get to your stop next to the river?"

"One day."

Blane mussed, glancing away toward the window over the makeshift sink. The rain had started, light at first, but now it was pouring, drumming on the roof and windows like it was the starring role in a musical. Mariel's thoughts went to what she would have done if she was stuck in this storm, in her tent, all alone. She shivered slightly, and Blane glanced back at her before getting up and going to the small fireplace. He opened it and shoved another log in. Mariel stared at the flickering flames, sadness rolling over her in waves like the rain outside. Goddess above, she really missed her powers.

"It will take us two days to make it down the mountain from here to my truck. Which gives us nine days..." Blane glanced back at her and shrugged his shoulders. "Stay with me for that time. We can try to get your powers back. We can get to know each other, and if by the end of it all, you still want to go on your way, you can."

Mariel stared at him, contemplating her choices. What he proposed wasn't the worst thing ever. And she did come up here to try to unlock her powers. Though, in her version, there wasn't a sexy as sin Lycan trying to help her. She sucked on her bottom lip and slid from her chair, padding over to sit on the bearskin rug. Blane went absolutely still next to her as she held out her hands, warming them on the heat and desperately wishing it was her flames that were warming them at the moment. Tears swam in her eyes before she blinked them away and took a shuddering breath. "I don't know," she whispered before cracking a sad smile. "Do you think you can keep your hands to yourself... buddy?"

Blane relaxed next to her and sat, his side touching hers, before laughing softly. "I don't know, little brat. Think you can try not to escape into the woods barefoot and scantily dressed every moment you get?"

Mariel leaned back into him, knowing it was a bad idea. She already felt a pull to him, magnetic in nature, and knew it had to be the bond. She knew through teachings that a mating bond was magical in nature. And while it could be rejected in the early stages, the longer you were in contact with the person it was trying to tie you to, the harder it got to leave. And once it solidified, the only thing to break it was death itself. Learning about the bond in theory was entirely different from actually experiencing it, though. And to Mariel's surprise, she almost didn't want to fight it.

Almost being the optimal word.

Blane leaned into her harder, snapping Mariel out of her thoughts, and she glanced at him. The firelight danced across his features as he stared heavy-lidded at the crackling flames before them. "Thank you, by the way, for saving me," she whispered.

Blane grunted in response, and Mariel elbowed him slightly in the ribs. He smiled and glanced at her. Mariel's breath caught in her chest as wolf eyes stared back at her before he blinked, amber eyes turning brown once more. "How's your chest?" he rumbled.

Mariel placed her hand on her sternum in confusion. "A little sore, why?"

Blane smiled and shook his head, glancing back at the fire. "No reason."

She scrunched her eyes brows and reached out, tugging at Blane's arm. "No, that was a weird thing to ask. Tell me why?"

He took a deep breath and patted her hand before standing up, this time the yawn cracking his jaw. "Because, little flame, you weren't breathing after we went over the falls."

Mariel's breath caught, realizing what he meant. Blane had done CPR on her, which also meant...

Her fingers flew to her lips, and Blane smirked before taking a few steps back toward the ladder to the loft bed. He winked at her before turning away. He was halfway up the ladder before he called out over his shoulder, "It's been a hell of a day, little flame. Maybe after a good night's sleep, I'll kiss you properly."

Mariel watched him disappear into the darkness of the loft and scoffed.

The absolute nerve that man had.

She turned back to the fire, ignoring the heat cascading down her cheeks and neck that had nothing to do with the flames before her. Shaking her head, she glanced back at the dark loft as the sound of Blane getting into bed reached her level. His groan of contentment had Mariel pressing her thighs together and biting her lip. She shouldn't be turned on right now. She should be concentrating on her magic. Finding a way to release it from the invisible bonds trapping it within her.

She closed her eyes and concentrated on the sounds around her, from the crackling of the fire in front of her and the steady pattering of rain on the roof. Soon, the sound of soft snores reached her ears. With her eyes still closed, she focused on herself, thinking of a single flame, a candle in the darkness, the barest flicker of light in the darkness. Instead, she found something else.

The whisper of new magic, wild and untamed, weaving its way through her mind. She reached out to touch it in her mind's eye before pulling away. She knew what this was. The mate bond. It shimmered, swaying toward her as if it wanted her to touch it. To nurture it and...

Something deeper down inside of her shivered, her magic stirring like a great beast. Not yet waking, but almost as if acknowledging this new magic trying to gain a foothold inside of her, as if her magic wanted the bond to grow.

Mariel opened her eyes and slowly got up, tiptoeing to the ladder, and made her way up to the loft. She let her eyes adjust to the low light until she could make out Blane's form. He was laying on his stomach, spread out on the bed, his breathing deep and even. Every few breaths, a soft snore would emerge. The comforter was haphazardly wound through his bare legs and across his ass. Mariel bit her lip. If she was a betting woman, she would say he was sleeping in the nude.

If she concentrated hard enough, she could feel the bond pulling between them, and a small little piece of her wanted to crawl forward and snuggle right up against him on the bed. Which would be a disaster, because Mariel knew she would be tempted to allow other things to happen, and she shouldn't give in to her less logical frame of mind.

What she should be doing was making her way back down the stairs and to the recliner. To think over her new predicament logically, but her body didn't want to obey logic. Instead, she climbed up the last few rungs and crawled toward the bed. She stopped when she reached the mattress, resting her elbows on the edge. Her brain and heart were at war with each other. Her brain screaming that this was a bad idea, that it would be too complicated, and she had just gotten out of a disastrous marriage. She shouldn't be shaking her life up again and bonding with someone she didn't even know.

Yet, her heart pulsed to a different tune altogether. And last time she checked, a witch should always trust her intuition and the innate feminine magic that flowed through the soul. Her intuition was screaming at her to let go, to let fate guide her. That this was the way toward unleashing her magic.

Mariel sucked on her bottom lip, ready to push away and let logic win, but a sleep laden voice yanked her out of her thoughts.

"Are you going to get in bed, or continue staring at me?"

"Uh... I... it's not... I wasn't..."

She floundered her words and Blane moved, rolling over to capture her shoulders and yank her onto the bed with him. She landed in a heap, half over his chest and one of her legs flung over his hips. She gripped his shoulders as he wrapped his arms around her and nestled her against him like he was a pillow. He rested his cheek on her head and rumbled, "Go to sleep, little flame."

Mariel huffed against him and tilted her head, her breath mingling with his. She brought her hand up to trace the outline of his bottom lip, and he nipped her fingertip. "You're playing with fire, mate. I can only be a gentleman for so long before—"

Fuck logic.

Mariel sighed, her lips so close to his, all she had to do was tilt her head and she could kiss him. "I like playing with fire."

Blane's rumbling growl echoed from his chest and sent shivers straight down her spine. Her pussy clenched and Blane groaned as his hand moved from her waist to her upper thigh. "I don't doubt it," he whispered before moving, his lips trailing across her jaw. "Talk to me, little flame."

This time, Mariel groaned, his low whisper turning her on more than she expected. His hot breath trailed down her jaw to her neck, where he kissed her gently. "Talk about what?" she gasped, her nails sinking into his shoulders.

"What changed?"

Mariel blinked slowly, her brain stuttering to keep up as Blane placed featherlight kisses up and down her neck. He was getting dangerously close to her lips, and Mariel squirmed, trying to turn her head so she could finally feel his lips against hers. He chuckled and rubbed the tip of his nose against her cheek.

"Little flame?" he asked and pulled away to look down at her.

Mariel whimpered and pulled at his shoulders, not wanting to break contact. "I... I saw it," she managed to choke out.

Shadows played across Blane's face as lightning lit up the dark sky outside. Thunder rolled in seconds later, and then darkness surrounded them once more. The only thing Mariel could make out was his dark silhouette pressing against hers. "Saw what?" he whispered as he threaded a hand through her hair, his lips a mere breath away from hers.

"The mate bond. I... I didn't know it was a tangible thing, but it's there. A whisper of magic inside my head. And, and..." Mariel sighed. "I don't know anymore. I don't know what to think anymore."

Blane rumbled against her chest, but didn't say anything as Mariel tried to gather her thoughts. She sucked on the bottom of her lip before turning her head to the side. "I think... I think I'm just confused."

"About what?"

"The bond... I always thought it was a lycanthrope thing. We were taught it wasn't something that could affect others as deeply. But... but what I feel, it..."

"It what?" Blane rumbled and brought his hand up to tip her face back toward his.

She frowned. "It's hard to fight. And for some reason, something deep inside of me is telling me not to. That if I just give in, then everything will be alright. Everything will work out."

"Is this you giving in, little flame?"

Mariel closed her eyes and took a deep breath. When she opened them again, she could make out the faint glow in Blane's eyes. His wolf was staring at her, and she held her breath. Thunder rolled over them again, the rain picking up its tempo, and she nodded.

Blane sucked in a deep breath, and it was the only warning Mariel got before he dipped his head and kissed her.

Chapter Six

BLANE

BLANE COULDN'T HOLD BACK any longer. The bond screamed for him to take his dangerously delicious mate trapped below him. He was trying to understand, truly understand, what held her back. What she was scared of. There was something she still wasn't telling him, but when she nodded, he lost the fight and dipped his head to capture her lips with his.

He sank into the kiss, threading his fingers through her hair. When she opened her mouth, accepting his kiss, he deepened it, and Mariel groaned as he explored her mouth with his. By the time he pulled away, his mate was panting, gasping for more than air.

She wiggled against him and arched her back, pressing her beautiful breasts against his chest.

There was still the flannel shirt between them and he really, really wanted it gone. She went to shrug it off, but Blane stopped her, capturing both her wrists in one of his hands and pinning them above her head.

This time, she growled, and Blane could almost feel the impatience thrumming through her body. "I thought you wanted this? Wanted me?"

Blane nipped at her lower lip. "Of course I do, little flame. I'm just taking my time with you."

His mate blushed, heat radiating off her, and Blane smirked. In the darkness, he knew she couldn't see him, but with his heightened senses, he could still see her. And there was something so erotic about her searching eyes. She arched against him again, and he leaned down, sucking on her lower lip. Something she did constantly, and it was something Blane had been dying to do. He elicited a whimper, and when he pulled away again, she whispered, "Do you want me to beg? Is that it?"

A growl rumbled through Blane as he trailed kisses down her neck, nipping at her exposed collarbone. "You will never have to beg with me, little flame. Just let me worship you."

His words seemed to settle her for the moment, and she relaxed as he slowly unbuttoned the shirt she wore. As his fingers grazed her full tits, he brushed them over her nipples, and his mate moaned so beautifully it almost had Blane coming right then and there. He lingered on her breasts for a moment, sucking and teasing, until his little flame was thrashing and whimpering underneath him.

Only then did he release her hands, and she instantly thrust her fingers into his hair. Her breath hitched as he trailed soft kisses over her stomach and moved lower. Cupping the backs of her knees, he threw them over his shoulders before nipping and sucking his way over her full hips and inner thighs. Her hands tightened in his hair and her voice broke through his lust-crazy mind. "I've... I've never had, um... my ex... he never wanted..."

Blane growled and inhaled his mate's sweet scent just begging to be tasted. He decided then and there this would be his favorite place for life and was determined to be between her legs at least twice daily.

She tugged at his hair. "Blane? I know guys don't like—"

"Don't like what, little flame? Burying their face between the legs of a goddess and devouring the sweet nectar of life? Because fuck, Mariel, this is where I would like to live the rest of my years. Nested right between your thighs."

He didn't give his mate time to respond as he gave her pussy a long generous lick before flicking the tip of his tongue across her clit.

His mate's startled moan was all Blane needed to hear, and he dipped his head again. His tongue danced along her wet pussy, dipping in and out as he moved up to work her clit. Far from gentle, he devoured her like a starving man, but his mate responded in kind. Nails bore down on his flesh, Mariel's trembling thighs squeezing tight around him. Her moans turned to breathless screams, and Blane felt his little flame stiffen right before she screamed his name. He drank down her sweet nectar as she orgasmed on his face and gently licked her pulsating pussy. He stroked her clit one last time, eliciting a soft whimper from his mate, before trailing kisses across her thighs and draping an arm over her hips. Dragging his fingers over one of her still trembling thighs, he smiled.

"Blane?" she whimpered, and he arched an eyebrow before kissing her hip softly. He gave her a thorough look, taking in the way the shadows danced across her gorgeous body.

"Come here." She tugged at his shoulders and bit her lip.

Blane nipped at her hip softly before he crawled his way back up her body, heading her call for him. She arched against him, angling her face toward his for a kiss. Grabbing her by the chin, he devoured her mouth in the same way he had her pussy, and his mate moaned, wrapping her arms around him. He was blissed out, so in the moment that he almost didn't feel it. The bond pulled between them, so strong, almost as strong as if he had already marked her. He broke the kiss, chuckling. Whether his little flame knew it or not, there was no way they were leaving this cabin after a week unbonded.

Marie narrowed her eyes, sending shivers down his spine. "Why did you laugh?"

Blane shook his head and nudged her legs closed with his free hand, pushing her onto her side before nibbling gently on her neck. "Nothing, little flame. I'm just enjoying my time with you."

She groaned, thrusting her ass up in Blane's hands as he laid his weight back over her body. He dragged his throbbing cock over her wet pussy, coating it with his juices as he nibbled across her neck again. His teeth grazed over her pounding pulse as he ran his cock across her pussy. His mate brought a hand up, dragging it through his hair, and turned her head. "Wait."

Blane stilled instantly. Shit, how had he already fucked this up?

His heart pounded hard in his chest, matching his mates as she bit her lip once more. He groaned at the sight, wanting nothing to bury his cock and teeth into her. She opened her mouth to speak before snapping it shut. When she didn't speak, Blane nudged his nose against hers and whispered, "Tell me, little flame. We don't have to do this. We can stop right now. There is no rush."

She took a shuddering breath and wiggled her hips, causing his cock to slide against her wet thighs.

His grip tightened on her hip at the movement, and a groan spilled from his lips. His mate took a deep breath. "I... No, I want you, it's just... I'm not sure about the mate bond yet. I know I said I was, but..."

Blane hushed her with a soft kiss and dragged his hand down, fingers teasing her clit. "Sex yes, bite no."

His little flame nodded, her eyes searching as if he would reject her over such a trivial thing. He growled and captured his lips with hers, fisting a hand in her hair before lining up his cock to her tight, wet entrance. He broke the kiss as he pushed into her and watched as her eyes fluttered. Her moan was music to his ears as he pushed deeper into her tight pussy. She wiggled against his unyielding embrace, her hips demanding him to go faster than his slow assault.

With a whine, his mate tried to move against him as his cock slid another few inches inside of her. "More, please. I need your—"

She gasped, unable to finish her words as Blane thrust the rest of the way inside. He stilled and whispered, "You need what, my little flame? Me to fuck this sweet little pussy of yours nice and slow? Or do you want me to work it hard and fast? Either way, you're going to come on my cock before I'm through with you."

His beautiful mate choked on her words, her eyes widening as he pulled out slowly until only the tip of his cock was still inside of her. Eyes roaming, he took in the gorgeous sight before him. His little flame splayed out on her side, her skin washed in shadows and the dim light provided only by the fireplace below. He squeezed her plump ass in his hand before giving it a soft slap. Gasping, she fisted her hands in the sheets before finding her words. "Both," she whispered, the look on her face both a dare and a confession. "I want both."

A groan erupted from Blane as he gripped her hips in place and pushed into her pussy in one hard thrust. She moaned as one of his hands slipped to her clit, pinching and rubbing, making his mate buck below him as he continued his hard thrusts into her. The heavy slaps of their flesh overtook the sound of the pounding rain outside. "Like fucking music to my ears," Blane rumbled as the sounds his mate was making crested to new heights. He felt her pussy tighten around his cock, and Mariel's lips parted in a silent plea before her scream echoed out. Her pussy pulsated around him, and Blane almost lost it right then and there, but instead, he slowed, riding his mate gently through her orgasm.

He turned her slightly, letting her splay stomach first onto the bed, and draped his body over hers. As he pumped into her deep and slow, he kissed and nibbled the arch of her ear and down the side of her jaw. Cupping a hand around the front of her neck, he moved his kisses back up until he got to the arch of her ear again. His mate whimpered and shoved her ass up into him. Her pussy was tight as sin, and Blane felt the telltale tingle start at the base of his spine and cock. He pulled back, interlacing his freehand with hers, and she groaned again as he thrust into her deeply twice more before pulling out and coming all over her back. Releasing her hand, he grabbed the flannel shirt that had somehow never made it off the bed.

He wiped her down quickly before pulling her into his arms and kissing the back of her neck. His mate snuggled into him, her breathing slow and steady, even as her heartbeat thundered against his chest. He intertwined his fingers once more with hers and kissed her forehead. Mariel groaned and threw a leg over his waist, snuggling even deeper into his side, her head falling into the crook of his neck and shoulder. "I wanted to go for three, but I couldn't last against that sweet pussy of yours."

Mariel moved, making herself comfortable before she whispered, "Three... three what?"

"Orgasms."

"Two was more than enough."

"Absolutely not. Tomorrow, I'm giving you three."

His mate signed. "Then I guess we should fall asleep so tomorrow comes more quickly."

"That's a fucking perfect idea," Blane whispered and cuddled his mate.

He listened as the sound of his mate's breathing evened out, and he finally closed his eyes, letting the sound of the rain and his mate in his arms lull him back to sleep.

Chapter Seven

MARIEL

MARIEL GROANED AND SNUGGLED deeper into the warmth surrounding her. A low rumble vibrated through her, and she slowly opened her eyes. Blinking them a few times, she listened to the persistent patter of rain along the roof. Soft gray light flooded through the cabin, and Mariel took a sudden breath.

Holy shit, she had slept with Blane.

Moving her hair out of the way, she realized the warmth she was cuddling was his body, and the rumbling was coming from his chest and soft snores. Her eyes roamed his hard body, snagging on his abs, then gorgeous shoulders, before reaching his face. Goddess above, he truly was a handsome man.

She shifted slowly, extracting herself from his embrace and the warm covers. Her body protested, sore from her toes all the way up to the tips of her ears. She sat at the end of the bed, her neck and back popping as she stretched. Glancing over her shoulder, she saw Blane was still blissfully asleep.

Closing her eyes, Mariel took a deep breath and turned her mind inward, searching until she found the deep well that carried her magic and the mate bond. It had felt stronger, a heaviness weighing on her mind. The bond connecting her to Blane was stronger and brighter, just as she expected. Yet when Mariel turned to her magic, she found it to be the same. No flame, no spark, just snuffed out nothingness.

Fingers caressed down her spine, and Mariel opened her eyes. She glanced over her shoulder, the frown already forming on her lips. Blane's eyes shone in the dim light, and she took a deep breath before shaking her head slightly. She needed to get out of here, if only for a moment. "I... I need to use the bathroom. I'll be back," she stammered and all but flung herself down the stairs.

Mariel wasn't lying. She actually did need to use the bathroom, and now she stood with her hand on the latch to lead her back outside and to the cabin. The cabin she had fled in panic, completely naked and into the pouring rain. She could only imagine what Blane thought of her actions. That single thought had her squaring her shoulders, her sadness turning to anger.

That was the old way of thinking, letting other people's judgments command her actions. Her family and her ex-husband had dictated her life and how to live it. She had been forced to shape her life around their opinions and, in the end, it had cost her everything. She had come here to regain her magic and her independence. Mariel had come to the mountains to find herself again. She closed her eyes and took a deep breath; she was tired of running. She wanted to be brave and finally take a chance. And she wanted that chance to start with Blane.

But first, she had to leave the bathroom, and she had a confession to get off her chest. And if Blane still wanted her as his mate after all that, she would fully embrace it. She pushed the door open and stepped out onto the rain-soaked grass. Her eyes instantly found him, standing under the porch overhang, arms crossed across his naked chest. He was fisting a shirt in his hand, and it covered his lower half, barely. Blane was just as naked as her, and under other circumstances, Mariel would appreciate the view. He made a move to come down the stairs to her, but she shook her head and held up her hand. He stilled and Mariel dashed through the rain as thunder rumbled overhead. The second her foot touched the first porch step, Blane reached out to grasp her shoulders, pulling her the rest of the way and into his warm embrace. He wrapped the button-down shirt around her, and turned them both, backing up until her back hit the outside cabin wall.

Mariel gulped as a growl erupted from him. "Talk to me, little flame. Why the hell did you just run away like that?"

She read between the lines, and her heart shattered as his voice wavered.

Why did you run away from me? he truly asked. Or maybe it was the feeling she somehow picked up from the ever-strengthening bond between them. Gulping, she took a deep breath, her eyes finding his. She reached out to grip his forearms. "I want you. I want you, but I'm scared you won't want me after what I tell you. And you need to know before we take this any further."

Blane took a deep breath as to speak, but Mariel brought a hand to his lips. He froze under the touch and clenched his jaw. When he didn't say anything, Mariel continued. "I married far too young, not even nineteen before my parents found me a suitable warlock to marry. I come from an old, old witch line who traces their roots back to Europe. We, well... My family is a respected magical family in the community. And all I've ever known my whole life was their control, their control over me and my magic. And then my husband..."

A growl reverberated down her chest, and Blane's eyes flashed amber. Mariel gulped. "Ex-husband," she whispered, and that little word seemed to calm her wolf slightly.

That thought alone managed to make her pause. When had she started thinking of Blane as hers?

"Is that all? Do you worry I wouldn't want you because of some family name? Because I don't care about your past, only that you are here with me."

Blane's question snapped her back to reality, and she shook her head. "I wish that was all. But..." She sucked on her bottom lip, and Blane reached up, rubbing his thumb over it.

"Little flame, you can tell me. Just tell me. Tell me so we can get past what is keeping you from me fully."

"Fine," she snapped. "You want to know! I can't have kids. I can't have kids, and that was why my husband, my ex-husband, cheated and blamed me for it. And ultimately, that was what led to my family disowning me because I was defective. Then I got so fucking angry, I torched my house to the ground and was punished for it."

She pushed at his chest, her anger seeping into her veins. More at herself than him, knowing this was it. He was going to walk away, because that's what everyone did. Blane let her push him away, but stepping back into her space, he tangled a hand through her hair, forcing her to look at him.

"Is that all?"

Mariel froze in shock. That wasn't...

That wasn't how he was supposed to react. And that wasn't how he was supposed to be looking at her. The longing was still there. He still wanted her, even after her confession. The reason she was no longer on speaking terms with her family, the reason behind why her husband cheated on her, and the reason why she lost control, and with it, her magic.

"Is that all..." she spat his question back at him. This time, she punched him in the chest. "Is that all!" she screamed, fury and tears swarming her vision. She punched him in the chest again, and again. And he let her.

The tears streamed down her face, as she let the pain, sadness, and anger she had been harboring finally erupt from her.

She wasn't sure how long he held her as she beat on his chest and cried until her fists turned to hands desperately clutching his shoulders, trying to get closer to him rather than push away. She shivered as he kissed the top of her head, one hand still gripping a fistful of her hair as his other hand stroked her back. "That's it, little flame. Let it out.

Let it go. I have you, and I'm never letting go. I have you," Blane murmured, and Mariel sniffled slightly.

His hand in her hair tightened, tilting her head back so he could look at her. He angled his face and brushed his lips gently over hers, nibbling at her lips until she opened them for him. He didn't dive deeper into her mouth as she expected, instead slipping his tongue between her open lips and sucking on her upper lip. She groaned and closed her eyes as his hands found their way down her back to her ass, then to her thighs. He scooped her up without breaking contact, her knees resting over the crook of his elbows, his hands grasped firmly on her ass. Pressing his body into hers, he pinned her to the cabin wall. His erect cock nudged firmly against her lower stomach, and she moaned again as he slipped his tongue into her mouth. The kiss was gentle and deep, and Mariel threaded her hands through his hair, squirming against his hold. She rubbed herself against his cock as it hit her clit just right.

Blane pulled back slightly, and she whimpered until he hushed her. "Little flame, open your eyes."

She did as he asked and held her breath. The way he was looking at her dug at the wound deep inside of her, and when he started speaking, she almost started crying again.

"I'm your family now, little flame. I will never leave you, cheat on you, or hurt you. If you want kids, we can adopt. It makes no difference to me. Family is who you choose, not who you're born to. And I will never control you, except during sex." He smirked, and Mariel scoffed before he kissed her lightly again. "Speaking of which," he murmured against her lips, "I'm going to fuck you. Right here, right now. And you are going to come for me, on my cock, as I bury it deep into that soft little pussy of yours. Do you understand me?"

She tightened her fingers, pulling Blane's hair as he pushed her farther up on the wall, his cock teasing her entrance. She gasped against his lips as he sank into her with one thrust. The root of his cock brushed against her clit, pleasure already building low inside of her as he pulled out almost completely before thrusting back into her. With every thrust, he murmured against her lips, calling her his goddess, his little flame, his mate.

Mariel felt her orgasm build, her pussy tightening as his slow thrusts hit her deep and rubbed in all the right places. But she needed more. She moaned, "Bite me. Bite me, please. Do it. Bind us together."

Blane groaned against her lips and never faltered in his slow thrusts as he nibbled down her neck, teeth scraping over her thundering pulse. Her orgasm ripped through her as his teeth pierced her skin, and Mariel swore she saw stars as another orgasm washed over her first one. She screamed Blane's name as he ground into her, until he froze, his cock twitching as he came inside of her still pulsating pussy.

Chapter Eight

BLANE

BLANE PLACED THE DIRTY dishes to soak in a small tub on the makeshift kitchen counter before joining Mariel in front of the fire. A soft smile crept over his lips as he slipped into the recliner and stared at his mate's exposed shoulder and neck. She had her hair braided to the side, his flannel shirt too large for her and sliding down to show the mating bite he had given her earlier that day. He didn't disturb her and instead watched as his mate meditated. Trying to speak to her magic, she had told him an hour ago.

Cocking his head, he stretched out his legs and waited. He didn't have to wait long as his little flame muttered a curse before opening her eyes and slapping her hands against the bearskin rug. "Damn it all the hell."

Blane tapped his foot on her thigh, letting her know he was behind her, and she yelped in surprise before turning around fully to face him. "No luck?" he asked.

She shook her head and leaned back on her hands, shaking out her legs. "No, I just don't understand it. Before... everything, my magic was just there, begging to be used. I never had to be taught; it was instinct. I just knew how to use it. Yet now I can feel the bond, and I can see where my magic is supposed to be, but it just won't..." She lifted a hand and made a swooshing motion.

Blane snorted. "Light? Explode? Whoosh into existence?"

His mate pointed a finger at him. "Exactly."

"But you can feel the mating bond?"

A blush rose to Mariel's cheeks, and Blane almost groaned from the beautiful sight. Fuck, his mate was gorgeous when she blushed. "Yes," she whispered, her voice hoarse as if remembering what had transpired earlier that morning.

"What does the mating bond feel like?"

She startled slightly at his question before taking a deep breath and closing her eyes. He felt her then, touching the bond, and a shiver ran down his spine. When she finally opened her eyes, they blazed with fire before she blinked quickly, and her beautiful blue eyes stared back at him. "It feels untamed. Heavy and wild, like a rushing river. How can anyone control that? Is that what lycanthrope magic is like?"

Blane shrugged. "Maybe you are asking the wrong question. We are taught that magic can't be controlled, that it is a gift, and you must treat it as such. Like a wild animal that gives you the gift of not eating you. It will only allow itself to be treated like an equal, not a servant."

Mariel frowned and shook her head. "That's... that's not how...that's not how witch magic works."

"Why not?" Blane whispered, and his mate looked at him with such confusion on her face that he almost laughed. She shook her head and glanced away from him as if thinking. When she closed her eyes again, he felt her caress their bond.

"Mariel," he growled, and a shiver of pleasure ran through him again.

She opened her eyes and sucked on her bottom lip, feeling it too.

"Mariel, come here," he growled again, and she got to her knees, placing her hands on his knees.

"I'm tired of talking about my magic," she whispered as her eyes hooded.

The fire flickered shadows across them, and Blane sucked in a deep breath. He didn't say anything, but he swore the fire twisted, reaching toward them, toward his mate like the hand of a lover. It settled back down a second later, and Blane's concentration slipped back to Mariel.

She slid her hands up his thighs and up the planes of his stomach. Her fingers toyed along the waistband to the sweatpants he was wearing, and he groaned. "What did you have in mind, little flame?"

She smirked. "Oh, nothing much. Just something to pass the time."

Blane held his breath as her hand slid into his pants and grasped his already hard cock. She pushed his pants down slightly, letting his erection break free. He threaded his hand through her hair as she dipped her head and tentatively swirled her tongue around the head of his cock. His grip on her hair tightened, and he let his head fall back, groaning as she licked along his length before putting his cock in her mouth.

"Fuck," he whispered as she started to bob her head, one hand wrapped around the base of his shaft. She licked and sucked, twisting her hand around the base of his cock in the same rhythm as her mouth. All too soon, Blane felt the telltale tingle in his balls and at the base of his spine. If she kept this up, he would come right in his mate's mouth. And he wasn't ready to do that quite yet. He tightened the grip on her hair before collaring her gently with his other hand. She hummed in the back of her throat, protesting the gentle tug at her hair, and Blane almost came right then and there.

"Up, on my lap now," he growled and glanced down at his mate.

She hummed again before releasing his unbearably hard cock from her mouth and glanced up at him with a grin.

"Now," he growled again.

She complied this time and shifted higher up on her knees, crawling into his lap. Moving her slightly, he draped her legs over the arms of the chair and released his hold on her hair, but not her neck as positioned his fingers over her glistening pussy. As his fingers slid across her entrance easily, she groaned against his hold, nails sinking into his shoulders. His mate bucked her hips against his hand as he pushed two fingers into her wet pussy. He pumped them into her three times before pulling out and spreading her juices over his cock, lubing it up.

"Blane," she pleaded as he pulled his fingers out of her, and he lifted his head to capture her lips in a deep kiss before lining his cock up with her entrance. He pushed into her tight pussy slowly, and she moaned into his mouth. Once he was fully situated inside of her, he broke the kiss and pushed away, leaning her back against his legs.

"Oh, fuck," she whispered as she dangled over his legs backwards, her head tipped back, and arms curved down to touch the floor.

Blane chuckled softly and trailed his finger over her exposed clit, pinching it slightly. A shudder racked through her entire body, and Mariel's high-pitched moan echoed out. He pressed his forearm across her hips, trapping her from moving against his cock. Then he moved his legs to trap her shoulders and arms. Mariel whimpered and gasped once she realized how easily he had tied her up just using his body.

"Easy," he murmured. "I'm just warming my cock in your sweet pussy, you know. Just to pass the time."

He pinched her clit again before softly rubbing the tip of a finger in a circle over it.

"Blane!" she squealed, her hips bucking into his hand.

He smirked and settled back into the recliner, continuing his assault on her clit as she desperately struggled against his hold. "Just tell me to stop, little flame, and I will."

She took a deep breath, and for a moment, Blane thought she was going to tell him that this position was too much for her. Instead, a high-pitched keening reached his ears just as her pussy clenched down around his cock in a stranglehold. As her orgasm rippled over his cock, she whimpered his name, her voice cracking. Her pussy didn't release its hold as the orgasm continued to roll over her, and he pulled her upright until they were facing each other again. His mate breathed heavily, dropping her head to the crook of his neck, and he cradled her gently against his chest before moving his hips slowly. She whimpered and kissed his neck, as he trailed his hands under the shirt she was still wearing. He caressed her back as he moved gently inside of her. Another shudder rippled through her as he dipped his head and teased his teeth along the mating mark at her neck.

"I... oh, I think," Marial gasped, and her pussy fluttered around his cock as she came again. This time, her pussy pulsated around his cock gently, and he thrust deep as he his own orgasm rolled over him.

The crackling of the fire mingled with their panting breaths, and Blane closed his eyes as Mariel rested against him. He opened his eyes slightly and noticed once again how the flames seemed to reach toward his mate as she rested against his chest in a blissed-out state. She mumbled something, and he grunted, "What did you say, little flame?"

Nuzzling at his neck, she shook her head. He ran his fingers up and down her back, rocking the chair.

Now this was a state of pleasure he could stay in forever. With his mate still recovering from an orgasm and warming his cock next to a crackling fireplace. He could stay here forever, except they shouldn't fall asleep in the chair. That would just cause a backache he didn't want to deal with later. Not if he had to keep his mate happy and satisfied.

With a grunt from him, and a groaning complaint from Mariel, he shifted them out of the chair and onto the bearskin rug. His mate blinked up at him and a satisfied grin lined her lips. He brushed his fingers over them after he laid her on a warm rug. Moving behind her, he pulled her in close and rested his arm under her head. Blane kissed the back of her neck as she curled his arm around her waist and tangled her hand in his. She sighed again, fluttering her eyes open slightly.

"Hmmm?" He kissed her neck again. "Was that a sigh of satisfaction? Because if not, then I need to step up my game."

Mariel chuckled. "That was definitely a sigh of satisfaction. That was... I don't have the words."

Blane nibbled on the back of her neck. "Good. I just want you to be happy and satisfied tonight. Tomorrow, we can tackle your magic again."

He felt her nod and pulled his arm tighter around her waist. Waiting until her body relaxed, slipping to sleep, he followed right after her.

Chapter Nine

MARIEL

MARIEL WOKE TO THE sound of birds chirping and the utter lack of rain pounding on the roof. Soft light streamed in through the windows and played across her face and body. She grumbled, not ready for the daylight, and rolled over in the warm arms surrounding her.

Cold air attacked her backside, and she shivered before throwing a hand over her head, pointing it toward the fireplace. The crackling of fire soon filled the room and Mariel snuggled back in the arms of her mate, warmth coming at her from both sides.

She bolted upright with a yelp, comprehension dawning, staring wide-eyed at the piece of wood alight on the top of the wood stack. "Holy fuck," she whispered before rushing to the piece of wood and throwing it into the fireplace.

"Well, that was entertaining to watch." Blane chuckled, and Mariel glanced over her shoulder, still in shock and trying to process what had happened. She took a deep breath before snapping her finger.

A small flame fluttered into existence before slowly extinguishing. It wasn't much, but it was so much more than she could have expected in the past few years and tears began to fall. Blane moved quickly, wrapping his arms around her, and squeezed. "Please tell me those are happy tears?" he murmured while peppering soft kisses along her jaw and neck.

Mariel nodded, still holding her hands up in front of her, silent sobs shaking her body. "Yes, yes," she managed to hiccup between breaths. "I can feel it. It's small, but I can feel it. The warmth of my magic inside of me."

She closed her eyes, allowing her mind to fall into the well that was her power. While the mate bond felt like a roaring river inside of her, her magic was a trickle next to it. It twisted its way next to the bond, touching and feeding into it at some places. She reached out into those places and took a deep breath.

That was it.

The magic from the bond had not only restarted her magic, but it had fused itself to it in certain places, feeding it like how a raging river fed the outlets and streams around it. Mariel opened her eyes with a smile playing on her lips and turned in Blane's arms. She grabbed his face and kissed him deeply. He kissed her back with such ferocity, she lost her breath. Pulling away, she rubbed her nose against his. "I can feel every flicker of flame. From the one inside of me, to the fire behind us and the..."

Mariel sucked in a breath, her eyes growing wide. "Oh..." She jumped up, running to the front door and burst out onto the porch. Blane was on her heels, his arm encircling her waist when she stopped, his large body cocooning her with his.

The raging storm had ceased sometime during the night, leaving behind dew laden grass and crystal-clear skies. Except for the trail of smoke wafting up from deep within the forest. Mariel stretched out her magic and felt a raging fire deep in her bones as she watched in horror. The smoke thickened by the second, the fire growing until flames flicked beneath the smoke eating along to tops of the trees. She brought a shaking hand up, pointing to the smoke Blane had no doubt already seen.

His grip tightened around her waist. "Fucking damn it all to hell." Then he was tugging on her, bringing her back into the cabin. She followed, her body growing numb from the adrenaline coursing through her. She was barely able to catch up with everything Blane was doing around her. He shoved one of his shirts in her hands before shrugging on a pair of actual hiking pants. It was only when he reached down to tie his hiking boots that Mariel's brain finally caught up. Shaking her head, she shrugged on the shirt Blane had shoved into her hands.

They were making a run for it.

That was the only logical thing to do, except...

She glanced down at her bare feet before feeling her magic along the uncontrolled fire sweeping closer by the second. They wouldn't make it. At least not if Blane was carrying her down the mountain. She moved closer, touching his shoulder tentatively. "Blane," she whispered, and he glanced up at her with a hint of his wolf flickering across his gaze.

"Don't worry, Mariel. I'll carry you. We will be fine. We can make—"

She shook her head, cutting him off. "You need to trust me. That fire is moving fast, and I'll only slow you down."

Blane stared at her, and for the first time, she saw anger weave its way into his expression. "Are you seriously asking me to abandon you here? My mate, the one thing every Lycan lives and breathes and prays to one day have. I know we don't know each other as well as you want, but you should know the absolute truth in my next words. I will never leave you."

His words brought tears to Mariel's eyes. She felt his statement radiate all the way down their bond. She knew Blane would rather die than leave her, and she couldn't fault him for feeling that way, because it was entirely mutual.

Mariel nodded, and Blane strode forward, wrapping his hand in hers. He pulled them both out the door and down the front porch before halting. "Shit."

Shit was right.

Mariel lifted her arm over her face on instinct, the smoke already thick in the air. She lived and breathed fire, and she knew this was bad. Really, really bad. Her mind raced as her own magic tugged at her, and in the back of her mind, a plan started to form.

It was a long shot, suicidal even, with barely a chance of working, but if Blane refused to leave, then she had to try. For both of them.

"I have a plan," she cried out through the intense smoke and sudden breeze. "Wet down some shirts to put on your body and cover your nose and mouth. I'll use my magic. Fight fire with fire."

Blane stared at her, a crazed look entering his eyes, his wolf still at the surface before he nodded and dashed back into the house. Mariel wiped her hands on her sweaty thighs, the heat from the impending fire already affecting her. Then she sat and closed her eyes, diving deep into the well of her power. And there, she began to weave.

Mixing the power of their mate bond, wild and unyielding magic, with hers. She expected resistance at first, but was pleasantly surprised when the magic gravitated like water toward each other. But it still wasn't enough. She needed something more...

Blane's body wrapped around her from behind, his fingers weaving with hers as he murmured in her ear, "I'm here. I felt the magic call. It wants you to take it, take the magic from my side of the bond too."

Mariel gulped, the fire licking dangerously close as she dove into the bond and wrapped the heavy magic around herself and Blane. She drew from the both of them, letting the fire inside build until she could barely hold on any longer. It crested, until it was suffocating her mentally and physically. And still, she held on by the barest of threads, feeding even more magic into her. If her plan was to work, she needed to access every iota of power at her disposal. Her entire body burned as she opened her eyes, and she stood, stepping out of Blane's comforting grasp. She stretched out her arms and let it all go in one rage-filled scream.

Her scream rang crystal clear, her magic flowing from her hands to build a wall of dancing blue fire around what was hers. The cabin, the land, and most of all, her mate. Time flickered, holding its breath between one second and the next as both waves of fire collided in a deafening blast.

Mariel began to chant, and pushed toward the fire, moving slowly until her chant grew and she thrust her own wall of fire forward a quarter of an inch. Then she did it again, even as her voice lost its battle against the surrounding smoke. She felt blood drip from her nose, trailing its way over her lips and chin, dripping down her body, and yet she pushed further, draining every drop of magic she had pulled out of her mind.

Mariel's knees gave out first, the ground coming up fast, and she closed her eyes, waiting for the impact, but it never came as strong arms wrapped around her. She coughed and sputtered, trying to slap off the damp cloth wiping at her face. Then the most handsome voice she had ever heard cut through the roaring sound of her own blood in her head.

"Mariel, Mariel, Mariel, please don't make me do CPR on you again. I swear to the moon goddess, if you pull this shit again—"

Mariel's eyes were heavy, but she managed to crack them open and lift a soot-covered hand to place on her mate's cheek. "I did it."

Her whisper had Blane scooping her tighter against his chest, crushing her in his arms as he shook. "Yes, yes, my little flame, you did."

She held him back and glanced around, her blue flames slowly flickering away into nothingness. The land around them was scorched, the natural fire having laid waste to the forest before them, but behind...

Mariel smiled, tears streaming down her face. The forest behind them was safe, the cabin was still intact, and her mate was still alive.

Blane coughed slightly before standing up and taking her with him. He swept her up in his arms. "Let's get the hell out of here. Let's go home."

Mariel nodded and kissed her mate. "Home sounds good. But..." She glanced down at her bare feet. "How will I get down the mountain?"

Chapter Ten

THREE DAYS LATER - MARIEL

"YOU'RE GOING TO PACE a hole in the rug, mate."

Mariel stopped to glare at Blane, who relaxed in a chair, his feet kicked up on a glass coffee table.

"Easy for you to say," she murmured and started to pace again. She glanced around the room, in all its decked-out elegance, from the peachy-white painted walls, and soft-colored furnishings. It reminded her of the life she left behind, screaming old money. She just hoped the owner of the house, Blane's alpha, didn't hold on to old beliefs too. Mariel sucked on her bottom lip, and a low growl emanated from Blane.

Mariel spared him a look, and he patted his knee. "Little flame, stop pacing and come here. I promise everything will be fine."

"You keep saying that, but I'm the fly in the spider's web, so to speak."

Blane's eyes lit up amber. "Mariel, it will be fine. Trust me. You know I won't hurt you, and that extends to anyone who tries to hurt you too."

He patted his leg again, and Mariel gave up her nervous pacing and sat. Blane wrapped his arms around her waist before whispering, "That's my good little flame. After this, we can go to my place, and as an award, I'll let you sit on my face."

Mariel's giggle was interrupted as a tall woman, dressed in a stylish cut suit, stalked into the room. She flicked her curly honey-brown hair over her shoulder and hit Mariel with a sensual smile, her ruby red lips entrancing and full. "Who's sitting on whose face? And can I join?"

Blane's chest rumbled, and Mariel stammered, "I... um... are you, is that the, are you the alpha?"

The woman snorted before leaning across the bar situated at the far side of the room and grabbing a decanter of liquor. She uncapped it and pointed it toward the both of them. "You want any?"

"That's Sasha. She is second in command. The alpha's twin sister. And speaking of which, where—"

"Funny choice of words, Blane." Sasha's eyes glowed hot for a moment and she took a huge inhale of the air. "It will be fun to have two witches in the house."

Mariel stiffened on Blane's knee. "Two?"

Blane shook his head. "It's supposed to be a secret, and I couldn't say anything until approval."

"Which you still don't have until we ask a few questions," a voice rumbled through the room, and Mariel turned back around in time to see a man and woman stalk in. The similarities between the siblings were uncanny, but it was the red-headed woman and the magic surrounding her that drew Mariel's attention. She stood slowly, her magic testing the air, snapping forward instinctually to say hello to a fellow sister.

The woman's magic did the same, and she gasped before giggling. "I don't know if I'll ever get used to that. It's so weird. I'm Lily, by the way."

Lily reached out to shake Mariel's hand before the alpha pulled her back. "Bunny, love. I know you want another witch to be part of the household, but we don't know her."

"Oh hush, Hunter. I know her, or actually, Breena knows her. Mariel was supposed to show up for a coven meeting last month, but apparently chickened out. Or at least, that is what Breena said."

Lily giggled again as Mariel listened to the exchange about her between the two of them, and the feeling was absolutely surreal. So surreal she felt faint and leaned against Blane. "We died, didn't we? We are charred husks of meat sitting on top of that mountain."

Everyone stopped to stare at her, and Blane kissed her temple. "Quite the vivid imagination, little flame. But we are still alive, and if these three hurry up, I can show you how alive we really are."

Sasha chuckled from the bar stool across the room. "Cute. Still want to know if I can join in on the face sitting, though."

The alpha, Hunter, clapped his hands to get everyone's attention. "Okay, let's make this quick, as I have other things to attend to. You and Blane are mated now; I can see that clear as day. What I need to know is if you have any nefarious intentions toward the pack and the local coven, especially now that we are meeting with the supernatural council in a month... What was your name again?"

Lilly bounced on her toes and spoke at the same time as Blane.

"Mariel."

"My mate's name is Mariel. And the only nefarious intentions are mine."

Mariel held up her hands, and everyone silenced. "Wait... wait, your pack and the local coven are working together? When did this happen? And what is this about the supernatural council?"

"Yes," Hunter said, and Mariel blinked, waiting for more elaboration. When none came, she took a deep breath and leveled her stare at the alpha.

"Yes? That is all you are going to say?"

Hunter stared right back at her, and Blane tightened his arms around Mariel's waist. "Yes, that is all. That is all until we determine if you are a threat or not."

Mariel was more than ready to snap right back at him, but the grip on her waist, and the way Blane took a deep breath and held it, stopped her. She swallowed her pride, but didn't break the stare-off she was having with the alpha. "I would never be a threat to my mate. And because he is part of your pack and you seem tolerant toward witches and possibly bringing this stupid vendetta between the races to a halt, then I will confidently say I have no nefarious intentions toward anyone here."

Hunter tilted his head and nodded. "Good enough."

He turned toward Lily and pointed to the door. "We are going to be late."

She gasped, her eyes going wide before waving to Mariel. "It was nice meeting you. I'll formally introduce myself tomorrow."

Sasha snorted again as Lily grabbed Hunter's hand, and all but dragged him out the door. She took another swig from the bottle before looking back at Mariel and Blane. "You're not the sharing type, are you?"

Mariel shook her head and gave Sasha a small smile. "You're really pretty, but you're right. I don't like to share."

Sasha shrugged and slipped off the bar stool, disappearing out the same door as Hunter and Lilly. Which just left Mariel sitting on Blane's lap.

He leaned in and whispered, "Want to see my place? We can TV and chill?"

Mariel chuckled and turned in Blane's embrace, kissing him passionately. When she finally pulled away, his eyes sparked with amber.

"Please tell me that was a yes."

Mariel nodded, and Blane swept her up in his arms, rushing out of the room.

Blane had all but run out of the house and tossed Mariel into his truck. She laughed, throwing her head back, and let the wind ruffle her hair as his truck sped off down a dirt road on the alpha's property and Mariel watched the trees whip by. She smiled as the mansion disappeared in less than a minute. Ten minutes later, they pulled into a small lot, and Mariel's jaw dropped as she scrambled out of the truck. "It looks like a bigger version of the cabin."

He came up from behind and threw her over his shoulder. Mariel screamed and giggled as she watched the ground pass by upside down. She heard the jingle of keys, and then low light illuminated the interior of the cabin. Blane slid her into his arms, and she took a good look around. Her eyes danced over the golden-hued wood furnishings, marble countertops, and the bearskin rug in front of the fireplace. Her face warmed, thinking back to the cabin in the mountains. While this one was more modern, with indoor plumbing and what looked like an even bigger loft, Mariel couldn't help but miss their mountain sanctuary.

Blane set her down on her feet gently. "It's modeled after it, but..."

"It's pretty, but..."

She turned in his arms, and he nodded. "I know, little flame, there is just something about the cabin in the mountains that isn't here."

She nodded before glancing around again. "We will just have to visit our little mountain sanctuary more often."

Blane cracked a wicked smile. "Our?"

"You heard me. And didn't you promise me a face sitting if I was good? Or were you just being a tease?"

Blane's grip on her hips grew tighter, and he growled before capturing her lips with his. He had her on the bearskin rug before she could take her next breath. The buttons on her shirt scattered across the wooden floor, and she arched into Blane's hands as they cupped her tits, massaging and pinching her nipples until she cried out. Moving her hands to her jeans, she unbuttoned them and shoved them as far down as she could.

She wanted his mouth and hands all over her naked body, and she didn't care if he had to rip the rest of his clothes off.

Chuckling, he pushed her down with one hand on her chest. His eyes wandered over her body, and she whimpered, arching her hips up as he dragged a finger down the plane of her stomach to the top of her lacy underwear. "I don't know if I'm upset that we stopped by your place last night to shower and rest or not. On the one hand, this matching bra and panty set is sexy as all hell. But it does mean that you have clothes on... and shoes that you can use later to run away from me with."

Mariel huffed and tried to sit up, but Blane held her in place. She wiggled against him and moved to roll up again. This time, Blane settled his weight over her and leaned down to suck on a nipple through the lace of her bra. She cried out, shoving her hands through his hair. "Stop teasing me. I was good. I want my reward.

Blane released her nipple with a pop and glanced at her with a wicked smile. "You are quite right. You were good... ish."

Mariel snorted at his words, but held her breath as he continued tugging her pants down until they got to the top of her beat-up tennis shoes. They went flying across the room, her pants close behind. Her stomach dipped as Blane took one finger and drew it up the seam of her underwear. Her pussy began to throb as those fingers pulled her panties to the side and rubbed against her wet entrance. Mariel moaned and arched her back as Blane teased her clit and outer lips with his fingers. "I need you inside of me," she whimpered, her pussy already tightening with anticipation.

"Mmmmm, we will get to that later."

Mariel was about to protest, the words ready to spill from her lips as Blane pulled away, but the look on his face stopped her. Carnal desire danced through his eyes as he gripped her hips, and in a move she couldn't follow, she was suddenly straddling his face.

"Ohhh! Oh, fuck, fuck, fuck," she screamed out as Blane spread her legs and sucked hard on her clit. He continued his assault on her throbbing pussy through her panties, and Mariel screamed again as the unexpected sensation threw her into a deep orgasm. She dug her hands into the bearskin rug, slumping over as the orgasm ripped through her entire body. Blane caught her as spots overtook her vision. Her pussy continued to clench as Blane laid her gently on her stomach and removed her soaked underwear. The cool air against her sensitive flesh was too much, and Mariel whimpered.

Blane hushed her as he settled over her, interlacing his hands with hers, his thick cock nudging at her entrance. They both groaned as he entered her gently, sliding in without resistance. He took her slow and deep, rolling in and out. Blane leaned down and licked the mating mark on her neck, and Mariel gasped as warmth ran down her spine, all the way to her pussy. He nibbled at the mark, and she sighed, falling into the steady rhythm of his cock rocking in and out of her. A second orgasm built low inside of her, weaving through her body, and her pussy pulsated softly around Blane's cock. She squeezed his hands as he thrust deeply before his cock twitched and he released inside of her.

"I love you, little flame," he whispered in her ear, his weight like a warm blanket settled over her.

Mariel smiled as pure bliss settled over her. "I love you too, my wolf. My mate."

Epilogue

THREE MONTHS LATER - BLANE

A NEW DUSTING OF snow danced around Blane's paws as he slunk through the shadows of the bare trees. He skirted their mountain cabin, coming around to the side the fire had decimated three months ago. His mate had proposed bringing building material up, wanting to make the cabin habitable year-round, and Blane was more than ecstatic. Getting the stuff up the mountain wasn't as hard as he thought it would be, hiring a supply company who used pack animals to get the materials to their destination. Mariel and Blane showed up a few days later and got to work with installation and a partial roof for the outdoor shower.

Then Mariel smirked and pulled out one more plan.

A wood fire hot tub.

Blane crept forward on silent paws; his mate currently bent over, ass at the perfect level for a little love bite.

She screamed in alarm and spun around, flames flickering from her fingers as Blane danced away, his tongue lolling out of the side of his mouth.

Mariel narrowed her eyes. "Really, Blane? What if I had flambéed you into a little wolfie crisp?"

Blane woofed softly and wiggled his butt in the air before turning around and pelting snow toward his mate with his hind paws.

Her mouth dropped open in shock before she shook the fire from her palm and reached down to scoop up a snowball.

Blane easily dodged it, and then the chase was on, his mate sliding around the cabin after him, snowballs raining down around him. He sprinted around the cabin one more time, losing her quickly before shifting back into a man. He turned just in time to wrap his arms around Mariel as she collided into him. They rolled through the snow, Blane coming out on top. Flashing his surprised mate a smile, he kissed her deeply. She arched into him, her breath rasping against his as he groped her ass through her snowpants.

She pushed away with a giggle, fire swimming through her eyes, and Blane reached out in his mind to caress their mate bond. A shiver that had nothing to do with the cold ran through his mate and her eyes hooded. "You know, we should test out that hot tub. While you were out patrolling, I got it finished and the water pumped in. The fire is already going, and the water is heating up."

A wicked smile played along Blane's lips, and he pushed away, grabbing his mate as he went. "That sounds like a wonderful idea. Except for one issue."

A split second of confusion flashed across his mate's face before she narrowed her eyes. She knew he was up to something, and it made Blane happy that in such a short time his mate already knew how playful he could be.

"And what issue would that be?" She looked down, her hand caressing his hard cock, unaffected by the cold air.

Blane growled as she continued to stroke him. "The issue..." He paused as her grip tightened, his thoughts scattering as Mariel took her other hand and began to massage his balls.

He groaned and grabbed her hands. "The issue is you're still dressed. And you are being extremely naughty."

Laughing, she shook her head. "Says the wolf who bit my ass earlier."

"And I plan on doing it again, my little flame."

His mate released his cock and took a step back, mischief twinkling in her eyes. She took another step back, and as Blane went to follow, she tsked him. "Stay right there. We are going to play a little game."

Blane groaned, but nodded, interested in what his mate had in store for him.

"You're going to close your eyes and count to fifteen. Then you're gonna find me."

Blane closed his eyes quickly, a smirk playing across his lips as he heard his mate spin on her heel and take off as he counted. Once he got to fifteen, he sprinted around the house, following her footsteps. He skidded to a halt as he stumbled across the pile of her clothes and chuckled. "You naughty girl."

Mariel's laugh echoed out, and he shook his head as he stalked toward the hot tub she was lounging in.

"You're not that good at hide and seek, little flame."

"Who said anything about hide and seek? I just told you to come find me after counting to fifteen."

Blane snorted as he vaulted over the side of the tub, splashing his mate as landed. Before she had any chance to protest, he had her in his arms, his mouth covering hers. She sank into him and straddled his legs, his cock lining up with her pussy perfectly. Grabbing her hips as she sank down slowly, her pussy stretched to accommodate him, and she groaned into his mouth.

He rocked against her, thrusting up to meet her and slide in the rest of the way. His mate broke the kiss to cry out, her nails sinking into his shoulders as her pussy tightened around his cock. "Oh fuck, yes. Just like that," she whimpered as Blane ground into her, only pulling back a few inches before thrusting back in. The water splashed around them, mixing with the sound of Mariel's cries and his low growls.

"Touch yourself," Blane growled as he concentrated on keeping the pace and not on how good his mate's warm pussy felt on his cock. He needed to last until she came, but she had to come soon.

One of her hands slid from his shoulder and trailed down his abs before his mate followed his order and started rubbing her clit. She groaned, and Blane closed his eyes, letting his head fall back as he listened to his mate's whimpers. He felt her pussy tighten and clenched his teeth. "That's it, little flame. Come for your mate. Come on my cock."

"Fuck, oh, ohhhh fuck," his mate screamed as her pussy pulsated around him and she melted into his arms. He held his thrust, grinding deep inside of her as his mate whimpered against his neck, her hands threading through his hair, and he finally let go, allowing himself to come deep inside of her.

Mariel sighed as he held her, his cock twitching against her throbbing pussy for a few more moments. He kissed her forehead and murmured, "Best game ever. We should play it again."

His mate snuggled against him and smiled, kissing and nibbling at his shoulders. "I agree."

She moved off his cock and across the tub before Blane realized what was happening. He growled as she jumped out of the tub and glanced over her shoulder before taking off toward the cabin.

His cock roared back to life, ready for the next round as he sprang out of the tub and raced after his sexy little flame.

The End

Enchanted Moon

Wicked Fate Lusty Mates

Astrid Vail

Blurb & Content Warning

He was supposed to be dead. She was the one who killed him.

The last thing Silina ever wants to do is think about her past.

A past that died along with her heart twelve years ago in a dirty city she never called home.

But now her past is back: tall, dark, and handsome, growling about claiming his mate. Claiming her.

Yet something else lurks in the shadows, scheming to pull them apart again.

But Silina isn't ready to lose her mate all over again, and this time she is ready to fight tooth and nail to keep him.

WICKED FATE, LUSTY MATES

Content warning includes spicy on page sex scenes, abduction, murder, death, past child abuse, and language.

Chapter One

ROMEO

THE STEADY CLANKING OF metal on metal mixed with Romeo's steady breathing as he hung upside down. Muscles screaming at him, a sheen of sweat covered his entire body as he finished his last round of sit-ups. The guards shouted, the echo reverberating through the cell block as the lights began to shut off. His eyes adjusted immediately as darkness engulfed his surroundings and the fellow prisoners. Murmurs and sighs whispered among the darkness, the rustling of beings settling down for bed.

Romeo stilled, letting the blood rush to his head as another sound made its way through the dark. The slight rasp of a hand grasping the outside of his cell door was his only indication that he was no longer alone. Even with his heightened senses, he couldn't see or smell the being that stood just out of reach. The only being in the supernatural prison who had free rein day or night. A being who chose to spend his life here, instead of out there in the free world.

"You are leaving tomorrow," the being rasped, shadows playing across its body, obscuring him from view.

Romeo grunted and let himself go, twisting in the air to land heavily on the cold ground. Wiping the sweat from his face with a towel, he meandered over to his cell door. He leaned against the cool metal bars, nodding, knowing the being had better eyesight than he did in the dark. "Ya, tomorrow is the day I finally leave this hellhole."

The shadows twisted again, and Romeo caught a glimpse of a hand and forearm before they disappeared. "This hellhole isn't a place meant for someone like you."

"And it's meant for someone like you?"

The being didn't answer, and Romeo shook his head. "The outside world isn't that bad."

The being chuckled this time, and the shadows around its head swirled, shaking back and forth before red orbs illuminated the darkness. An involuntary shiver rolled down Romeo's spine as the dry rasp of the being echoed toward him.

"This place might be a prison for everyone else, but it is my sanctuary. I am the only one of my kind, and I intend to live my life here, in solitude. Plus, the blood of the wicked tastes much better than that of the innocent."

Romeo pushed back slightly, habit by now when talk of blood spilled into the conversation. He remembered his first night here, twelve years ago, when the being made itself known to him. A tradition to keep the newbies in line, letting them know something bigger and badder than they could ever imagine roamed these halls. Something that couldn't be locked away. Phantom pain rippled across his neck and Romeo swallowed heavily.

"You are not one of the wicked ones, young wolf. You know I will not sip from your veins ever again."

Romeo shook his head. "Force of habit. I know your philosophy. Even if I still think you are wrong after all these years. I'm here for a reason. I am one of the wicked ones."

"The blood never lies, young wolf," the being whispered, his voice seemingly farther away, and that was Romeo's sign their conversation was over.

The being let him be, hunting for its nightly snack, and Romeo shrugged his aching shoulders before cracking his neck. He lay down on his cot with a sigh, staring up at his one and only personal item taped to the wall. The only thing he had on him when he was dragged into this place, covered head to toe in blood. The only thing he needed as he paid his dues for the violence he had inflicted all those years ago. He reached out, tracing the fading picture of the two young kids embracing each other. The girl smiled at the camera, happiness radiating off her like the sun itself.

The boy in the picture stared at the girl with pure love written on his face, and Romeo closed his eyes. He let his hand fall and rubbed his chest. The ache in his heart the day he was ripped away from her had never dissipated. Romeo sighed and flipped over onto his side, closing his eyes, and like every night before drifting off to sleep, his imagination painted a picture of what his life could have been if he hadn't been taken away from his mate all those years ago.

Morning came early, like every day before. The lights flickered on, and the guards yelled, batons clanging outside the cell doors. Romeo's head was filled with fog, his sleep restless and permeated with dreams he no longer tried to control. He shuffled to his cell door, running a hand through his shaggy dark hair before stepping out of his cell and getting in line. Everyone shuffled forward like sheep until he got to the front. As he was about to turn left—a habit formed from his time here—a guard blocked his path. "Wrong way, criminal. You're going that way today."

Romeo's head snapped up, and it all came flooding back, the fog of his sleepless night washing away. Today was the day he was leaving this place. He straightened his shoulders, coming to his full height, before turning on his heel and letting another guard lead him down a different corridor. A corridor he had glimpsed only once before, twelve years ago. The light seemed brighter, the hallway cleaner, as they led him down the only entrance and exit to this hellhole. Days of his incarceration overlapped with the new memories he was making striding down the hall. Only this time, he was going the other way. Only this time, they were shoving real clothes into his hands instead of prison red. He spied the elevator before him, through the impenetrable glass and security gates. When he stepped through hesitantly, no one stopped him. To be honest, the guards seemed to be more annoyed with him for taking so long than anything else. One of the guards swung the electric baton absently back and forth before sighing and moving his hand in a hurry-up motion.

Romeo didn't need to be told again as he rushed through security and into the elevator. No guards came with him, no one tried to stop him. After a few seconds, the elevator doors opened, and he stepped out into another hallway, this one filled with natural light. The air smelled clean, and the noise of office work hummed around him. Another guard looked up from behind a security gate and pointed to a door next to Romeo before the intercom crackled and his voice washed over him. "You can change in there. Just leave your prison clothes on the floor."

Romeo obeyed, and within five minutes, he was dressed in a simple pair of jeans, a dark flannel shirt, a plain undershirt, and scuffed biker boots. Everything was worn in, but it fit him well, and it was only when he shrugged on the leather jacket that he heard the crinkle of paper. He shoved his hand into the pocket of the jacket and extracted a piece of paper, along with the picture he had taped to the wall for all these years.

Young Wolf,

I hope these clothes are to your standards and fit. I also took it upon myself to do some digging and I have included an address. Do with it as you will.

May your wolf finally run free.

The note ended, unsigned, but Romeo knew it was from the being who he had grown accustomed to speaking to all these years. He would even go so far as calling the being a friend, a vigilante within the darkness of this prison.

He shoved the paper back into his pocket before making his way out. The guard from before sat behind the security glass, with two more guards next to him, waiting. A loud buzzing permeated his senses, and the gate swung open. Romeo took a deep breath and stepped forward. The guards escorted him down a few halls, and the air took on a crisp, unfiltered scent. Until suddenly, he was in a lobby, with no gates, no security glass. Just a plain lobby with another guard sitting behind a large desk. The guard stood and pulled out a few papers and an ID, handing it over with a smile. "There you go, kiddo. This is all the paperwork you will need out there to start fresh. You probably don't remember me, but I was manning this desk when you were hauled into here as a scrawny little sixteen-year-old."

The other guards took a step back, leaving Romeo alone with the smiling older guard. Romeo nodded and gently took the envelope. "Ya, I remember you. You told me to hold strong. That one day I would be right back up here, leaving this place."

The guard nodded. "That's right, kiddo. Now don't dawdle. Go on now. You are a free man. Turn left on the dirt road and that will take you into town."

A lump grew in Romeo's throat, and he heeded the old guard's words, heading toward the steel door, the neon exit light flickering. He pushed it open and took his first deep breath of the outside world as a free man. Pine and fresh rain assaulted his senses, and he held up his hand to block the sunlight. The sound of birds and traffic far off finally registered, and Romeo turned left, just as the old guard said. Heading toward the dirt road that would eventually lead to the tiny town on the outskirts of the prison, he pulled out the note in his pocket and glanced at the address again. His wolf moved under his skin, and Romeo shrugged his shoulders before stepping off into the woods. It was time to change and finally hunt down his long-lost mate. Here was hoping she still wanted him after all these years.

Chapter Two

ROMEO

ROMEO WALKED INTO A little town three days later. He ran most of the way in his other form, sticking to the wilderness, not wanting to attract attention to his monstrous wolf. Plus, after all these years, his wolf deserved to stretch its legs. He shrugged on his clothes quickly after shifting back and kept his head low. Small towns always made him nervous back in the day. Their inhabitants were more hyper vigilant in ways the big city brethren weren't. And Romeo was an outsider. A huge, muscle bound, tattooed outsider.

The icy drizzle of rain started not long after he had changed back into his human form, and Romeo couldn't help his sense of relief as the weather drove people inside, seeking the comfort of warmth. This was also the last place he would have expected to find his mate.

He scented the air, carefully picking up whiffs of the town, and there on the breeze, a siren call beckoned to him. Following the faint scent over worn-down sidewalks, he stood under the little overhang of a coffee shop. Inside, the staff and customers bustled about, but there was no sight of her. Yet her scent was the strongest here, and Romeo debated just sitting on the wet cement until she showed up again. But the last thing he wanted was to bring attention to himself, and if he stayed any longer in this town without further invitation, he would do just that.

The search for his mate would have to wait, much to his displeasure, as Romeo turned on his heel and followed another scent leading out of the small town. Rain continued to fall as he followed the winding blacktop for the next few miles, until he found himself outside a set of wrought-iron gates. The thick forest behind the gate kept what Romeo would only assume would be an estate from view. His wolf inside paced, annoyed that they had to rest in their hunt for their mate so soon. But protocol was protocol, and the last thing Romeo wanted was to be on the bad side of a wolf pack so soon after his release. He quieted the wolf in his head and pushed the intercom button on the gate.

The crackling of static was loud against the steady drum of the rain until a curt voice finally answered.

"Alpha Hunter Residence. State your business."

"New wolf in town. Would like an audience with the alpha," Romeo growled into the speaker box.

The rain started to come down in earnest, the sky opening fully. Icy shivers ran down his body from head to toe as Romeo waited and waited.

"Do you have an appointment?" The intercoms crackled to life once more, and Romeo shook his head before answering.

"No."

"The alpha keeps to a busy schedule. The next opening we have is in two weeks to see new wolves. We suggest waiting with your old pack until then."

This time, Romeo growled and contemplated molding the intercom box into a more smashed version of itself. Instead, he sighed and muttered, "I have no pack. I am a lone wolf, and I will be in the area for business."

The intercom buzzed and clicked before going quiet. Romeo waited as the seconds ticked by, then, much to his surprise, the gates slowly started to open. He squeezed through quickly before whomever was behind the intercom changed their mind, and started up the winding drive.

Chapter Three

SILINA

THE DAMN RAIN WAS not going to let up, and Silina grumbled as she kicked the door to her car open, sprinting to the back door of the nightclub. She quickly punched in the door code and stepped inside. The bouncer at the back door looked her over with a frown before handing her a towel. She smiled gratefully as she began drying off her face and hair. The smell of alcohol, sweat, and cleaning supplies wafted by her. A smell she had gotten used to in the last eight years while working the club scene. She took the towel with her as she made her way along the back hall.

Music vibrated through her bones, heavy on the base, and Silina felt her body relaxing. Her magic swirled around her as she dragged her fingertips across the wall and grinned. She could feel the lust and power in the air, her magic nipping at the patrons inside the already crowded nightclub. Through her magic, she could feel the life force of every single being and knew it would be a good night to replenish her magic stores. A siphon like her was rare, and because of that, she knew very little about her magic. But the one thing she knew was the need to feed, and her magic was hungry tonight. Lucky for her, a packed nightclub was the perfect place to do so, without hurting anyone.

Silina picked up her pace and opened the door near the end of the hall. The low chatter of the dancers and waitresses hit her first, followed up by a mixing of perfume fighting back against the ingrained sweat smell that seemed to permeate the entire establishment. Silina made her way over to her designated locker and spun the dial, popping open the door easily. She was already buzzing from the anticipation of feeding tonight as she grabbed her clothes and accessories. Quickly, she shrugged off her clothes and changed.

A hush fell over the room, and Silina looked behind her to see a handful of the women whispering and giggling yet keeping to themselves as usual. A few of the newer girls scoffed and stuck up their noses, gossiping to one another, and Silina rolled her eyes. She wasn't here to make friends, something she had made quite clear when she started bar backing at the club. Over the years, she had worked her way up to bartending and had no complaints. The job paid well, and it fed her magic.

She grabbed her makeup bag, jostling the back of her locker. Her indifferent mood turned dark as a faded picture, usually obstructed from view, dislodged, and floated through the air. A lump grew in her throat as she snatched it up and gently placed it back in its rightful place. She didn't need to look at the photo. She knew every inch of it, inside and out. Hell, she could sketch the damn thing from memory if she wanted.

But that was the issue.

It was a memory she desperately wanted to erase from her mind. The memory of the best and worst day of her life. Life lessons painfully taught to a couple of lovesick teenagers who thought they could take on the world.

She shut her locker with a loud bang, startling the rest of the women still in the room. No one approached her and Silina didn't offer an apology.

Most of the women here knew to stay clear of her when her mood changed. Even her magic shuddered before creeping its way back to her, surrounding Silina in an invisible cloak of miasma.

She stepped over to the mirror and started in on her makeup, layering the dark coal and even darker shadow along her almond-shaped eyes. Matching her makeup with her mood, she stalked out of the room without a word to anyone.

The music of the club rushed in around her, the pop-infused music grating along her nerves as she made her way to the bar and slid behind it. The other bartender took a long look at her before making their way to the opposite side of the long bar. *Good*, she thought, because she wasn't in the mood to converse. She was here to do her job, and nothing else. She tried to push the memories of the night twelve years ago out of her mind. Of the night that altered her life so drastically, she didn't even know who she was anymore. But they came surging back, and Silina gritted her teeth against the phantom pain in her heart.

She shook her head and gave a feral smile to one of the bouncers who came wandering up to her side of the bar. He gulped and tried to offer her a soft smile. It evaporated from his face as she glared at him.

"I don't have all day. Do you want water or Red Bull?"

"Water, please."

Reaching down, she threw a bottle of water from the mini fridge designated for the work staff drinks, and pointed her chin to the live DJ. "Tell him to put on my mix tonight."

The bouncer scrambled from his chair, obeying her like she owned the club instead of just working there. Though, being fair, she was one of the longest-lasting employees in this place. The manager let her do what she wanted most of the time, so long as she didn't cause too much trouble.

Soon, the music changed, the low bass hitting hard under the pop, turning it darker and more sensual. Silina let her magic leak out, letting it sip the lust and desire from the air as the dancers in the suspended cages started moving to the shift in rhythm. The crowd on the ground floor gyrated to the new music, and Silina got to work. As she moved behind the bar, sinking into her work with the music pumping around her, the familiar ache of regret and loneliness faded away. She eased into the euphoric feeling of using her magic and drowned out the pain in her heart. Swaying to the music as she worked, she tried to forget that today was the anniversary of the day her heart died. The day she lost her one and only.

And it was her fault he was dead.

Chapter Four

SILINA

HER MOOD WAS STILL dark as Silina made her way to the back room at the end of her shift. All the other girls were already heading home as she sat in an empty chair in front of a cracked mirror. Magic bubbled under her breastbone as she kicked off her shoes, becoming a toxic well of grief and anger. She wanted to scream, to cry, to rage. She wanted to let her magic snap out and steal everyone's breath from their lips, to drink down their life essence until the pain went away.

Instead, she calmly reached over for the pack of her make-up remover and pulled out a wipe. With practiced strokes, she ran it over her entire face until it was clean. She didn't dare look in the mirror, unwilling to see if the bruised little girl she always felt like on this day was peeking out. Tears threatened to fall, but she took a breath and tilted her head back until her eyes dried. She refused to cry because the crying got her nowhere. It couldn't erase the hurt or the past, so there was no point.

Getting up, she moved slowly to her locker and spun the dial. It popped open with ease, and she quickly removed her outfit for her comfortable sweats and flip-flops. She bound her raven black hair up into a messy topknot and grabbed her purse, shoving the money she had earned tonight inside. She needed to add a reminder to go to the bank tomorrow. The last thing she needed to do was carry around a week's worth of earnings at the bottom of her purse. As she unlocked her phone, her eyes widened at the five missed calls, one voicemail, and fourteen text messages. Four of the calls and thirteen of the text messages were from her best friend, Lily. But it was the remaining call and text message that made Silina's blood run cold.

The high priestess of the little coven she belonged to, the person she had known the longest in her life, wasn't one to leave voicemails or text messages unless it was insanely urgent. She tapped the icon for the voicemail and gulped as her high priestess's voice echoed out.

"Silina, it's Gwen. I know you're working, but we need to talk. Now. Come straight home. Promise me you will come straight home."

Her normal no-nonsense tone wavered at the end, almost as if she was begging. Never in the ten years Silina had known Gwen had she ever heard her beg. She gulped as she opened the text message.

Come home right away.

It was straight to the point, and Silina felt the all too familiar defiant streak in her blood boil to the surface. She didn't like being commanded to do anything, and she was damned sure she wouldn't be following blind orders until she knew what was going on.

Her thumb hovered over Lily's name, ready to read her text messages to see if her friend had a better insight as to what was going on, when a knock echoed on the closed door. Silina glanced at the cheap clock on the wall and inwardly cursed as a bouncer's voice intruded into the space. "Five minutes until lock up!"

Dropping her phone into her purse, she fisted her keys. As she opened the door to the stone-faced bouncer, who had given her the towel earlier in the night, he nodded. Silina maneuvered her way down the hall as the bouncer followed and opened the back door for her. He kept watch as she stepped out of the club and picked her way across the cracked blacktop to her car. The sky was still filled with storm clouds, but luckily, it had stopped raining, for now. She walked through the lingering puddle surrounding her car and shoved the key into the lock. Shaking off her wet feet, she locked her doors after getting in and waved to the bouncer. He motioned to her, mimicking locking the doors, and she gave him a thumbs up. The bouncer nodded and stepped back inside. Once he was out of sight, Silina sighed and leaned back, rifling through her purse for her phone. She clicked on Lily's text messages, and they flooded her phone.

Bile rose in the back of her throat as she read through them, the anger she was pushing down finally boiling over.

> Silina, WTF ?

> You need to call me ASAP.

> Why didn't you tell me you had a MATE!

> He is here. In the FUCKING LIVING ROOM. And he is quite a hunk.

> HEY!

> Why aren't you picking up my calls?

Oh, Wait… Are you working?

Shit, you are. Okay, we will keep him here until you get off.

Eakkkk. I'm doing a happy dance. I can't believe you have a mate.

Actually, hang on. Is he dangerous? Are you running from him?

Do we need to kick his ass?

Just tell me if I need to electrocute his furry wolf ass out of here.

SHIT. Okay, call when you get off work.

Silina jammed her keys into the ignition and turned over the engine to her old beater car with so much force she was amazed it didn't sputter and die instantly. Her mind was a rampage of thoughts and emotions as she peeled out of the parking lot and onto the highway leading out of the city. Her whole body ran hot, then cold, her arms shaking, and she clenched her jaw as her phone started vibrating. It didn't matter who was calling. Her single focus was to get to Lily and Hunter's place and find out who the hell was there. Who the hell this imposter was, and what did they want? Because they were indeed an imposter preying on something they had no right to prey upon.

Silina screamed, letting her anger out as she took the exit off the highway too quickly and slammed on her brakes as she skidded around a turn. She fishtailed onto the main road that led through the small town and barely had enough thought to maintain the speed limit, less she got pulled over. That was the last thing she needed.

The moment she passed through the main part of town, she stepped on the gas, taking the winding road in front of her at breakneck speeds until she found herself idling outside of the wrought-iron gates to her best friend's and her mate's mansion. They opened before Silina had the chance to buzz herself in, and she clenched the steering wheel as her whole body vibrated from anger. She made her way up the winding drive and skidded to a stop at their front entrance like a bat out of hell. Kicking open the door, she lost a flip-flop in the process. She was so livid she didn't even bother turning off the engine and instead stomped up the stairs, kicking her other flip-flop off for good measure. She didn't bother knocking, and instead flung the door open, marching inside before yelling. "I don't know who the fuck is here. But when I find out..."

She trailed off as her gaze found an imposing silhouette making its way into the foyer. Her anger snuffed out instantly, leaving behind only pain and confusion as the man stepped forward. The ghosts of her past hovered over him as his tantalizing voice wrapped around her numb body. Silina gaped, unable to breathe as he smiled softly and ran a hand through his gorgeous chestnut brown hair. Her eyes swept over his strong body and face, lingering over the spattering of tattoos peeking out from behind the edges of his clothing before meeting his eyes.

Eyes that have haunted her every moment for the past twelve years.

"Hey, baby. Did you miss me?

Chapter Five

SILINA

HER MOUTH WENT BONE dry as she took in the man before her, dressed in battered motorcycle boots, worn jeans, and a threadbare t-shirt. She could see the shape of every single muscle, from his abs and chest to the way the shirt strained against his biceps. She tried not to look at his face again, unable to believe the person standing before her was truly him.

When he took a hesitant step toward her, she raised her hand to stop him. She stared at the tips of her fingers, and the way her hand shook. A hysterical giggle bubbled out of her as she felt her magic shift, reacting to the only man she had ever lusted after in her life. Even after all these years, even after all she went through, her magic was ready to betray her again. She reined it in, and her eyes looked back up of their own accord, finding him once more.

A mistake.

Silina felt her knees get weak as she took in a face she knew she would never see again. She felt herself fall all over again at the sight of his chiseled jaw and sinfully full lips, but it was when his dark brown eyes caught hers that the memories of that night came rushing back. When the light in those vivid brown eyes glazed over with the finality of death.

The memory locked her weak knees in place, and Silina lowered her hand. "How are you alive?"

Her whisper filled the silence between them, hovering in the air as a confession and a question at once.

Romeo shook his head slowly. "I'm a lycanthrope, baby. It takes a lot to kill us. Even when we are young."

As her eyes searched the man before her, she tried to understand how this could be possible. "I... You... You were dead. You weren't breathing... There was—there was so much blood. I held you in my arms. I wept over your lifeless corpse, and then I..." Her eyes grew wide as she took a step back. "I left you there. I abandoned you. You were still alive, and I abandoned you."

Romeo clenched his jaw and reached toward her. "Silina... Baby, it wasn't your fault."

"I thought I killed you!" she screeched before slapping a hand over her mouth. Shaking her head, she took another step away, retreating toward the still open door. Romeo followed her slowly, his hand out, as to calm a feral beast, and she couldn't blame him. That was exactly how she felt in this moment, a beast on the edge. She took another step back, and Romeo followed. Her mouth was dry and yet still wet as she sputtered. "Where... where have you been all these years?"

She needed to know. She needed to know if he had been alive all these years, why he would make himself known now.

Romeo winced and drew his hand back. "Prison."

That one word was like a knife through her heart, and Silina gulped in a shaky breath. Her Romeo, her mate, had never been the violent or troublesome type. This couldn't really be him. What could he have done to get him thrown into prison for the last twelve years?

"Prison? For what?" She heard her voice say the words, like it had a mind of its own. Her body felt numb, like she was floating from above and watching this all take place before her.

"It doesn't matter, baby. I'm here now. That's all that matters."

"No, it does matter. Tell me."

Romeo ran a hand through his hair and blew out a long breath. "For murder. Murdering *him*."

Silina gaped at the only man she had ever loved as her whole world turned upside down. "Murder?" she whispered. "You don't mean..."

He nodded and tears threatened to fall as her lower lip quivered. The man before her, the love of her life, had not only survived the rampage that night, but also the deadly blast of magic that exploded from her twelve years ago. But he also took the blame for a murder.

The murder she had committed to save them both.

Her nastiest secret she had kept hidden all these years. She would have traded places with him in a heartbeat. She was the one who should have gone to prison, not him. Silina took a step forward, a single tear trailing down her cheek as her magic snapped out, trying to caress the man before her. Her eyes widened in horror as she tugged it back into herself. It struggled against her hold like a live snake, and she knew instantly that she would never be able to control her magic around this man, her mate, the love of her life. She also knew if she lost even a tiny bit of control, her magic would suck the life force out of him, and she couldn't go through the tragedy of losing him again. She was stronger now, and there was no way he would survive the onslaught of her magic if she even loosened her grip in the slightest. The reality of their situation crashed into her, ripping away all their possibilities of a relationship.

Nausea built in her chest, Silina turned on her heel and bolted out the front door.

She had to leave.

Get as far away as possible.

She knew she would have to run forever, always be one step ahead of Romeo if she wanted to preserve his life. She felt her heart break all over again as she launched herself into the still running car. She slammed the door, and her foot was already on the pedal when a heady and masculine scent washed over her. He had followed her.

Of course, he had followed her.

Her passenger side door slammed shut, and he smacked the dashboard. "I would suggest going. Quickly."

Her body moved on its own, obeying the man she would always love, throwing the car into gear, pushing the gas pedal down as far as it could go. She jerked the wheel, tires spinning. Out of the rearview mirror, she saw the silhouette of her best friend and her mate running after them.

Adrenaline spiked through her veins, her mind finally catching up with her actions. "Wait, why are *we* speeding out of here? I'm supposed to be running from you. Not us running from them."

Romeo's full-bodied laugh curled up the base of her spine, and memories of them running down the back alleyways of the city without a care in the world bubbled to the surface. They had never been innocent, but they had been young and so in love.

Tears sprang to her eyes, and she knew she should stop the car, kick him out, and run for the hills. The longer she was in his presence, the less likely she would be able to reject him. She shook the thought away as they approached the gates to the property. Here was hoping whoever was operating them knew she wasn't stopping. Whipping around the last corner, she saw the gates opening. She pushed the gas down harder and swung her car out onto the main road.

"Okay, baby. Where are we going?"

Romeo's voice brought Silina to the forefront of her mind, and she felt her magic move toward him once more. A frustrated scream erupted from her chest, and she pointed at him, taking her eyes off the road. "We?! We shouldn't be going anywhere, Ro-Ro!"

He grabbed the wheel, pulling it to the side, just as a truck blared its horn and they swerved, tires crunching over the gravel on the side of the road. She slammed on the brakes and threw the car into park.

"Don't you understand? I can't... my magic... even now, it wants you, and I can't... I can't."

Romeo sighed, his face going slack, and he closed his eyes. "I know, baby... I just... I just wanted to see you again. I'm a selfish bastard for wanting to see you. But I needed to just once more, even if... even if you rejected me. I needed to see you again."

Silina reached out, her hand trembling. Her fingertips hovered over his face, so close, and yet she knew if she touched him, it would be all over. All her anger and sadness mixed into a single plea. "It's not fair. I know. Believe me, I know. I want to be your mate. I don't want to reject you. I've only ever wanted you, but..."

Romeo opened his eyes, jaw clenched so tight she could hear his teeth grinding. "I can't fight it. You know that. My wolf wants his mate."

Silina shook her head and dropped her hands to her lap. "I don't know what to do. If we give in, I will lose control, and you will die. But..." She sniffled, a single tear falling down her cheek. "But I can't stand you leaving again. Now that I know you are alive."

"I—" Romeo cut off his words as a low rumble came from the roadside.

"What the fuck?" Silina whispered, as the truck they had almost run off the road earlier pulled up beside them. The driver was shrouded in shadow from the dark cab, but when they motioned to roll down the window, Silina cringed inwardly.

Romeo pushed the window button, lowering it until it was fully down. "Not the best time, buddy."

The dry popping sound of a gun only registered as a stinging sensation hit her in the neck. Romeo lunged out the window, only to fall back in shock. Silina moved in slow motion as she reached up and pulled out the dart. The shock and pain running through her veins dissipated slowly, being replaced by whatever drug had been in the dart. It fell from her hand on its own and she slumped against her seat. Moving her head to the side, she saw the same darts, five in total, sticking from Romeo's chest. He was already slumped against the seat, head down, eyes closed. She opened her mouth, trying to speak, but she couldn't make a sound as her body started shutting down.

The sound of a truck door slamming and her door opening a second later barely registered as hands grasped her shoulders, pulling her out of the car. She couldn't feel her body or her magic as the mystery man shoved her into the covered bed of her truck. Her eyelids fluttered, and she tried fighting the drugs coursing through her, but it was no use. The harder she fought, the more it pulled her under. Her only solace was the feel of Romeo's body next to hers, and she used the last of her strength to wrap her hand around his before she finally succumbed to the darkness.

Chapter Six

SILINA

SILINA MOANED, HER HEAD pounding as the smell of cheap cologne, whiskey, and smoke filled her senses. It was the smell from her past, and Silina knew this all had to be a bad dream. She must have fallen at the club, hitting her head, and none of this was really happening.

Then a voice from her nightmares crawled its way over her skin, and her stomach revolted as memories of the worst night in her life swam to the surface. The dilapidated house from her youth, her mother's pimp waiting for her when she got home that night.

That night... that night...

Whimpering, tears fell freely, unable to stop them as the memory continued to play out. Feeling the pawing hands all over her body, she screamed. "Romeo!"

Silina's scream ricocheted all around her as her eyes snapped open. Her arms and back ached, and when she tried to move them, chains rattled overhead. Whatever drug she was injected with had finally worn off, and she blinked into the darkness. Her toes barely scraped the floor below, and Silina realized she was hanging, tied up by her arms and wrists.

A rasping chuckle crawled over her skin again, and this time, she focused on where it came from. "You're supposed to be dead. Romeo spent twelve years behind bars because you were dead!"

Her voice cracked as a small flame lit up in front of her, the pox-marked and wrinkled face of the man from her nightmare staring at her. "Oh, little girl, I am dead. You and your whelp of a boy saw to that."

That was when she smelled it, the scent of rot under the cologne. "I don't understand."

The flickering flame in front of her went out, and she was met with stillness, the quiet eating at her senses until the illumination of lights blinded her. She blinked rapidly until she could see, and her breath shook. She was hanging from the ceiling of a small barn. Chains hung in a few places, mercifully empty except for one set far off. She squinted and her gut clenched.

Romeo was hanging in the corner, still passed out from the drugs. Anger rolled over her, and for once in her life, she purposely lashed out with her magic, ready to suck the life force out of the man before her again. On purpose this time. Except nothing happened.

The man laughed, then hacked, covering his mouth with his hand. When he pulled it away with a grimace, she saw black, putrid blood covering it. Silina shook her head, brow furrowing. "What...What are you?"

"Dead, you daft bitch. Or were you not listening to me? This is all your fault, but finally, finally, I found you and that whelp. Now I can live again. That was the deal." The man smiled, and Silina gagged as two of his teeth fell out. Now that she could see him fully, she had no doubt in her mind that he was telling the truth. Which could only mean one thing.

Someone used black magic to raise this nightmare. And they wanted her for some goddamn reason.

Pins and needles slid down her spine as Silina pushed back on her tiptoes. She was going to get out of this one way or another, and she was going to save her mate. It didn't matter that they couldn't be together because of her magic; she would always love him, and she would save them from this nightmare. As the dead man drew closer,

Silina launched her feet forward with a snarl and kicked his knees out from under him. He went down with a satisfying crunch, and Silina reared back her heel, striking him in the ribs. She felt his flesh give under her bare feet and gagged. "Fucking disgusting. Tell me who raised you from the dead, you piece of filth. Who wants me? Who wants him?"

The dead man scuttled backwards, dragging his legs, and spat more black bile on the ground. "You're lucky someone wants you in one piece, bitch. And as far as who raised me, why don't you ask your high priestess?"

Silina stilled, her ears ringing from his words. There was no way. Her high priestess wouldn't betray her like this. "You're lying."

The dead man's rasping laugh filled the barn, only to be cut off by the sound of high heels ringing out through the darkness. An immaculately dressed woman stepped into view, her light pinstriped pantsuit pressed and polished to within an inch of its life. Her dark hair was pulled back into an immaculate bun, and gray eyes met with Silina's.

Her stomach dipped, nausea and betrayal running through her as Gwendolen, her high priestess, and the woman she had trusted for ten years of her life, stepped into the light. "You fucking bitch," Silina whispered before thrashing against her chains. "If you harm Romeo, I will kill you."

She kicked out again, this time trying to get enough momentum to break from her chains. She knew better than to use her magic. It wouldn't work on the woman in front of her, nor the dead man who was still laughing. The only person her magic would affect was Romeo, and she would be damned if she ever hurt him that way again.

Gwendolen held up her hand and raised her voice just loud enough to be heard. "Enough, Silina. I'm not your enemy."

She stilled as the dead man stopped laughing and turned, eyes wide, as Gwendolen's words sank in. Blinking rapidly, her mind tried to process what was happening as Gwendolen reached out quickly and the snapping of bones and tendons filled the barn. The dead man's head rolled off his body and across the floor, and Silina sucked in a ragged breath. "Gwen, what the fuck is going on?"

"What is going on is fifteen years of hard work being obliterated because of stupidity and impatience. That's what." Gwendolen mumbled before sidestepping the already rotting corpse, and moved behind Silina.

She felt her chains loosen, and the moment her feet touched the floor, Silina clawed her way out of them and ran across the barn. Reaching up, she released Romeo and caught him as he fell. He was still completely out of it, and his massive body took them both down to the ground, but Silina didn't care. All she cared about was her mate being safe. Even if she was going to have to leave him again.

Tears sprang to her eyes, heart twisting in despair as she ran her hand over his forehead, pushing his hair out of his eyes. His breathing was easy, and Silina could feel his steady heartbeat under the palm of her hand as she pushed away. She stood quickly, keeping her wayward magic close, even as it tried to wrap its way around Romeo. Gwendolen's heels rang across the hard floor, getting closer, and Silina turned to face her. "Tell me what is going on. How is he here?" She points to the now truly dead man halfway across the barn, before stabbing her finger into Gwen's chest. "And why are you here?"

Gwendolen shook her head. "I'll explain in the car. Now, grab your wolf, and I'll help you get him out of here."

"I can't," she whispered, still wrapping her struggling magic around her.

Gwendolen glanced from between Silina and Romeo before tsking slightly. "We have a lot to talk about, but believe me when I tell you, your magic won't kill him."

Silina swore she got whiplash as she turned her head quickly, staring at Gwendolen. "What did you just say?"

Her high priestess reached down, grabbing Romeo's ankles, and lifted with a grunt. "I said your magic won't kill him. Now grab his shoulders so we can get him to the car. Unless you want to leave him again."

Silina felt rage pulsate through her body, along with her magic, and had half a mind to argue until she glanced back down at Romeo. She hesitantly reached out, grabbing him under his shoulders. Her magic snapped out, coating all three of them, but it didn't react negatively. Silina shook her head, trying to understand why twelve years ago it had stolen his energy, his life force within seconds, yet now it lay over him like a warm blanket, as if to protect him. She would have to ponder her magic later as she lifted with her legs and grunted. "Fuck, you weigh a damn ton."

Gwendolen snorted slightly as they shuffled out of the barn and managed to shove her still unconscious Romeo into the back seat of the waiting SUV.

Silina crawled in after him, placing his head on her lap. With a deep breath, she very slowly loosened her hold on her magic, little by little. She waited for it to start, waited for her magic to betray her, yet all it did was continue to hover.

It wrapped around them both, as if this was what Silina and her magic had been looking for all their life. The slamming of the car door and the rev of the engine brought Silina back to reality, and she growled low in her throat, "Gwendolen, tell me what the fuck is going on. Now."

Chapter Seven

ROMEO

His head was filled with sand, body fluctuating between hot and cold. Romeo knew he had to wake up, had to fight. But he couldn't remember why.

The most enchanting voice, the voice of an angel, floated through his subconscious, and Romeo latched onto it. The angel wasn't speaking to him directly, but he concentrated on her words anyway.

"So, what are you? A double agent, or some bullshit like that? And why did you have to bring me into it?"

Another voice, one Romeo had never heard before, answered his angel. "I have my reasons. But your involvement was necessary. It always has been, and it was better me taking you under my wing than *them*. You are an asset to the witches, and the council, it seems, has decided to make their move."

Something shifted under Romeo's head, and he realized his head was lying on a lap. Shaking hands gripped his shoulders, and the night came rushing back to him.

His mate. His mate was in trouble.

Light fingers danced across his skin, up his arm and across his throat. A hand cupped his face, and he leaned into it with a moan.

"Shhhh. You're safe now. I have you."

Romeo calmed slightly, taking a deep breath as his mate's hand skirted his flushed skin. He sank into her touch and listened to the surrounding noises, trying to get his bearings. Whatever he had been dosed with was still raging through his system, but it was slowly dissipating. The swaying of the vehicle was not helping, though, and nausea swelled. He ground his jaw slightly until it passed and homed in on the conversation once more between his mate and the mystery woman.

"Your magic is unique. You and I know this. And I have been keeping you out of their hands for a while now. For your own safety," the mystery woman said, and Romeo felt his mate tense underneath him.

"You still should have told me I was in this sort of danger," his mate hissed back, and Romeo felt his lips twitch into a soft smile. They might have been apart for the last twelve years, but Silina's fighting spirit was still the same. And it was one thing he loved the most about her.

Romeo continued listening as his mate sighed and brushed her knuckles across his cheekbone. "I know what I am, Gwen. Siphons are rare, and I have done what you asked over these twelve years. But you betrayed me, in more ways than one."

He stiffened at her words, the venom evident in her voice against this Gwen person. If his mate felt betrayed by her, then that meant he wouldn't let his guard down around this mystery woman, even if she was helping them at that moment.

Romeo opened his eyes slightly as he heard the steering wheel creak under the driver's hands. Glancing around quickly, he was able to ascertain it was only Gwen and his mate in the vehicle.

"I had to do what was necessary, Silina. And I didn't know he was still alive when I took you in. I only found out a few years ago."

That confession had his hackles raised. This woman had known Romeo still lived and never told his mate. This Gwen had let his mate suffer in her own mind. That alone made him hate her.

"You knew... you knew and didn't tell me."

"It wasn't relevant at the time. And it would've caused complications."

The silence rang thick in the air, the tension nearly suffocating. Romeo opened his eyes all the way and stared up at his mate. Her jaw was clenched, nostrils flared from anger, and he could feel her magic dancing around them. It snapped and popped, swirling like the raging storm it was. He reached out, covering her hand with his. She sucked in an angry breath, but when she glanced down at him, her beautiful chocolate eyes softened, and the tension lifted slightly from her face. "Hey, Ro-Ro," she whispered and squeezed his hand. "How are you feeling?"

"Better. Now that I'm in your arms," his voice rasped, and he shifted as the vehicle banked to the left. His mate nibbled on her lower lip, one of her brows creasing slightly. He studied her face, from the dried streaking of tears to the dust peppering her pronounced cheekbones. She was absolutely beautiful, even after the ordeal they had gone through. He released her hand to brush aside the stray hairs that had escaped her haphazard bun. Leaning into his touch, she kissed his palm before averting her gaze.

"Why did my magic hurt him all those years ago? Why doesn't it work on him now?"

Romeo canted his head, looking at the back of the driver's seat, and wondered the same thing. The vehicle slowed slightly, and Gwen threw on the blinker before answering.

"Magical bursts, like the one you experienced years ago, are wild and erratic. They only happen in dire circumstances and are like a nuclear bomb of power. Simply put, the only reason why Romeo lived was because he was truly your mate. Your magic can still affect him, but he will bounce back."

He glanced back at his mate and didn't like the look of pain radiating across her face. But the look soon turned questioning, and Romeo wondered if this Gwen person was holding out more pertinent information from them. Feeding his mate breadcrumbs about her magic when it suited her the best. It seemed like his mate suspected the same thing.

Silina ground her jaw, and her eyes glistened, rage, sadness, and suspicion clearly written across her face. Romeo stroked her cheek and grasped her jaw. "Look at me."

When she finally did, he tightened his grip. "Don't think about the past, Lina. We are here now, together. We can be together. That is all that matters. Okay, Baby?"

She sighed, slumping into his grip, and nodded. "You should listen to him."

Romeo growled and loosened his grip, directing his pent-up anger at this Gwen person. "And you should fuck off, Gwen."

His mate stiffened before letting loose a snort and started to giggle. "Ya, Gwen, how about you fuck off entirely in my life going forward? I'm done following you blindly."

Gwen's sharp inhale filled the vehicle, but she didn't say anything as she slowed and rolled down the window. The crackling of the intercom and the creaking of gates opening had Romeo sitting up finally, and he took in their surroundings.

They were back at the alpha's house, meandering up the long winding drive, and Romeo pulled his mate into him, lopping his arm around her small waist and shoving his face into her neck. He breathed in her scent under the layer of filth they were both covered in. But he didn't care. They were both together and alive. That was all that mattered.

Silina held him back, her magic wrapped around both of them like an invisible barricade. Only when the SUV finally stopped did she move, fumbling for the door handle. She pulled him out with her, and Romeo blinked rapidly. He leaned in, wrapping his mate in his arms as the alpha's mate, another witch he had met before, bounced down the steps. She skidded to a halt, hand reaching out to touch his mate, but she pulled back slightly. The witch tilted her head and looked back and forth between everyone, with burning questions filling her eyes.

Silina sighed and gave the witch a sad smile. For the life of him, Romeo could not remember the redhead's name. Truly, when he had shown up at the alpha's house, he had one thing on his mind, which was to find Silina.

Romeo watched as the witch's mate, Hunter, the alpha of the local pack, made his way down the stairs. He placed a hand on the redhead's shoulder. "Lily, sweetheart. Take them inside. I need to talk to the high priestess."

Lily nodded and grabbed Silina's hand, essentially pulling her and Romeo inside at the same time because he was unwilling to part with her on any level. The moment they stepped over the threshold, Lily shut the door and took them both in, her gaze full of scrutiny. "You guys look like absolute shit. What the hell happened? Why did you run?"

His mate shook her head again, and dust and dirt floated down to the floor. "Can we shower and crash here? I promise to fill you in on everything later. I promise."

The redhead, Lily, scowled at Romeo's mate before sighing and pointing up the stairs. "Of course, Lina. You're welcome here anytime. Mi casa es tu casa. You know that."

Silina nodded and glanced back at him with a slight smirk. "Come on, dirty boy. Let's get cleaned up."

Chapter Eight

SILINA

HER MIND WAS A jumbled mess as she pulled Romeo up the stairs behind her. She was spinning out of control and needed to get away from anyone who could accidentally be affected by her magic. She didn't know what to do about Gwendolen's betrayal, but she wasn't going to dwell on it at that moment. The only thing that mattered was the hand she was gripping and getting them alone in a locked room.

Romeo didn't utter a word as he let her drag him down the hallway. She peeked over her shoulder to see he was staring intently at the ground. When he stumbled slightly, Silina cursed under her breath. She stopped and pushed him against the wall. He took a deep inhale and cracked a slight smile. "Hey, baby."

Silina frowned and ran her hand through his hair, pushing it out of his eyes. "Shit, you're still dosed with whatever we got hit with, aren't you?"

He let his head drop into the palm of her hand. "It's wearing off, but ya. I got a pretty hefty dose. I should be good in a few minutes, though."

Silina groaned, clenching her thighs, as Romeo kissed the palm of her hand. She shouldn't be thinking about his hands on her when all they really needed was a shower. Hell, she really should be thinking in smaller steps. Shower, talk... not think about those hands running down her naked body now that she learned her magic wouldn't harm him.

Her thighs clenched again, the all too familiar warm tingle rooting itself low in her abdomen. And she really shouldn't be thinking about how good it felt as Romeo's arm snaked its way around her waist, pulling her closer as he trailed his soft lips over the palm of her hand and up her wrist.

Silina felt her heart rate skyrocket as Romeo tipped his gaze to meet hers, their eyes locking. It was as if all the air was punched out of her in that moment, time screeching to a standstill. Instinctively, she felt for her magic, but it was calm. Placid and content like it had never been before. Silina drew in a shaky breath, breaking the moment as she pulled away. She refused to lose contact with him, though, and gripped his hand, pulling him once again down the hall. He must have sensed her urgency, because he followed without a word. His presence wrapped around her like a warm blanket. He was so close that she could feel his chest against his back, and the second they stepped into the huge bathroom at the end of the hallway, she turned.

Screw shoulds and shouldn'ts. She wanted and needed this man.

Her lips were on his within seconds, and Romeo reciprocated, pulling her closer and lifting her up with one arm. She wrapped her legs around his waist, her hands threading through his hair. She felt him move, shutting the door behind them before her ass met with the cool marble of the sink countertop.

Then his hands were on her, under her sweater, fingers grazing across her touch-starved skin, and she whimpered. Romeo pulled back from the kiss slightly, much to Silina's dismay. He nibbled at her lower lip, growling, "Baby, if I keep kissing you like this, I'm not going to be able to stop myself from marking you, claiming you. Making you mine."

Silina arched against his hands, still under her sweater, and tightened her legs around his waist. She could feel his cock straining against both their pants, and she opened her eyes to meet his gaze. "Ro-Ro, I've wanted this all my life. I've always been yours; don't you dare stop now."

She watched as his pupils dilated, then his mouth was on her once again. He dove in deep, stripping all the air from her lungs as his hands skated up to cover her breasts. Arching into his hold, she loved the feel of her nipples against his rough hands. She whimpered again as one of his hands dropped, moving to dip low against the waistband of her sweatpants.

She did the same, grabbing the front of his pants, quickly unbuttoning and releasing his cock into her palm.

It was thick and heavy as she fisted it, and Romeo groaned against her lips, his hips thrusting into her. "Fuck," he growled as he roughly pulled at her sweatpants.

Silina lifted, allowing them to be pulled down over her ass and thighs. Romeo shifted his weight, pulling back ever so slightly. His other hand, still under her sweatshirt, snaked up to grasp the back of her neck.

She tipped her head with a moan as Romeo kissed her exposed neck before whispering into her ear, "Are you wet for me, baby? Tell me how much you need me."

Silina gasped as she felt the head of his cock nudge at the entrance to her pussy, but he didn't push in any farther. She bucked her hips, but Romeo held her hips in place.

"Tell me, baby," he whispered again.

Silina groaned, "I need you. I need your thick cock buried inside of me. I need you to mark me, claim me as yours. I never want to be separated from you again, even for a moment. Make me yours."

Romeo hissed, sliding in a little deeper, and Silina squirmed against his girth. At this angle, he felt impossibly big, and she leaned back, gripping the edge of the sink. The movement lifted her hips and Romeo slid in another inch. They both groaned as he pulled back, leaving just the tip inside. "Fuck, baby. You feel amazing."

He lifted her hips, and Silina put her foot on his shoulder as he pushed in, slowly filling and stretching her pussy until he was halfway inside. "Look at that," he whispered, as he trailed his fingers over her opening. "Look how well your pussy takes my cock, baby."

Silina opened her eyes, and she felt her core tighten as she did just as he said. She glanced down, watching his cock push farther into her until he was filling her completely. He bottomed out, hitting her just right, and Silina whimpered. "Oh fuck. I think I could come just from watching you thrust into me."

In response, Romeo pulled out and thrust back into her hard. Silina felt her body respond, her pussy tightening as he slowly pulled out, only to follow up with powerful thrusts. She gripped the sink with whitening knuckles, her eyes still trained on how they were connected, watching how his cock stretched and filled her. His length glistened under the light every time he pulled out, her pussy juices drenching it fully. Her orgasm crested, surprising her by how fast it had built up. She cried out, her hands flying to Romeo's shoulders as he continued his onslaught on her pussy. Nails sinking into his shoulders, she clawed him closer. She cried out again, her pussy pulsating even as she felt his teeth on her neck. He bit down, and Silina's eyes rolled to the back of her head. The magic of the mating bond slipped between them, her own magic curling around it like the lovers they were. She felt Romeo's release, his cock twitching inside of her as he buried himself deep inside of her.

Her pussy continued to flutter, clenching slightly every few seconds as they held each other, their panting breaths filling the bathroom. Letting her foot fall from his shoulder, she wrapped her legs around his waist once more. She wanted to keep his half-hard cock inside of her as long as she could. She still couldn't wrap her mind around the fact that he was not only alive, but they were wrapped in each other's arms, mated, and her magic wasn't lashing out. She arched her back as Romeo's fingers glided down her spine, absolutely loving the contact of his body against her bare skin.

When he made a movement to pull out of her, Silina shook her head and tightened her legs around his waist. "Just...just another moment. I love feeling you inside of me."

Romeo chuckled and kissed the mating bite on her neck. "And I love the feeling of being inside of you. But I've got to pull out if we are going to shower. I promise you we will do this again, over and over and over."

Silina growled low in her throat, "We have a lot of years to make up for."

"Don't worry, baby. I plan on making all those years up to you."

Silina cracked a smile as he kissed their mating bite again, then groaned as he pulled out of her fully. She sighed as the feeling of emptiness enveloped her pussy, but perked up as he stretched his arms overhead, pulling his shirt off with the movement.

Her hands moved of their own accord, feeling all the hard groves of his chest and abs. He grunted in response and pulled her sweater over her head. As his eyes fell to her breasts, a hot blush pinkened Silina's cheeks.

"Do you like what you see?" she rasped, as Romeo ran his fingers over her nipples.

"Baby, I'm gonna fuck these tits later and come all over them."

Silina giggled, loving how her mate was talking so dirty to her. His hands tickled over her nipples again, and she arched into them. "Why later? Do it now."

Romeo huffed, a shine rolling over his eyes before shaking his head. "No, we are getting clean first. Then I'm gonna make you very, very dirty."

Silina snorted, "Shower then?"

Romeo nodded and lifted her up with one arm around her waist. "Yes, baby, shower... and shower sex. Then later, I'm gonna fuck those tits, and that mouth, and then I'll fuck your pussy again. Got it."

Silina nodded and threaded her hands in his hair. "You better uphold that promise. Now let's get clean, you dirty, dirty boy."

Chapter Nine

ROMEO

STEAM FILLED THE AIR as warm water flowed over both of their bodies. Romeo couldn't stop touching his mate, the need for constant contact overwhelming every one of his senses. Lucky for him, she seemed to be feeling the exact same thing. His hands were currently in her hair, massaging shampoo as her body draped against his. She sighed, rubbing against him, and Romeo inhaled sharply, his hips moving on their own as his hard cock slid across her ass and lower back. He gripped her hair, moving her head slightly to expose her beautiful neck and their mating mark. Dipping his head, he ran his tongue along it before trailing kisses along his mate's shoulder.

"Ro-Ro," Silina moaned and pushed her ass into him harder, placing her hands out in front of her.

He growled, keeping a fist in her hair as he smoothed his other hands down the front of her body. His fingers found her clit, and she shuddered as he began circling it slowly. "Do you like that, baby?" he whispered, knowing full well from the sounds his mate was making that she was enjoying the hell out of what he was doing.

Silina panted, and Romeo grinned as he took in how her fingers tried to grip the shower wall. Her hands slid through, and in the end, it was only his grip on her hair that held her up. Her back and neck arched beautifully in front of him as he continued his slow circles on her clit, shudders racking through her body. The way she leaned over and lined his cock up perfectly with her sweet pussy, Romeo could have easily started fucking her. Which he planned on doing in earnest, but first...

He dropped his hold on her hair and grabbed her hips to keep her in place before lowering to his knees. His mate's startled gasp turned into a high-pitched moan as he placed his mouth on her delicious pussy, driving his tongue into her.

"Romeo! Fuck, oh... Oh, fuck."

His mate shuddered against him, her moans turning to soft, strangled gasps as he continued to circle her clit and fuck her with his tongue. She rode his face, bucking against his mouth until her whole body shook and he felt her pussy pulsate. He quickly leaned back and tugged at her hips. His mate came willingly, her legs giving out as he pulled her down and aligned his cock up with her dripping wet pussy, still clenching and unclenching from her orgasm. He worked himself inside of her, stretching her out to accommodate his girth. Reaching out, his mate used the wall to push against, grinding herself deeper onto his cock. His grunts filled the steamy air, mixing with her low moans, as they picked up a grueling rhythm, and he pounded into her from behind. Her moans turned to hoarse whimpers, and he felt her pussy tighten again.

"That's it, baby, come on my cock. Come for your mate, you dirty girl."

His mate turned her head slightly, staring at him over her shoulder with hooded eyes, mouth slightly opened as Romeo slapped her ass. It pushed her over the edge, and he felt her pussy clamp down, her delighted scream echoing through the shower stall. "That's my baby girl," he growled.

"Yes, fuck, yes, I am," his mate panted through her orgasm. She winked at him as he continued thrusting. "Now come for me, dirty boy. Fill my pussy up even more."

Romeo's jaw slacked slightly as his mate matched his dirty words, but more so at how he responded to them. He came moments later, and they both closed their eyes. Their soft moans intermingled, and Romeo wrapped his arms around Silina's waist, pulling them both back to lean against the shower wall.

The water was still pounding down around them, and his mate giggled in his arms. He squeezed her tight against him and kissed her wet head. "What's so funny?"

"I'm pretty sure everyone heard our sexcapades. Not that I'm complaining, but we might want to go somewhere more private next time."

Romeo snorted. "I mean... do you really think they thought we were just gonna shower quickly and rejoin them downstairs?"

Silina turned in his arms slightly, her eyes growing wide. "Ro-Ro, do you think they are just sitting down there... listening and waiting?"

His laugh reverberated off the walls, and he squeezed his mate tight. "Well, what is done is done. Might as well actually clean up and see what everyone is doing."

His mate blushed, but nodded her head. They both stood and quickly washed up before Romeo reached over and turned off the water. He was in the process of drying his gorgeous mate, fluffing her hair while she growled and swatted at him, when the sound of yelling reached their ears.

His mate scrambled for the door, dressed in nothing but a towel, and bolted down the hallway to the stairs. Romeo cursed, following quickly behind her, and managed to wrap an arm around her waist, halting her. The raised voices came from a room right off the foyer, and Silina tossed him a dirty look before hissing. "Let me go in there. They are fighting about me."

Romeo shook his head and held her tighter. "How about we assess the situation before running in half-cocked. Last thing I want is to be knocked out... again."

Silina's face softened slightly, her scowl dissipating. She adjusted her grip on the towel she was wearing before placing her hand gently on his forearm wrapped around her middle. "Don't worry, Ro-Ro. I can handle whatever is happening in that room. Pretty sure there isn't anything else that can shock me tonight."

Romeo scowled, but released her just enough so they could get into the room where the commotion was unfolding. An icy blanket of air wrapped around them the moment they stepped in and, all of a sudden, all of his senses were dulled. He growled, glancing around to see Gwen standing near a flipped over and smoking chair. Her hands were by her sides, and her face was devoid of all emotion. On the other side of the room, a large man was holding a cursing blonde woman around the middle, keeping her in place while the alpha stood with his mate behind him. The redhead, Lily, was gripping his shirt and murmuring soothing words as the alpha's eyes glowed. To his surprise, Silina took the whole scene in stride and calmly asked, "What the fuck is going on?"

The icy chill dissipated, yet still not enough for Romeo to regain his heightened senses back. Gwen didn't flinch at his mate's words, though he noticed her indifference faltered ever so slightly. His mate turned on her heel, glancing around at the chaos. The struggling woman stilled, but the man held her like his life depended on it.

"Drop the null and face me like the bitch you are," the blonde woman snarled, and his mate's eyes widened.

His mate squeaked, "Are you talking to me?"

The blonde shook her head. "No, not you, Silina. I'm talking to our manipulative and lying bitch of a high priestess."

"Enough!" the alpha's voice rang out, and his mate gripped his arms tight. "Blane, get your mate under control."

The blonde scoffed but quieted as the man whispered in her ear. Silina gulped, holding her head high as she took in the room. "I'm not sure what is going on, but I would like some answers about tonight." She paused and glanced over her shoulder to Gwen. "Because you are obviously not telling me everything. I knew you were holding back in the car ride here."

"If you don't tell her what she is, I will." The blonde spoke up again and tried her best to look empathetic toward Silina, all while giving Gwen the evil eye.

His mate's face scrunched up; the look of confusion clearly painted on it. "What... What I am? I'm confused."

Gwen's frosty voice echoed through the room. "I knew I shouldn't have brought you into the coven, Mariel. You're too smart for your own good."

The blonde snapped her head back, as if Gwen's words had physically struck her. Then her eyes narrowed, and she turned her gaze to Silina.

"You're not a siphon. You're something much more rare and powerful. I had my suspicions. When I found out our high priestess was a null and learned about the mysterious witch who never seemed to use her powers, and worked in a place high with emotions and a even higher body count, I put two and two together."

Romeo inched forward, wrapping his arms around his stunned mate. She gaped at Mariel as the silence grew heavy within the room. Finally, his mate grasped her words and turned to look at Gwen. "What is she talking about? You told me I was a siphon. If I'm not, then what am I? And why would you lie?"

"Careful, Silina. This is not a path you want to walk yet. Just forget about tonight," Gwen murmured, and Mariel shot a look of pure hatred at the high priestess.

He felt his mate start to shake as venom coated her words. "No... No, tell me everything right now."

Gwen sighed and shook her head. "Fine. But remember, when this is all said and done, I was protecting you." She glanced around the room at everyone still there. "I was protecting all of you. There is more at stake than you can even fathom."

"Just tell them," Mariel gritted out through her clenched teeth.

"You're an enchantress, Silina. Something that only comes along every century or so. Your magic is unique, easily confused to be that of a siphon. Except a siphon can only steal magic, the energy of other supernatural's, then they harness those powers for a short time. You, on the other hand..."

"Can harness a life force and drain anyone, and anything fully," Silina whispered.

"And in the process, you make pure, undiluted magic," the blonde whispered, and Silina glanced at her, the pain clearly radiating across her face.

"I still don't understand why that's so important."

Gwen sighed. "We can stop here. You all can trust me. What I am doing, have been doing, is to stop the possibility of a war."

Mariel laughed, and the alpha shook his head. "No, enough. Enough of this withholding of information. Tell us everything. I need to know my pack and mate are safe."

Gwen sighed, and the iciness surrounding everyone fell. Suddenly, Romeo's senses were back, and he could feel the high emotions and the taste of lingering magic in the air.

"I am a null, as has been already stated," Gwen started, "meaning I can nullify all magic around me within a certain radius if I so choose. Silina is an enchantress who can produce unfiltered raw magic. All we need then is a siphon who can be given that magic, and you have an unstoppable trio. What is known in the witch world as the Trinity. And that is why tonight happened. They have known for while I was harboring the enchantress. I've been keeping them at bay for a while now, saying she wasn't ready yet. But it seems they are tired of waiting. They want the magic Silina can provide. I have been going to clandestine meetings for years. But their plans are numerous, and they are suspicious of me. The alpha knew what I have been doing, but I'll admit, I haven't been telling him everything."

Romeo had no idea who they were, but from the looks of it, neither did Silina. The alpha, on the other hand, looked like he was ready to reach out and strangle Gwen.

"They have a siphon."

Gwen answered with a curt nod.

"Who are they?" Lily asked the question everyone was seemingly dancing around.

The alpha ground his jaw and took a deep breath before answering. "The witch council has decided to play their hand once they found out about us. That Gwen and her coven were trying to bring actual peace between our species, inside of the tense truce we currently have. The council wants control over the lycanthrope population once more. And apparently, they are planning to do it much sooner than we anticipated."

Chapter Ten

SILINA

SHE WAS TIRED. SO, fucking tired of the last twenty-four hours and the constant bombshells dropping around her.

First, her mate was alive.

Then she was drugged and kidnapped.

And then, she found out that Gwen, the one woman she had trusted all these years, was lying and holding information back from her.

And lastly, she found out she wasn't even a siphon but something so much more.

Silina's mind was buzzing and enough was enough.

She glanced at Gwen, who was standing ramrod straight against the hostile crowd as the alpha of the pack pointed a finger at her. "We are going into lockdown. I'm not putting my pack or their mates into any more danger until we figure out exactly what is going on."

At his words, Mariel's mate, Blane, tossed the still fuming witch over his shoulder and stalked right out the door.

Gwen side-eyed Silina and sighed. "It's better you stay here. You will be better protected in the alpha's territory. Breena cast a spell over the property a few months ago, and it's airtight against prying eyes."

She turned, as if to leave, and the alpha growled low, "Where the fuck do you think you're going? I said we are on lockdown. That includes you."

Silina couldn't help but shrink back into Romeo as Gwen shot the alpha an icy glare. "I am not part of your pack. You don't get to boss me around."

"We are trying to forge alliances. Part of the agreement we signed was I protect your coven. That includes you until I figure out if you are still on our side or not."

Gwen ground her jaw and crossed her arms. "Fine then. I'll stay till morning. I can't be holed up here forever. We need to brainstorm the best course of action against the witch's council."

"Great," Lily drawled, and gave her mate, the alpha, a long, hard stare. "I'll get bedrooms set up for the impromptu sleepover. Then you and I are talking. I don't like that you withheld information like this from me." She turned on her heel and marched out of the room, and Silina moved to go after her.

Romeo followed as she dashed after her best friend. Hushed angry voices filtered out after her, but she didn't care anymore. She knew eventually she would have to figure out what the witch council was planning, because it obviously involved her magic, but for tonight, she just wanted to sleep.

She caught up with Lily, who had charged ahead and up the stairs. "Are you angry with me?"

Her breath caught as the air crackled with electricity—her best friend's specific brand of magic—but when Lily turned around, her face seemed more tired than angry.

She gave Silina a quick shake of her head. "No, I just don't like that I was kept out of the loop. I'm mad at Hunter, but I'm feeling betrayed by Gwen. I still don't really understand what is happening."

"Me neither," Silina whispered before reaching out to give her friend a quick hug. "But maybe everything will make more sense in the morning?"

Lily nodded and pushed open a door before flicking the light on. "You both can crash here for as long as you want. There are some spare clothes in the dresser."

Whispering goodnight, she gave Lily another hug before she departed, and Romeo ushered her into the room. She moved like a zombie, tiredness clouding her mind as she dropped the towel she was still wearing and flopped onto the bed face first. "This is such a fucking mess."

Romeo chuckled and patted her ass as he came to sit down next to her. "Let's just rest, then. The problems will still be there in the morning."

Silina turned her head to look at him. "How are you doing with all of this?"

Romeo shrugged and leaned over her, pulling the blankets down and maneuvering her underneath them. He snuggled against her back, and Silina fought a yawn.

Kissing her shoulder, he ran his teeth over their mating mark. "I'm perfectly content as long as you are in my arms. Now let's go to sleep."

Silina nodded, her eyelids already shutting as she snuggled into his chest. "Mmmkay, just for a few hours. Then we are having sex again."

Romeo's chest shook with silent laughter. "Whatever you say, baby. Want your morning wakeup call to be my dick?"

She knew he was joking, but Silina didn't care. "That actually sounds wonderful. If I'm not waking up with your cock inside of me, then I will be really, really angry."

Romeo snorted. "As you wish, baby."

Silina moaned, on the cusp of waking, as a tingling sensation swept through her lower back and between her legs. She arched her back slightly as a rasping voice whispered, "Hush, baby, just relax and let me take care of you."

Warm breath lingered, sweeping down her neck, and she felt pressure at her core. Moaning again, she bucked her hips as the pressure increased, filling her up to the brink. She felt herself start to move, the pressure inside dipping in and out, at the same rhythm of her body. A smile touched her lips as she squirmed under the warm, heavy weight at her hips. "Ro-Ro?" she gasped, as she started to wake up. It was still dark as she opened her eyes, pleasure cresting through her body.

A warm weight hung over her, and her mate kissed her, nipping at her lips with a sigh. "Ya, baby. It's me. Time to get up."

She wrapped her arms and legs around him as he continued his slow movements inside of her. At this angle, with every thrust, he rubbed against her clit, and she moaned against his lips. He continued to nip and suck, peppering kisses on her face as her orgasm crested. It washed over her in waves and Silina cried out softly. She felt him come inside of her two thrusts later, and Romeo rolled over until she was on top of him. He caressed her bare back as she snuggled her face into his neck.

"Best wakeup call ever," she murmured. "I should go back to sleep so we can do it again."

He chuckled, and Silina kissed his neck before sitting up in a straddling position. She wiggled her hips as he massaged her thighs, their mess of fluids already trickling down her legs.

"Oh shit..." Romeo whispered as his hands stilled. "We haven't been using protection."

Silina sucked in a breath as their gazes locked. "Crap, and it's not like I'm on anything. I don't have sex with, like...you know, real penises."

Romeo blinked slowly. "... come again."

A blush crawled over her cheekbones, and she licked her lips. "I've only ever done it with toys. Or were you asking about birth control?"

Romeo reached up and brushed her cheek. "I'm your first... real penis?"

They both snorted, laughs echoing out of them at the same time, and Romeo pulled her back down onto his chest. "Well, you're my first in every way," he managed to wheeze out between gasping laughs fits.

Silina still had a grin on her face as she pushed off him and bit her lower lip. "You know it wouldn't be so bad, would it?"

"What?"

"If you know..." She motioned at them both. "If we accidentally made a..."

She trailed off as Romeo smiled. She remembered back when they had talked about running away together. He had wanted a huge family, and Silina hoped he hadn't changed his mind.

"You remember before everything happened? When I told you I wanted five kids?"

Silina nodded. "Is that still the case?"

Romeo tugged her back into his arms and kissed her. "Fuck ya, baby."

She giggled as he grew hard underneath her again, and she turned around, straddling him backwards. "Well then, I think we should practice more. You know, just to make sure we get it down right."

"We just practiced. Now it's time to be naughty," Romeo growled before grabbing her hips and tossing her onto the bed. He was over her a second later, straddling her waist and leaning over to place both of his hands next to her head.

Silina licked her lips, his hard cock at eye level, and Romeo winked at her. "I think I remember saying something about fucking these gorgeous tits, baby."

"And my mouth. Don't forget that."

She watched his eyes glow slightly as she arched her back, squeezing both her tits together. Romeo slid his cock between them and started rocking, in and out, and every time the head of his dick got close enough, she gave it a little lick.

"Fuck," Romeo growled. "Keep doing that and I'm not gonna last."

Silina laughed and squirmed a little lower, so with his next thrust, she could lick more of his cock.

"Baby, fuck... I'm going to come."

"Come on my tits, just like you promised, my dirty boy."

Romeo grunted, and she felt his cock swell and pulsate, releasing all over her. His hot sticky cum ran down her chest and collarbones, even splattering a little onto her chin and lower lip. He reached out to wipe it off and Silina lifted her mouth to capture his thumb. He sucked in a breath as she sucked the cum off.

"You taste good," she murmured.

Romeo cocked his eyebrow, before looking down at her chest and trailed a finger through his sticky release. He brought it up to her mouth, and Silina eagerly sucked his fingers clean.

"That's so fucking hot, baby," he whispered. "Next time, I'm coming in your mouth."

Silina sighed and arched her back. "I'm not opposed to that happening right now."

Romeo snorted and shook his head before rolling off her, much to Silina's disappointment.

He pulled her up and circled his arms around her. "Shower, food, then I think we should talk to your coven members."

Silina sighed, and Romeo tipped her chin up so he could meet her eyes.

"Then I promise you another few rounds with my cock, wherever and whenever you want it."

Silina cracked a smile. "That sounds like a perfect plan."

They both moved at the same time, wrapping their forgotten towels from the night before around them before peeking out into the hallway. Silina rushed out the door toward the bathroom, with Romeo hot on her heels, and she giggled as he slapped her ass. They slid into the bathroom at the same time, and Silina pushed her mate up against the wall, kissing him deeply.

Pulling away slightly, she whispered, "You and me, Ro-Ro. Nothing's going to tear us apart again. Promise me."

Romeo grasped her hair, tilting her head up so she could meet his eyes. "I promise you, baby. I'm not going anywhere. Not without you, ever again. Now get into the shower so I can worship this body."

Silina smiled and dropped the towel, loving how his eyes ate her up as she stepped into the shower and turned on the warm spray. She sank into his arms as Romeo stepped in after her, and closed her eyes, letting the pleasure of just being in her mate's arms overtake her.

Epilogue

HIS BROWS CREASED AS Romeo concentrated on the road, hands gripping the wheel tight. His mate sat next to him, curled up in the seat, her magic radiating off her in waves. She was absolutely glowing from the first night back at her work, her magic fully satiated. They hadn't been out of each other's vicinity since finding each other again, and Romeo even got a job as a bouncer at her work. The lockdown the alpha had everyone on lifted a week ago, and Romeo didn't even want to think about the mess that had happened between the witches and lycanthropes during all that time. It wasn't a straight-out war, just as Gwen promised, but it sure felt like a small one. But they won in the end, coming out even stronger as a community.

Romeo glanced at his mate, her eyes hooded as she played with a wisp of her hair.

"Eyes on the road, dirty boy," she murmured, and Romeo felt his cock start to swell inside his jeans.

Fuck, he really did love it when she called him that. But she was right. He had just started learning how to drive again, and she was technically his teacher. Every night after work, they would drive around for a bit, and it was some of his favorite times. Just him, his mate, and the dark blacktop before them.

The thought brought up all sorts of naughty images in his mind, and Romeo smirked. He reached over, caressing his mate's face. "I think I'm hot for teacher."

She scoffed, "You think? Well, obviously, I need to up my game."

Moving in her seat, she glanced around before smiling seductively.

Romeo's breath caught as his mate reached over and unzipped his jeans. His throbbing cock fell into her hand instantly, pre-cum already leaking out. He stole another glance her way, and Silina licked her lips. "Eyes on the road, dirty boy. And try not to crash."

He gritted his teeth as his mate dipped forward, her sweet lips kissing his shaft before opening her mouth. Fitting the head of his cock in her mouth, she swirled her tongue, licking and teasing his tip while she fisted the rest of him, moving her hand up and down slowly.

Romeo dipped his head back with a groan, before jerking his eyes back to the road. One of his hands fell off the steering wheel to grip Silina's hair with his fist. His eyes fluttered as she took more of his cock into her mouth, and he pulled the car over, slamming on the brakes. There was no way he would have kept the car on the road with the way she was sucking his cock so well. He already felt the telltale tingle at the base of his spine and his balls felt tight and heavy.

He felt his mate groan in the back of her throat as he thrust a little deeper into her mouth until he hit the back of her throat. She continued sucking, her small fist still moving around the rest of his shaft. His grip on the back of her head tightened, and he groaned as he felt his cock twitch.

His beautiful mate groaned with him, swallowing down his cum as he spurted into her mouth. As his cock stopped twitching, she lifted up, licking her lips and looking smug as she winked at him. Romeo growled and pulled her into his lap. He kissed her hard, not caring that he could taste himself on her lips.

She kissed him back with just as much vigor, and when they finally broke apart, their panting breaths filled the silence of the night. She made a move to crawl back into the passenger seat, but Romeo tightened his grip on her waist. "No, you are staying right where you are. We aren't done yet."

Her soft chuckle made his cock harden again, and she shifted her weight until his cock dug into the front of her sweatpants. She kissed his jaw, nipping her way up to his lips. "I love that you bounce back so fast."

He bit her lower lip, causing his mate to groan. "And I love that you can take me every time. Now put my hard cock in that soft pussy of yours and hold on tight."

With a smirk, she pulled her sweatpants down just enough for him to gain entrance, and he hissed as his sensitive cock sank into her hot, wet pussy. He waited until she settled in on him before putting the lights back on and putting the car in shift. His mate's eyes widened, and he got back on the road.

"Holy shit," she whispered. "I never thought about driving sex."

Romeo shifted under her, eliciting another moan from his mate as she started riding him slowly. It felt magnificent, and before either of them noticed, they had turned off the main road, taking an alternate and less maintained way home. Romeo made sure to hit every bump and pothole he could, and the extra jostling was making his mate squirm and wiggle all over his lap. She squeaked as he hit a particularly aggressive bump, and he felt her tighten over his cock before her pussy started pulsating.

She came with a loud shout, her nails digging into his shoulders as her pussy strangled his cock until he couldn't take it anymore and came with her. A few moments later, she slumped against him, and his cock softened until it was half hard. He was still inside of her and was going to stay that way until their next round.

Their home, a little mother-in-law suite located on a piece of property shared with his mate's high priestess, came into view and he parked. He let the car idle as he wrapped his arms around his mate and kissed her on the forehead. "How was that, baby?"

She lifted her head, her eyes brimming with satisfaction, and grabbed his face, kissing him deeply before whispering, "We need to do that again."

His cock twitched inside of her, getting full again as his mate shifted her weight. "Right now?"

His mate nodded her head, and Romeo chuckled as she moved her hips, his cock burying deeper into her warm pussy. Groaning, he slammed the car into reverse and gave his mate exactly what she wanted.

The End

Arctic Moon

WICKED FATE, LUSTY MATES

ASTRID VAIL

Blurb & Content Warning

**She never believed in happily ever after,
until he came along.**

They call her cold hearted, but Gwendolen never
cared.
The only thing she ever cared about was
freedom.
Freedom from a life no one, not even her coven
knows she is living.
Never cared about anything else until *he* came
along and uprooted her carefully laid plans.
Plans that never involved a lycanthrope claiming
to be her mate.
When the life she is trying to escape comes
knocking, Gwendolen is faced with a choice.
She can have the freedom she desperately wants,
for a price.

WICKED FATE, LUSTY MATES

All she must do is betray her coven, and her
newfound mate.

Content warning includes spicy on page sex
scenes, murder, death, past child & spousal abuse,
and language.

Chapter One

CHASE

BLOOD DRIPPED FROM A cut above his eye, trailing down his face and onto his lips. A smile stretched his face as his opponent swung wide. Ducking, he stepped in to land an uppercut. The bear shifter before him groaned and shook his head as Chase danced away.

He was already sporting several bruises from his ham-fisted opponent, and his lungs stung with the salty intake of sweat, blood, and violence hanging in the air. His wolf, a raging beast inside of him, relished the violent release. It was the only release Chase would give him.

In the fighting rings.

It was a mercy that Chase was even alive with a wolf like his.

"He's a fucking psycho."

The hushed whispers floated under the cheering of the crowd, and Chase grunted as the bear shifter tackled him. He hit the hard ground with a grunt, something popping in his back, followed by a sharp crunch. Chase ignored the pain as he began wailing on his opponent's ears and head.

Everything was legal once you stepped into the ring, except shifting, of course. The people came to watch people fight, not animals.

His knuckles split, drenching his wraps in more blood as the bear shifter shook off his punches like a bear swatting away an annoying fly.

Pun intended.

A meaty fist slammed him square in the face, and Chase's head smashed back against the ground, his nose gushing blood.

His ears rang and even his demented wolf inside gave a pause as pain exploded through the back of his skull. As the bear gave his jaw another love tap, Chase felt a rush of darkness creep in.

The bear shifted his weight on top of him, a veteran of a shifter covered in scars and sporting salt and pepper hair, who grunted before shaking his head. "Do you yield, wolf?"

Chase's wolf snarled but slunk to the back of his mind, content with the happenings of the night. He could finally rest, his rage subsiding. Which meant Chase was left by himself to either continue getting his ass handed to him or yield.

Without his wolf snarling in his ear, Chase chose the latter.

"Yield," he spat out, blood still dripping down his face.

The crowd booed and protested as the bear shifter got to his feet and offered Chase a hand. He took it with a savage smile and his opponent gave him a once-over. "Wolf," he rumbled, "you have a demon living inside of you. I wouldn't want to face you in animal form."

"That's what they all say," Chase murmured as they broke apart.

He ducked through the metal gates holding the crowd at bay and pushed through them. A few people patted him on the back, but he was invisible to most of them as they rushed to place their bets on the next round of fighters. He made his way to the backrooms, heading straight to the showers, and turned it on full blast.

Pain lanced through him as the cold water rained onto his already healing bruises and open wounds. His eyes watered as he lifted his face up, letting the cold water numb his mangled nose. He could feel it healing and it hurt worse than receiving the punch in the first place. After rinsing most of the blood off him, he stripped off his fighting clothes and gave himself another rinse. The sting of his wounds was already gone by the time he turned the water off and pulled a towel around his waist.

Chase made his way to a locker and grabbed his duffle bag. Pulling on a pair of sweats and a dark tank top, he shoved his sopping wet fight clothes inside. He checked his phone before cursing silently. He had to hurry if he was going to catch the bus back into town from the city.

Slipping on his beat-up sneakers in a hurry, he waved to the other fighters with a shit-eating grin on his face.

"See y'all later," he called out before sprinting to the door that led to the stairs that would ultimately drop him off on the street side and into a shitty city neighborhood.

"That guy is a fucking psycho." The whisper hit his ears just as the door slammed shut behind him.

Chase sighed before taking the stairs two at a time.

Psycho, demon, devil incarnate.

The words played through his thoughts as he reached the deserted street and made his way over to the bus stop.

All the things his wolf was. And he was driving Chase insane.

The only relief he found inside his head was through violence. But soon, Chase knew these fights would not be enough.

Soon his wolf would demand to be set free, to run on four legs.

And if that ever happened, Chase was as good as dead. Unless he could find another way to calm his wolf for good.

He hopped off the bus, the night crashing around him like a blanket, and glanced up at the sky, the stars and moon hidden under a blanket of invisible clouds. Popping his neck, he gave the bus driver a wave as they pulled away from the only drop-off point in the small town he lived in.

At this time of the night, or really, early morning, there wasn't a soul about. For someone like Chase, with a demented wolf in his head, being alone was a curse. He needed to surround himself with people, with his pack, to keep his wolf under control. Unless it was after a fight night, then his wolf left him alone in peace for at least a few hours. Enough time for him to get some undisturbed sleep.

He jumped slightly as his phone buzzed in his hand. Glancing down, he saw his alpha calling.

"Heya, boss man, whatcha calling me so late for?"

His alpha's curt voice cut through Chase's smile. "We had a situation, and I need you to come in."

"I'll be right there."

"Wait." His alpha paused, muttering something under his breath, and Chase heard a female's voice in the background.

It was his mate, Lily. Chase was so happy for his alpha for finally finding the one. His alpha sighed before addressing Chase again.

"Long story short, I need to figure out if the high priestess of the Witch coven we have a contract with is still on our side, or if she has been betraying us all along. But..."

"But what?"

"But, until we can figure *that* out, she still needs to be protected in case the coven comes after her, like it did with one of the other coven members tonight."

Chase swore, jogging to the small apartment he rented above the local bakery. He was up the steps within moments, jamming his key into the lock. "You got it, boss. So use my charm to get the high priestess to lower her guard and simultaneously protect her from possible witchy threats. Easy peasy."

His alpha snorted over the phone. "I would love to see you charm this witch. Bring your blow torch. She is as icy as a woman can get."

Chase didn't have time to respond as his alpha hung up.

With a shrug, he tossed his duffle bag and phone onto the bed. It didn't matter, anyway. His alpha had laid down a challenge for Chase, even if he didn't know it. He was going to charm this ice queen of a witch just to prove he could.

Throwing his wet clothes into a hamper, Chase set about repacking his duffle bag. He did not know how long he would be on protection detail for, but if he was going to make it to the alpha's place by dawn, he would have to start walking now.

Chapter Two

GWEN

GWEN WRAPPED HER MAGIC around her like a shield in case of any magical attack. Then she took a deep breath and doused out any and all emotions. It wasn't a side effect of her nullifying magic, like everyone assumed. Shutting off her emotions and being a "cold-hearted bitch," as people liked to call her behind her back, was a side effect of her upbringing. Because emotions and feelings were weaknesses in the household she'd grown up in. It was better to be logical. Logic always prevailed, no matter what.

Logic dictated she should have stayed with her family instead of running away all those years ago. Logic also dictated when the rare elemental witch landed in your lap a decade ago, she should have brought her to the witch council immediately.

Instead, she hid her, protected her.

Because Gwen hated logic, contrary to popular belief. Most people assumed, with her stick-up-the-butt attitude and icy heart, logic was her favorite thing in the world.

They couldn't be further from the truth, but Gwen had an end goal. And once she met that goal, she would be free of her family with their secret initiative. It would finally be over.

That was all that mattered.

And in doing so, she burned a lot of bridges tonight. She needed her coven to turn against her. She needed the lycanthrope pack to suspect her motivations to give her more breathing room. But what she didn't need was a babysitter, which was what the alpha of the pack was demanding. Somehow, this part of the plan backfired.

She couldn't have a wolf following her every move if she was going to pull off the next part of her plan. Which she voiced adamantly, "Absolutely not. Trust me, I can take care of myself, and a babysitter will just slow down my plans."

The alpha, Hunter, glared at her with amber eyes. "Which are?"

Gwen fisted her hand tight until her nails dug into her palms. "Like I said before, just trust me."

She couldn't voice her plans out loud. The alpha didn't understand, nor could she fully come clean.

She wouldn't jeopardize her end goal, the one thing she had been working at for over a decade.

Hunter pinched the bridge of his nose. "Woman...you tell me to trust you, yet you can't tell me why. And after tonight's events, I am really wondering why I signed a contract with you in the first place. Take one of my wolves. That is the only offer I can make. Take a wolf and I'll stop asking questions and trust you."

Gwen conceded and turned on her heel. There were things she needed to get done, and it was just better to give in to his ridiculous command. "Send him to my place in the morning."

"No."

She stopped and slowly turned around, making sure her emotions stayed hidden. "Excuse me?"

"You stay here till morning. Then you and one of my wolves will leave together. That is the condition."

Gwen wanted to fight him on this, needing to get home as soon as possible and see where her plan had gone wrong. Because tonight shouldn't have happened. Someone in the witch council had jumped the gun, so to speak, in abducting Silina. It had forced Gwen into rescuing her and she needed to make sure her cover with the witch's council was still intact. She didn't have time to sit around, twiddling her thumbs and waiting for some babysitter.

Opening her mouth, she snapped it shut quickly. Logic dictated she should voice this very concern. But somewhere deep down, it conflicted her. She wanted to stay; she wanted to be surrounded by such fierce protectors, something she had never had in her life. Logic dictated burning this last bridge, completely annihilating the lycanthrope pack she worked so hard to infiltrate, per the witch council's request.

There were so many moving parts in her plan that Gwen honestly didn't know if she was the hero or villain anymore, but there was one thing she was certain of: she was tired of being alone.

So instead of protesting, she let one word slip from her lips and hoped it didn't cost her everything in the end.

"Fine."

Daybreak did not come quickly. Instead, it took its time as Gwen sat in a hardback chair within the guest room they set her up in. Sure, she could have slept, but she didn't want to chance the haunting nightmares that always seemed to find her outside her warded bedroom. Instead, she stared blankly out the window, waiting for the first touch of gray against the dark sky. Her mind was a whirlwind of thoughts, though, picking apart every aspect of her carefully crafted plan. She still couldn't figure out what went wrong. Perhaps she hadn't accounted enough human emotion to drive the head of the witch's council. But in her experience, that man was the epitome of logic, emotion be damned. No, it had to have been her. She slipped up somehow, and a sick feeling nestled itself low in her abdomen.

As dawn finally crested, Gwen shook herself out of her thoughts and stood, making sure her pantsuit and hair were in meticulous order. She didn't bother putting on her shoes yet, as she didn't want the noise of her high heels to disturb the other sleepers in the house.

She didn't sneak, though, instead she walked diligently down the hall with her head held high, face impassive as she made her way down the stairs, and only then, in the foyer and next to the front door did she slip on her high heels.

When she took a step outside, it did not surprise her to see the alpha waiting for her, leaning against her car. Nor was she surprised to see another man with him. They were speaking in hushed tones, no doubt plotting on how her mystery babysitting wolf would pull pertinent information out of her and report back to his alpha.

Gwen scoffed internally, her heels ringing loudly into the silent morning. As she approached, she took in the mysterious lycanthrope, from his shaggy blonde hair and broad shoulders, all the way down to the tips of his scuffed running shoes. He was wearing sweatpants, a threadbare shirt that was fraying around the edges, and when he finally turned, Gwen took in his deep blue eyes and a boyish charm that emanated from his face.

Emphases on boyish.

Gwen pegged him to be in his mid-twenties, at most.

She stopped in front of them both and, in the early morning light, she barely made out the yellowish hue of healing bruising on the lycanthrope's face.

He smiled at her and looked her up and down before offering her his hand. "Name's Chase, beautiful. It will be a pleasure to watch you."

Gwen raised an eyebrow. "You may address me as Gwendolen, ma'am, or preferably, not at all." She ignored his outstretched hand and turned to the alpha. "This is and will be an inconvenience. Reconsider."

He just shook his head and walked away slowly. "You two kids have fun."

Gwen outwardly scoffed this time, and Chase called out after his alpha. "We sure will, boss. Me and Not At All will become fast friends."

Gwen side-eyed the grinning lycanthrope. "You are not funny. Now get in the car. I have things to do, and I don't have all day."

Chapter Three

CHASE

CHASE THREW HIS BAG into the backseat before sliding into the ice queen's SUV. His alpha wasn't kidding. The woman currently putting the car in drive had an icy exterior with an attitude to match. But what he wasn't expecting when she stepped out of the mansion with the morning dawn rising at her back was how his wolf would react.

His wolf had whined.

Fucking whined.

His wolf had never whined in its life. It was a vicious, feral thing that lived inside of him, only allowed out once a month under alpha supervision.

But he had a moment of clarity in his head, for once in his life. His wolf calmed slightly at the sight of *her*.

And Chase needed to know why.

She couldn't be his mate, because he would have known instantly through scent. Though he really couldn't scent her either. The more he tried to hone in on her, the more his senses dulled. His alpha had warned Chase about this, that the high priestess was some sort of magic deleter ... Called her a null or something. But Chase hadn't been paying enough attention to remember the name.

He glanced her way, his eyes taking in the high priestess's features. To call her pretty was an understatement, and she was much younger than he had expected. Couldn't be over forty. Her hair was dyed dark, making her lethal light gray eyes stand out even more in her angular face. With high cheekbones, pouty lips, and curved jawline, in another life, Chase could have seen this woman strutting down a runway for high fashion.

Squinting slightly, he smiled like a fool. Her makeup was smudged, and Chase could tell under her foundation she was covering up a smattering of light freckles across her nose.

She glanced his way as they reached the gates to get off the alpha's property and promptly scowled at him. "Look, Chase. You seem like a decent kid, and I understand you are following your alpha's orders. But just stay out of my way and don't get involved with my life in any way, shape, or form. This will all be over soon enough."

Goosebumps ghosted down his arms at her words, his wolf sitting at attention. He needed to know what she had planned. Not just because of his alpha's orders, but because his wolf insisted it would involve them also, whether the high priestess knew it or not.

"What will be over soon enough?"

She flinched subtly, her hands gripping the steering wheel a little tighter than necessary. He knew she was going to lie before the words even came out of her mouth. "You having to babysit me, of course."

Chase wanted to press but knew it wouldn't be of any use with a woman like this, so instead he settled back into his tried-and-true method of getting people to open up to him.

Charm.

He relaxed his whole body and put a sloppy, boyish grin on his face before fiddling with the radio.

Or at least, tried to.

She tsked. "I don't drive with music. It's too distracting."

Fucking psycho woman.

Chase kept his smile on his face, even though he wanted to roll his eyes. "Well, okay then. So what should we do in the meantime? Oh, I got it. Ice breakers!"

The look the high priestess gave him was worth those words coming out of his mouth. A mix of confusion, horror, and just plain exasperation. She shook her head, but Chase plowed forward, pretending like he didn't see.

"Right, so I'm Chase. Twenty-six years old and a Cancer sun sign. I like action movies, pizza, long walkies in the forest..." He winked at her, but the high priestess stared dead ahead, completely ignoring him.

"Come on, Gwendolen," His voice lowered an octave as his wolf moved to the forefront of his mind slightly. "Play with me."

He watched her stiffen, and warmth colored her cheekbones slightly. She didn't answer him and instead gripped the steering wheel so tight it squeaked. When the silence ticked by long enough, Chase sighed and gave up. He leaned his seat back and closed his eyes, letting his mind drift. He would pick up trying to crack the ice queen's exterior later, after a nap.

The car jerked, a small hand pressing against his sternum as his eyes flew open. Chase made a move to sit up, his wolf rushing to the forefront, ready to protect at all costs. The pressure on his chest doubled and suddenly his wolf was gone, leaving behind only panic in its fold.

For the first time since his first change, his mind was silent and empty, his wolf put into a status.

"Fuck, what the—"

"Shut it, wolf." Gwendolen's voice frosted over his body like a winter day, and Chase slowly turned his head.

Her hand was still on his chest, her eyebrows crushing together as she searched the road ahead of them. From his position, he could see the trees surrounding them, but nothing else.

"We have a problem," Gwendolen whispered before training her eyes on him.

"What type of problem?" he whispered back. "And what did you do to my wolf?"

Gwendolen searched his face, and Chase watched her perfect icy mask slip briefly. Fear peeked through her gray eyes before she glanced away and back to the road. She swallowed roughly before lifting her hand from his chest. He still couldn't feel his wolf, all his senses dead to the world.

"The problem is in my house, and I threw a nulling field on you."

"But you're no longer touching me."

"I only need to touch you briefly for my magic to work."

A shiver ran down Chase's spine, a bitter taste on the back of his tongue. Never once did he think he would miss his wolf. But he missed that fucking violent psycho and his heightened senses at the moment.

"I need you to listen to me, Chase. And listen closely." She turned back to him, her mask back in place, only her cold demeanor shining through. "My magic will wear off in fifteen minutes once you get out of my sight. I need you to get out of the car, then head toward the back of the big house right down the road."

Chase opened his mouth to interrupt, but she pressed her fingers on his lips. "Dammit, don't interrupt. We don't have time."

He nodded slightly, and Gwendolen continued.

"Stay silent. Don't let anyone see you. Climb the flower ladder at the back of the house and use it to get to the little balcony. It goes to my bedroom. One of two places in my house that is heavily warded. *He* won't be able to sense you, but *you* will be able to hear everything. And whatever you do, do not make yourself known. I can't help you if you get caught. Got it?"

Her fingers slipped from his lips, and Chase clenched his jaw. "Gwendolen..."

She shook her head. "Trust me, just trust me. I promise I'll explain everything later... Please, I promise this isn't me trying to get rid of you. I promise. Please, just do this."

It was her ever-increasing plea that had him nodding slightly and slipping out the car door. He didn't turn around as he sprinted down the road and prayed he wasn't making a huge mistake.

Chapter Four

GWEN

GWEN RELEASED HER BREATH as Chase disappeared, praying to the goddess he didn't get caught. He wouldn't be detectable by magic, not with her nulling field wrapped around him, if he reached the warded room in time.

Because she wasn't lying; she wouldn't be able to help him if he got caught.

Her heart clenched at the thought, and it made Gwen pause. She didn't know this wolf. He was just one of hundreds she was trying to save from the council and their devious plans. But for some reason, she didn't want to see him as one of the casualties. She shook her head, deciding to ponder why he affected her so deeply later. Right now, she had other things to worry about.

She put the car in gear and wrapped even more layers of her nullifying magic around her. She would need it for who was waiting in her house. He hadn't even tried to sneak in, just walked in and triggered every alarm she had built around her property.

Gwen pulled into her drive and parked next to the gleaming black sedan and got out. She didn't glance at the driver leaning against the hood, smoking a cigarette. Instead, she looked at his feet and the butts littered around them.

Three...

Which meant he had been waiting for about an hour.

This was not good.

Gwen straightened her shoulders and stalked up the stairs to her front door, which was already unlocked. Her heels clicked across the tiled foyer, and she continued into the open-concept floor of her home.

Her stomach dropped, acid burning its way up her chest, as she took in the man sitting at her dining room table. He was reading the newspaper and drinking coffee.

Her fucking coffee.

Out of her favorite mug.

She wanted to hiss like a pissed off cat. She wanted to rip the paper out of his hands and throw the coffee in his face.

Instead, Gwen iced over her rage, and she stalked to the coffeepot, pulling out a mug from the cupboard. After filling it to the rim, she turned around and took a sip.

"To what do I owe the pleasure of having the head of the witch council at my table?"

"You know," the man drawled, before carefully folding the paper. "I really need to change that name. As warlocks are also part of the council."

Gwen pressed her mug to her lips, concealing her grimace as the man finally met her eyes.

Once she thought him handsome, commandeering, and even kind. Now all she saw was a venomous snake hellbent on world domination.

Or at least, supernatural domination.

"Gwendolen."

"Robert." She didn't let her voice waver. Even as she felt a mess of emotions inside. She would never show weakness in front of this man. Never again, not after everything he had put her through.

He had the audacity to laugh. "Gwendolen darling. My wife, tell me where you have been for the last twenty-four hours."

"I am not your wife."

Inside, she snarled and snapped. On the outside, her words flowed out, emotionless. Just like she had to pretend to be for most of her life.

"Semantics." Robert waved off her answer. "The old families follow the ancient laws, and you were one of my promised four."

"Then go bother one of your three other women. I have work to do."

Robert placed his mug on the table with an aggressive click and rubbed his head. "You are testing my patience. Just answer the question."

In her mind, Gwendolen hurled her coffee mug, hell, the whole coffeepot, at his head.

She sighed and put the mug on the counter. "Cleaning up your mess, Robert. Why did your lackeys jump the gun and abduct the enchantress? I told you she wasn't ready yet."

The muscle in Robert's jaw jumped, and he stood quickly, quick enough to make Gwen flinch. She hated herself even more for the chink in her armor.

Because he saw it.

And the fucker grinned, before straightening his suit jacket. "Where is she, Gwendolen?"

"At the alpha's house. With her mate. And she knows."

Robert went still, his eyes turning predatory. "What do you mean, she *knows*?"

"The new witch told Silina what she is. What she truly is."

Lie number one.

In her experience, she had about two more lies before her tell showed. Then she would be well and truly fucked.

"And you're standing with the pack? Do they know about you, my beautiful snake in the grass?"

"Do you think I would be standing here if they did?"

Lie number two.

Robert narrowed his eyes and strode forward, grabbing her by the chin and forcing her to look him in the eyes. "Gwendolen, are you lying to me?"

"No."

Lie number three.

Robert narrowed his eyes before releasing her face and taking a step back. He straightened his tie and turned, his shoes clicking across the tiled floor of the foyer. He opened the door before turning back to look at her. "I want the enchantress in a cage, in my dungeon, by week's end. Do you understand me? That is the price of your coveted freedom from your duties to me, as your husband. Don't forget that."

The door slammed behind him, and Gwen felt her eyes water. Gripping the counter behind her, she tried to fight the panic engulfing her mind. She sucked in a shaky breath just as the door to her bedroom creaked open and Chase stepped out. She met his glowing eyes, his wolf at the forefront as he prowled closer.

She couldn't go through another round of verbal sparring. Not today, not after dealing with *him*.

Pushing away from the counter, she skirted the kitchen island, putting it between Chase and her.

He paused, and she shook her head.

To her surprise, the glow in his eyes faded, leaving behind inquisitive oceans of blue in their wake.

"Are you okay?" he rasped.

Gwen didn't bother answering his question, not trusting her voice. She was screaming on the inside, and she needed to be alone. She needed to clean off the dirty feeling being in *his* presence always left on her. Almost reaching up to touch her face, where he had touched her, she caught herself.

As she nodded slightly, she managed to croak out, "Help yourself to any food you want. I need to shower and change into fresh clothes."

Gwen kept her eyes down as she quickly made her way to her bedroom and shut the door behind her. The shield wrapped around herself fell along with the tears in her eyes. She crossed the floor to the master bathroom and turned the shower on full blast, as hot as it could go. Shrugging off her clothes, she stepped under the scalding water and sank to the ground, wrapping her arms around her knees and rocking back and forth as silent sobs racked her whole body.

She was well and truly fucked.

Chapter Five

CHASE

His wolf snarled behind the invisible cage of his mind. Begging to follow, to protect, to mate.

To mate.

The thought was jarring enough to make Chase stumble back as Gwen shut the door to her bedroom. He stared at the closed door as time ticked away minute by minute. His wolf finally settled enough for Chase to take a deep breath for what felt like hours later. When he glanced at the clock on the stove, he saw only ten minutes had passed.

"Fucking crap. What the fuck?" he groaned and thrust his hands into his hair. Pulling out his phone, he thumbed over the unanswered text message from his alpha, asking him for an update.

His wolf growled, a warning in his head. They couldn't betray their mate. But they also couldn't go against their alpha's orders.

Chase shook his head.

The high priestess couldn't be his mate. His wolf was fucking wrong. They hadn't even gotten a scent from her yet. She was always hiding behind her power.

His wolf tested its invisible bonds again, angry at being called a liar.

A wolf knows, it always knows. It doesn't need scent, just a feeling. A tug in the right direction. One wild flame calling to the other.

Except this flame was freezing him out, locked behind a cage of their own making.

His wolf whined in his head again, and Chase made his way over the couch and collapsed. He shut his eyes, chest heavy, as his wolf tried to get out again. He was torn between hunting down and murdering the man who was just here, or barging into Gwen's room and holding her close to him.

Because his wolf was right; he didn't need to scent Gwendolen to know she was his. His wolf knew the second it set its eyes on her, and it just took his human brain this long to catch up. He should have put two and two together the second his wolf whined in her presence. Tugging at his hair again, he glanced at the dark flat-screen TV across from him.

He could see his reflection staring back, the wolf in his eyes begging for release. But his wolf was fucking insane and there was no way he was letting him out, let alone in an immaculate house like this. Knowing him, he would start peeing over everything to show anyone and everyone that Gwen was his territory now.

His wolf huffed, as if approving of the act, and Chase groaned, falling on his back, and putting a pillow on his face. With another groan, he pushed the pillow harder onto his face, hoping to suffocate himself, and put him and his wolf out of what was about to be a complicated turn of events.

As his phone buzzed, Chase lowered the pillow just enough to read the text from his alpha.

> **You left me on read. Is anything going on?**

Chase started typing, and he swore his wolf laughed in his head once he hit send.

> **Absolutely nothing, boss.**

> **Will update tomorrow.**

Glancing at the ticking clock again, he watched the hands move, and swore after a minute they stopped moving altogether. He growled softly and strained his ears, trying to pick up any noise from Gwen's bedroom. Whatever spell she had placed around her bedroom was preventing him from hearing with his heightened senses. Though, funny enough, when he was in the room, he could hear everything Gwen and that man, her supposed husband, had spoken. It had taken every ounce of willpower he had in his arsenal to not bust out of the bedroom and go full wolf on him.

With a shake of his head, he bolted off the couch. He should probably look like he was doing something instead of just sitting on the couch and waiting, staring at her door.

And panting and drooling after our mate, his wolf interjected.

Chase rolled his eyes and padded over to the kitchen, pulling open the fridge and looking inside. He frowned at the neatness, the perfectly portioned out and ready to reheat meals laid out in perfect rows. The need to move everything around, to make a dent in the perfection surrounding him, grew wild inside of him.

Fuck, his mate was a god's damn perfectionist and he...

Chase glanced down at his worn-out tennis shoes and sweatpants he was wearing. Fuck, even his shirt had an old stain on it. He couldn't be bothered to get out, and he was pretty sure there was a hole or two somewhere, too.

He was a fucking mess, that was what he was.

The sound of the door opening had Chase turning quickly and shutting the fridge door with much more force than necessary.

Gwen cocked one of her perfectly sculpted eyebrows in his direction and Chase let his eyes roam. He took in the way she had braided her hair around her head like a crown and the way her cream-colored sweater hugged her curves just right. He might have lingered a little too long on her slim fitting yoga pants and how they showcased her lean legs before he finally made it to her bare feet and painted toes. His eyes stayed on those toes, painted a vibrant blood red, as they moved closer and closer. Only when they stopped right next to his battered sneakers did he finally lift his head. Gwen's face pulled tight, her eyebrows scrunched together in a way that made Chase want to reach out and smooth them down. She looked...worried and annoyed, and he couldn't help but think it was kind of adorable.

She cleared her throat, and Chase realized he was staring at her, not saying a damn word like some sort of creep.

He ran his hands through his hair quickly and put a big smile on his face. Here was hoping she didn't see how fake it was. "Did you enjoy your shower?"

Dear goddess, he did not just say that. Who the fuck asks how someone's shower went?

Gwen blinked slowly before shaking her head. "I'm going to pretend you didn't ask that. So did you tell him?"

Chase dropped his smile. "Tell who what?

Gwen scoffed and made a shooing motion with her hands. Chase moved out of her way as she opened the fridge. "Did you tell the alpha about what happened?"

"Mmmm, no."

Gwen glanced at him sharply and slammed the fridge door shut. "What do you mean, no?"

"Here, if you don't believe me." Chase pulled out his phone and held it out for her to take.

She grabbed his phone and tapped at the text message app before frowning and giving his phone back. "Why would you lie?"

Chase shrugged before pocketing his phone. "Because I feel like there is more to what meets the eye with you, and I don't want to give my alpha half-truths and speculations."

Also, you're my mate, and I will protect you at all costs... Chase swallowed the words lingering on the tip of his tongue and his wolf growled.

Gwen pursed her lips before turning back to the fridge. Chase watched as she opened the door once more before closing it a few seconds later. She locked her gaze with his. "I've had one hell of a twenty-four hours. How do you feel about pizza and beer?"

Chapter Six

GWEN

"PINEAPPLE ON PIZZA IS clearly the superior choice," Chase laughed before tipping his head back, taking a huge bite out of the dangling slice in his hand.

"You are clearly delusional and need to have your head checked." Gwen laughed right along with him. She discreetly watched him eat the rest of his pizza slice before chugging the rest of his beer. He shook his head and ran his hands through his hair again. Something Gwen noticed he did a lot. She was still trying to figure out why. Everyone had tells and fidgets and this was certainly one of his, but she didn't know what it meant.

Was he nervous? Uncomfortable? Holding something back?

She sipped on her second beer of the day, because it was most certainly still day out, and tried not to feel bad for day drinking. She needed it after the last twenty-four hours.

Chase caught her gaze from across the couch. "I'm the one who needs their head checked?" He pointed to the TV that was currently streaming one of her favorite true crime series. "You watch this for fun."

She pointed at him with her beer bottle. "Fun and informative. Remember that, wolf."

Chase gasped, placing his hand on his chest. "Who, me? I am nothing but your faithful little wolf at your beck and call. No need to threaten. I have sisters. I know my place."

She snorted. "You are certainly charming, Chase. I'll give you that."

He gave her a wink, and Gwen sobered slightly.

Shit, he really was charming, and charming was not something she was used to dealing with.

Powerful men. That was where her strengths lay. She could navigate those types of men. She had navigated that world her whole life. Gwen sighed and placed her beer on the coffee table before turning to face Chase.

"Uh oh." He mirrored her position. "The mood has suddenly changed."

Gwen grabbed the remote and muted the show. "We should actually talk. About earlier. I'm sure you have questions. So, you can tell the alpha everything."

Chase cocked his head and nodded slightly. "We could talk about that, or..."

Gwen arched an eyebrow. "Or?"

He smiled. "Or we could finish the icebreaker from earlier, and then play Truth or Dare."

"Interesting tactic," she murmured.

"Tactic?"

Gwen shook her head, ready to tell him to stop with the games, but an invisible force stole her words. She wanted to know more about this man in front of her, and he was willing to talk. Plus, she never had the luxury of playing Truth or Dare before. She had always wanted to, but never had the childhood for such a game.

She reached for her beer and downed it before answering. "Fine. Let's play. Let's see, from before, the icebreaker. You already know my name..." Chase smiled, and she continued, "Age thirty-seven, I'm a Scorpio, and I dislike hiking through the woods."

"What do you like then?"

"Painting."

Chase's eyes lit up, and he leaned toward her. "Ahhh, an artist. What type of painting do you do?"

"That's two questions." Gwen smirked. "It's my turn."

Chase lifted his hands in mock surrender. "Sorry, sorry."

"Truth or dare?"

Chase mussed on the question, and Gwen rolled her eyes. "Come on, choose."

"Fine, fine, I can see that you have more questions for me, so truth."

Gwen opened her mouth, ready to steer the conversion back to the problems at hand, but stopped. Logic dictated she should get as much information as possible. She should be planning, scheming, and counterattacking.

Screw, logic. "Do you want to see?"

"Yes," Chase answered instantly. "Hard yes. Show me your art."

Gwen jumped off the couch and swept another beer off the table before heading over to the door. She didn't have to look back to see Chase following as she slipped on a pair of flats and opened what everyone assumed to be a closet door. She reached out and flipped on the lights before heading down the hidden stairs that took her to the garage.

Chase whistled slightly behind her. "Hidden stairs. I like it... Holy shit."

Gwen stepped to the side as Chase slowly wandered into her studio. She leaned against the closed garage door, sipping on her beer, and watched him take in the chaos that was her sanctuary. He turned slowly, eyes dancing over every painting until his eyes finally found hers. "I knew there was a wild side to you under the mask you wear."

Gwen shrugged. "What can I say? I enjoy painting people."

Chase snorted before turning again and stopping in front of her current work. "Nude people. In sexual acts." He glanced over his shoulder at her. "Very dirty, sexual acts."

Gwen pushed away from the garage door and padded over to him. "Sex sells. The kinkier, the dirtier, the better the price I get."

"You're very talented," he murmured before turning her way. "Truth or dare."

Gwen sucked on her teeth. In for a penny, in for a pound. "Dare."

A grin slowly pulled at Chase's lips. "Dare... Hmmm." He tapped at his chin before snapping his fingers. "I got it."

"Oh?" Gwen mussed.

"Drop your shields."

Gwen paused, the bottle halfway to her lips. Fuck, she wasn't expecting that. She didn't drop the magic she had wrapped around herself for anyone. She couldn't afford anyone to see her as anything but ice cold and logical to a fault. "Pass," she whispered. "Choose something else."

Chase shook his head. "That's not how this game works, sweetheart."

Gwen put her beer down on a paint-stained table and crossed her arms. "Why do you want me to drop my magic? You want to know if I'm lying when you ask the hard-hitting questions? Hmm?" She turned around, heading for the stairs. "I'm done with the game. I'm going to sleep."

"Gwendolen, wait."

Chase grabbed her waist, spinning her around. She threw her hands up in time to press them on his chest as he dragged her close. Her eyes widened slightly. The last thing she would have expected was for him to grab her. She pushed at his chest and growled, "Release me, wolf. You have no right to manhandle me."

"You're my mate."

Gwen's jaw went slack as Chase's words rang out. "Excuse me?" she whispered.

That couldn't be right. She couldn't be a lycanthrope's mate. He had to be mistaken.

Chase pulled her closer, his arm wrapping around her waist protectively. She met his eyes, blue eyes softening as his wolf moved closer to the surface. Her face warmed as Chase's eyes dipped to her lips. She licked them on instinct alone, her thoughts turning dangerous.

Wanting and lust. Something she hadn't allowed herself to feel for a very long time. But she felt them with this man, this lycanthrope she barely knew.

"You're my mate. That's why I want you to drop your shields," Chase whispered before lowering his head.

"But, but you can't scent me. How can you be sure?" Gwen gasped as his lips grazed her ear and he nipped at her. She flinched slightly as he breathed in deeply, the growl in his voice doing something wicked to her body. Her thighs clenched, unaccustomed to feeling this out of control.

Because that was what she felt. She felt her control slipping slowly as Chase pressed a featherlight kiss against her neck.

"Drop your shields and we can find out how right I am."

Somewhere below the roaring of her heartbeat filling her mind, Gwen knew this would be disastrous. Mating with a lycanthrope would shatter every one of her delicately placed plans to take down the witch's council. Logic screamed to push Chase away, to walk away.

Gwen gulped as Chase moved, his lips hovering over hers, so close that if anyone of them spoke they would touch. And fuck did Gwen want their lips to touch.

"I hope you're wrong," she whispered as she pushed logic aside and closed the distance between their lips, dropping her shields at the same time.

Chapter Seven

CHASE

THE SWEET SCENT OF jasmine and honeysuckle blasted into Chase like a freight train as succulent lips collided with his. His wolf howled in his mind as the scent of his mate surrounded him fully. He lifted her off the ground and moved, pressing her back against the wall. As he growled into her mouth, he felt her legs wrap around him. She moaned, her hands moving from his chest to tangle into his hair. The need to take her, to mark his mate, overwhelmed all other thoughts.

His wolf rose to the surface, propelling his need tenfold, and he lost any semblance of control. He swiped his tongue deeper into Gwen's mouth, his hands roaming over her body, caressing her strong thighs and ass. Thrusting them under her large sweater, she gasped as his hands caressed her sides.

Chase scraped his thumbs over her hard nipples and growled as his hands massaged his mate's tits. She wasn't wearing a bra, and that thought alone made him go slightly feral. He needed his mouth on her luscious tits. Fuck, he needed his mouth everywhere on his mate's body.

He broke the kiss long enough to hoist Gwen farther up the wall and duck his head under her sweater. There wasn't enough time to undress her. He needed to ravish every inch of her. When he sucked one of her nipples into his mouth, his mate arched into him.

He could barely hear her moans over the roaring in his head as he switched over to her other nipple. Her hands left his body briefly and suddenly they were in his hair again, his mate having ripped her own sweater off. He glanced up at her body, a wolfish grin plastered on his face as his knees buckled and he rolled them both to the ground. Clattering sounds echoed around them, but his mate seemed oblivious, or just didn't care as she settled her weight on top of his thighs. Chase caressed her bare torso, in desperate awe of her. With his gaze locking onto Gwen's face, she reached up and pulled her hair out of the complicated braid. His breath caught as she shook her head, letting her long hair fall down her back like a waterfall. He reached up, threading his fingers through the waves before clasping the back of her neck and sitting up. Brushing his thumb over her bottom lip, he cupped her chin.

His mate moaned against his lips, this time their kiss soft and unhurried. Chase nipped at her lips before drawing back, his gaze colliding with hers. "You look like a fucking goddess, sweetheart," he whispered, as his hands trailed down her upper half until they got to her hips. He dug his fingers in slightly on her ass and lifted his own hips to grind his throbbing cock against the seam of her yoga pants.

"Fuck," his mate groaned and grabbed his shoulders, tearing at the shirt he still had on. It was off an instant later and Chase watched Gwen's pupils dilate as she ran her hands over his chest and abs. Her short fingernails left red marks, and he arched into her hands as they trailed down to the band of his pants. He hissed in pleasure as one hand dipped inside and fisted his cock. His mate's strangled moan was like music to his ears, her small hand warm and tight, fingers dancing up and down his shaft slowly.

Chase watched his mate's face as she bit her lip, eyes trained on his throbbing cock. Finally, she looked back at his face. "I want this. I want you right now. Consequences be damned."

He sucked in a breath as his mate stood and shimmied out of her leggings. She bared herself to him, and Chase whispered, "Fuck, sweetheart.

Bring that gorgeous body back down here, and I'll give you everything you ask for and more."

A blush scorched across his mate's cheeks as she kneeled back over his body. He went to sit up, but Gwen put her hand on his chest, pushing him back down. It was slightly wet and when he glanced down; he saw her fingers dripping in paint. He arched up into her hand as her fingers traced across him. When he glanced at her face, he almost stopped breathing. She was solely fixated on his body and the symbols she was drawing on his skin. He chuckled when she finally sat back, admiring her work. He gave her about three seconds before grabbing her waist and flipping her over, landing them both in the spilled paint all around them. Gwen laughed and arched into his hands as he dipped them in the paint and started at her hips, dragging them to her neck, leaving red and blue all over her body. He dragged his hand back down, swirling the paint back and forth, making a mess all over her beautiful flesh until he got to her thighs.

Chase left handprints behind as he spread his mate's legs open, and growled, "I'm going to worship this sweet pussy of yours first." He dipped his head before she could respond. The taste of his mate was like coming home after a long day, and he lapped at her, his tongue fucking his mate's pussy as she rolled her hips up to meet every one of his thrusts. Her hands slipped into his hair as he ravished her, her rasping gasps and moans echoing around him.

"Please, please. I need you inside of me. I need you to come with me," Gwen screamed and pulled at his hair.

Chase growled and licked upward over her clit, sucking hard before lifting his head fully. "My mate, I want you to understand one thing. You never have to beg for me. Command me. Because you are a fucking queen. No, you are more than that. You are a fucking goddess. My fucking goddess."

Gwen's breath hitched, and she leaned up on her elbows. "Fine," she rasped. "I want you inside me now. I want to ride you until we are both exhausted from pleasure. That is what I command."

Chase grinned and gave his mate's clit one last kiss before removing his sweatpants and rolling over. He grasped her waist on the way, anchoring her firmly over his hips. "As my goddess commands, she gets."

They both groaned as his cock lined up perfectly with his mate's pussy and he slid into her fully in one thrust. Gwen took control, moving her hips back and forth, riding him slowly with his cock nestled deeper inside of her. He swore he saw stars as she leaned over him, entangling her hands with his. She pushed them over his head, positioning her tits right over his face. Chase growled and lifted slightly, catching a nipple in his mouth. As she gasped, her pussy tightened around him. "Yes," Gwen moaned, leaning into him harder. "Just like that. Come with me. Come with me."

Chase switched to her other nipple, and he felt her pussy tighten even more as she ground down onto him, her clit rubbing against the root of his cock. He felt her start to come, her breathing hitching again, and Chase surged up, burying himself even deeper into his mate's pulsating pussy, and wrapped his arms around her waist, pinning her hands behind her back. He groaned, kissing her quickly on the lips before moving to her neck and biting down.

Gwen screamed in pleasure, their mate bond snapping into place, her pussy strangling his cock again. He came within seconds, roaring with her and licking the mating bite, his claiming mark on her. She shuddered as he released her arms and she placed them on his shoulders, her nails digging into his flesh. He shivered slightly, euphoria still rolling down his spine as his mate's pussy fluttered endlessly around his cock.

Gwen laid her head between the crook of his neck and shoulder, giving him gentle kisses between panting breaths. He would have been content with sitting there all night, covered in paint and his mate's slick juices, but Gwen pulled back a few minutes later. He reached up and fisted her hair slightly, giving her a kiss on the forehead and holding her in place. She kissed him back with a smile before frowning and rubbing at his cheekbone. "We've made quite a mess," she murmured. "Why don't we get cleaned up?"

Chapter Eight

GWEN

GWEN FUCKED UP.

She knew she fucked up, but it didn't matter to her now. There was no stopping this beautiful train wreck once she let her magic fall away. And after the bond snapped into place...

Gwen smiled as she dried her hair with a towel. The bond was a steady rippling flow of magic between the two of them, and only the two of them. She wasn't even sure if her shields, once put back up, could block out the mating bond. If she concentrated, even the slightest, she could pinpoint the exact location of Chase, could almost see him in her mind's eye. If this was how her coven members felt, then Gwen understood. Hell, she understood everything now. The mating bond was undeniable, and she knew at this moment she would do anything to keep her mate safe. Which royally screwed over any plans she had in dealing with the witch's council and Robert. Gwen shivered slightly and tossed the towel in the hamper before taking a deep breath and stepping out of the on-suite bathroom.

Chase, her mate, sprawled out on her bed.

Gwen blushed as a shiver ran along their mate bond and down her spine. She was instantly horny again. Just from looking at him. And from the way he was looking at her, she knew he felt it, too.

She padded over to the bed and Chase immediately sat up to wrap his arm around her waist, pulling her in close, her body nestled between his legs. Threading her hands through his silky blonde hair, he kissed her neck. And as much as she wanted to go another round with her mate, Gwen was exhausted. She also knew they should call the alpha, letting him know that all of Gwen's plans were now dust in the wind and that she had bonded with one of his wolves. Also, that the head of the witch council technically had demanded the enchantress by the end of the week. And there were some other secrets she needed to get off her chest.

Chase continued his slow kisses up her neck to her jawline, and all her thoughts melted away as Gwen dipped her head. His lips found hers, and they rolled, arms and legs twining together like they had been lovers for years, instead of just hours.

Desperation suddenly swept through Gwen's whole being, dread pooling out of nowhere. She deepened their kiss, turning it from sweet to consuming, like he was her lifeline in this moment in time. Somewhere in the back of her mind, she knew that if this were to last, if she were to escape the clutches of Robert and her fate in the witch's council, she would have to do something insanely drastic. She was done with this chess game she played over the years. It was time to tell the pack alpha everything. But first...

Gwen broke the kiss with a gasp as Chase ground his hard cock into her center, stimulating her already sensitive clit. He had his hands threaded through her hair and their eyes met as he moved his hips slowly, eliciting another moan from her.

"Fuck, you're gorgeous," he murmured, "and smart, and talented. And I don't know what I did to be deserving of you as my mate."

A yawn escaped her even as butterflies swarmed her stomach, and Chase chuckled before tucking a stray hair behind her ear.

"We should, we should probably—"

"We should probably rest?" he whispered.

Gwen nodded. "Yes, rest would be good. I've been up for over twenty-four hours."

Chase smirked. "Hmmm, then maybe I should help you relax and fall asleep?"

He didn't wait for her to respond before diving under the covers, his hands already tugging at her pajama shorts. Gwen's startled squeak filled the air before turning into a moan as her mate's hot breath tickled the inside of her thighs. Her pussy clenched in anticipation, already growing wet as he trailed kisses up the inside of her thighs. She fisted her sheets as his mouth finally found her aching center, her mate's tongue caressing her core. Starting gently, his tongue slipped inside of her, tasting her fully before moving up to her clit.

With a whimper, she tried to move her hips with him, but Chase had placed his hand around her waist, holding her in place. He licked her again before growling, "Relax and let me pleasure you, sweetheart. Let me worship my goddess."

Gwen felt her pussy tighten, almost coming from his heated words alone. She closed her eyes and concentrated on the feel of her mate's mouth on her pussy, the way one of his hands snaked down over her clit, his fingers strumming her like a guitar. How the hell he already knew what she liked, which pressure was enough for her, was beyond words.

It didn't take long before she was gasping and bucking her hips. Her hands fisted the sheets so tight if she had been in her right mind, Gwen would have worried about ripping them. Instead, her toes curled, her orgasm crashing over her in waves as she screamed out Chase's name.

He growled against her throbbing pussy before giving it one more lick. "That's my beautiful goddess."

Crawling back up her body, he languished soft kisses across her hips, stomach, and breasts until he reached her neck and their mating mark. He gently bit it, and Gwen arched under him, warmth spreading through her body as her eyes rolled back and she moaned. As he nibbled his way up to her ear, he whispered, "Relaxed, sweetheart?"

Gwen wrapped her arms around him, sinking her nails into his strong shoulders. She nodded, knowing a smile decorated her lips. He moved to kiss her reverently, the tip of his tongue tracing along her bottom lip before sucking on it. She tightened her hold on his shoulders, anticipation of what was to come next, driving her basic instincts. All she could think about was the way he would feel when the press of his hard cock against her aching core finally dipped inside of her.

He released her lower lip and gave her another soft peck against her lips. "Good. Then let's go to sleep."

Gwen's eyes flew open as he moved off her and landed against her side, nestling her body into his chest. "Wait...but, what?" she squeaked out as Chase buried his head against the back of her neck. She felt him smiling as he tightened his arms around her waist and pulled her in closer.

"Sleep," he murmured against her neck again before yawning.

"But you're still hard as a rock. Let me at least—"

Chase tightened his arms and growled, "Better get used to me being constantly hard around you. Twenty-four seven, three sixty-five. But right now, let's just go to sleep. I know you're exhausted."

Gwen grumbled, but snuggled into her mate's arms. "That's just ridiculous. Being hard twenty-four seven, I do believe is considered a medical condition."

Chase chuckled, his body shaking hers.

She sighed and closed her eyes, sleep already whispering its enticing melody. "Fine, but I command I suck your cock in the morning."

"I won't argue against it. Whatever my goddess commands, she gets," Chase murmured into her hair.

Gwen smiled, and was asleep within the next breath, with her mate's arms wrapped tightly around her. And for the first time in a long time, she felt a sense of tranquility wash over her that she wished she could keep forever.

Chapter Nine

GWEN

ONE, TWO, THREE, FOUR... Boo! I found you.

Gwen woke up with a start.

The unhinged giggling from her dream faded into the darkness, replaced by the sound of her frantically beating heart and the soft breathing of the man beside her. The dread filling her body slowly dissipated as she touched the mating mark on her neck.

The man in her bed was her mate and the dream...

The dream was a memory. A memory of someone she wasn't anymore. She was no longer that scared, hurt little girl. She had power, and she knew how to take care of herself.

Gwen reached out and caressed Chase's face, running her hands through his hair before leaning over to give him the barest of kisses. His lips quirked into a grin, but he didn't wake.

She had a mate now to look after and vice versa. She might not know much about him, but she knew the lore and truths about lycanthrope bonds with their mates. And Gwen knew mates would lay down their life to protect each other.

She touched her neck, their mating mark, again before slipping out of bed and grabbing her dressing gown from the bedpost. Warmth flooded her veins, and the tranquility, the rightness she felt last night before falling asleep, returned as she glanced back at her sleeping mate.

She was no longer dealing with her past alone. She finally had someone in her life she could let behind her shields, and for once, she could feel safe again.

Gwen took stock of her sleeping mate and couldn't suppress her grin as her eyes connected with the sheet tented out in one particular area. She bit her lip and had to physically restrain herself from reaching out and waking him up with her hand and mouth on his cock. They hadn't set ground rules yet, on what they could and couldn't do to each other. She backed away slowly until she got to her bedroom door and stepped out as quietly as she could.

An itch right between her shoulder blades, the feeling of being watched slithered down her spine, and Gwen shut her eyes, counting back from ten in her head. She refused to be paranoid in her own home, her safe place. Plus, the wards around her property would let Gwen know if anyone entered without permission. By the time she got to two in her head, the feeling had slipped away. Gwen opened her eyes and whispered to herself, "See, it was nothing. You're just not used to having your personal shields down for so long."

No one answered her back as she glided over to the coffeepot and turned it on. It was just starting to gurgle, the warm aroma of coffee in the air, when a rough, sleep-laden voice wrapped around her body. "Sweetheart."

Gwen turned toward the voice, toward her mate ,and was blessed with a goddess sent vision standing in the doorway. He pulled his hands through his already messy hair, his muscles flexing in his chest and arms. Gwen could stop her eyes from dipping lower to see he was completely naked and still standing at full attention.

She gulped, simultaneously feeling like she couldn't breathe, but hyperventilating at the same time. As she ripped her eyes from her mate's sculpted body back to his handsome face, he lifted his hand and curled his finger. "Come here, sweetheart. Come back to bed with me."

Gwen's body was already moving, running into his open arms, and then she was touching him, pulling his head down to hers. Their lips collided, tongues tangling, and Gwen moaned into Chase's mouth as he picked her up. The next thing she knew, her back was hitting the mattress, her mate's warm weight already sinking onto her. With physical effort Gwen didn't know she possessed, she broke the kiss and sucked in a breath. "Wait."

He stilled, his whole body going tense. "I'm sorry. Did I hurt you?"

Gwen shook her head, a smile spreading across her lips. She wrapped her hands around his shoulders, her fingertips gliding across his warm skin. "I promised you something when we woke up."

Chase's eyebrows scrunched together, and a low rumble echoed through his chest. Gwen laughed as the confusion on his face turned to understanding in a split second. "Sweetheart, I told you. You don't have to—"

She pressed her fingers against his mouth. "I command it."

Chase kissed her fingers before flipping them both over and stretching his arms over his head. "Okay then, my goddess. This body is yours to do whatever you want with."

Staring down at his chest again, she flattened her palms down his hard muscle, and she felt her core clench. "We probably should go over rules and safe words."

Chase arched up into her hands as she scratched her nails lightly down his chest to his stomach. "I'm sure there is nothing you can do that I won't like."

She snorted and raised an eyebrow. "Oh, really now? So, you wouldn't complain if you woke up with me fucking you from behind with a strap-on?"

It was an extreme example, not that Gwen even had a strap-on, but she wanted to make him get the point behind rules and safe words.

He choked slightly, "Okay, maybe...well...maybe not that yet."

Gwen snorted. "See...rules. Rules are needed for what I can and can't do to you."

"Wait, do you really have a strap-on? Because that would be kind of hot."

This time, Gwen sucked in a breath and felt her face grow warm. "No, but we can definitely get one if you want to explore that one day."

Smiling, he nodded.

Gwen felt her core tighten even more, a flush overtaking her whole body. Fuck, her mate was adventurous in bed, and she really liked that. But for now... "Figure out a safe word, for later. You shouldn't need one for what I'm about to do to you now," she whispered before slipping off him and grabbing a pillow. Getting off the bed, she fell to her knees. Chase sat up, and she put herself between his legs, fingers trailing up his shins to his muscular thighs. He fisted her hair as she dipped her head and kissed his inner thigh. Gwen felt her mate shudder slightly as she let her tongue dart out. He groaned as she teased him, touching everywhere except his cock and balls. Gwen smiled as he squirmed under her touch, breath coming out in sharp exhales, fist still tight in her hair.

"Fuck!" Chase growled, his hips bucking slightly as she finally gave him what he needed and trailed her tongue up his throbbing cock. He was going to be too big for her to take in her mouth completely. Gwen already knew this as she fisted the lower part of his shaft with one hand and started massaging his balls with her other hand. He jerked in her hands as she sucked on his tip, swirling her tongue around. She flicked it over his slit and groaned herself as she took him deeper. Fuck, her mate tasted good.

Gwen continued sucking, taking as much of his cock into her mouth as she could before going back up, licking, and flicking his head. She moved her hands in a rhythmic motion and knew he would not last long. She felt his balls tighten in her hand, his pre-cum coming out faster.

"Fuck, fuck, fuck, Gwen, sweetheart, I'm going to..."

Taking him as deep as she could, she hummed in the back of her throat. She glanced up to see Chase's head thrown back, his jaw clenched just as tight as his fist in her hair.

"Fuck!" he shouted, and Gwen would have smiled if she didn't have her lips wrapped tightly around her mate's pulsating cock. His hot cum slipped down her throat, and Gwen swallowed as fast as she could, determined not to let a drop escape her grasp.

Chapter Ten

CHASE

THE BEST ORGASM OF Chase's life rolled through him as his mate hummed in the back of her throat, his cock buried deep inside. He watched as she swallowed with glee before dragging the tip of her tongue up and over the sensitive head of his cock. His hand still fisted her hair, and he tugged, bringing his mate to her feet, then to his lap. Gwen chuckled softly as she draped herself across him, caressing his back before kissing his neck. He trailed a hand down his mate's side, pushing back her dressing gown to reveal...nothing.

Chase sucked in a breath as he realized Gwen was completely naked. He felt his cock harden almost instantly as he racked his hand down her front, finger teasing lightly at her entrance. She was already soaking wet, and Chase grinned. "Did my goddess enjoy playing with my cock?"

She growled in his ear and bit his earlobe. Her tongue darted out, licking down his neck before answering him. "Of course, I did. It is quite the masterpiece."

This time, Chase chuckled, his laugh turning to a groan as Gwen reached between them, her hand grasping his cock once more.

"Fuck, sweetheart," Chase whispered as Gwen coated his cock with her juices. "I need to be inside your sweet pussy."

"We can arrange that."

Gwen moved her hips, the head of his cock touching her entrance, twitching in anticipation until they both froze.

His mate's eyes grew wide as she scrambled off him, pulling her dressing gown tight as the sound of a door slamming shut echoed through the house.

Gwen shook her head, brows crinkled in confusion. "That's not possible, my wards..."

Chase was already on his feet, grabbing his sweatpants, when he glanced up to see why Gwen had stopped mid-sentence. Her face was ghastly pale, and she swayed on her feet slightly before regaining her composure. "No," she whispered before running out of the room.

Chase was quick to follow, the wards his mate had surrounded her room, suffocating and clawing at his senses before he stepped out and wrapped an arm around Gwen's waist to keep from plowing her over. His senses were still dulled, and Chase realized with a start that his mate had thrown a nulling field around them both. But that was the least of his concerns.

His hackles would have arisen if he had access to his wolf form, but he still managed a snarl rising upon his face as he glared at the man smirking in front of them.

Robert.

The bastard his mate was running from. The reason she was in such a mess in the first place. He felt his mate tremor under his arm, and Chase knew the moment he got his hands on Robert it was lights out, forever. He honestly didn't care about the consequences. Chase needed to protect his mate, at all costs.

And he almost stepped forward, too. To make good on his instincts to eradicate this slime ball from the earth, until another person padded into view.

She was delicate, wearing a blue sundress, with a devious smile plastered across her face. But that wasn't what made Chase pause. It wasn't even the gun in her hand that she raised toward them once she stopped next to Robert's side.

It was the stunning resemblance this unknown woman had to his mate. The only difference Chase could pinpoint was their hair color. This woman was sporting long ashy blonde hair, and he had the feeling if his mate didn't dye hers, it would be the same.

Chase didn't dare take his eyes off the pair, especially since his wolf was completely cut off from him because of the nulling magic Gwen wrapped around them. He wasn't sure if it was because she wanted them to think he was a regular man or if she was protecting him. His arm turned to steel around Gwen's waist when she tried to step away.

Robert smirked, and it took everything Chase had in him to grab the nearest thing and throw it into that smug bastard's face.

"It isn't often that you drop your guard and act like a lovesick child, Gwendolen. And to do so with a Lycan, a filthy beast. Well, that is just something that needs to be rectified."

Chase eyed the mystery woman as she waltzed around Gwen's kitchen, dragging the gun across the stand-alone island. His mate ignored Robert's barbed words, instead turning to keep the woman in view. "Since when did you think it was wise to give a crazy woman a gun?"

The woman in question giggled, and unease flowed through Chase, settling in the pit of his stomach. "Crazy, me? Do you know they call you the crazy one at home?" The woman sighed and glanced out the window over the kitchen sink. "It's been a long time, sister. And that's how you greet me? You don't even want to introduce me to this pretty thing wrapped around you?"

The woman turned and finally focused on him and stepped close, her hand raised as if to touch him as Gwen snarled, "If you touch my mate, Annabelle, I swear to the goddess, I will kill you."

Annabelle's hand dropped, and instead she raised her gun, pointing it at Gwen. Chase tried to pull her behind him, and Robert laughed.

"Ladies...you know how I detest your petty squabbles. Even as kids, you two could never get along. Anna darling, I told you. You can't shoot your sister. We still need her. They both are, because through him and their mate bond"—Robert pointed toward Chase—"we can take this Lycan pack to its knees and finally retrieve the enchantress."

Gwen and Anna hissed at the same time, glaring at Robert, and Chase swore he glimpsed a flash of fear briefly run through the man's eyes.

Anna smirked before lifting the gun. Chase was moving before processing where she was pointing the blasted thing, his body engulfing his mate and taking them to the floor. To his surprise, Gwen managed to wiggle out from his grasp, and before he could stop her, she flung herself at her sister. The two women fell back, tripping over the couch, and

Chase roared, setting his sights on Robert, who was just standing there with a stunned look on his face.

The nulling effect surrounding him fell away, his sense snapping back into him just as he reached for Robert, fisting his shirt in his hand. Blood coated his senses and his wolf snarled, telling him to shift and protect his mate at all costs. Chase wrestled with his wolf in his head as Robert's babbling words finally registered.

"She shot me. The bitch shot me."

His body slumped forward, and Chase snarled, pushing the man away. Robert hit the wall with a sickening thud and slid, crumbling to the ground. He was still breathing, unconscious from shock, and Chase took a step forward, reaching to snap the bastard's neck to end it all. To finally free his mate from this life.

Chapter Eleven

GWEN

GWEN KNEW THIS WAS it, the endgame. No planning, only instinct when she felt her twin's intentions deep within her soul. The roar of the gun filled her home, and Gwen was launching herself out of Chase's arms before the sound even ended. She didn't want to save Robert, hell, she hoped the gunshot killed him. But she couldn't let her sister turn that gun on Chase or her, because she knew without a doubt Anna would pull the trigger again.

And Gwen would not lose her mate, not today.

She tackled her twin, arms around her middle as they both toppled over the back of the couch. Gwen heard more than felt the small TV table buckle under their weight. Anna's unhinged laughter filled Gwen's ears as she scrambled for the gun. Her sister grabbed Gwen's arms and pulled her down, hissing in her ear. "It's over. You can't shield your mate bond from me. I will drain it down to nothing, then I will take your mate from you and kill you in front of him."

Gwen wrapped her power over herself tighter, trying to block her sister from accessing the magic tying Chase and her together. But she knew her sister was right. She already had her hooks in Gwen's head, siphoning the magic from the bond.

"Not today. Not in this lifetime," she snarled and broke the grip her twin had on her arms. Fumbling the gun into her hands, she pointed it at her sister and pulled the trigger.

Wetness splattered across Gwen's face and chest as all noise ceased to exist. The shocked look on her sister's face melted away to neutral, blank eyes staring up at Gwen as blood pooled out from beneath her, staining the light tan run a muddy brown. She dropped the gun as hands grabbed her, hauling her up and away. The buzzing in her head dimmed, and Gwen blinked slowly, as sound and time seemed to catch up all at once. She snapped back into the present, her body already aching, and realized Chase had her wrapped up in his arms, face buried in her hair.

"Gwen, Gwen, fuck, sweetheart. It's okay, I have you. It's over. It's over."

She gulped and whispered, "Robert?"

Chase pulled back and cupped her face in his hands, forcing her to look at him. "Dead. Bled out. Gwen, look at me. It's over. It's going to be okay."

His gentle tone, and the warmth of his hands, two small things in the grand scheme of events that just transpired, pushed Gwen over the edge. She felt the tears slip from her eyes as her sobs spilled out.

Chase wrapped his arms around her once more, rocking her gently. "Don't worry, sweetheart. I'll take care of it. I'll take care of everything."

Gwen stared at the clothes in her closet, her towel clutched in her hand. Voices echoed in from under the doorway, a handful of wolves and part of the witch's council mingling in her living room and kitchen. She reached for a pantsuit, gray pinstripe with a tight cut, and paired it with a silk off-white shirt. Pulling back her hair, Gwen put it in her patented bun. Contemplating shoes, she decided against it. She never wore her shoes inside her own home, and to start just because she had unexpected people over was not her style. She wrapped her magic around herself and reached for the door, stepping out into the mess that was her home.

Her eyes involuntarily searched for their mate, and Gwen breathed out a sigh of relief when she found him. He stood in the kitchen corner with his alpha, along with their second. He caught her eye, and Gwen almost laughed when he did a quick scan of her. She could feel the heat of their bond caressing her body and knew instinctively that he liked what she was wearing. Not that it mattered, but for some strange reason, it gave Gwen the confidence boost she didn't know she was missing. The clearing of a throat next to her brought Gwen back to the matters at hand, and she turned, acknowledging the older witch who made their way over to her.

"Rebecca." She tilted her head in greeting, and the older witch nodded.

"Gwendolen, you have made a mess of things. The council wants to know if this was a hostile takeover or just an unfortunate accident?"

Gwen felt the bond between her mate ignite, a low growl echoing through her mind. She almost smirked at the protectiveness. Her mate was listening, even if it didn't look like he was. "If you are asking if the rest of the council needs to watch their back, the answer is no. You, along with the rest of the council, knew the tumultuous relationship Robert, Annabelle, and I had. This was not a power grab, but..."

Rebecca held up her hand and finished her sentence. "But now there is a power vacuum."

Gwen nodded slowly, and Rebecca sighed.

"So be it. We will call for a vote tomorrow. Prepare your statement of the events that transpired here and bring the wolves. Change will be good for the old ones. Me, included... Now!" she called out to the other witches mingling in her living room, turning away from Gwen, their conversation abruptly over. "Let's go. We have other things to do. Preparations to make."

Gwen held her tongue as Rebecca and the other witches left. The second the door slammed shut, Chase had her in his arms and her body went limp. "Where did the bodies go?" she heard herself ask, her voice trembling.

"They took them while you were in the shower," he murmured into her hair and kissed her temple.

"Well, isn't that adorable?" Hunter's sister, Sasha, the alpha's second, broke the moment.

Gwen straightened her shoulders and pulled away from Chase's grasp. She ignored Sasha's comment and nodded to the alpha. "I am not sure what Chase told you, but—"

Hunter held up his hand. "He told me everything. All of it seemed justified, and from the supernatural council, we will see it as a mate protecting her own."

Gwen clicked her mouth shut, glanced back at Chase. He shrugged and pulled her back into his embrace. "I told you I would take care of it."

Hunter cleared his throat. "Now what I want to know is if we are still in danger of this whole trinity bullshit now that the head of the witch's council is dead?"

Gwen shook her head. "Ohhh, I guess... I guess you didn't know."

"Didn't know what?"

"Annabelle was the siphon. And...and she is..." Gwen's voice cracked. "I'm finally free of him and her. We all are."

"You can stay with us until—"

"No, no. Those bastards will not have the last laugh and drive me out of my home," Gwen interrupted this time. "I want to see where they died every day and know I am still free."

Sasha tilted her head and chuckled softly. "Damn. I would not like to be on the wrong side of you."

Hunter shook his head. "I guess I leave you two until tomorrow. Then we will see where the pack and you stand with the witch's council."

Gwen reached up to give Chase a kiss, smoothing her thumb over his bottom lip, before glancing over her shoulder at Hunter. "You don't have to worry. Without Robert in charge, the council will be more accepting. They never wanted to go back to the old ways, but he was intimidating or blackmailing anyone who could oppose him. Me, included."

Hunter nodded silently and pushed away from the counter he was leaning on. Sasha followed suit, and he didn't speak until they got to the front door. He stopped, hand on the doorknob, before calling out over his shoulder. "To the start of a new beginning, then? A real truce between the Lycans and witches?"

Gwen smiled, her gaze still on her mate. "To new beginnings. Yes, I think we can manage that."

Epilogue

CHASE

THE STEADY BEAT OF rain hit his shoulders as Chase turned from beast to man and he let his head fall back. The rain came down over him in soothing rivulets, and when he opened his eyes again, a smile etched his face as the mating bond pulsed through him. He took the stairs two at a time until he reached the door to his mate's home, their home, and dashed inside just as thunder rumbled through the sky. Scooping up the towel waiting for him just inside, he quickly dried off the rain from his body and the mud from his hands and feet.

Chase didn't need to reach down the mating bond to find his mate, but he did all the same just to feel the warmth of it filling his body. His wolf calmed instantly, eager to find and hold his mate in his arms.

Fuck, it had only been a week, and he still couldn't believe Gwen was his mate and all the shit that had already transpired since then.

Death and pain.

Happiness and hope.

With a shake of his head, he instantly reached for the small door next to the coat closet. He padded down the interior stairs leading to the garage turned studio, passing through the wards on the interior door easily enough, and breathed in the scent of his mate.

Staying silent, he took a chair on the opposite side of the room and watched as his Gwen painted, the steady brush strokes mixing with the pounding fall of rain outside. He wasn't sure how long they sat in silence, his mate lost in her own seductively creative world, and he lost in watching her.

Chase held his breath as Gwen finally lowered her brush and turned to look over her shoulder at him. Her soft hair tumbled down her back in a loose braid, and Chase didn't fight the urge to walk over to her, fisting her hair and leaning in to give his mate a long overdue kiss. She groaned against his mouth, sucking on his bottom lip as he pulled away.

"Did you enjoy your run in the rain?" Gwen asked.

Chase chuckled and kissed her forehead. "Land perimeter still looks good. I could still feel your wards everywhere you told me to check. And I detected no strays, witch or Lycan alike."

His mate's eyes glazed over slightly, lust painting her cheeks pink as her eyes roamed down his naked body.

Chase shivered in anticipation as Gwen trailed her fingertips over his chest and down his abs. Then she leaned forward and let her tongue drag over his hardened nipples.

"Fuck, sweetheart," Chase groaned and tightened his hold on his mate's hair.

His cock had already been hard from the moment he laid eyes on his mate, and he hissed in pleasure as she grabbed hold of it, giving him a few swift pumps. He gulped as she licked and kissed her way down his stomach, her breath hot and teasing over his shaft. As her tongue snuck out to lick his tip, Chase let his head fall as his mate swallowed his cock in her mouth. Her other hand teased his balls, applying just the right amount of pressure.

He felt the telltale sign of his orgasm ready to crest, his balls tightening under her skillful fingers, and groaned. "Gwen, sweetheart. Fuck, your mouth is goddess sent, but if you want anything from me this first go-around, you're going to have to stop."

In response, his mate hummed in the back of her throat, making his cock leak even more pre-cum, before she leaned back and let his cock fall from her mouth. She glanced up at him with a smirk.

"As a matter of fact, I want something from you."

Chase matched her smirk. "And what would that be, my beautiful goddess?"

"Pick me up and fuck me against the wall like the good, obedient wolf you are."

Chase didn't waste time obeying his mate, scoping her up and pinning her against the wall just as she asked. His hands needed her ass, already pulling at the form fitting leggings she had on. He nipped at their mating mark on her neck and Gwen gasped, her hands fisting in his hair.

"Fuck me already, wolfy. I need it hard and rough," his mate growled in his ear before biting down his neck.

Chase growled right back and lined up his cock to his mate's already wet pussy. Her sharp, groaning gasp was music to his ears as he thrust into her hard and deep. He didn't stop to let her accommodate his girth, doing exactly as his goddess instructed.

He pounded into her, feeling her pussy tightening around his cock as his mate whimpered.

"Fuck, fuck, Chase. Don't fucking stop. Yes, yes, fuck, I'm going to come."

His mate screamed, her hands fisting his hair painfully, and Chase groaned. The pain, just on the right side of pleasure, was ecstasy.

Gwen screamed again, her pussy rippling around his cock as he grunted and came with her. He managed two more deep thrusts before stilling, post orgasm bliss washing through their mating bond and panting breaths mingling with the storm thundering down outside.

His mate peppered soft kisses across his jawline before grasping his neck in her soft hands. "You disobeyed me, wolfy," she whispered and gently bit his earlobe. "You stopped when I told you not to."

Chase groaned as his mate pulled away to look at him. He pulled out of her and let her feet touch the ground before falling to his knees before her.

This was his favorite game to play already, loving his mate's kinky and wild side. He also loved disobeying her in the bedroom just to see how far she would go in dominating him.

"Are you going to punish me, my beautiful mate? My goddess?"

His mate groaned as he kissed her pussy, sucking on her clit before she forced him to look back up at her.

"Oh, wolfy. You have no idea what I'm about to do to you."

His cock hardened at her words, ready for their next round already.

Gwen moved, tugging his hair, and Chase followed on his hands and knees, following his mate towards the stairs leading back up to the main house.

A shiver rolled down his spine as Gwen looked down at him and cooed, "That's it. Be obedient and I might go easy on you."

In response, Chase grinned before biting his mate's ass, hard. He didn't want easy today. He wanted his mate's sinful punishments.

She squeaked in shock before sucking in a deep breath, her eyes hooding. "Ohhh," she whispered, fist tightening in his hair, "You want it naughty, then. I think I know just what I'll do to you."

His mate didn't elaborate, instead tugging him up the stairs, and Chase followed, crawling all the way to their bedroom.

Gwen pushed him toward the bed, releasing him before sauntering over to the closet and the chest of toys they had hidden inside. He groaned as she pulled out a studded collar, ropes, and a soft leather horse riding crop.

His mate smirked. "Now, who has been a bad fucking wolf?"

Chase held out his hands. "I have. Now please punish me, my beautiful goddess."

Thunder rumbled through the air again as his mate stalked toward him with his punishment in hand, and Chase moaned as she clasped the collar around his throat.

"Remember your safe word?" his mate whispered as she clipped the end of the rope to the collar, then the D-ring fasted to the bed frame.

"Yes."

"Good, now take your punishment, you naughty fucking wolf."

The first smack of the riding crop against his exposed balls had Chase arching, moaning for more.

By the fourth smack, he was moaning, the stinging pain mixing with pleasure. "Sweetheart, Gwen. Fuck, I need you." He gasped before his mate struck his balls again.

Gwen smirked as she trailed the riding crop across his thighs and up his stomach. She circled his nipples slowly before placing it onto the bed.

Chase licked his lips, cock throbbing violently as his mate shrugged off her clothes and climbed on top of him. She leaned in, lips a hair's breadth away from his, and teased his lips. He groaned, thrusting his hips up, hands enticing with hers as his mate sank down, owning his cock with her warm pussy. She moved her hips, taking him deeper as she set a slow and sensual pace.

They both groaned as the storm picked up outside, the sound of their fucking mingling with the pounding raindrops on the roof. Gwen picked up her pace and Chase thrust his hips, matching her quickening pace until he felt her pussy tighten, pulsating over his cock as she threw her head back with a soft scream.

He continued thrusting into her, holding back his own release until his mate folded over him and breathlessly moaned into his ear. "That's my good fucking wolf. Now come for me in five...four..."

His eyes rolled back as her words pushed him over the edge, and he released her hands to wrap his arms around her waist, thrusting into his mate's still pulsating pussy as she counted down.

"One..." his mate whispered, and Chase shouted, thrusting one last time, burying his cock deep as he filled her up with everything he had.

His orgasm threatened to make him pass out as it rolled through him violently. Gwen's soft kisses brought him back to the present moment later, and he turned into them, pressing a soft kiss to her lips.

"You're fucking amazing," he whispered. "And I'm never letting you go."

His mate kissed him back. "Good, because I feel the same fucking way, my love. My mate. My everything."

The End

Feral Moon

Wicked Fate Lusty Mates

Astrid Vail

Blurb & Content Warning

His mate is a witch, and all witches must die.

After escaping a secret experimental location, Wolf tries to forget that magic exists and goes back to his simple life until the day he catches a scent on the wind.

His mate.

There is only one problem. She is like those who made him.

A witch.

Which makes her a monster, and he will kill anyone who tries to use magic on him again.

***

As a nature witch, Breena lives her life in solitude, within her remote mountain home. When a mysterious lycanthrope shows up on her land, feral and ready to attack, she traps him accidentally. Forcing Breena to see the truth in this lycanthrope. He is her mate and perhaps the only one who can heal her fears, if she can heal his first.

Content warning: Graphic sex scenes, references to past abuse & animal experiments, blood, murder, and explicit language.

Chapter One

THE WOLF

THE LIGHTS FLICKERED, CAUSING a clammer in the cages. He felt the suffocating magic in the air and surrounding the cages, pulsating once before flashing out completely.

That piqued his interest.

Opening his eyes fully, he stood, shaking out his aching muscles. He was taller than all the others in confinement. He also had more muscle, more grit, and more tolerance for all the experiments the magic users had performed on him.

Witches ...

The word floated through his mind, reminiscent of the two-legged they had melded into him through magic.

But that was all that remained.

Human words that held no meaning to him.

For he was still a wolf, just like all the others here with him.

He tested the cage, pushing his weight against it, using the extra strength given to him through the experiments.

The cage didn't bite like it normally did. Didn't throw the magic back at him as it had for the many moons he had been held captive.

Snarls and the sound of bending metal filled the room, yips of excitement mixed with pain as the imprisoned wolves broke their cages and made their escape.

He was slower, more careful. More observant than the rest.

He listened to the sounds beyond what was in the room.

Because they were still captives, with just a bigger cage to roam.

A few of the wolves who escaped their cages started snarling and biting at the others.

Completely feral, giving in to their instincts. Seeing everyone and everything as a threat.

He was the same, but he was also more.

The magic users had paid special attention to him, cooing and whispering about how he was the one they were waiting for.

Test subject *Thirteen*, they called him. The Alpha others called him. But he didn't care. Names were useless to him. He was just a wolf, even if they gave him a human shape. A shape they only allowed him to wear once a pregnant moon. A shape that came with haunting memories and a mind full of strange words and meanings. Luckily, the memories had faded away to nothing. The words, though...they stuck around. Even when he didn't know the meaning of most of them.

He stopped pushing on his cage door, not wanting to break the locks until the internal fighting around him ceased. He could have easily stopped them, but he wanted to be in good shape when he finally made his escape. Not just from this cage, but from the room they were still trapped in.

Time never mattered, so he didn't try to discern how much of it had passed while he waited.

The others paid him no mind, instead prowling and pissing on everything. Marking territory he didn't care about.

He laid down and waited, the rumble in his stomach ceasing to nothing but a dull ache. But he didn't close his eyes because, under the sound of the others with him in the room, his ears had picked up on the panic outside.

He didn't know why, but he had a feeling.

Gut feeling... The useless words infiltrated his mind.

Either way, it was a feeling, and it told him that his time for true escape lingered in the outside panic.

He just had to be patient.

And so, he did, and true to the feeling, his time came.

The outside door opened, and the others attacked. Blood-curdling screams rented the air.

He took this time to push the door open to his cage, the bending of metal and popping of locks drowned out by the screams. He didn't join the bloody fray; he didn't enact his revenge against the magic users.

No, those things didn't matter.

The only thing that mattered was true freedom.

And that freedom lay beyond the door, standing open to him.

The door of the magic users had no time to close before the others attacked.

He ran, leaving them all behind.

His fur raised along his back, his ears picking up the sounds of the other wolves following his path. Glancing over his shoulder, his paws hit hard packed dirt.

Four others had followed his lead and escaped fully. They raced past him, scattering in different directions.

Good, he didn't want to be responsible for them. He didn't want to form a new pack.

He just wanted his freedom.

He wanted to feel the wind caress his fur and smell the rainstorms in the wind. He wanted wilderness and solitude.

Lifting his nose to the soft breeze, he scented which way he should go. Nothing in particular piqued his interest, so he turned toward the darkest parts of the surrounding woods. He wanted to make sure he couldn't be followed by any of the two-legged monsters. As he picked up his speed, nose to the ground, his ears stayed on high alert.

As time passed, he let his pace turn steady and slow through the forest, his legs eating up the miles beneath him. When he grew thirsty, he found a small stream and drank. When his hunger came back, gnawing at him fiercely, he hunted. Finding small rabbits and rodents, and even smaller nests of bird eggs easily within his reach.

Once the sky finally turned dark, he stopped to rest, lying down within the crook of a fallen tree and a burrow some animal before him had made. And when the darkness turned to a soft light, he awoke and started all over again.

He didn't count how many moons had passed, only that he was content in his solitary life. Wandering the wooded expanse that in turn was his home, and so he continued to wander, until the air turned colder at night.

The useless words in his head had long ceased, gone quiet, and in some moments, he wondered if everything that had happened to him was just a dream.

But wolves did not dream. They only existed in the here and now. So he knew that his memories of becoming a two-legged were real. That magic was real.

Then one day, a day like all the rest, he lifted his head, scenting the air, hunting for his next meal, when a longing filled him to the very core.

And the magic inside of him stirred.

Mate.

The word rasped through his mind, and he paused.

Did he long for a mate? Was that the scent he just picked up on?

Whoever or whatever it was, it smelled of power and nature. Of the very woods he had lost himself in long ago.

He wanted to turn away, never wanting to interact with another two-legged again, but the dormant magic filling his veins compelled him, and for the first time, he felt himself wanting to obey.

For he had always been a curious wolf.

When he caught the scent again, he followed it.

Chapter Two

BREENA

BREENA STARED OUT HER kitchen window as the morning dawn shed light through the paned glass. She watched as the birds played in a puddle left over from last night's storm. The wind was light, barely stirring the treetops, and Breena signed. Normally, she would already be outside, walking the perimeter of the forest surrounding her home, taking stock of her gardens and land. Listening to the surrounding nature. The fruit trees were chatty in the mornings. But that was to be expected, as they were still young and in need of a nurturing hand.

She glanced at the antique clock hanging on the wall behind her. As much as she would love to be outside doing her duties as a nature witch and protecting her land, she had to wait.

As if on cue from her thoughts, her pocket vibrated.

Pulling out her cell phone, she answered the incoming FaceTime from Gwen, head priestess of their small coven, and recently appointed head of witches for the greater territory surrounding them.

She smiled as their normally prim and proper head witch looked utterly frazzled. Her hair was skewed, and Breena squinted. Yup, those were definitely whisker burns on the side of her neck. Gwen straightened her blouse before shooting a glare at someone off camera.

Breena couldn't help herself and laughed, "So how's mate life treating you?"

"Can't keep our hands to ourselves," Gwen mumbled. "Even when we have important calls to make!"

She yelled the last bit of her sentence, still glaring off camera, and Breanna heard a male laugh before the sound of a door shutting cut him off.

"Sorry about that," Gwen sighed.

Breena shrugged. "It's fine. I'm happy for you. How was the head of the coven's meeting?"

"Fine. I would say normal, but I wanted to give you a heads up. Things that Robert and Anna had brewing in the background before their demise. The pack and a few select witches raided some acreage they owned in the middle of the forest and found a few dead witches, along with a ton of empty animal cages. We are still trying to go through the research left behind and see what they were doing."

"Right." Breena nodded. "I'll see if the forest is in a talkative mood today. See if the trees know what was happening out there."

Gwen nodded. "Just be careful, Breena. I'm not sure how far Robert's reach was, and you are all alone out on your property. Plus, I don't have a good feeling about what was in those cages. It was a bloodbath."

"The land protects me, as I protect it."

Gwen sighed and rubbed her head. "That's what I told Hunter and Lily. They really wanted to send a wolf out your way to babysit you until we figure out how deep this mess goes."

Breena snorted. "I know. Lily called me the other day. I told her no thank you and if they did send a wolf, I would just have the forest snatch it up and spit it back out on their property."

"All right. I would love to see that. But..." Gwen paused and looked off screen again before muttering, "I've got to go. I'll update you later if we find anything. And send a SOS in the group chat if something does happen, okay?"

Breena nodded, and the screen went black.

She sighed, not knowing if her sigh was one of loneliness or relief.

There were reasons why she was alone out here. Reasons why she never left the confines of her property. Her coven, and now the lycanthrope pack, knew her power was connected to the forest. They knew she was only powerful here on her own property and that was why she never left.

But that wasn't the whole truth. Sure, if she left her property, she would have no magic, but her issues lay deeper than that. Without her magic, she was completely helpless, and Breena feared being helpless. In her experience, helplessness brought out the worst in people.

Only Gwen knew the extent of her fears. A fear that had taken root at such a young age. And now Breena lived alone, unwilling to leave the confines of her own prison.

The internet was a saving grace, though, and Breena had paid extra to get it installed in her remote cabin. With it, she could still speak to her friends, work from home on freelance designing jobs, and schedule anything she needed to be delivered.

Breena sipped her tea, thinking about what could have been going on in those cages, and a shiver slid down her back. Experiments, cages, witches...it was all hitting too close for comfort. She knew her past was just that, the past, but unease filtered into her gut, and she quickly put her cup down and ran to the front door. Swinging it open, she raced down her porch steps, bare feet hitting the hard packed dirt within seconds. She bent down, coming to her knees, and let the cold from the soil seep into her hands and into her bones. The magic of the land and her own collided. It whispered through her mind, reminding Breena that she was safe as long as she stayed on her land.

A few breaths later, she opened her eyes and got to her feet. Brushing the dirt from her hands and flowing maxi dress, Breena pushed her wild hair out of her face and began to walk toward the adolescent fruit trees.

She had duties to perform, and the fruit trees were already complaining that she was late for her visitation.

Sweat beaded on the back of her neck, the sun beating down on her as Breena tended to the garden. It was midday, her morning call with Gwen already lost in the recesses of her mind. She focused on the here and now, not on the past and not on the future. Just the way she liked it. With her hands buried in the soil of her land.

She was currently tending to her flowers, weeding, and humming the latest rock song by her favorite band, Twisted Coven. A breeze curled around her and with it a whisper of something large and predatory lurking within the forest.

Breena paused, letting her magic fan out, searching until she found the creature hiding in the shadows. She turned, eyes widening as the largest wolf she had ever seen prowled out of the forest and into the sun. Its russet brown coat gleamed, fur thick and shaggy, and its golden eyes met hers, brimming with knowledge an ordinary animal should not possess.

This was no normal wolf.

It was a shifter.

And he was looking at her like she was his prey.

Chapter Three

THE WOLF

HE GROWLED, PROWLING CLOSER and closer to his intended target. This woman's scent beckoned to him, called to him. The magic coursing through him screamed mate, but he couldn't deny one obvious flaw. She held the strange magic in her body. The same magic as those who tortured him and made him into this being. And he would not fall prey to a magic user again.

It was just best to end this here and now.

The woman turned, staring at him with wide eyes, her hair as wild and dark as the forest at his back.

As the eyes of his mate bore into his own, he almost hesitated. He was unable to see vibrant colors in this form, but it did not matter. He didn't need to know the eye color of his mate before he killed her and relieved himself of this incessant pull toward her.

It was magic, and all magic ever did was bring pain.

He leapt, snarling like the beast he was as the woman in front of him screamed and held up her hands. He didn't know what magic she would try to use on him, but it didn't matter. These magic users needed to mutter their curses and touch objects to perform their torturous acts. And he would kill this woman before her hands could touch him. He would rip out her throat before she could utter a single word. He would —

Out of nowhere, vines and roots exploded from the ground, the forest turning on him to protect her.

The forest, the one he had made a home, was protecting *her.*

The vines wrapped around his legs, his chest, his throat, holding him in place.

He struggled against the roots that held him mid leap, snarling and biting, trying to get free. The roots twisted tighter and then he was flying. This time in the opposite direction of the woman, toward a small building near the edge of the forest.

Struggling more, he knew what was about to happen as the door opened on its own and he was thrown into the darkness.

Trapped, he was trapped once more by a foul magic wielding monster.

He lifted his head and howled, low and mournful. A howl full of agony. He struggled some more, but the roots only tightened until he could hardly breathe. He stopped his struggle briefly to take in his shadowed surroundings.

A new prison.

He might be trapped for the time being, but this magic user would eventually slip up. They always did. And when she did, he would not hesitate to kill this one while making his escape.

Chapter Four

BREENA

Chest heaving, Breena flinched as a long agony ridden howl echoed out from the shed. She glanced at her hands, then back at the shed. That was most definitely not where she projected her magic. In fact, she had tried to do exactly what she told Gwen she would do. Throw the wolf back onto pack land, or at least out of the forest. Just anywhere but here.

Instead, her magic was hijacked by the forest itself.

Apparently, the forest did not want her to get rid of this particular wolf so soon.

Getting to her feet, Breena hesitated, glancing back to her house before eying the shed. What she should do is call Gwen immediately, or the alpha of the Southern Moon Pack. She had told Hunter and Lily she didn't need a babysitter. And yet they sent one. Mind made up, she took two steps toward the house until a tightening in her gut stopped her.

She glanced back over her shoulder at the shed. The way the shifter had looked at her, his eyes wild, almost as if he was feral, sent a shiver down her spine. Hunter and Lily would not have sent a feral animal her way. They would have sent someone in human form.

Gwen's conversation from this morning popped back into her head. Cages, animals, experiments...empty cages.

Breena closed her eyes and tilted her head, reaching not to the well of her magic but to the heart of the forest itself. She wanted to know why it allowed this wolf to get so close to begin with, and why it wanted to keep it here.

The breeze picked up, a storm brewing on the horizon of her senses. She concentrated harder on the pulse of the forest itself. She bit her bottom lip as the forest pushed at her mind, gravitating toward the shed.

Opening her eyes with a sigh, she turned back around. Breena didn't hear a sound as she placed her hand on the handle and with a sharp inhale, magic at the ready, she threw open the door.

She squinted into the darkness, finding the back of the shed covered in shadows, until she made out the form of the wolf. The forest still had him restrained. Struggled breaths and low growls reaching her ears. Breena left the door to the shed open, letting in as much natural light as she could. She stepped inside slowly and the wolf shifted against its restraints, his golden eyes darting from her to the outside.

"Shhhh," she crooned. "I won't hurt you. I just want to know why the forest wanted to keep you here. Why don't you shift, and we can talk?"

The wolf glared at her, hatred radiating from his eyes.

Breena frowned and slowly reached out with her magic. What she found made her stumble back, a gasp slipping from her lips. Twisted, corrupt magic surrounded this wolf, warped against the very grains of nature.

Now she understood why the forest held on to this wolf.

He needed her help.

Slowly, she advanced, a hand held out in front of her. Breena knew now that this lycanthrope was feral and would attack like any other wild animal backed into a corner. But she also couldn't let him go without first undoing the corrupt magic surrounding him. She was a nature witch, after all, and if anyone could help, it would be her.

The wolf growled low in warning, but Breena trusted the roots holding him at bay would not falter. When she was about a foot away, she stopped and lowered herself to a sitting position. The wolf tried to lunge for her, but she didn't flinch, the roots holding just as she knew they would.

"I can help you," she crooned. "I'm going to help you. Don't be afraid."

The wolf growled, saliva dripping from his mouth, spittle flying as his eyes lifted from hers and to the still open shed door.

Breena used the wolf's slight distraction to her advantage and closed her eyes, reaching toward the warped magic with her own. She let the forest guide her and it pointed to a tangled web at the back of the wolf's mind. It was definitely witch magic, a binding of sorts, and it did not belong.

So, she went to work untangling it.

When Breena finally opened her eyes, the wolf had stopped struggling. Position changed to sitting and staring intently at her. She realized a weight had settled in on her shoulders, back aching something fierce, and the natural light from outside had dimmed.

Hours...

She had been sitting there working on the nasty binding spell for hours. A spell put in place to keep a lycanthrope from turning. How long he had been in wolf form, Breena couldn't know, but with a deep breath she pushed with her magic once more and whispered.

"Shift."

The wolf before her howled in agony, struggling against the roots as a sparkling, dark mist engulfed him. Breena sat frozen in place, fear coursing through her veins as the howl turned into a scream and then nothing.

Shit, what if she had miscalculated and killed it?

Finally, the mist settled and where a wolf once sat was now a very naked man, with golden eyes staring back at her. Breena gulped and scooted back slightly as those golden eyes scraped down her body and back up.

The man scowled, and a rumble emanated from his chest.

His voice, gravelly and deep, sliced through the silence, making Breena quiver slightly. "Release me, Monster."

Breena gulped. "Mon... Monster?"

The man tested the hold of the roots, muscles flexing, and Breena couldn't help but to look at his body. He was naturally tanned and tall. His muscles, not overly huge but toned, like a runner's or a swimmer's. Breena's eyes settled in on his chest and the clawing scars decorating his skin.

"Monster. Magic user," the man growled, and his words pulled her eyes back to his face.

She shook her head. "Witch, not a monster. Though perhaps you are right. Only a monster would have bound you in such a way." She motioned toward him, and the man shook his head.

"Witch." He tested the word upon his tongue and growled, staring over her shoulder outside. "Free me. Turn me back to my natural state. Not this filthy human form."

Breena blinked as the realization settled over her. When she had been in the wolf's mind, she had noticed something different. Something seemingly out of place. She thought it was because of his feral state, but now she was not quite sure.

"What do you mean, natural state?" she whispered. "You are a Lycan. Both human and wolf. The fabric of your being is both."

The man slowly turned his eyes back to her. "Lycan. Is that what you monsters turned me into?"

Breena stared at the man, knowing her mouth was slightly ajar. Her brain sputtered and spun like an old modem trying to connect to the internet. "Turn... turned you?"

The man blinked slowly, and his eyes once more turned back toward the open shed door. His muscles flexed against the roots, holding him in place. He didn't elaborate, but Breena had already formed her theory.

They had been taking wolves and turning them into lycanthropes. Which should have been impossible. Magic like that long banned and lost to time.

A shiver ran down her spine. Impossible was staring at her again. Golden eyes narrowing, head cocked.

"Why are you breathing like that?"

Only then did Breena realize she was starting to hyperventilate. Memories of her past pushing against the locked box in her mind. The box she pushed into the furthest recesses of her brain. Memories that kept her confined here, on her property, in the prison of her own making.

She knew about monsters.

And she refused to be one.

Breena wobbled to her feet. "Please don't kill me."

She waved a hand, and the roots fell away, releasing the man, and he was on his feet in seconds. He stumbled and, on instinct alone, she reached out to catch him. They both tumbled to the ground, his heavyweight crushing her. Breena's breath caught as something passed between them. A spark of magic echoing through her mind that was not her own, yet tasted so familiar, as the wild-eyed man pushed off her and ran. Breena rolled to her stomach and watched as he disappeared into the darkness, the forest swallowing him whole.

Chapter Five

THE WOLF

DARKNESS SURROUNDED HIM AS he fell to his knees, pine needles digging into his human flesh. The cold rushed in around him, something he was not used to, and he cursed his naked skin. He had to get up. He had to run. The monster was after him.

He growled, reining in his panic-ridden mind. Now that he could catch his breath, his ears picked up on nothing. No footsteps, no shouts. No one was following him. The monster... No, the pretty witch had let him go. Her green eyes burned into his mind as she whispered for him not to kill her before releasing his binds.

With a shiver, he remembered his wobbling legs, like those of a newborn deer, betraying him, and he fell. But she had caught him. Touched him, but inflicted no pain.

He grabbed at the weird fur on his head. Hair, he thought it was called, but the words didn't matter to him. No, he had to get his mind under control. What had the witch done to him? Instead of pain when she used her magic on him, he only felt relief, like she was releasing a pressure in his mind. Then she told him to shift, but it wasn't like with the monsters. She didn't re-bind him with her magic.

He could now change shape at will, no longer being controlled by another. And more than that, she had released him without hesitation. Without even thinking of the harm he could have inflicted upon her.

Huffing, he shook his head. She was like a pup, unaware of the danger he posed. He shivered again as a breeze caressed his shoulder. The shoulder he was now looking over. With his night vision, he could see that the witch had gone inside. The light from her home shining through unbarred windows. Easy to break into. She stared out the window, lifting something to her mouth.

The words came unbidden from his mind, like they did before his escape.

Cup. Tea. Coffee. Water.

The wolf shook his head. All these words from the meat suit that was forced upon him. He didn't want them, yet there they were, at the ready in his mind.

He continued to watch the witch from the shadows until the light from inside blinked out, and soon, only the sounds of the night filtered forth.

Why had he lingered so long to watch her?

He should have changed the moment he stepped foot in the forest. Back to his natural state, yet he had lingered.

Watching the pretty witch with wild hair and bright green eyes.

Mate...

The word filtered through his mind again, and he shook his head once more.

He would not be claiming a witch, a monster as his mate...

Yet the pull of magic was strong, stronger now that he had seen her. Some part of him wanted a mate, someone to protect. To hunt for. To live his life with.

To form a pack with.

Yes, that was it. He wanted a pack and a proper mate. Not one of the two-legged, and definitely not that one in the dark house. Even if she had been somewhat kind to him.

A low whine filtered out from him, but he clamped it down. Burying it with the longing inside him deep, deep down.

He needed to leave before he was pulled in by her scent again. He needed to change back to his natural state and leave immediately, because no good could come of him staying here.

The witch might have said she wasn't a monster, but deep down, he knew she was like all the magic users. This had to be some sort of trick.

She was a monster, and her true self would show, eventually. And he refused to be trapped again.

He closed his eyes and concentrated. Concentrated on his natural form. Wild magic surrounded him, shifting his form, but then it abruptly stopped and when he opened his eyes, he growled and clenched a fist that was supposed to be a paw.

It took him a moment with his two-legged ears to hear the tinkling laughter echoing through the forest.

The forest was laughing at him. More than that, the forest was forcing him to stay in this inadequate form.

He growled once more.

Fine then, he would leave on foot.

Turning on his heel, he made it about three steps before a strong wind pushed him back.

This time, the surrounding bushes rustled as if warning him.

"I will not stay," he growled.

The wind pushed at him again and on it came a faint whisper.

"Once wolf, now man... the moon goddess holds your fate and your mate's in the palm of her hands. Stay... Stay... Stay... "

The wolf growled again, "Why? This is not my place. I will not be held against my will by another monster."

"Protect... protect the one favored by the forest gods. Protect your mate."

The words rang through him, triggering his most basic instinct. Protect his mate.

It didn't matter if he didn't want her. It didn't matter.

He was a born protector, and that need was overriding everything else inside of him.

The wolf growled and turned, peering back at the dark house.

Fine, if the forest wouldn't let him leave until he protected the witch, then he would figure out what danger she was in and eliminate it. Then he would run away from this nightmare of a forest. He would make a real pack and forget about his monstrous human mate forever.

Chapter Six

BREENA

THE DREAMS CAME THAT night. Haunting as ever. Always around this time of the year. The year she escaped death. The year she learned that monsters hid all around her.

Breena tossed and turned all night, knowing her dreams were just memories and she was safe. She was safe within her naturally made prison. Nothing could touch her as long as she stayed within the confines of her property. Yet, throughout the night, she felt it.

A dangerous yet intoxicating presence, watching, sitting at the edge of her domain. The Lycan had never left, and Breena wondered why.

She figured he would be gone by now as she opened her eyes to the soft rays of sunshine dancing across her skin. As she rolled over, though, she saw that was not the case. She didn't startle, yet her pulse rose slightly as she gazed into golden eyes, staring back at her through her closed window. Sitting up, she swung her legs over the bed and cracked her neck before softly padding over to her window. The Lycan watched her with predatory eyes, but instead of fear, all Breena felt was protected.

Not one to question her gut, she opened the window and leaned out slightly. "I figured you would be long gone by now, wolf."

"Same," he growled back to her.

"Well, you're always welcome around as long as you don't try to eat me again."

The man scoffed and glanced away before catching her eye once more. "The forest. It wants me to stay. It won't let me shift."

Breena sucked in a breath. "Shit. Have you been out here all night in your human form?"

The man nodded.

She took a step back. "Well, get your ass in here and warm up. You must be freezing. I'll make some tea and food."

Breena turned around without waiting to see if he would follow. Giving him the choice as she walked out of her bedroom and through her small home to the kitchen. She was in the middle of prepping tea when she heard the telltale footsteps of someone moving through her house. She smiled to herself as a chair squeaked behind her.

He didn't say anything as Breena continued prepping the tea. She turned, tossing some muffins she made the other day on a plate, and deposited them in front of the man.

Keeping him in the corner of her eyesight, she watched as he cocked his head before picking up a muffin and sniffing it. Slowly, he bit into it, and Breena turned back toward the teapot. As the tea seeped, she stared out the window like she did every morning, letting the surrounding nature and trees speak to her. It was quiet today, almost as if they were the ones watching her. Watching to see how this interaction between Lycan and witch would play out.

Her shoulders stiffened slightly as the man moved from the table and stood directly behind her. But Breena did not turn. Not even when hot breath caressed the side of her neck as the man leaned over her, hand reaching out to snag another muffin before retreating back to the kitchen table.

Breena waited a moment before following, grabbing two cups and the teapot. The man watched her silently as she sat down and poured them both a full cup. "Careful, it's hot," she mentioned, as she placed the steaming cup in front of him before picking up hers and blowing on it.

The man's gaze intensified as she sipped from her cup before placing it down on the table. Silence filled the space, silence that Breena loved in the mornings, but this time, it felt stifling. She wanted to say something, anything, but she didn't know where to start. Lucky for her, the man did.

"Pup," the man growled, "do you not eat?"

Pup... Did he really just call her a pup? She wasn't quite sure how she felt about this nickname for her, but she let it slide for now.

"No... I mean, yes. Just not really in the mornings. I prefer my cup of tea first."

The man continued staring, the intensity of which was starting to make Breena blush. She sipped her tea again and looked out the window.

"It's quiet here," the man whispered, and when Breena glanced back at him, she saw he too was looking out the window just as she had been doing.

"Yup," she breathed. "I enjoy the quiet solitude. One with nature and whatnot."

The man titled his head before closing his eyes, letting the sunbeams from the window wash over him.

Breena took this chance to really look at him. From his wild light brown hair that fell to the edge of his collarbone to his full lips and chiseled jawline, all the way down his impressive and still naked physique to his feet. She frowned slightly, noting how insanely dirty he was, covered in grime and dried mud caking on his feet. When she glanced back up at him, he was staring at her again. She cleared her throat and gave him a slight smile. "Like I mentioned earlier, you are welcome to hang around. But perhaps I could request something?"

The man's eyes darkened, his face hardening slightly.

Breena gulped at the sudden change, but continued talking. "Perhaps you could bathe? I know you probably didn't need to wash up in wolf form, but humans...we like to be clean. Hygiene and whatnot."

The man blinked and glanced down at himself, brushing at some dirt on his chest. "Bathe..." he muttered. "Ahh... yes, I think I can do that."

He glanced back up at her. "There is a river nearby, yes?"

Breena snorted. "There is, yes, but you can use my shower. No need to walk down to the cold river when I have warm water in the house."

The man narrowed his eyes, as if he was thinking, before nodding slightly. "Shower. I can experience a shower. Show me the way, Witch."

She held back her giggle that wanted to escape as the man stood completely naked, giving Breena all the eye candy she could ever want from a man. He stared at her, as if trying to read her mind, and Breena sipped at her tea once more before standing to join him. "Come on. I'll show you where the bathroom and shower are. Also, you can call me Breena. What's your name?"

The man shook his head, a furrow creasing his brow. "Names are silly things. I am a wolf."

Breena shrugged. "Okay, then. I guess I can call you Wolf, if that's what you want." She padded forward, angling around Wolf and heading toward the small bathroom attached to her bedroom. "It's just this way. Follow me."

Chapter Seven

WOLF

SHOWER... HE WAS GOING to take something called a shower.

He narrowed his eyes and followed the monster.

No, Breena. She said her name was Breena.

It was silly. Names and the like, but Breena wasn't acting like the monsters who had trapped him and forced this body upon him. Though he was still trapped, except this time by the forest. The forest who seemed to like this witch.

She also gave him a name.

His name was now Wolf, and he somewhat liked the way it sounded.

Wolf followed closely to the room where he had climbed in this morning after watching the witch all night. She moved a lot in her sleep. She even whimpered a bit like a pup. A part of him wanted to wake her. The part that knew she was his mate. But another part, the part who knew that magic meant pain, raged against the cage of his human body. It was her people who did this to him. Which meant she should be like them.

Kill her, the battered and scarred part of his mind raged.

Comfort her and protect her, the other half willed.

Wolf was confused, and he didn't like it. A growl trickled out of his mouth, and the witch turned, eyes wide.

"Is something wrong, Wolf?"

He shook his head and instead inspected the weird small room the witch had led him to. It was white with a few plants hanging in holders above them. There were a few different types of textures below his feet. One cold and hard, the color of the walls. Another soft and fluffy in two places, the color of the trees outside. Then there was smooth dark rock on the other side of a clear door the witch was holding open. She smiled hesitantly. "If you want to come over here, I can show you how the water turns on. There are temperature controls."

He had no idea what she was talking about, but he also didn't want her to continue making words come out of her mouth. They were starting to give him an ache in his head. Wolf stalked forward, invading the witch's space. She tried to move away from him, but he snaked an arm around her waist. If this was a trap, then he was taking her with him.

She made a soft sound as he pressed up against her, looking back at him with a bewildered face. He motioned toward the strange things on the wall. They were the same metal color as the instruments that had hurt him, and he was wary. "Show me this thing you call a shower."

The witch snorted and reached up, moving something toward the wall before bending at her waist to turn the shiny metal. He grew hard between his legs but ignored the heat flooding through him.

This was a word he knew.

Arousal.

His mate was bending over in front of him, after all. But he wasn't going to entertain the thought. No, he wanted to turn back into his natural state and find a pack again. Act like nothing had ever happened to him.

Wolf jerked slightly as water started pouring out of the contraption facing toward the wall. He loosened his hold on the witch and reached up, touching the water.

It was warm. Just as the witch had promised.

The witch straightened, her clothes rubbing something awful against his arousal. She gulped, looking down at him before pointing at the contraption leaking water. "Just move that back over toward you and stand under the water. You can use this too—"

The witch yelped as Wolf turned the contraption, drenching them both in water. "You get clean too. Take off these clothes."

The witch glared up at him, water streaming over her entire body, and it reminded him of the time he fell into the river as a pup.

"Excuse you, but I will not be getting naked in front of you. And how do you know what clothes are, but not what a shower is?"

"Because the monsters wore clothes. Weird furs that are not fur, to protect their naked bodies. And they just threw water on us in our cages. Not this shower thing."

The witch gasped, her glare turning soft. "Oh... that's... that's terrible. I'm sorry."

She reached up, touching his chest, and Wolf stared at her hand. It didn't bring pain like the monsters. And she hadn't tricked him with the shower.

He cocked his head, bringing his gaze back to the witch. "Why are you sorry? You didn't do it."

And there it was.

The howling, broken part inside of him settled down slightly. This witch, his magic-using mate, had not harmed him. She had been nothing but kind to him. Her face turned pink, and she looked down again before looking away quickly, muttering something he didn't quite hear.

"What?" Wolf growled.

His witch shook her head and pursed her lips before reaching for a bottle. "Shampoo, for your hair."

Wolf grunted as she pushed it into his chest. "What do I do with it?"

"I... you... How do you not know what shampoo and showers are? What of your memories?"

Wolf shrugged and took the bottle from her. "Maybe, I did once. But any memories from this human have long since faded."

The witch stared up at him with a shocked look on her face, her mouth slightly ajar. "So... so all you have is a human meat suit and somehow the ability to speak?"

Wolf blinked slightly. Yup, that sounded right. He nodded instead of using his words.

"Did... Do you know who this meat suit is..." The witch paused and made a face. "I can't believe I'm using that word. Do you know who this human was before you two got intertwined?"

Wolf snorted. He quite liked calling the two-legged meat suits. It fit their description quite well, yet from the face the witch had made, perhaps it was not a pleasant word. He shook his head and answered the witch the best he could.

"The human had succumbed to a long sleep before I was put into his body. His body was still alive, but not his mind. The words came to my mind, some with meaning, some not."

The witch pinched the bridge of her nose and shook her head. "Holy fuck."

Wolf squinted at her through the water pouring over his head. "You want to mate?"

"What!"

"You said fuck, which is mate."

"No! It's a ... it's a saying. No... no mating," the witch stammered and ripped the shampoo bottle out of his hand.

Wolf narrowed his eyes as the witch tipped the bottle over and squirted a thick liquid into her hand.

"Dip your head. I'll wash your hair."

Wolf complied, getting closer to the witch, and sighed softly as her hands threaded through his hair. It felt good, and he slowly relaxed. His head dipped lower, and he leaned forward, resting his hands against the wall.

His movement crowded the witch, and she made a sound. Somewhere between a moan and a choke. But she continued to move her hands through his hair, and that was all he cared about. It felt marvelous.

Wolf closed his eyes and let his head fall to the witch's shoulder. Taking a deep breath, her scent hit him full force. Arousal mixed with her main scent of freshly turned earth and sun-drenched skin. He took another deep breath as the scent of her magic, smelling of the forest itself, triggered a memory from before all this madness.

A young girl with dark hair and bare feet, happily frolicking down a small path in the woods. Wolf was young then too and strayed from his pack. Toward where a group of humans had begun settling down in a meadow near the edge of the forest. The girl turned as a branch cracked in the woods, her clear green eyes meeting his. She smiled and bent down, reaching out her hand. Her soft voice floated on the wind, warm and inviting, just like her.

He trotted forward, sniffing her hand, and she let him with a giggle until another voice, harder and full of malice, called out. The girl shot up, panic coating her scent, and he watched the happiness in her eyes leach. She whispered and flung her hands out, urging him to run, and he did.

The next night, the pack left the territory, and when they returned, the girl was gone. The only thing remaining in the meadow was the scent of death and sadness.

As the memory faded, Wolf raised his head. "I know you. We have met before."

The witch paused, and her lips turned down in the corners. "I don't think so. I would have remembered your face."

Wolf shook his head. "In the forest long, long ago. When I was still just a wolf pup."

The shampoo bottle fell from the witch's hand, her scent changing rapidly to one of immense panic. She pushed against his chest, ducking under his arm, leaving Wolf all alone as water drenched him from head to toe.

Chapter Eight

BREENA

THERE WASN'T ENOUGH AIR in the world to fill her lungs or stop the panic rolling through her body as Breena rushed outside. She sucked in massive breath by massive breath, feeling herself going lightheaded. Putting her hands on her head, she rooted her feet to the ground and stared up at the clear blue sky. She concentrated on her breathing and the feel of the ground beneath her bare feet. She needed to think, but the memories of that night and the next day were too raw in her mind even after all these years.

And for Wolf to bring up that day so casually. To have seen her in the forest minutes after her powers blossomed...

It couldn't be a coincidence, could it?

With him showing up so near the anniversary of her parent's death and the day she escaped the cult they belonged to.

She closed her eyes as the memories of that night tried to take over, hungry to turn her into a broken shell of who she used to be.

Breena gritted her teeth and refused to let the tears fall.

Wolf's presence was hard to miss, his energy as wild as the forest itself, and just as soothing in some inapplicable way. She knew the moment he came outside looking for her. She didn't even need to open her eyes to know he was heading toward her. The way his energy scraped at her skin, but not necessarily in a bad way...

It confused her. Made her want to give in and see what it would be like to kiss him. To touch him.

Breena opened her eyes as his presence rolled over her, much closer this time.

Wolf was standing directly in front of her, a frown pulling at his lips. The crinkle in his brow cut a handsome but concerned look. Her eyes wanted to roam his masculine naked body again, but she needed to stay sharp. She needed answers to why he was here.

"Why are you here, Wolf?"

The crinkle between his eyebrows deepened. "I hurt you somehow with my words. I scared you."

Breena shook her head, the tears in her eyes threatening to fall once more. And here she thought she had gotten them under control.

"No, Wolf. Why are you *here*? Here in this forest, on my land? Why isn't the forest letting you leave? Letting you shift? Why are you here? And why would you bring up *that* day?"

A tear slipped from her eye, trailing down her cheek, and Breena flinched when Wolf reached his hand out, fingers grazing her face. He pulled back slowly and ground his jaw. "Because you called me. Your scent floated on the wind, entrancing me, pulling me toward you. Just like that day long ago. I remember it now. I knew it felt familiar."

Breena huffed. "And I'm just supposed to believe you? How do I know you're not part of some scheme to get me off my land, to make me powerless once more and back in their hands?"

Wolf's face hardened, and he stepped forward, crowding her space. "The forest wants me to protect you. I... I want to protect you. I don't know who *they* are, but their hands will never touch you again."

"Until the forest lets you shift again," she whispered. "Then you will leave."

Wolf looked away from her then, and Breena knew she was right. The moment the forest let Wolf shift, he would be gone.

"Maybe..." he growled, and Breena glanced at him through teary eyes. "Maybe I would like to stay a little bit longer.

"Why?"

"Because you have been kind to me, and as much as I try to fight it, you are my mate."

Mate...

The word pierced her to the core, and she took a stumbling step back. Wolf watched her warily as she hugged her arms around her waist. It all made sense now. Everything he had said, the way she felt toward him, and the reason why he was so protective.

Breena shook her head again and took another step back. "I ... I need to think. I need some space right now."

Wolf glanced at the foot of space between them. "You have space."

"No... No, that's not what..." Breena paused and sucked in a deep breath. "Just don't follow me."

She turned and walked away, back to her home. Her sanctuary. She needed to change out of her wet clothes and get on with her duties for the day. And she needed to think, in peace.

Clear skies changed as the day moved forward. Just as the day always did. Predictable in that way. The day always moved on to bring night fall and then it did it again. The days and nights never worried about something as small as human troubles.

It was a weird comfort to Breena, knowing that no matter how her day or night went, she had a clean slate in the morning. Which was why, as she stood and dusted the earth from her bare knees, she was easy to forgive and forget... most things, that was. Time always moved, people came and went. It was the way of life.

She made her way back to her home, glancing at the edge of the forest the entire time. Wolf was still here, somewhere on the edges. But he had done what she told him. He hadn't followed, and he hadn't pestered her all day. Her stomach growled, and she silently cursed. If she was hungry and starting to get chilled from the upcoming change in the weather, Breena could only imagine how Wolf felt. Taking the porch steps in one leap, she rushed inside and hurriedly made two sandwiches, adding extra meat and cheese onto the one she planned on giving to Wolf. She ate hers while preparing his and stepped outside with the plate.

"Wolf," she called out, the wind stealing away her words. Damn, the wind had picked up in the short time she had been inside. Breena glanced at the storm clouds moving in. They were coming closer, and she swore she heard the rumble of thunder. "Wolf!"

This time, she yelled, and Wolf appeared out of the forest, his stride long and eyes alert. He stopped at her porch railing and stared up at her. The plate of food hovered between them, a peace offering in her mind. Hopefully, he saw it as that too. "A storm is coming. Why don't you come inside and eat. I don't want you out in this weather."

He nodded and took the plate from her. Breena took another look at the sky, the hairs standing up on her neck from the electricity. They both barely made it inside before the rain started coming down in heavy sheets. She shivered as a blast of cold wind nipped at their heels and hurriedly shut the door. Rushing through the kitchen and the bedroom, she made sure all windows were shut and locked before heading into the living room.

Wolf had wandered over to the threadbare loveseat, keeping her in his line of sight as she moved quickly. Giving him a hesitant smile, she went to walk around him, toward her small fireplace, when his arm snaked out to grab her around the waist. Her breath caught as he plopped her down on his lap. The now empty plate discarded to the side, and Breena turned her head to meet burning golden eyes.

"I want to learn. I want to learn more about you."

The low rumble of Wolf's voice echoed through the small room, drowning out the heavy pounding of rain on the roof. Breena held her breath, not sure what to say, and positive from the look on Wolf's face that he wasn't done speaking.

"For the first time, I wished I had the human's memories. So, I could understand you better, so they could guide me somehow. But all I have are my own memories and human words I only know from when the magic merged this body with mine. I wish I understood all their meaning, because then maybe I could understand what I have done that hurt you."

Breena's eyes burned, her heart aching at Wolf's confession. She brought her hands up, threading her fingers through his hair. "You didn't hurt me, Wolf. I can't be the reason you become stuck here. I know you need to be free, but you wouldn't have that if you stayed here. I can't leave this place."

He frowned, cupping her face. "You are trapped here? By the forest?"

She nodded slightly. "Yes. By my own choice. If I... If I leave, then I am powerless. Helpless, and I can't be helpless. Never again."

Wolf didn't say anything, instead his eyes took in her face, as if memorizing every line and freckle. She fully expected him to get up and leave, yet as the pressure built between them, his gaze searing into her by the second, Breena knew she should stay reasonable. She should explain in more detail why it would be a bad idea for this feral Lycan to mate with her. Instead, her gaze dropped to his lips, and she leaned forward slightly. He leaned into her at the same time, as if fate truly was drawing them together.

"We shouldn't do this," she whispered, her lips almost touching his.

She felt Wolf take a deep breath, arms tightening around her waist. "Do what?"

"This...we are teasing fate. It wants us to be together and me sitting on your lap. It's becoming hard to think."

Wolf shifted under her slightly. "All that matters is the here and now. Not the past, not the future. And if this fate you speak of wants us together, do you think it wise to deny it?"

Breena groaned. What he said made sense, be it in wolf logic, but had she not just been thinking the same thing earlier today. Was not living in the moment, in the present, how she lived her life?

Wolf lifted his chin slightly, and her core tightened, an all-too-telling flutter in her stomach. There truly was no denying fate, and Breena finally gave in and kissed him.

Chapter Nine

WOLF

Soft lips outlined his and a wave of bliss, the feeling of rightness washed over Wolf as his mate kissed him. He knew this word. Kiss. He also knew what it led to.

And this was something he thought about while giving his witch space. What it would be like to mate with her. Start a pack with her. It was an undeniable pull, and he decided to stop fighting it. So long as she did the same.

All too soon, his witch pulled away, face flushed, and eyes turned downcast. He could hear the heavy beating of her heart, her chest moving in deep breaths. Wolf reached up and collared her throat gently, not wanting her to move.

His mate met his eyes, and this time, Wolf moved. "Again," he rasped, initiating the kiss. She opened her lips in a soft gasp and Wolf nibbled at her bottom lip. Some instinct buried deep inside of him urged him to do these ridiculous things. As a wolf, they would have already been mating, him rutting into her from behind. But his mate was not a wolf, and he had a human form now.

And he wanted to experience mating this way.

His witch shifted in his lap, his arousal between his legs aching and stiff. He desperately wanted to relieve himself of it, but Wolf also knew that humans did things differently. He had seen it in the woods a few times before and, always, the male had waited on his mate's cues.

She moved again in his lap, turning her whole body until her chest was flush against his, the heat from between her legs colliding with his own. His witch broke the kiss, her eyes glazed over and her own arousal permeating the air. She threaded her hands through his hair, and Wolf groaned, closing his eyes and tilting his head back.

He growled softly as her lips glided over his neck, trailing across his overly warm flesh. One of her hands moved down his chest, and his arousal twitched as his mate's hand gripped it. Wolf opened his eyes and threaded a hand in his witch's hair, pulling her head back up. Their eyes met as his witch gripped him with her hand. His hips moved on their own, pumping.

A whimper left his witch's throat, and Wolf leaned in, teeth grazing her neck. Instinct screamed at him to bite her, claim her, protect her. Mark her and make this witch his forever.

Make her his mate.

His witch whimpered again as he teased a spot on her neck, sucking at it. Her hands were rough in his hair, pulling, and finally, he glanced up with a growl.

"Bedroom," she whispered, and Wolf sucked in a deep breath.

"Why?"

His witch flushed even deeper and stammered, "Um... well... I mean, we need protection."

Wolf was suddenly alert, glancing around the room, looking for the danger. "Where is the danger?" His mate's choking giggle drew his eye back to her, and he tilted his head.

"I... How do I explain? It's not like danger, danger. But more like, safety between us when we get intimate."

Wolf growled softly, "I would never hurt you."

His witch sighed and shook her head. "No, it's not like that. It's—"

Wolf cut her off, kissing his witch roughly. "Whatever this protection is, I will do it for you. Even if I don't understand."

His witch gulped as Wolf stood and she wrapped her legs around his waist as he walked them both to the witch's other room. The one she called a bedroom. Wolf was smart enough to know she wanted them to mate in her soft sleeping area. He leaned in, putting her down softly before standing and glancing around. "We are protected now?"

His witch smiled, face flushed and shook her head. "We are closer to the protection."

Wolf's arousal twitched, drawing his witch's eyes, and she licked her lips, her breath growing heavy once more. She got on her knees, beckoning Wolf closer. He grunted as she gripped his hips and leaned in, taking his arousal into her warm mouth. Fisting his hands in her hair, he threw his head back, the scent of his mate's own arousal saturating the air. Her mouth worked over him until Wolf couldn't bear it anymore. He wanted to spill himself inside of his mate, but not this way. He pulled away and pulled his witch to her knees. "No more playing," he growled, stroking her bottom lip with his thumb. "I need to..."

He paused, remembering a word and its meaning.

"Fuck you," he breathed. "Turn around and let me fuck you."

His witch's eyes got wide, and she moved slowly to the side. Wolf kept his hand on her waist as his witch rummaged around in a hidden compartment next to her bed before opening her hand.

"For protection... I need to put this on you."

Wolf nodded, not caring at his moment so long as he could start rutting his witch soon. He found himself barely breathing as his witch moved toward his arousal and rolled something onto it. It was tight, but not so much to be uncomfortable. She glanced back up at him and nibbled on the bottom of her lip. "Ummm... that's it. We can now—"

His witch squeaked as he moved her quickly to hands and knees, coming in behind her. She arched her back and glanced over her shoulder at him, a heavy-lidded gaze on him. He paused and moved one of his hands from her waist. She had touched his arousal, and it had felt good. Now he wanted to touch hers. He dragged his hand through her legs, coating his fingers with her wetness.

His witch gasped, whimpering slightly and pushing back on him. But he had already removed his hand, bringing her wetness to his mouth. He sucked on his fingers and shuddered slightly. His witch tasted amazing, and he wanted more. Holding her waist, Wolf got to his knees and lowered his face to her wet center.

She sucked in a deep breath as he licked her, and when he shoved his tongue where his arousal would soon be, his witch's breathless moans came out in short bursts. He continued lapping at her, tasting and sucking, as his witch grew louder and louder until her body started to quake.

Only then did he pick up on the words she started panting, "Wolf. Please. I need you. I need you to fuck me. Rut me. Mount me. Just fucking get inside of me, please!"

With a growl, he pulled away and lined up her arousal with hers, and with one long thrust, he was finally inside of her.

"Fuck!" his witch screamed, her hands fisting in her soft bedding.

He leaned over her, his own body buckling at how good his witch felt squeezing around him. Hands placed in front of his witch for balance, his body flush against hers, he began to move in and out with long, fast thrusts. Heat built low in his body, tingling sensations flooding him as his witch moaned and whimpered. She arched her back even more, pushing her rump into him, and he took one of his hands and fisted her hair. Exposing his witch's neck, he leaned down, teeth scraping against her tender flesh as he pounded into her faster. Wolf bit down just as the tingling sensation in his body overtook him. His witch screamed, squeezing around him in small bursts as he roared in time with his release.

Chapter Ten

BREENA

THUNDER ROLLED OVER THE cabin and Breena shifted, blinking her eyes open to find it was still dark outside. She turned her head as a band of lightning flashed outside, illuminating Wolf's sleeping form, and a smile touched her lips. Another rumble of thunder broke over her cottage, and Breena counted.

One, Two, Three, Four...

Lightning illuminated the sky again.

She shifted as quietly as she could, suppressing a shiver as her bare feet hit the cold floorboards. She didn't bother covering her naked body as she moved silently from the bedroom to the hallway and finally to the living room. As she stoked the fire, she watched the dying embers flare back up and fed it a few new logs before shutting the fireplace door and moving toward the large window.

It was a heavy darkness outside, illuminated only by lighting. The moon and stars hidden by the clouds. Rain hit hard, sliding down the glass panes in force, the only light coming in from the digital clock on the oven. Because of that, she could somewhat see out her window into the darkened forest beyond. Narrowing her eyes, Breena got closer to the window, hand pressed against the cool glass. Now that she thought about it, she wasn't positive it was the thunder that woke her. Her gut was tugging at her, her subconscious trying to guide her.

Closing her eyes, Breena reached for her magic, nurtured and connected to the forest surrounding her home. With a shake of her head, she opened her eyes and nearly shrieked as a shadow passed over the window in front of her. Breena turned quickly and slapped her palm against Wolf's chest.

"You scared me."

Wolf glanced down at her hand, then back to the window, his eyes scanning like she had just moments before. "Did you see something, pup?"

Breena shivered as his rough voice wrapped around her like a blanket and took a step toward him, closing the distance. She didn't need to see him to notice when his attention shifted from outside to her. His hot breath scorched down her neck, over the bite he had given her earlier. She leaned into him as his teeth scraped over the mark, heat blossoming low in her abdomen. Her pussy clenched and as she glanced up to golden eyes. "The bite, it's a mating mark, isn't it?" Breena whispered, only now realizing the significance.

"Of course it is. You are my mate. Why would I not mark you?"

She almost snorted from his nonchalant answer and decided the mating mark was something they could talk about later, when it was light outside, and consequences of actions seemed more significant. Instead, she tilted her head so her lips could brush against Wolf's. He reciprocated the kiss instantly as thunder rolled overhead. Breaking the kiss, Breena glanced back to the window, counting in her head until the lightning flashed. She breathed out a sigh of relief, the tension she was holding floating away. The lightning illuminated her backyard fully and the edges of the forest, revealing nothing. The feeling that something was off, something lurking out in that darkness, dissipated slightly and she turned back to Wolf.

"Sorry, I just..." She shook her head. "I'm just overthinking."

Wolf studied her face before glancing back into the darkness. "Do you want me to scout our territory?"

Breena smiled at his use of *our,* instead of *your,* and it made her heart flutter a bit. She shook her head again and took his hands. "Absolutely not. Not in this weather. Let's go back to our warm bed and have some fun."

The golden hue in Wolf's eyes darkened, and he growled, pulling her in flush with his chest. "The kind of fun we had earlier?"

Breena laughed and tugged at his hands. "Yes, that type of fun."

She squealed as Wolf grabbed her by the waist and threw her over his shoulder in one move. Between one moment and the next, they were back in the comfort of her bed, the mattress bouncing as the view of the world flipped once more and she was staring breathlessly up at her mate.

Mate... yes, that felt insanely right. And she would hold on to that feeling for as long as she could.

Her mind tried to take hold, telling her they needed to figure out the logistics. She couldn't leave this place, which meant Wolf had trapped himself here with her. She never wanted to trap him here; she wanted him to have the freedom to come and go as he pleased. But she squashed those thoughts for tonight and instead took in the gorgeous feral man that stood before her.

He truly was breathtakingly gorgeous as lightning feathered through the sky once more, illuminating the bedroom. Darkness flooded back seconds later, and Breena got to her knees and reached out, caressing the outline of Wolf's chest and strong arms. He grunted and leaned in, kissing her lips and jaw, making his way down her neck. Inhaling slightly, he pulled away. "How do I make you more aroused? You are not as aroused as our first-time mating."

Breena sputtered slightly, "What... how... Oh! Can you smell how wet I am?"

"Wet," Wolf growled, as if filtering the word through his mind before nodding. "Yes, I can smell how wet you are. How ready you are for me. And you need to be...more."

"Wetter?" Breena whispered as heat blossomed across her cheeks.

"Yes."

Breena reached out and grabbed Wolf's hand. It was a little rough, but she liked the feeling of it. "Do you trust me?"

Wolf growled, and the sky illuminated the room once again. It didn't last as long, as the storm was already moving away, heading toward the mountains. As darkness settled back in, Breena shivered, waiting for his response.

"I trust you, my mate. You and no one else."

Breena sighed in relief before the heat in her cheeks came back and she balanced a hand on his shoulder while bringing his other hand to her pussy. "Then I'll show you another way to get me wet for you. Though the way you devoured my pussy earlier was really good too."

Wolf threaded his hand through her hair, pulling slightly until she was looking up at him staring intensely at her face as her fingers guided him. She parted her folds with his fingers, rubbing slightly before moving his thumb to her clit. Gasping, a shiver rolled down her spine. "If you touch my clit, it's a good type of sensitivity. And it makes me wet. Very, very wet."

She slipped his hand farther down, guiding one of his fingers into her already slick pussy. Her breath hitched. "And you can fuck me with your fingers too. Like you would with your cock."

Her hand left his as he took over, exploring her pussy with his fingers, and trailed a hand up, cupping one of her breasts. "I also like..." Breena moaned and panted as Wolf pressed another finger into her and she widened her knees slightly.

His hand worked her pussy, thumb moving to her clit, and Breena gasped, leaning into him. She forgot entirely what she was saying, but Wolf didn't.

"You also like what?"

Breena moaned, grinding her pussy into the palm of his hands. "My tits, I like my nipples being kissed and sucked on too."

Wolf grunted, and the next thing Breena knew, she was on her back. Wolf pumped his fingers into her, all while playing with her clit, and the second his mouth touched her overly sensitive nipple, she arched into him with a soft scream.

He moved, kissing her tits softly before licking her other nipple, and Breena gripped the sheets so hard she thought she was going to tear them. As his fingers changed position inside of her, curling up slightly, she felt her orgasm crash over her. She whimpered, trying to get enough air in her lungs as her pussy spasmed around Wolf's fingers.

He slowed, then stopped completely, her pussy still clenching and unclenching as he glanced up at her.

"Orgasm," she whispered weakly. "It's a good thing."

Wolf huffed before taking a deep inhale. "I like how your orgasm felt. Do it again. This time around my..." He paused slightly, as if searching for the word.

"Cock?"

"Yes, make your pussy orgasm on my cock."

Breena threw her head back in laughter before pointing to the bedside drawer. "We are going to need some protection."

Chapter Eleven

WOLF

SUNLIGHT DANCED ACROSS HIS mate's soft skin, and he traced the flickering light with his fingertips. His witch's breathing hitched, and he sensed her coming out of the deep sleep she was in. She muttered something he couldn't quite catch before rolling over and burying her head in his chest. Growling softly, he pet her hair before grazing the line of her neck to the mating mark he gave her last night. It wasn't a mistake, even if his mate thought it was. She didn't voice her concerns, but he felt them through the bond. He could also feel her magic and through it the forest surrounding them. He could feel the borders of her land, and the way the forest nurtured her magic. It made him pause for a moment. His witch mentioned that she was powerless beyond the borders of her land, helpless. Panic slowly coursed through his veins at the thought of his witch being helpless. No, that would never happen. Not with him around.

The forest might have trapped him here in the beginning, but now he was determined to stay. He liked being with her, and that was enough for him. He was a wolf, after all, and was quite simple, even if he wore a human suit at the moment.

His mate in question sighed, cuddling closer to him. Wolf smirked as he continued tracing the mating mark.

As his witch squirmed slightly, he felt her lips start to caress his chest, going lower and lower until she scooted fully out of his grasp and down his body. He grunted as she positioned herself in between his legs, her fingers tracing his skin softly. Tossing her wild hair out of her face, she gazed up at him with her sweet eyes, reminding him of a doe in the forest. She blinked her pretty innocent eyes a few times before the hands tracing his skin moved closer to his arousal.

No, she had called his arousal a different word last night.

She had called it a cock.

Wolf reached down and slid his hand into his mate's hair, keeping it out of her eyes as she slowly ran her hand up and down his cock. The other massaged the sack underneath and Wolf felt himself shutter slightly.

Then he groaned, letting his head hit the soft sleeping area as his mate took his cock in her mouth. The telltale tingling was back, and Wolf wondered if this was what his mate felt too before orgasming. If it was, then he was happy to give her this type of pleasure. His hips bucked slightly, losing control as his mate took his cock deeper into her mouth. Her tongue swept around his cock as her hand caressed his sack, and he knew he was about to come undone soon. With a growl, he pulled at her hair, and his witch let his cock slide from her mouth and grinned. He could smell her wetness in the air, her arousal coming from giving him pleasure. He remembered what she had said last night. That she liked it when he had devoured her pussy.

"Come here," he growled, and his witch obeyed to an extent before stopping and straddling him. Her pussy, warm and soft, rested against his painfully hard cock, and she rubbed herself against him.

Wolf grabbed her hips. "Sit on my face so I can taste you, mate."

His witch's face flushed like a sunrise, and she bit her lip, her pussy growing wetter from his words alone. "As much as I want to do that, I kind of want to ride your cock instead."

Wolf snorted and reached the hidden place his witch stashed the protection. Taking it out, he handed it to his pretty mate. "Fine, then. Show me how you ride a wolf."

His mate grinned and the soon quiet room filled with the sound of groans and whimpers as she sunk onto his cock, bobbing up and down on top of him. Gripping her hips, he took control as the tingling feeling grew in his lower back and sack. His mate whimpered, hands clutching her nipples as her breathless moans grew heavy. He felt her pussy tighten on his cock right before she screamed, arching her back, and Wolf started driving into her faster. Her pussy gripped his cock, his mate's orgasm triggering his own.

He released himself into her as his mate collapsed on his chest, breathing heavily as he buried his face in her hair and smiled.

With a sigh, she rolled off him and helped dispose of the protection before giving him a shy smile. "How about I make you some food?"

Wolf's stomach rumbled in response, and his witch laughed until a loud sound echoed through the house.

His witch's eyes grew round, color leaching from her face as she turned toward the sound. It came again, like a woodpecker pounding on a tree. Confusion and fear wafted from his mate and Wolf stood quickly.

"What is it?"

"I... that's not possible. How is someone at my door? My magic, the forest..."

His witch trailed off and shut her eyes, her face becoming contorted.

Wolf knelt and grabbed his mate, shaking her slightly. When she opened her eyes, her panic suffocated the room, and she shook her head. "Wolf, I can't... I can't feel my magic. I can't feel anything. My magic is gone. I'm helpless."

Anger boiled through his veins and bloodshed flashed before his eyes. He stood, stomping out of the room and toward the incessant noise coming from outside. His witch stumbled behind him, tears streaking her beautiful face. She was saying something, but all he could feel was the deep well of rage taking over him. Whatever was on the other side of the door was making his mate cry.

And he was going to fucking kill it for making his mate helpless in her own home.

Chapter Twelve

BREENA

SHE COULDN'T BREATHE.

The rising panic was stifling, consuming all her senses as she tried feverishly to reach for her well of magic. But she was coming up against a wall. The forest could have been screaming at her and she wouldn't have heard a damn thing.

Then a new panic set in.

Whoever had done this had to be powerful, and they were knocking on the door. The door Wolf was barreling toward right at this moment. And she couldn't let whatever this monster was take him away.

Breena ran after him, her cell phone falling to the floor. She couldn't remember reaching for it, and somewhere in the back of her mind, it screamed for her to call for help.

It didn't matter anyway. She was already chasing after Wolf. Her mate, and protective instincts overrode the screaming, whimpering mess her mind was at the moment.

Her worst fear.

To be helpless and without her magic had just come true, only for Breena to realize it was no longer her worst fear.

Losing Wolf was, and she would be damned if that was happening today too.

She screamed at Wolf not to open the door, but it was too late as Breena skidded to a halt. She still couldn't see who was there, but she didn't miss the double pop that resonated in the air. Her mind screamed gun, but she was already so numb all she did was stand there as Wolf snarled. He reached out and whoever was at the door squealed like a pig before falling to the floor and she watched Wolf step over them and disappear outside.

Breena stared at the man on her stoop, eyes lifeless, his head at a weird angle. Her brain was still in a fog, but what it did register was the gun lying next to a lifeless body. She dashed to the door, leaping over the dead guy, and skidded to a halt.

There were three people in her yard, and she didn't recognize a single one. There was another male, and a female dressed the same, in black fatigues, guns trained on Wolf. A strangled sound came from her throat, Wolf, on his hands and knees, in front of the house. Darts scattered around him and finally her brain clicked that these were dart guns. The barest hint of relief coursed through her as Breena glanced away from her mate and to the third man striding forward. He was younger, wearing a teal and black suit, its color harsh against the backdrop of the forest. His shiny blond hair was slicked back and stylish, yet oddly unappealing to her and when he grinned his teeth gleamed an unnatural white.

Breena instantly hated him. He reminded her of a snake waiting to strike.

The man held his hand up to the other two, not even sparing her a glance. "Don't dose him up too much. We need him alive."

The woman glanced over to Breena, her eyes taking in the thigh length band shirt she was wearing and nothing else. "And what of the witch? What do you want to do with her?"

When the younger man in the suit finally glanced her way, there was something in his facial structure that looked vaguely familiar. Nausea filtered through her as he approached Wolf, completely passed out on the ground.

"Oh, I'll deal with the little witch in a moment, but first..."

The man reached down and put two fingers against Wolf's shoulder, and Breena's body moved of its own accord. "Don't fucking touch him!"

But it was too late as the man whispered and fur rolled over Wolf, his body contorting in weird angles, and between one breath and the next, he turned human to wolf.

Breena landed on her knees, hands catching his body and yanked him toward her, onto her lap as the man laughed.

"Oh, sweet little witch, don't worry, I have something stirred up real nice for you too. Especially after what you did."

Hot tears fell from her eyes, burning her cheeks. She snarled at the man, "I don't know who the hell you are, but I'll kill every single one of you for touching him."

The man chuckled again and put his hands out to wave away the other two who had been advancing on them, guns trained on her.

"You don't remember me? Oh, of course not. I was but only a child when you killed my father."

All the blood leached from Breena's face, her hands tightening in Wolf's fur. Now she knew why this man looked familiar, but she couldn't place him. He had the same facial structure as another monster, a monster from her past. The reason why she had come looking for sanctuary on this land so many years ago. "I didn't kill him," Breena found herself whispering. "The forest did."

But even then, Breena knew the truth; the forest had been protecting her. Protecting her against the monsters for a very long time.

The boy from her past snorted and shook his head. "You and I know that is a bunch of bullshit. Now I'll be honest, I only came here for our little escapee experiment. But finding out it was you on this land. That it was you who..." He glanced at her neck and chuckled. "You mated with him. Oh, this is rich. This is just the cherry on top of an already glorious day."

He took a step back and snapped his fingers, pointing to his two henchmen, or really one henchman and one henchwoman. "They are both coming with us. Let's hurry before the spell wears off and the witch can use her power again."

Breena stood, readying to fight with everything she had, power be damned. They were not taking her or her mate off this land. She would claw, kick, and bite. Become as wild as the land itself. But in that moment, a distant buzz prickled at the back of her subconscious before reaching her ears, her brain registering only then that it was the sound of a car flying down her gravel and dirt drive. Dust billowed in as it skidded to a halt, and Breena almost cried as Gwen stepped out of the vehicle.

Her coven leader took in the scene with cold eyes, her hair perfectly styled, suit clean and pressed. She took a step away from the car, wearing heels Breena could never figure out how she could walk in.

The two lackeys the man brought raised their guns at her, and she tsked, her voice full of icy rage. "I would think twice about that."

Growls rose from the forest, and behind Breena, wolves filtering out to surround them. One prowled toward Breena, glowing eyes taking in the scene before a dark sparkling mist encased him, and within a blink the Alpha of the Southern Moon pack stood before them. Breena averted her eyes, not wanting to see Lily's mate naked.

Gwen smirked, clapping her hands together. A deep rumble followed by an echoing snap filtered through the back of Breena's mind, and suddenly the forest was screaming, raging, begging to be used as her cut off power roared into her like a hurricane.

She threw her head back and laughed.

Now it was her turn to show these interlopers how much they had fucked up.

She made quick work of them, leaving the two lackeys trussed up like Christmas presents in the shed, while she hung the boy from her past upside down in a tree. He wiggled and squirmed the best he could, but the vines erupting from the ground and trees held strong.

The forest wasn't in a kind mood, and neither was Breena. She made sure this man would be bruised with a few broken bones by the time she decided to release him.

The alpha helped Breena drag Wolf back into the house, while the rest of the pack bled back into the forest, except the wolf, who stayed close to Gwen. Eventually, he changed to, and the next thing Breena knew, she had the head witch of the coven in her living room, sipping tea while her mate and the alpha stood vigilant over Wolf's body. Thankfully, they had brought spare sweatpants to cover their nakedness.

Breena sipped at her tea and leaned forward, barely hearing what Gwen was saying to her. She had already explained who Wolf was, and that they were mates. That was all that mattered in her mind. She didn't care about any lycanthrope politics or the fact the alpha and Gwen were arguing about feral wolves and rogue witches. The word *cult* sprang up a few times, directed toward her, but Breena paid them no mind. She was laser focused on Wolf, watching his steady breathing, and waited silently. Plus, she figured Gwen would fill the alpha in on her past. She really didn't care now. The only thing she cared about was lying unconscious in front of her, and it would take the armies of hell to break her concentration at the moment.

Wolf suddenly twitched, and Breena threw her cup to the side, the crash startling everyone but her as she launched herself into the sparkling smoke currently encasing her mate.

Chapter Thirteen

WOLF ~ ONE MONTH LATER

WOLF SNARLED, HIS BODY colliding into another, fur and teeth clashing. As they pulled apart, a dark mist rose and Wolf dove deep inside himself, pulling out his human half. He was a full second too slow as a thick forearm...

Yes, that was the word, forearm snaked around his neck, and all the blood rushed to his head. He tapped frantically on the arm and the pressure released. Rolling to his back, his opponent was already on his feet, offering a hand. "You're getting better. Now tell me in detail how it went wrong."

Shit, Wolf hated this part. It was part of his lessons. A condition for not being eliminated immediately by the Alpha of the Southern Moon pack for being feral. Because that was technically what he was. A feral lycanthrope. A wolf wearing a human body.

But much to the alpha's surprise, Wolf was learning how to pass as a human at a rapid pace.

He glanced up to the porch where his mate sat with her coven leader, and she smiled, blowing a kiss his way before going back to her conversation.

He was doing this for her. His mate. Nothing would tear him away from her, even if it meant he had to learn to be human.

He let his opponent help him to his feet.

"Thank you, Chase," he grumbled, and Chase patted him on the back roughly.

"Hey! Bonus points for using my name!"

Wolf shook his head. Chase was a pup in his eyes, a bit younger and way too joyful. But he did respect his wolf. Craziest thing he had ever set his eyes on and fiercely loyal to his mate.

He let his eyes wander again to the porch. He had a habit of doing that now, after what happened. After he learned she tried to protect him with only her body, pushing away all her fears of being helpless without her magic. He rubbed his face and glanced back at the still smiling Chase.

Wolf growled, "I wasn't fast enough when you shifted. I should have sensed you reaching for your..." He paused, searching for the word. "Lycanthrope magic, and I should have reached for mine at the same time. Because you turned quicker than me, you were able to take my back and choke me."

Chase nodded. "Choke you with what?"

"Your forearm."

"Which is?"

Wolf sucked in an aggravated breath. "It is part of the human body. Part of the lower arm."

Chase chuckled and shook his head. "Good. Good. I'll tell the alpha you are studying. To be honest, man, your wolf is much less troublesome than mine ever was. If you're considered feral, then mine is fucking psycho."

"Agreed," Wolf grumbled and took off toward the porch. He had been away from his mate long enough and he wanted to be next to her.

Chase laughed, and out of the corner of his eye, he saw the man toss something his way. He caught the soft gray fabric on instinct and grumbled under his breath.

Fucking clothes.

Luckily, when it was just him and his mate, she never insisted on him covering up. Only when they had visitors, though, was he supposed to wear these things called sweatpants.

Wolf tugged them on quickly and made his way over to his mate. She was in the middle of a conversation, but he didn't care. Grabbing her by the waist, he picked her up and sat in her chair, depositing her plump ass on his lap.

That was one good thing about human lessons; he was learning all sorts of juicy words that made his mate whimper in the bedroom.

His mate burst out laughing as her coven leader gave them both a startled look. Then she glared at Chase. "Don't even think of it."

Her mate laughed and pulled up a chair beside her.

"As I was saying, the three who came on your land and attacked Wolf..."

"Four," Wolf interrupted as he caressed his mate's lower back. "There were four."

The coven witch titled her head.

Cool eyes assessing in a way that made Wolf briefly wonder how Chase and his mate worked. He was so easygoing, and she reminded him of a snake.

"Gwen," Chase murmured and reached out, taking her hand.

Gwen blinked, and the coldness slipped away slightly. "Yes, four. Yet you broke one's neck, so in simple math, there are now only three."

Wolf almost growled, but Breena shifted, wrapping her arms around his neck and giving him a soft peck on the cheek. It calmed him enough to avoid the coven witch's eyes and look elsewhere.

"As I was saying," Gwen continued, "those remaining three zealots have been tried and sentenced for these current crimes, plus a few more in their coven who were part of the Lycan experiments. As far as what happened in the past, your past. There isn't enough evidence for the council to charge the entire coven and its members, unless you bear witness. And even then, it would be your word against theirs. Technically, it isn't illegal to start a cult or have followers, and there is no proof about what happened. As for the followers, the handful left after all these years have scattered. As far as we know, they had no idea about the illegal experiments and forbidden magic being used. But I would say, stay vigilant."

His mate scrunched her face slightly, eyes growing haunted for a moment. Then she shook her head and met his eyes. "I've got Wolf now. If my past and that damn cult try for me or the zealots try for him again, I'll be ready. I'm not scared anymore."

Smiling at her words, he gave her a long kiss, gripping her jaw in his hand. His mate pulled away with a gasp, a pretty pink flush creeping across her face.

"And that's our cue," Chase muttered and finally grabbed his mate, pulling her into his arms. "We have some...painting to do."

Gwen gasped, even though Wolf didn't quite understand why he would be talking about painting. It must have been some sort of human thing he had yet to learn.

"Just send the SOS to the group again, if you run into any trouble. Everyone was lucky we were close by when this went down. But there is no guarantee that will happen again," Gwen called out over her shoulder as her mate tugged her down the stairs and to their car.

His mate waved goodbye, and Wolf muttered, "Painting? What is so urgent about painting?"

His mate laughed. "Keep this a secret, but I've heard Gwen is an excellent painter. In the more erotic arts."

"Erotic?"

"Mating... They are going home to mate."

Wolf snorted.

Now that, he fully understood.

Just the thing he was going to do with his witch sitting all cozy on his lap. But first...

He leapt up, swinging his mate over his shoulders, and stalked around the house and into the back part of their territory. Once he got to their territory line, he put his mate down and took a few steps forward.

"What? What are you doing?" His mate's voice wobbled slightly, and Wolf's chest hurt slightly as her confusion tainted the air.

He turned and quickly stripped out of the sweatpants he was wearing and took an extra two steps back.

"I heard you speaking to Gwen over the past month. She suggested you start trying to face your fears and take a step off your land. You are not powerless. You and I both know this. You were ready to defend me tooth and nail, without magic. You can take four steps off your land."

His mate whimpered, glancing back at her house, then to him.

"Come on, pup. I won't let anything happen to you. Trust me."

Her eyes snapped up, catching him as he asked his mate to trust him. She had said the same to him once. Wolf watched her take a deep breath before sliding a foot forward. She visibly shivered, wrapping her arms around her waist. "This feels weird," his mate whispered.

Wolf grunted, reaching out his hand to her. "Tell me. Tell me what it feels like."

She slowly untangled an arm from around her waist and leaned forward, reaching for him, and Wolf grasped her hand. But he didn't pull her. No, his mate would have to do this on her own.

"It feels like my magic is still there, but it's diluted."

She took the final step over her invisible boundary and visibly shuddered. This time, Wolf pulled her into his arms, wrapping her in his embrace. "And now?"

"I... I can still feel the forest, but not its magic. I do still feel the lycanthrope binding us. Not my magic, but ours."

Wolf lowered his head, resting his chin on the top of her head. "Our mating magic?"

"Ya, can you feel it? It's different from my own, but... but it still feels like home, you know?"

Wolf chuckled. "I feel it. It feels like you. Like home. Like I can't wait to lick every inch of you and lay you down right here and fuck you until you're screaming my name."

His mate giggled and lifted her chin. "Oh, is that so?"

He didn't answer, instead kissing her deeply until they were both on the ground, his beautiful mate straddling him. He grabbed her thighs and the flimsy shorts she was wearing. His mate gasped as he tore them away before lifting her higher upon him. Within seconds, he had her where he wanted her, straddling his face. She moaned, already wet for him, and he gave her a long lick before burying his face into his mate's pussy.

Yes, this definitely felt like home.

Epilogue

BREENA ~ SIX YEARS LATER

WITH A SIGH, BREENA hung up her cell phone and went outside. A bluish gray tinge clung to the night sky, dawn yet to make its presence known. Her eyes searched the toy strewn yard until she found exactly what she was looking for. Hopping off the porch as stealthily as she could, she snuck up on the shed and its open doors. She was halfway there when a voice growled from behind. "We really need to work on your situational awareness."

Breena jumped and squealed, turning fast to throw her arms around Wolf's neck. They shared a short kiss before she stepped back. "You know, it still throws me off guard any time you are fully dressed."

Her eyes roamed over the worn-in plaid button-down he was wearing and the equally loved hiking shorts. He wasn't wearing any shoes, unlike her, but that was where Wolf drew the line. It was his deal breaker. He never went anywhere that required shoes.

Wolf bent over, slinging the large hiking bag over his shoulder before moving in to cup Breena's face. "Are you ready, mate?"

She nodded, and a pain tugged at her heart, but she nodded, nonetheless.

Wolf must have sensed something off because he pulled her close, kissing her again. "This will be fun. Just you and me. I heard you speaking to the kids last night, and then Silina this morning. The twins are in great hands."

Breena hugged him back fiercely. "I know that. It's just... This is the first time that we won't be near a phone while they are away."

Wolf chuckled softly. "I know, but remember, I have a connection whenever I turn into my wolf form. I'll be able to sense if anything is amiss."

Breena pulled back slightly. "Oh, I know. That, in and of itself, is why I agreed to go on a half-day hike to wherever this beautiful oasis within the mountains is."

Wolf snorted and took a step back, tugging at Breena's hand. "Well, come on, then. Daylight is wasting. I know just the place to watch the sun rise too."

Her legs hurt, her back hurt, and for the umpteenth time, Breena questioned why she allowed her mate to talk her into this. This was the farthest she had been from her house since practicing leaving her property, and with every step, she clung harder and harder to the mating bond magic that flowed between them.

Finally, she stopped in the middle of the trail, her chest heaving from the upward climb, and called out. "Wolf. My mate. Love of My Life." She gasped in another breath as he turned toward her and grinned. "Please tell me we are almost there."

Wolf chuckled and started walking backwards. "Just a little longer. Then it is all downhill, I promise."

He winked at her and continued walking backwards. Breena dragged her feet, but when she finally crested the hill where Wolf was waiting at the top, she saw the little oasis in the forest he had promised.

Trees on all sides but one, the little clearing sported a beautiful crystal-clear lake, with a sandy shoal, and a small waterfall on the opposite side. It churned the water slowly, making it lap the edges of the naturally made pool, and all Breena could think about was dipping her achy body into that glorious water.

It was all the motivation she needed to pick up her pace, and Wolf chuckled softly by her side. She made good time and started peeling off her sweaty clothes immediately, throwing them onto a large, smooth rock that looked excellent for sunbathing later.

Wolf dropped their pack next to the rock, and Breena felt her mate's gaze on her back as she dipped her foot into the water. It was cold, but not unbearably so, and her body loosened up, cooling off drastically as she waded into the water. She dove under with a sigh and the water moved around her in waves as Wolf dived in after her. He swam toward her and circled his arms around her waist. They shared a kiss underwater until Breena needed to surface.

She giggled, kissing her mate's face softly and circling her legs around his waist as he held them afloat. Leaning back, she let her eyes close as she drifted and let the warm sun beat down on her.

Wolf growled and floated them back to the shore, and Breena giggled as he lifted her up, walking back to the large rock that she had flung her dirty clothes on. He pushed them off before laying her down, and Breena groaned, letting the warmth from the rock soak into her. The cold from the water and the heat from the sunbaked rock felt amazing. She felt heat build between her legs as Wolf's hand trailed between her thighs, and arched her back as her mate leaned over, taking a nipple into his mouth. She caressed his back and chest as his fingers found her clit and slowly started working her.

After six years together, he knew the exact spots to pleasure her, and within moments, Breena was panting, her whimpers echoing through the forest.

"Please, please. I need your cock. I need you inside me," Breena moaned as Wolf continued to play with her clit.

He lifted his head, golden eyes catching hers, and he grinned before sliding a finger inside of her pussy. She clenched down immediately, her body's reaction to knowing what was coming. Breena growled, "I said cock. Not a finger."

Wolf chuckled before adding another finger and then another.

Gasping, she watched as he worked three of his thick fingers inside of her before pulling out completely. Her strangled moan of losing the feel of him turned into her almost coming as she watched her mate lick his fingers clean.

He winked at her before gripping his cock, and Breena sat up and spread her legs, her knees slightly up and she thrust out her tits. She wiggled a bit, and Wolf groaned, grabbing her by the knees and pulling her closer. His cock hovered at her entrance, and they met for a kiss before Breena moved her hips slightly and the tip of his cock slid into her.

She moaned as Wolf deepened the kiss and pushed into her fully with one long thrust. Breena held on, hands tangling in her mate's hair as he set the pace, sliding in and out of her, hitting deep and hard every single time. She came within seconds, her pussy pulsating around Wolf's thick cock, her scream echoing throughout the forest.

He continued fucking her through her orgasm, and she felt her second one building already, feeding off the first as he trailed kisses across her jaw and down to their mating mark. She moved her hands to her nipples, rolling and pinching them as Wolf picked up the pace.

Heat spread through Breena once more, her second orgasm taking over her body as Wolf bit the mark on her neck and thrust into her deeply, holding himself there. This time, she came with a whimper, unable to get enough air in her lungs as mind-blowing bliss coursed through her veins. She felt him come inside, her pussy still pulsating around him, and her mate's heavy body pushed her into the rock.

Wrapping her arms around his shoulders, she buried her head into the crook of his neck, their heavy breathing mixing with the sounds of the forest. All too soon, Wolf pulled out of her as he rolled over. She snuggled on top of his chest, one leg sprung over his hips, and he traced fingertips of her thighs and ass lazily. As she spared a glance at his face, she sighed. He looked peaceful and just as handsome as the day they had met. She traced her fingers over his chest, playing with his nipples, and he growled, swatting her ass gently.

"Keep that up and we will be going for round two right here and now."

Breena glanced down at her mate's cock, seeing him already starting to harden again. With a grin, she let her hand slide down, gripping his semi-hard cock. She started stroking him, and Wolf opened his eyes to look at her.

"Insatiable," he growled, before grabbing her waist and pulling Breena on top of him.

She let go of his cock as he moved her down, rubbing her pussy and clit on top of his cock, and Breena moaned from the sensations.

She was still sensitive from her orgasms a few minutes ago as Wolf finally pushed into her and slapped her ass.

Shivering, she took her mate at this new angle, filling her up to the brink before pulling out and doing it again, over and over.

Her orgasm hit suddenly, and she gasped, digging her nails into her mate's chest as he took over, moving her hips with the rhythm of his own. Breathless pants once more filled the forest and

Wolf came not too soon after her as she collapsed onto his chest.

"Six years, and it still feels like the first time with you," he murmured, and Breena chuckled.

She pushed on his chest, sitting up with a grin. "I love you. I loved you from the first time I saw you."

Wolf chuckled. "Really? Because the first time you saw me, I was not in my right mind."

Breena snorted. "What can I say? You were a very pretty wolf, and my sense of preservation was very low that day."

Wolf sat them up and kissed her, caressing her back, and Breena's eyes grew wide as she felt him harden inside of her once more.

"Again?" she gasped as the root of his cock ground against her over sensitive slit.

"Always," he growled and thrust into her gently.

Breena moaned, tipping her head back as Wolf rocked back and forth inside of her. She gripped his hair tight, just how he liked it, and let the bliss of just being with her mate overcome her.

Heat pooled into her pussy, tingling sensations lighting up her body once more. Breena smiled, and Wolf licked her neck, placing kisses across her chest.

"I love you, Wolf. Always and forever," she managed to whisper between breathy moans, and her mate chuckled.

"I love you too, my witch. Always and forever."

The End

Scarlet Moon

WICKED FATE LUSTY MATES

ASTRID VAIL

Blurb & Content Warning

A second chance at love never tasted so good.

Sasha

When a call for help reaches the Southern Moon pack, Sasha is more than willing to take one for the team. Anything to get her brother out of her hair and her mind off the personal demons plaguing her.

Add one annoying pit stop at the supernatural prison, and now Sasha must add a pompous vampire to her list of things she would like to run away from.

But he has information the lycanthropes need to fight a growing terror in the swamps of Louisiana, and Sasha is willing to play nice, for now.

The only issue is she can't stop wondering what it would be like to kiss this damn vampire.

And what it would cost her in the end if she did.

WICKED FATE, LUSTY MATES

Rhekr

He is the last of his kind, or so he thought until a beautiful she-wolf shows up demanding to know how to kill vampires.

Not one to forgo a challenge, Rhekr invites himself to Louisiana with the grumpy she-wolf, determined to prove two things.

One,

Whatever is attacking the lycanthropes in Louisiana is not vampires.

And two,

that he can stich up the she-wolf's broken heart.

Even if it means doing the same with his.

Scarlet Moon is the final instalment to the Wicked Fate, Lusty Mates series. Inside these pages you can find morally grey heroes, spicy sex scenes, redemption, and a second chance at love for both characters.

Content warning includes:

on page sex scenes, rough sex, primal chase, blood, death, sibling fighting, mentioned past family abuse and trauma, unhealthy coping to trauma, losing a loved one, patricide, thoughts of suicide (not acted upon), and adult language.

Chapter One

SASHA

Sasha growled as the incessant buzzing grew louder and louder until she blindly groped for her phone. Or at least, she thought it was her phone. It was a tossup between hers and the two other bodies she was cuddled up against.

"Hello?" she groaned as her head started to pound.

"Hey, it's me. I need you at the house. Urgent pack matter."

She sighed as her twin and pack alpha, Hunter, didn't wait for a response before hanging up. What she really wanted to do was close her eyes and sleep off her hangover. Technically, she could refuse his orders. Sasha was older and stronger, but if the pack found out about that, it would lead to all sorts of things Sasha had no need for. Like formally fighting her brother and becoming the pack leader herself. No, she would rather be drinking and fucking, two things she did best. Not take care of a pack.

Sasha rolled to the side and carefully crawled over the two naked bodies in the bed. She was at their home, some human married couple, who had been looking to get a little freaky at a seedy bar she had been playing pool at.

Her demons had been on a warpath last night, and she was more than glad to shut them up with a good old-fashioned threesome. Plus, the humans had offered her some really fucking good whisky. The hangover was worth it. Her demons had settled for now.

She was out the door within minutes, swinging her leather-clad legs over her Ducati sv4 and revving the powerful engine. With a grin, she snapped her helmet visor down and let the vibrations of her bike fill her body and soul. Peeling out, she blasted through the small suburb the random couple lived in right outside of the city, and hit the on ramp within minutes. Weaving between traffic and ignoring speed restrictions, the wrought-iron gates of her brother's estate greeted her within forty-five minutes.

The estate was technically both of theirs, but Sasha liked to avoid this place as much as she could. She really didn't understand how her brother stomached living there. Didn't understand how the walls didn't haunt him the way they did her.

Then again, maybe it did, and he just processed their collective childhood trauma in a healthy way. Plus, he had an amazing mate to help him in ways Sasha never could.

She zipped up the winding driveway, pushing away the growing agony in the pit of her stomach, and parked next to a familiar SUV. As she pulled off her helmet, she glanced around with a frown. The whole pack and coven were here, minus the nature witch and her new mate.

Clipping her helmet to her Ducati, she jogged up the front steps and into the house without knocking. Following the voices into the main living room, she hesitated at the door, seeing everyone lounged out on the furniture and ground. Couples sprawled in each other's laps and held hands. It was modern bliss, and it put a stranglehold on Sasha. She cleared her throat even though all the Lycans knew she was already here. Hunter glanced over his shoulder, arms around his mate, and sniffed.

"You smell like cheap cigarettes and booze." His eyes roamed her body, his frown deepening at her disheveled state. She knew what she looked like. Her makeup was deeply smudged, and her hair was an absolute terror zone. The patented red lipstick she wore daily was long gone, and Sasha knew she looked like a hot mess. And not in a good way.

Her brother shook his head slightly before turning away from her. He would never say anything in front of the pack, but Sasha knew a *talk* was coming. They would yell and fight, but in the end, he would be right. How she coped with her demons was not healthy. But she didn't care. She actually didn't care about much these days.

No one else said a thing to her, but she did nod back to Lily, who gave her a tight smile.

"Alright, now that everyone is here. Gwen, did you want to cue up the call?"

Hunter's voice took on his typical alpha tone, and Sasha had to hide her smile as Gwen, the head witch for the region, stiffened and arched an eyebrow. She didn't like taking orders any more than Sasha did. But she didn't say anything back, no icy one liner, and that was when Sasha knew this pack meeting was truly urgent.

She focused on the TV screen as it lit up, one side of the screen showing Breena, the nature witch and Wolf, her mate. The other side showed a lived in and worn-down cabin, along with a face Sasha hadn't seen in ages.

Once happy, clear blue eyes were now lined with worry and the woman's long, braided black hair was lined with silver and gray. "Fuck, Nancy. You're not looking too hot."

Nancy, the second to the pack down in Lafourche Parish, spared Sasha a look before shaking her head. "You don't look so hot either right now, Love."

Hunter growled, pulling the attention back to him. "You two can catch up later. Nancy, please relay what is going on down in Louisiana."

Sasha shivered as a haunted look overcame Nancy.

"Right, well... things have taken a turn down here. It started in Baton Rouge. Rumors be flying as they do, but we just ignored them until we couldn't anymore. Until the rumors turned out to be real."

Sasha crossed her arms, her brows crinkling. Last she checked, Nancy and their Alpha kept the pack small, out of the way, and minded their own. They never interacted with the big city politics and they were happy about it. Sasha knew the only reason they would reach out would be because of something catastrophic. And the fact that Nancy reached out to Hunter and not her... Whatever these rumors come to life were, was bad. Really fucking bad.

"Where's Apollo? Why isn't he on the call?" Sasha growled when Nancy paused. Apollo was the Alpha, and technically, his second shouldn't be bearing all of this on her own.

Nancy shook her head, tears forming in her eyes. "Dead... he's dead. I've taken his place, but we need help. I know it sounds ridiculous, with us being

Lycans and all, but there is... there are monsters out there in the dark. You wouldn't believe me if I told you."

Sasha sucked in a deep breath, along with everyone else in the room, as Nancy dropped bombshell after bombshell.

"Monsters? Tell us what makes you think there are monsters?" Hunter asked, and Nancy swiveled her attention to him.

She hunched in on herself and shook her head. "They are fast, cruel, and cannot be resonated with. Worse than a feral. We caught one and..." She made a face Sasha couldn't quiet place, equal parts embarrassment and disbelief, probably, but she couldn't be sure. "If I wasn't so desperate, I wouldn't even entertain the thought, but I think... I think we have vampires."

Silence filled the room as everyone stared at the TV. Hunter finally spoke up. "Did you say vampires? As in, suck your blood vampires?"

Nancy nodded. "Like I said. I know it sounds ridiculous, but the one we caught had fangs. He was ravaging the neck of a Cajun, drinking his blood. And... and he was fast, oh so fast. We barely caught 'em before sunrise. And the thing screamed when the sun touched 'em, steam and everything. Like in the movies, but how is that possible?"

Gwen sighed, pulling everyone's attention to her as she rubbed at her head. "It shouldn't be. But a lot of *should nots* seem to happen a lot lately. Did you bring this up to the New Orleans coven?"

Nancy paled slightly, her dark skin taking on a sickly tone. "I tried, but relationships between the practitioners and the Lycans here are not the best. We stay out of each other's way. That is how it always is. The last Lycan who thought to speak to the coven was cursed for two full moons. It wasn't pretty."

"I'll make some calls, then."

Nancy smiled and glanced back at Hunter, who shook his head. "Like Gwen said, we will make some calls. You hang tight. We will all figure all this out."

Silence filled the room as Nancy signed off, and Hunter gave Sasha a look she could only describe as 'big brother is about to give you a talking, don't go anywhere.' Except he wasn't her big brother, and she wasn't going to stand around waiting to get lectured.

Ignoring his glare, she turned to leave, planning on calling Nancy back on her phone to really talk to her old friend, just as one of the wolves spoke up. "I'm not sure if it helps, but I might know someone."

Sasha glanced back over her shoulder at Romeo, one of the newer pack members and one who had done twelve years behind bars. His mate was sitting in his lap, hands interlaced with his, and she glared around the group, daring anyone to interrupt what her mate had to say.

Hunter nodded, and Romeo continued.

"In prison, there was... let's just call him a shadow. No one knew his face, but he was the monster that monsters fear. Technically, the prison was built around him, so he can leave whenever he wants. But apparently, he likes his solitude and scaring others."

"And why do you think this monster can help us with this so-called vampire problem?" Gwen asked.

Sasha watched Romeo's face go ashen before rubbing his neck. "Because I'm pretty sure he is one."

Chapter Two

SASHA

HER HEADACHE CAME BACK tenfold as everyone in the room erupted in a flurry of words. They got louder and louder by the second and Sasha cracked her neck slightly, rubbing at her temples.

She really needed some quiet and a hot shower asap, not pack drama. Plus, she had a plan forming of her own. She hadn't been to Louisiana in far too long, and she wasn't going to leave Nancy just sitting out in the bayou waiting. No, she was going to go help her friend instead.

She turned away without a word, slipping out unseen by her brother amidst the chaos. She even made it halfway up the stairs before the pitter patter of feet following her grabbed Sasha's attention. Glancing over her shoulder, she smiled at Lily. Her brother's mate and the first witch to wiggle into the heart of the pack. She knew fate had to have had a hand in getting every single witch in that particular coven to become mates with most of the pack.

It elated Sasha to see so many happily mated wolves, yet her demons howled behind her genuine smile. They had been getting louder and louder over the past year, and soon Sasha knew they would break her.

But she planned on being far, far away from here before that happened.

Lily finally caught up with her and they continued up the stairs and onto the second floor, landing together.

"I need to get back down there, but I saw you sneak off, and I wanted to give you something."

Sasha's curiosity took over, and she paused as Lily darted into the room she used as her office. When she emerged with a little basket in her hands, Sasha blinked in disbelief. It was overflowing with bath and body products. Shaking her head, she reached out slowly, taking the wicker basket. "What...what is this for?"

A blush crept up Lily's neck, and she shrugged slightly. "It's the anniversary of me mating with Hunter. And...it's a thank you for convincing me to make the right choice. Without you, I wouldn't have the most wonderful mate and husband in the world."

Tears threatened, misting her eyes, and Sasha pulled Lily into a single armed hug. She kissed the top of the witch's head. "You never need to thank me for that. You are fated mates. It would have happened one way or another."

Lily wiggled out of her embrace and scrunched her nose. "First of all, I will always and continue to thank you because you are also the best sister-in-law ever. And secondly...you really need a shower."

Sasha laughed and waved Lily off. "Silly witch, where do you think I was going?" She shook the basket slightly. "And now, thanks to you, I get to pamper myself."

Lily snorted and turned on her heel, heading back to the stairs. "See you after? We are overdue for some girl time."

Sasha forced a smile and nodded. "Yes, we are really overdue."

Sasha prowled the walk-in closet of her childhood room, still filled with leftover clothes and shoes from her past. Things she didn't feel the need to take with her to her small studio apartment. Plus, she was around the main house weekly, spending enough time to have some belongings still here. Never knew what could happen.

Supernatural politics and all.

She wrapped the towel tighter around her as it tried to slip from her grasp. Normally, she wouldn't care, but with so many mated wolves and witches in the house, she decided modesty was key.

Grabbing a pink crop top with a stitched butterfly on it, Sasha rolled her eyes and threw it over her head and onto the floor. Damn, some of this stuff was from her teenage years. A snort erupted as she nudged a pair of clear platform sandals. Definitely from her teenage years... There had to be something somewhere in this closet that fit her current look and the reputation she had built.

Simple, yet still badass.

A flash of black and white caught her eye, and she lunged, pulling a pair of plain black leggings out of a pile, along with a tattered and holey white t-shirt. Letting the towel fall, she shrugged on the t-shirt and wiggled her way into the leggings. Turning toward the full-length mirror, she eyed the t-shirt critically before surpassing it wasn't see-through. No free nipple show. Sasha didn't have big tits to begin with, and she rarely wore a bra or underwear, for that matter. But just because she chose to go sans underwear and bra didn't mean she wanted everyone to get a look.

Sneaking into the laundry room, she snatched a pair of her brother's clean socks before heading downstairs. She sat on the bottom step and pulled them on before tiptoeing over to her coat and boots by the door. She even got one boot on before her senses tingled, letting her know someone was watching her.

With a sigh, she dropped her other boot and kicked off the one she had got on before turning around.

Hunter stared at her, arms crossed with a scowl on his face. "Really?"

"Can't blame a girl for trying," Sasha mumbled.

"Can and will. But right now, I need you in the living room."

He turned and walked away, expecting Sasha to follow him obediently. With a growl, she glanced back at the door. She should take the fuck off right now, ride her bike back without her boots and jacket. That would show her brother...

Except she really liked her boots and jacket.

And it would show him how pig-headed she was in her current state.

Grumbling under her breath, she followed him to the living room and sat down with a huff. Hunter and Gwen were the only ones seated, while Blane, the second of the pack, looked over a map on the bar top out of the way.

Sasha arched an eyebrow at her brother. She didn't say anything, though. He wanted her here, so she was here. She wasn't going to start up the conversation too.

Hunter clenched his jaw, and Sasha met his gaze with a smirk. They could do this all day, and Sasha always won. But apparently, whatever her brother wanted to speak to her about was more important than their battle-of-wills game they always played, because he broke the silence within thirty seconds.

"Not sure if you heard before running off, but Romeo knew someone in prison who could give us information about vampires."

"I heard," Sasha purred.

"We decided to send Blane out to speak to him, which means—"

"That I need to step in and do his duties while he is gone, like always." She turned her attention to Gwen. "Why aren't you going? This is obviously a witchy thing."

"Unfortunately, I have back-to-back meetings and a gala I have to attend this week. And *we* have decided it is more important to act quickly."

"And what about Romeo? He knows the guy."

"Would you want to go back to a place you have been imprisoned for half your life?" Hunter growled.

Sasha blinked slowly, leveling her eyes on him. "I seem to do it more often than not these days. Can't see why another person couldn't do the same."

"That is enough! This attitude has got to—"

"Attitude! Attitude! I'll show you a fucking attitude," Sasha yelled and stood up. So much for not fighting in front of people. "You know what, I'm out. I've had enough of this... this... this fucking bullshit. Enough of you, and the pack, and this fucking place!"

Hunter leaped from his chair, and Sasha met his stride, getting up in each other's faces. "Promises, promises, Sasha. Yet here you still are. Leave. You will come back in a week like always. Tail tucked between your legs and act like nothing happened. You need to—"

"To what?" Sasha hissed. "Forget what happened in this place all those years ago. Mind my manners like a good little wolf."

"Maybe it's time to let go," he growled back.

She inhaled sharply and raised her hand, preparing to strike her brother across the face. She didn't care if it was technically assaulting an alpha, which always led to a formal challenge of the pack. Insult her, yes, but to insinuate she had grieved enough. To forget. That was crossing the line.

A vise gripped her wrist, stopping her, and Sasha glanced over her shoulder. Blane held her back. Sasha knew she could take him on. She could take them both on in the mood she was in. And she was willing to do so. Who the fuck cared about pack politics? She would kick the Alpha's and his second's ass, then never be seen again.

"Sasha should go." Gwen's cool and calculating voice broke through the impending violence, stifling the room. She stood up and smoothed down her dress pants before picking up her stylish suit jacket from the back of the chair. Stepping forward, she met Sasha's pissed off glare. "You should go meet the monster in the prison."

Blane slowly loosened his grip, and Sasha let her hand drop.

"We discussed this. Blane is going," Hunter growled.

Gwen rolled her eyes, and Sasha almost wanted to reach out and hug the cold, confident woman before her. "You didn't even give us the option of suggesting your sister. You immediately ruled her out because, and I quote, 'I don't think she is stable enough.'"

"Gwen," Hunter growled in warning, but Sasha took a step back already, heading toward the map Blane had been examining. A couple of mysterious looking spots were circled in the middle of the woods. It was a map for three states over, and Sasha quickly folded it up.

"I like this plan. I'll head out now. Thanks for the vote of confidence, Gwen."

"Sasha."

Sasha ignored her brother and stalked across the room, heading toward the main doors.

"Sasha!"

Only when his voice cracked slightly did she stop. But she didn't glance back.

"Just don't do anything stupid, okay? You're still my sister, and I don't know what I would do without you being a pain in my ass."

She took a deep breath and clenched her fist, crinkling the map in her hand. "You don't need to worry about me. I'll come back. Just like you said, I always do."

Chapter Three

RHEKR

SCREAMING. PAIN. DARKNESS. SO much darkness.

Rhekr groaned softly and opened his eyes. The familiar sound of heavy breathing, gruff whispers, and tapping against cell doors was blissful music to his ears compared to his nightmares.

Which was why he didn't sleep much. Not like he had to, but still, after some time, it was nice to just close your eyes and drift away. His internal clock told him it was early morning and Rhekr frowned. Normally, he could shut his eyes and days would pass by, even months, but his instincts told him it had only been mere hours. A blink of an eye to his kind.

He laughed softly.

His kind...

Who was he kidding? There was no one left in the world who was like him.

Immortal.

Blood sucker.

Spawn of the devil.

Take your choice in what you wanted to call him, though his favorite was vampire. Because that was what he was. One of the original blood-sucking beasts. Developed through magic to do one thing.

Protect the witches and destroy everything in their path. Especially the lycanthropes.

That was all his kind were made to do, and in the beginning, that was exactly what his ancestors did. Rage bloody, endless killing sprees until they developed beyond the witch's control. Just how the lycanthropes did as well.

A prickle against his senses had Rhekr cocking his head. A low, steady pulse of magic flowed through his veins. Begging for release, begging for something he couldn't quite put his finger on.

Shifting from his magical cell, a cell none of the prisoners and guards knew anything about, Rhekr pulled at his internal magic and cloaked himself in shadows.

He followed the pull toward a little square hole carved into the prison walls. He himself was not a prisoner like everyone else here, instead making this place his solitude. Away from the fast-moving world and those who would love to get their hands on a specimen such as him.

The guards knew he existed and left him alone, mostly because he kept the prisoners in line for the most part.

He moved a shadow toward the hole and grabbed the small piece of paper left behind.

Rhekr almost laughed when he read the note.

Southern Moon Pack. We seek your possible expertise in a matter about your kind. Meet me topside. I won't wait long.

xoxo

It wasn't exactly begging, more demanding than anything, but it was the little XOs at the end that had almost made him chuckle. Made him want to come topside to see who the hell would demand his presence, then sign off with hugs and kisses?

He brought the note to his nose, inhaling the convoluted scents. The most prominent was the upstairs office. So obviously whoever sent this note hadn't come prepared. Which was also interesting.

Of the handful of people who knew Rhekr's location through rumors and old family lines, he would have expected them to pen and mail a formal letter. Letters he usually ignored, though sometimes wrote back if he was feeling generous in his information.

But this one... He knew only one person that could be acquainted with the Southern Moon Pack.

A new—or at least in his eyes—lycanthrope pack that only spanned a few generations.

Only this paper did not smell of the young wolf who he had befriended over the years. A killer the courts had titled him, but Rhekr knew the truth when he tasted his blood. A killer the young wolf was not. No, he was a protector and one of the good ones. Which was the only reason he became close to the wolf. Romeo, he had called himself.

But this note was not from Romeo.

It was, though...

He sniffed the note again, a muted scent caressing his tongue and senses.

It tasted of longing and pain, and darkness. This scent reminded him of his nightmares and that intrigued him to no end.

It was also a woman, and she was quite powerful.

With a grin, Rhekr quickly placed the note in his pocket and made his way back to his hidden cell. He would answer this wolf's call tonight.

If she was still waiting for him, of course.

Chapter Four

SASHA

SASHA LEANED AGAINST HER Jeep, a frown pulling at her lips as she glanced down at her watch for the umpteenth time. Looking up to the sky, open blue without a cloud in sight, the warmth of the sun encapsulated her. With a growl, she pushed away from the Jeep and ran her hands through her long, curly hair.

She hated waiting.

She wanted answers now, but the front desk wouldn't let her into the prison. Apparently, this wasn't even a prison. Just a building in the woods, heavily guarded with underground facilities.

It was a load of bullshit.

This place was a heavily guarded secret and most of the prisoners were here for life. As a matter of fact, in the email Gwen had sent her yesterday when she was still sniffing out the exact location of this place, Romeo was one of the first to be released in over twenty years. And he didn't even know the exact location. That was why it took her so long to find this place. And the old grumpy guard at the front desk couldn't even confirm or deny if her note would actually make it to its designated party.

Sasha glared at her Jeep with a sigh. She missed her Ducati, but it was the sensible thing to do, bringing the Jeep. She hadn't wanted to waste her money at run down motels just for a few hours of shuteye, plus she didn't know exactly what terrain she would encounter hunting for this prison.

Growling, she kicked at the tire.

What she really wanted to do was drive straight through to Louisiana. She would have been halfway there by now. It was the plan she had come up with in the shower at the estate. She hadn't seen Nancy in such a long time, and it rubbed Sasha the wrong way when Nancy didn't call her immediately. Running her hands down her face, she huffed, leaning heavily against the Jeep door. Had she really let one of her few real friendships slide?

Sasha was overdue for a change of scenery, and she needed to repair her friendship with Nancy. If she got to fight mysterious monsters also, that was just a plus.

Yet, here she was, waiting. Waiting for the mysterious stranger who lived in a prison to ask him how to kill these newbie monsters.

Sasha scoffed.

It was probably something simple, like ripping off their heads or setting them on fire. Yet Sasha had never seen Nancy so rattled before, so worn down. Plus, she said they were fast. Too fast for her pack to defend themselves against.

Sasha growled again and looked at her watch. It was already mid-day. She had delivered the note this morning.

What was taking this monster so long to show itself?

"Fuck! I'm so stupid," she whispered to herself.

Of course, sunlight. The monster probably couldn't go out in broad daylight. Nancy had said the newbie vampires couldn't handle the sun. Which means this monster probably couldn't either.

Fine then, if she had to wait for nightfall, then she was going to go for a run. She stripped quickly, throwing her clothes into the driver's side seat, and let the magic deep inside eat her alive. Or at least that was what it always felt like to her. One second, she was surrounded by hazy mist, nipping and scratching at her skin, and the next, she was on four legs, shaking out her honey brown fur. She stretched, digging her claws into the forested floor before sprinting into the tree line.

Shadows played across the trees, dusk in its final descent before nightfall as Sasha made her way back to her Jeep. Her nose picked up another scent briefly as she skirted around to the driver's side door, but when she glanced around, all she saw was shadows and forest. Her senses prickled. She knew something was watching her, but Sasha wasn't afraid. She rarely was. If there was something out there that could take her on, she would relish the fight.

Staring at a suspicious gathering of shadows near a large tree, Sasha waited a moment before letting her human side emerge.

A fleeting thought crossed her mind a little too late. If the monster knew anything about lycanthropes, then they knew this was the time she was most vulnerable. Between the seconds of change.

As she fully straightened and glared at the shadows again, a shiver ran down her spine. They had moved slightly, and her instincts screamed at her to attack. She instead put her hands on her hips and lifted her chin.

"Do you like what you see?"

A soft chuckle emanated from the shadows before they disappeared, revealing a tall man. Sasha quickly took in his features from his old-world face and raven hair that fell to his shoulders. He sported a worn leather jacket, something Sasha swore she had seen in cop shows from the early 90s, along with a black shirt and equally worn-in jeans. She glanced down at his scuffed boots before making eye contact. His green eyes matched the surrounding forest and held her paralyzed for a second before he blinked and smirked.

To his credit, he didn't let his eyes drift, instead holding her gaze with his.

When he didn't answer, Sasha huffed and shrugged her shoulders before opening the door to her Jeep. She slipped on her equally worn-in jeans, along with her sleeveless gray shirt. She didn't bother with her shoes and shut the door with much more force than necessary.

The man stood eerily still, waiting it seemed for her to speak, but Sasha could wait too, and she did, leaning against the Jeep with her arms crossed. Finally, the man chuckled and pulled a folded piece of paper from inside his jacket pocket. He held it up between two fingers, and when he spoke, a shiver rolled down Sasha's spine.

"You requested my presence, little she-wolf?"

His voice was rough and soft and at the same time, felt otherworldly, and Sasha knew for a fact that this being was old. Much older than one lifetime. Also, his voice made her horny as hell.

She hadn't been thinking of seducing the monster or whatever this man was before now, but damn... now she wanted to try.

With a hooded gaze, she let a rough purr infect her voice before prowling forward slightly. "Mmmm... maybe I did, maybe I didn't."

His gaze turned heated, but the man still didn't take his eyes off her face. "Little she-wolf, I know it was you who penned this note. Your scent is all over it."

Sasha closed in until about a foot stood between them and licked her lips. "And what do I smell like? Something decadent and irresistible?"

The man grinned slightly before leaning in and whispering, "You smell like my nightmares. Pain and darkness. Now tell me, what do you want?"

Sasha stumbled back slightly, all pretense of seduction over with. This man, this monster, could smell the turmoil within her soul, and that was just not something she was ever willing to explore. She would rather ignore it and drown herself in booze and one-night stands.

That was the healthy thing she wanted to do.

She hardened her demeanor and glanced back into the man's face. "Fine then. Let's cut to the chase. Vampires are in Louisiana. How do we kill them?"

Sasha drew some satisfaction as the man before her blinked twice, his jaw tightening slightly. Seemed she struck some sort of nerve.

"Impossible. I am the last of my kind."

Ahh, so Romeo had been right. This monster was a vampire.

She chuckled. "Sure. Maybe you were, but you are not anymore. How do you die? Decapitation? Fire? Sunlight? Bathing in holy water? Walk into an Italian restaurant?"

The man narrowed his eyes slightly and finally gave Sasha a once-over. When his gaze came back to her face, his jaw was tighter than ever. So tight Sasha swore she could hear his teeth grinding.

"We are hard to catch. Harder still the longer we live. But if you can catch us, then decapitation during the day, and burning us to ash works. Then you must sprinkle our ashes into a fast-moving river within twenty-four hours or else we resurrect."

Sasha sucked in a harsh breath before shaking her head. "You just— You are just giving me the information, just like that? Aren't you worried I'll use it to kill you?"

This time, the vampire before her smiled broadly, his fangs shining in the moonlight. "Sweet little she-wolf. You may be strong." He paused and took a long inhale. "Very fucking strong. But I am old. And far stronger than you."

Sasha growled as his words hit a nerve. "Fucking prove it."

She barely finished her sentence when all the breath left her body, her ass hitting her driver's side seat all within a second. "Fuck," she squeaked, lust and violence filtering through her veins, along with a hint of something she hadn't felt in a long time.

Fear.

She was slightly scared of the man in front of her. The vampire had moved so fast he managed to open her Jeep door and deposited her in the driver's seat before she even had time to blink. His chest still pressed against hers, hands at her hips. She was so fucking turned on she could scent her own arousal.

No doubt he could, too. But he held her gaze and Sasha nodded slightly. "Okay, then. So, you're faster than me. Doesn't mean shit."

Chapter Five

RHEKR

WHAT THE HELL WAS he doing?

Rhekr took a step back and tried to ignore how aroused the little she-wolf smelled. Fuck, he was glad he could mask his scent and she couldn't smell the same on him.

Speaking of which, the little she-wolf raised her eyebrow. "Interesting. You don't have a scent. I mean, I can smell the clothes you are wearing, but everything else... Your emotions, I can't smell them."

Her caramel-brown eyes brightened, and she licked her lips. "That's why the wolves have been getting jumped. We are relying on scent when we should be using our eyes... and ears."

He grinned slightly, letting her believe he didn't have a scent. "Smart little she-wolf. But..."

"But what?"

Rhekr had to steel his spine against her breathless words. He couldn't remember the last time someone elicited such a response from him. He wanted this little she-wolf more than he liked to admit. Being as old as he was, he was subject to ennui quite often. Yet there was something he couldn't put his finger on, something about this little she-wolf that invigorated his mind. Something that snapped him out of his dull existence. She had caught his full attention, and he wanted more.

"But *what*?" she asked again, this time with an annoyed growl.

"But they can't be vampires. Like I said, I'm the last."

"Are you calling me a liar?"

His grin dropped, face becoming serious once more. "Never, little she-wolf. I would never insinuate such a thing. Just that someone must have lied to you."

His hearing picked up the little wolf's heart rate beating erratically, and anger permeated the air. "Fine," she growled. "Then come to Louisiana with me and tell me that there are no vampires there."

Rhekr cocked his head, glancing at the vehicle before him. He had never ridden in one before, having locked himself away in the cave system turned supernatural prison long before vehicles were a thing. Sure, he had access to the internet, and information at his fingertips, but actually experiencing a vehicle outside of the prison?

He trailed a finger across the side of the vehicle.

"Unless you're too much of a coward to leave." The little she-wolf mocked him, as he took too long to answer her question.

"That," he murmured, "is something I have never been nor have been accused of until the words left your pretty little mouth."

The little she-wolf snorted, but Rhekr didn't miss how a slight blush dusted her golden skin. Darkness had descended fully, but thanks to the light from inside the wolf's vehicle, they could still see each other clear as day.

"Well, are you coming or not?"

Of course he was. He was bored, and she was his much-needed relief. But he wasn't going to tell her that. He moved to the passenger side door and gently tugged on the handle. When the door opened without complaint, he slid into the seat. The little she-wolf stayed silent, watching as his fingers traced the entirety of the vehicle he could reach. When her eyes snapped back to his face, he met her gaze.

"You are acting like you've never been in a Jeep before."

Rhekr shrugged. "Motor vehicles weren't invented when I went underground. And when I woke from my sleep, my cave system had turned into a prison. Even when I leave briefly, motor vehicles aren't really on my radar. Not when I can move faster than them."

The little she-wolf swore, making him grin. He did love a strong woman who swore like a sailor.

"Well... I guess welcome to my Jeep, old-ass vampire. Buckle up. I don't want a ticket."

Rhekr raised an eyebrow. "Buckle up?"

The little she-wolf sighed and leaned over him, pulling something across his chest and snapping it in place.

That was right. Seat belts. He remembered reading about them in news stories and in the motor vehicle manuals he perused in the prison library back in the day. The little she-wolf shut her door with a force he didn't think the poor Jeep warranted, but he didn't say anything. Instead, he watched as she put her own seat belt on. The motor vehicle manuals flipped through his mind at lightning speed as she cranked the keys and the engine turned over. Its rumble filled the silence, and the little she-wolf turned a nob. Light reflected the entire forest around him, and she grinned at him. "Try not to get too overwhelmed by all this new technology, ol' man. I promise I'm the only thing that bites in the Jeep."

Rhekr chuckled and brushed his hand through his hair. "Oh, I highly doubt that, little one."

The little she-wolf wrinkled her nose slightly before looking out the windshield. They moved slowly at first, creeping through the forest. The beams of light reflecting through the trees. "It's Sasha, by the way."

"Rhekr," he responded before silence invaded once more.

It only lasted a few moments before the little she-wolf fiddled with her phone and the middle console of the Jeep lit up. "What type of music do you like, ol' man? And before you say classical, that is where I draw the line."

Rhekr snorted. "I once had the pleasure of going to an 80s festival. I was fond of the music."

She raised a brow at him just as her lights illuminated the blacktop and she took a sharp turn to the right. "1980s, right? Not some weird 1880s rave shit, right?"

"I've lived through many 80s, but yes, I was referring to the 1980s."

"Perfect. 80s hits, it is."

The little she-wolf smirked and hit the gas, jerking him back in his seat as a band called Metallica assaulted his eardrums.

Chapter Six

SASHA

SASHA TRIED TO STIFLE her yawn, but failed as she pulled into their second gas station for the night. Technically, she still had a half tank left, but her eyes were grainy as hell, plus dawn would be touching the horizon soon. As she pulled into a spot up front, she turned down her top-100 rap songs and couldn't help but smirk as the look of relief passed over Rhekr's face.

It was amazing how quickly you could pick up on facial expressions after being in a car with someone for five-plus hours. Rhekr absolutely hated what she was playing now, but she somewhat enjoyed the scrunch that happened between his brows when he was annoyed. His haunting dark green eyes caught hers, and Sasha realized she had been staring for too long in silence.

"We should stop for the night soon." They both spoke over each other and Rhekr shook his head.

"You first, little she-wolf."

Sasha yawned again. "We should stop for the night soon. We can grab a motel room so you don't explode in the sun."

He gave her a perplexed look. "Is that what these supposed vampires are doing in Louisiana?"

Sasha answered him with a yawn and a thumbs up. She made to get out of her Jeep, but paused as Rhekr placed his hand on her shoulder. "Little she-wolf, you need sleep. The sun does not bother me, and I do not need rest like other creatures do."

"Alright, then I'll get a motel for me to sleep in for a few hours then," she growled.

Rhekr leveled a stare at her. "Let me drive."

Sasha laughed and wiped her over-tired eyes. "You? You drive? Mister vampire, whose first time in a motor vehicle was five hours ago?"

To his credit, Rhekr's face only softened as Sasha laughed at him. "My sweet little she-wolf, I am a fast learner. And driving does not look that hard."

Sasha paused, thinking it over. She really wanted to get to Louisiana and Nancy as fast as she could. Plus, she really didn't want to pay for a motel when she already had a setup in the back of her Jeep for sleeping. "It is Texas. And mostly straight aways. But we still have the problem of you not having a driver's license. I don't want to deal with cops."

Rhekr smiled slyly and reached into his jacket, producing a license. Sasha snatched it up quickly and gave it a once-over. "This is an amazing fake."

He shrugged and took the license back from her. "Thank you. I made it a few years ago on a whim. But your kind words just made this old vampire's day. Now let me drive while you rest."

"Fine," she snapped and pulled her half-open door shut again. She crawled into the back, and the already setup blanket nest from her last two days sleeping in the back seat. "Just don't crash my damn Jeep. I'll fucking haunt you if I die."

"It would be a pleasure if you would haunt me, little she-wolf."

Sasha growled softly.

Damn vampire was annoying with his kind words, but she was sure, soon enough, she would push him too far with her abrasiveness. With a smile, she snuggled down into the blankets. She was looking forward to that day, but for now, she just prayed she wouldn't wake up from her nap upside down in a ditch somewhere.

Screaming.

She was screaming as pain lanced through her entire body, filling her with white-hot flames. Death beckoned her, but arms held her tight, constricting what little breath she had in her lungs still. Restraining her, keeping her grounded as her future died in front of her.

Sasha snapped her eyes open, trying to move, to run as her past collided with her present, but this time, the pressure around her arms and chest stayed. She fought against them, growling and howling like a hellhound.

After what felt like an eternity, Sasha's consciousness finally came to the forefront and she could understand the soft whispers in her ear, that the arms surrounding her were not trying to kill her but embracing her. A sob choked her as deep green eyes met with hers. But the pain was still there, a wound constantly festering in her heart, and she did the only thing that she could to feed her demons.

Rhekr didn't miss a beat as her lips collided with his, instead changing his grip around her arms to her hair. She wrapped her legs around his waist and growled in his mouth as his weight settled in over her. Back arching, she ripped at the button and zipper of his jeans until she shoved a hand down his pants. They both groaned as her hand wrapped around his cock, already so fucking hard, and Sasha grunted in approval that the vampire was fucking packing below the belt.

She stroked his thick cock as he shoved away from her and pulled down her pants. Sasha unwound her legs and managed to kick off one pant leg before he was over her again, his mouth already on hers. The head of his cock pressed against her entrance, and she screamed as he pushed into her in one long stroke. He knew exactly what she needed. Pain laced with pleasure as she dug her nails into his shoulders. He moved, holding one of her hips down as he pulled out almost fully and slammed back into her.

Sasha screamed again, ripping at the back of his shirt as her eyes rolled back from the pounding he was giving her. His hand wrapped around her neck, applying the perfect amount of pressure, and she moved her hands to grip around his wrist and forearm. Her screams turned to whimpers, and she bit her bottom lip.

Rhekr growled, "Open your eyes, Sasha. Fucking look at me."

She did, surprising herself at how fast she obeyed the order. No one ever ordered her around in bed before, though no one was ever able to fuck her how hard this vampire was, and she was already feeling her orgasm building. She locked her gaze with Rhekr's as he snarled, his features taking on that of a fucking warrior in battle. It just turned her on even more, and she felt her orgasm crest and release. Her breathless scream was lost in the sound of flesh pounding against each other. Two strokes later, she felt Rhekr find his own release. His growl sent shivers down her spine, and to Sasha's surprise, instead of falling over her, he pulled her forward with the hand around her neck. She ended up in his lap, her head resting in the crook of his neck as he threaded one hand through her hair, holding her there. He trailed his other hand down her spine, and she instantly melted in his arms, closing her eyes as their heavy breathing filled the back of her Jeep.

"That's it, my sweet little she-wolf. Don't think about the past. Think of what I just did to that delicious fucking pussy of yours. Let your demons take comfort in what we just did."

Sasha wrapped her arms tighter around his shoulders and sank into his words. She concentrated on the way his semi-hard cock felt inside of her. She sank into the feeling of his hands on her and the way his chest moved against hers. After a few minutes, she finally released her hold on him and moved away. She pushed her hair out of her eyes and avoided eye contact as she pulled her pants back on. Without a word, she crawled back up to the front seat of her Jeep, and turned the engine back over. She avoided glancing in the rearview mirror, not trusting that if she met Rhekr's haunting green eyes that she wouldn't immediately break down. The festering wound in her heart dulled slightly, her demons satisfied for now as she pulled out from the dirt turnout Rhekr had pulled into and hit the gas hard. She really needed to get to

Louisiana as soon as possible. It had been a mistake what just happened, and it could never happen again. It had felt way too good and in more than a physical way. No, she needed to get her damn demons under control and to get away from the vampire in her back seat.

Chapter Seven

SASHA

THE INSIDE OF HER thighs burned, her pussy aching in the most delicious way, and Sasha sighed. Her thoughts had been spinning for the last two hours. She gripped the steering wheel tight and continued to focus on the way her headlights illuminated the road in front of them. The scent from their frantic and intense fucking still permeated the Jeep, her inner thighs sticky from both their releases. She shifted slightly. Most people cleaned up right after sex, her included, less she felt like she was betraying the festering wound in her heart. It just felt way too intimate in her mind. She bit her lower lip and tried not to think about the way Rhekr had taken her, how it felt, and how she didn't want it again.

Nope, definitely didn't want the handsome vampire to pound her into a blissful orgasm again.

No, what she needed to do was find a motel or truck stop where she could shower and remove his scent from her.

Scent...

"What the fuck?" she growled and glanced over to Rhekr, who was tapping his finger slowly against the door upholstery.

He had gotten into the passenger seat fifteen minutes after she broke their embrace and ran away like a fucking pup, unwilling to face what had happened. To his credit, he never uttered a word, only spared her a sharp, assessing glance before buckling in and staring out his window, giving her the room and silence she desperately needed.

"What is it, little she-wolf?"

"What, what do you mean, what? I can fucking smell you, but I couldn't in the woods earlier. What gives?"

His shoulder tightened slightly. "I can mask my scent."

"Like... with magic?"

Rhekr stopped tapping his finger. "Yes and no. There are certain traits that are just part of being a vampire. Masking our scent and manipulating shadows are two of those things."

Sasha ground her teeth. "Why didn't you tell me?"

"You didn't ask."

"And I'm supposed to just know what to ask and what not to?"

Rhekr smiled softly. "I'll answer any question you ask, when you learn what questions to ask."

Sasha sputtered, "What type of bullshit answer was that?"

"Speaking of questions and talking. Did you want to?"

"Want to what?"

"Talk about what happened in the back of the Jeep?"

This time Sasha's shoulders tightened. "It was sex. It was good. We are both consenting adults. There is nothing to talk about."

Rhekr tsked. "The sex wasn't what I was asking about."

Sasha felt the pit of her stomach fall, nausea building. "That topic is off limits."

Silence filled the cab of her Jeep, and Rhekr turned to stare out his window again. The steady tap of his finger against her upholstery restarted.

"I know of demons, little she-wolf. The need to drown them in empty sex, drinking, violence, drugs... anything to make the pain go away."

Sasha swallowed thickly, tears stinging her eyes. She gripped the steering wheel tighter. "Does it ever stop?"

Her whisper felt more like a plea, hanging heavy in the air.

Rhekr shook his head. "The pain... it never leaves. But it does fade along with your demons when you find something out there that is worthy of your heart, of your time, of your light."

Her brow furrowed slightly. "What does that even mean?"

"It means, little she-wolf, that we nurture our demons with our pain and anger. Just like we nurture things or people with love, compassion, and understanding. Stop feeding your demons your pain and anger. It won't diminish the memory of the one you mourn."

Sasha's lips parted, ready to snap at him before shutting her mouth. She honestly didn't have any words. And it pissed her off to no end. She wanted to hit something, to cry and scream, but in the end, it would do just what Rhekr said.

Feed her demons. Grow them into something she couldn't control. Not like she could really control them now.

She let out a sharp breath. "I... I got into a fight with my brother before leaving to meet up with you. He told me it was time to let go."

Rhekr snorted. "Your brother sounds like someone who hasn't lost a piece of his soul."

"No," Sasha whispered. "No, he hasn't."

Minutes passed by, and Sasha's thoughts swirled like a tornado in her mind. Did she actually want to talk about the day her future died, when she stopped living and life lost all meaning, with the vampire sitting next to her?

A vampire who seemed to comprehend her pain and not just guess.

She opened her mouth once more, ready to spill her secrets, just as her phone started buzzing. With an aggravated sigh, she answered the call and put it on speakerphone.

"Sasha, what the fuck are you doing in Louisiana?" Her brother's disapproving voice filtered into the Jeep.

She rolled her eyes. "And just how do you know I'm Louisiana? Bug my Jeep? My phone? Or was it a boot?"

"Let's call it 'I feel my sister lose her shit over our psychic twin mind waves, then she ignores my texts, and I have to find a witch to do a locator spell.' And the prison isn't in Louisiana. Did you even fucking go there?"

Sasha winced.

Of course.

Of course, her brother would have felt her little breakdown earlier. He always knew when her demons took over like they had hours earlier.

She should have looked at her phone when the first text message ping sounded, but she had been too wrapped up inside her own pity party to think.

"Sorry, baby bro. I should have messaged you back. Everything is fine. I'm fine."

Sasha didn't miss the side-eye Rhekr gave her, and she rolled her eyes at him.

The other end of the line stayed silent so long that Sasha looked down to see if they were still connected before glancing back at Rhekr and shrugging.

She mouthed silently, "Do you want him to know you are here?"

He shrugged and crossed his arms, giving her a shit-eating grin.

Fucking ass. She sighed and broke the silence.

"To answer your question, yes, I went to the prison and met with the monster."

Rhekr raised an eyebrow and mouthed, "Monster?"

"Well, we didn't know who or what you were?"

"Sasha... is the monster there with you?" Her brother's voice held a hint of concern over the phone.

"Shit! I said that out loud," Sasha yelled, while Rhekr placed a hand over his face. His shoulders started shaking, and Sasha reached over to slap his thigh.

"Stop laughing at me, ol' man."

"You're the one who outed me, little she-wolf. Horrible secret keeper."

"Hey..." Hunter barked through the phone, trying to get their attention, but Sasha ignored him.

"Excuse me! You're one to talk. You spilled your secret vampire ways to me immediately," she retorted.

"That's because you are pretty, and I wanted to tell you." Rhekr laughed.

"Hello?"

"Pretty? Not devastatingly beautiful? Goddess incarnate? You did see me naked at first meet. Not that it seemed you noticed."

"Oh, I noticed, little she-wolf," Rhekr growled.

"Hello! Still on the fucking phone! I don't need to hear this shit about my sister naked."

"Then hang up!" Both Sasha and Rhekr barked at the same time.

Sasha suddenly giggled and shook her head, reaching back down for her phone, and saw her brother was still on the line. "Wow, look who stayed. Oddly perverted."

"Sasha," Hunter sighed, and she could just imagine him pinching the bridge of his nose. "Sasha, I don't have time for this. Just tell me what the fuck is going on."

"Fine, fine. I'll spare you the agony of dealing with me and actually talk to you."

"Thanksssss." His sarcasm wasn't missed by her or Rhekr, who glared at her phone.

"So I met with the monster, who is really a vampire, and his name is Rhekr. Then he told me how to kill vampires, but didn't believe me when I said vampires were killing off lycanthropes in Louisiana. So I said I was going and called him a coward when he didn't want to go, and here we are."

"That is a horrible recap, little she-wolf. You didn't give me enough time to answer when you asked if I wanted to go, then threw a tantrum."

"I did not throw a tantrum. I can show you a tantrum," Sasha hissed.

"Alright! Alright! Fucking hell," Hunter grumbled through the phone. "Just don't do anything stupid and let me know when you get to Nancy's. I assume that's where you are going?"

"Where else would I be going?" Sasha barked and gripped her wheel tight enough that it squeaked under the pressure. He was starting to give her orders again, and she wasn't really in the mood for it.

"I'll take that as a yes. We will need to set up a call with the two packs and the coven here to exchange information. Then talk about what you and Rhekr will do in—"

Sasha hung up on him mid-sentence and threw her phone as far back in the Jeep as she could. Rhekr raised an eyebrow as her phone started going off again, and Sasha shrugged. "I don't like taking orders."

He snorted and shook his head as Sasha turned the dial on her radio and found a channel that wasn't all static to drown out the annoying buzzing of her phone.

Chapter Eight

RHEKR

WIND RUSTLED THROUGH THE Cyprus treetops as his little she-wolf drove the Jeep down the blacktop turned dirt road. Rhekr rolled down the window and tilted his head back, eyes slitted against the sunlight even though he wore sunglasses. Sasha had thrown them his way, buying a matching set for herself at the last truck stop they encountered. They were also able to snag a shower there. Which they both desperately needed, even if Rhekr didn't like that Sasha no longer wore his scent.

It was fine. He would rectify that little problem later.

They continued down the dirt road, getting narrower by the minute, until he had to roll up his window, less he got a tree branch to the face.

His little she-wolf grinned at him, and he returned the smile. She was positively glowing, a type of feral radiance beaming off of her. He was also sure if he actually said those words to her that she would tease him mercilessly.

Rhekr straightened in his seat as they finally pulled into a turnout on the dirt road. It was littered with beat-up trucks, cars, and motorbikes. Sasha pulled in next to something he was pretty sure resembled more rust than a car and turned off the engine.

"It's on foot from here, ol' man. You think you can keep up?"

Rhekr grinned. "You're cute when you try to flirt. You know that?"

She sputtered slightly and threw her sunglasses on the dash. "Flirting? You... You think that was flirting?"

His little she-wolf batted her eyes suddenly, and her whole demeanor changed, a seductress shining through as she licked her lips. Her voice grew husky, and she trailed her nails down his arm. "You wouldn't be able to resist me when I actually decide to flirt with you."

He leaned in slightly, and she copied his movement, their lips almost touching. She was good. Really fucking good, but he liked teasing her more. Liked bringing out her feral side. "Oh really," he growled. "Watch me, little she-wolf."

Using his vampire speed, he was out of the Jeep within seconds and already walking down the trodden path. He chuckled slightly as Sasha realized what had just happened. Her curses were sweet music to his ears, and it took every ounce of willpower he had to hide his grin as she came tromping up behind him.

Magic filled the air and Rhekr wasn't surprised when he glanced over his shoulder to see a cloud of mist floating away to reveal Sasha's lycanthrope form.

Fuck, she was gorgeous. With fur the same honeyed brown as her hair and dark brown splashed across her toes. She even had a dark strip down her snout. His little she-wolf shook herself out and narrowed her caramel brown eyes at him. She lifted her head and trotted toward him. As she was about to pass, he felt a sting on his ass before his little she-wolf darted off into the swampy undergrowth.

Rhekr chuckled and shook his head, looking back at his pants. Two little holes decorated his jeans, right on his ass where his little she-wolf had bitten him.

He adjusted his sunglasses and grinned.

Yes, teasing her was much more fun. And yes, they would sleep together again, sooner rather than later, but that wasn't all Rhekr was looking for. No, he knew deep down, his little she-wolf wasn't some passing fancy. In all his years alive, he had only felt this way once before.

Shaking off his memories, less his own demons decide to try to drown him, Rhekr picked up his pace and followed the trail of footprints Sasha left in her wake.

Rhekr knew he grew close to the pack of lycanthropes even before he saw the raised wooden homes. The hairs on the back of his neck prickled, warning that something was watching him. The sentries were downwind, but he didn't need to rely on scent to tell him where the lycanthropes hid themselves. He was a much more seasoned tracker than they could ever be, given his age, and he had learned early on to use every one of his senses.

To track in all types of environments.

Rhekr grinned as he strolled right into the little lycanthrope village, his eyes only on one target. His little she-wolf, standing proud and naked in her human form, speaking in hushed whispers to another woman.

Sasha's shoulders tightened slightly as Rhekr approached, and he couldn't help the way his heart beat a little faster, the way his cock hardened slightly when she glanced over her shoulder to glare at him.

"Took you long enough," she growled.

Rhekr shrugged. "I was enjoying the scenery. I haven't been to these parts in a few centuries."

The woman beside Sasha looked him over before tentatively reaching out a hand, the bangles on her slim wrist jangling. "I take it you're the vampire expert my dear Sasha just informed me about."

Rhekr took the woman's hand in his and chuckled slightly when he lifted it to his nose. "Holy water and garlic. Did you make it as a spray or lotion?"

Sasha growled under her breath, "Don't mock her. They are just doing what they can to survive."

"I do not mock, little she-wolf. But holy water and garlic, unfortunately, is not a deterrent. At least not to real vampires. Which these cannot be."

The woman yanked her hand out of his and squared up to him. "And why not? Are vampires such a far stretch? And what are you anyway?" She sniffed deeply. "You don't smell like anything at all. Are you masking your scent? Are you a warlock of some kind?"

Rhekr side-eyed Sasha, who had moved slightly, putting her body closer to his. It was an interesting move, something most people without training wouldn't have seen. His little she-wolf was preparing to protect him in case of attack. Which was both cute and a fucking turn-on. It meant she liked him, even if she was still denying it.

He turned his focus back on the woman. "Because I am the last of my kind. And to make a new vampire, you must have the venom of an original vampire. Last time I checked, I didn't give any of mine away."

The woman's eyes shifted, going golden, and a growl erupted from deep in her chest. "Nancy," Sasha warned before stepping in front of Rhekr fully. "I told you, we can trust him to help us."

Nancy's breath shuddered slightly, but her eyes paled back to their normal deep brown, and she took a step back. "You didn't tell me what he was, Sasha."

"I told you, he can help you. Help the wolves here from getting slaughtered. Plus, I wanted to prove him wrong."

Nancy muttered under her breath before pointing toward an out-of-the-way shack in an open field. Sunlight filtered over it, showing its deteriorating state. "Fine, fine. Then tell me what the fuck we have captured in that shed over there, then." She glared at Rhekr. "And when you do, I dare you to tell me to my face it isn't a damn vampire."

The scent of excitement and violence touched his senses, and Rhekr glanced at Sasha as she started rocking on her feet. "Wait, you have one of them trapped?"

Nancy nodded to Sasha before turning on her heel, not bothering to look in his direction. His little she-wolf grabbed him by the hand and quickly pulled him along with her in a surprising manner. He managed to snag a button-down shirt that was line drying and shoved it in Sasha's direction.

"If it is indeed a vampire, as you all claim, then it will be a young one. They are more..." He paused, trying to find the right word.

"Bitey? Flesh obsessed? Hankering for the veins?"

Rhekr snorted. "I was thinking more along the lines of easily distracted and hungry."

Sasha grabbed the shirt from his hands and tossed it on. "There, look at me being modest."

He shook his head slowly and started buttoning up the shirt, pulling her closer with every small tug until their breath mingled. His little she-wolf growled softly, but she didn't move away. What Rhekr really wanted to do was forget all about this vampire nonsense and take his little she-wolf somewhere private. There were many things he wanted to do with her body, her mind and, eventually, her soul.

The clearing of a throat right next to them broke the spell, and Sasha pulled away, eyes glaring at him like daggers when they had been heavily lidded and full of lust only moments before.

"Riiight..." Nancy pushed her way between the two of them and unlocked the shed door, throwing it open.

Rhekr stepped into the dilapidated shed after her, Sasha pulling up behind him. He took in the sight quickly. There, huddled in the corner, a sickly emaciated thing, once a man, now turned something hideous and out of a horror show. It was on all fours, clothing hanging in tatters, showing all too white and taut skin. It snarled at them, its four canine fangs elongated, and saliva dripped down its blood-soaked face. It moved fast, its hand darting into the line of sunlight across the floor before slamming back into the corner, the stench of burning flesh evident in the air.

"What the fuck?" Sasha whispered from behind him, her hands clenching at the back of his shirt. He moved to the side a little so she could have a better look, but the shed was certainly too small to accommodate them all.

"See." Nancy ran a shaking hand through her hair. "Vampire."

"Indeed," Rhekr rumbled. "And it looks like whoever decided to dabble in dark magic took to horror shows in the literal sense. Whatever this thing is, it is not functional. Nor is it truly a vampire. I've never seen anything like this before."

"What if its function is killing?" Sasha asked as she sidled around to his front and picked up a stick. Or really, a broken off half of a rake. She waved it in front of the thing in the corner, and it snarled, ripping it out of her hand. It gnawed on the broken rake handle before screaming and throwing it to the side. Its bloodshot eyes hooked on Sasha's bare thighs, and it hissed.

"Ewww, creeper," Sasha whispered as Rhekr wrapped an arm around her waist. He didn't want to take any chances if that thing decided to brave the beam of sunlight.

"Come on, I've seen enough. I want to examine this thing before we kill it."

"And then what?" Sasha whispered.

"Then I go see an old acquaintance for some answers."

Chapter Nine

SASHA

SASHA GRUMBLED UNDER HER breath, poking at the ground with a long stick before throwing it to the side. "How long does it take to examine the wanna be vampire? It's been like an hour."

Nancy chuckled, sitting next to her on the porch of her house. It was raised a few feet off the ground for seasonal flooding and their feet dangled precariously close to a swampy patch of earth. Sasha swore something moved under her, and the violent side of her nature dared the creature to rise up and bite her. She really wanted to kill something. Or the alternative—fuck someone, but the only someone she really wanted to fuck was in the shed doing goddess knew what.

"Uhggg." She leaned, letting her back hit the weather warped wood. Nancy's face filled her view, and she scowled.

"That face doesn't scare me, Sasha. I've known you way too long."

Sasha rolled her eyes before closing them, letting the sun shine on her face. Nancy was one of the few who truly knew her. Knew her before her life was torn to pieces. Unfortunately, she hadn't been able to come up from Louisiana in the aftermath. But she had sent copious amounts of letters, letters Sasha still had and cherished, and when she had been able to crawl her broken soul out of bed, this was the first place she had gone all those years ago.

Fingers caressed her cheek, sweeping her wayward curls out of her face. When she opened her eyes, Nancy grinned down at her. "Your lover has emerged."

Sasha sat up quickly with a frown, her eyes scanning over Rhekr as he emerged from the shed. "He is not my lover. I mean, we had sex, but... not my lover."

Nancy laughed. "Sasha, I know you and I know that look. I've seen it before. You care for him."

Familiar pain floated through her heart, but she shook it off quickly. No, she didn't care about Rhekr. He was a good fuck. That was all. That was all it could be. She shrugged off Nancy's hand on her shoulder and jumped off the porch, her bare feet squishing through mud and stagnant water until they reached drier land. She had changed into one of Nancy's thin strapped maxi dresses. It was breathable against the humidity, and she had it knotted up on the side to allow better movement, exposing copious amounts of her thigh.

A stray thought passed through her mind, wondering if Rhekr would find the dress pretty on her, and then Nancy laughed, as if she could read Sasha's thoughts. She lifted a finger to flip off her friend, which only made her laugh harder. She finally reached Rhekr and scowled even harder, as she took in the front of his shirt and pants, completely drenched in blood. A shiver ran down her spine as she sniffed, and she sighed slightly when she only smelled the putrid blood of the thing that was in the shed.

Rhekr stood there, his eyes snagging on her shoulders before reaching out and sliding one of the thin straps back in place. "You look absolutely feral, little she-wolf."

"Don't know if that is a compliment or not coming from the man drenched in blood."

"It was, and now that you mention it, it looks like I am. Don't worry, none of it is mine."

Sasha huffed and crossed her arms. "Why would I be worried? Did you get what you needed?"

A sly smile passed across Rhekr's lips. "Yes, little she-wolf, I got what I needed. And the thing is still alive. Just tell your friend to toss it into the sun. That should take care of it."

"Wait, but I thought we needed to like, behead it, burn it, and throw it into a river."

"That would be for someone like me. Which that thing is clearly not."

"Oh really," Sasha huffed and turned to see Nancy heading their way. "I clearly see the resemblance."

Rhekr chuckled under his breath before addressing Nancy. "Sunlight will kill the one barely breathing in the shed. Scatter its ashes to the wind. As for the others, if they come tonight, make sure to surround this place with bonfires. Fire and sunlight will kill them. Beheading and hearts ripped out will incapacitate them."

Nancy nodded. "You are going so soon? Are you not staying for the night?"

"Mmmm, I have to go see someone."

Sasha turned quickly. "Where? Who?"

Rhekr graced her with a full smile. "Just an acquaintance from my past, little she-wolf. I will be but a few days."

Sasha sputtered and glanced back at Nancy. "I guess we will be back in a few days."

"Sasha..." Rhekr shook his head. "I don't think—"

"Exactly," she growled. "Most men don't, and I'm going where you are going, got it."

Nancy snorted and glanced at the ground, but Sasha caught the grin on her face. Rhekr, on the other hand, frowned before muttering something under his breath.

"Fine, but I'm going to warn you right now. I can't help you if you piss this person off. She is more powerful than both of us combined."

Her brows creased slightly, but Sasha didn't back down. "Contrary to popular belief, I can be downright inviting and cordial when I want to be."

Nancy barked out a laugh, and Sasha punched her in the arm.

"I'm not going to argue. Come if you must."

"Fine, then it is settled. When do we leave?"

"As soon as we get a boat." He glanced down at his bloodied shirt. "And a change of clothes."

Smells of the lush bayou surrounded her, the spritz of water sprinkling on her bare arms as they moved almost soundlessly. The small, flat-bottomed boat skimmed across the water, and Sasha lay belly down, letting her fingers trail along the lazy water. She knew what she did held a hint of insanity, as the creatures who made this place home could easily take her down with one well-timed bite, but she was never one to shy away from danger. Speaking of which, she pulled her hand up and turned her attention toward the silent vampire steering his way through the bayou like an expert. He had traded with a pack member, a fancy pocket watch for a set of jeans, a faded gray tank, and the button-down shirt he had snagged off the line to give to her. He was also wearing an old baseball cap, which changed his demeanor in such a way she hardly recognized him. Rhekr looked like he belonged here, in the bayou, just a simple country boy, until he turned his eyes on her. He smiled, and her stomach flipped at the seductive look on his face. Then he was back to paying attention to their surroundings once more.

Sasha turned to glance back into the dark water and bit her lip. Fucking Nancy. She was right; she was always right. Sasha didn't know when it happened, but she cared for Rhekr. She cared for his wellbeing, and she wondered if he thought the same about her.

She grumbled under her breath as the water seemed to slow in front of her. Except it wasn't the water. Rhekr had cut the engine, letting the boat move lazily on its own.

"We are coming up to our stop for the night. Believe me when I say we don't want to pay the price of staying the night with my acquaintance. Plus, I want a good night's sleep before bargaining with her."

Sasha sat up straighter and took a look around with a critical eye. "You said it's been centuries since you've been this way. How do you know someone and where they live?"

Rhekr moved silently, using a long pole to drift the boat toward a hidden inlet near the shore. "Because she lived here long before it was settled, before this continent knew the cruel touch of a civilized hand. Vampires, witches, lycanthropes... we are just a product of another's magic. Another who will be able to tell us what is going on. She can help us, but there is always a price for such things."

Sasha clenched her jaw slightly as they hit the shore, and Rhekr jumped out, his bare feet landing silently in ankle deep water. He tied them off at a tree and extended his hand. She took it, even though she didn't need the help. All the more telling that she actually was falling deeper into the rabbit hole that was Rhekr. He helped her to solid ground before grabbing a small bag from the boat that also contained their shoes.

Remaining silent as she followed, she mulled over her own thoughts as they traipsed through the undergrowth until Rhekr stopped and she glanced up and up. A small fishing cabin on stilts, hidden within the trees, greeted them, and Sasha raised a brow. It looked old, very, very fucking old, yet it wasn't falling apart. Instead, it blended in with nature, and when they finally got to the door, Rhekr flipped up the outside latch, and magic nipped at her skin. A spell then, to keep it from falling to the elements.

Rhekr pushed open the door and stepped aside. "Ladies first."

Chapter Ten

SASHA

SASHA STEPPED INTO THE surprisingly dust-free and sparse open-concept space. A tiny area in one corner acted as the kitchen next to a small stove that had freshly chopped wood next to it. Another corner sported two twin sized beds. She glanced at a small space built into the room with a closed door—she was guessing the bathroom as she wandered over and opened the door. And she was right, as a small composting toilet along with a built-in standing shower greeted her. Shutting the door gently, she turned to find Rhekr sitting on one of the beds.

"What is this place?"

He shrugged, and the bed creaked as he lay down on his back, tucking his hands behind his head. "It's set up for those visiting Madam Marie. Showing what she is capable of. She's updated it since the last time I was here."

"Which was?"

"A couple hundred years ago."

Sasha hummed slightly, running her fingers over a small windowsill, and looked out. "So how far away are we from the lovely Madam Marie's?"

"About two hours."

Sasha spun on her heel. "Two hours! We totally could have made it. We have at least three before nightfall."

The bed creaked again as Rhekr sat up and tossed his hat down, shaking out his hair. "It's best not to deal with her at night. Her price of payment gets steeper the later in the day it gets."

"Worried she might want a threesome?" Sasha joked.

"As much as I would be open for that, it would not be with her. You can sleep with whomever you want, little she-wolf, but take my warning and do not sleep with Madam Marie."

"Have you?" she growled softly.

"Why, are you jealous, my little she-wolf?" Rhekr purred back in her direction.

Sasha turned away from him and stared out the window before whispering, "What if I am a little jealous?"

"Then maybe you should do something about it," Rhekr whispered, his presence suddenly behind her, breath hot against her neck.

She spun quickly, and their lips collided, Rhekr pushing her back against the wall. His hand gripped her hair tightly, and she moved, wrapping her legs around his waist. She ripped at his button-down, pushing it off of him, and took the lead on the kiss as he released his hold on her hair. Wrapping her hand around his jaw, she bit at his lips playfully, and Rhekr growled.

She broke the kiss as he removed his tank top, and for the first time, she saw his sculpted chest. Sasha licked her lips as her fingernails scraped over the swirling tattoos decorating his chest and shoulders. Moving lower, she grabbed the button of his jeans. She could already feel how hard he was, the outline of his cock straining against the zipper.

To her surprise, he removed her hands, and she growled, "Oh, come on. I want you to fuck me, now."

Rhekr ignored her command, kissing his way down her neck, and in a move too fast for her to follow, he was on his knees before her, throwing her legs over his shoulders. She threaded her hands through his silken dark hair as he took his time running his hands up her thighs and under the summer dress she still wore.

His lips brushed across her inner thighs, licking and sucking until she felt his warm breath tickling across her pussy. She gripped his hair, and a low moan erupted from her as he licked pussy all the way to her clit. His hands gripped her ass hard, hard enough to leave bruises as he buried his face into her. She moved her hips to the rhythm of his tongue, grinding roughly against his face. Fuck, she loved the mix of pleasure and pain, and it seemed Rhekr knew it. She felt her orgasm building, riding the crest, ready to break, when Rhekr stopped and pulled away.

Sasha gasped and tried to put his head back between her thighs. "Why did you stop, fucking fang face! I was so close."

Rhekr's laugh filled the small room, and he grabbed her hands from his hair, swinging Sasha around to land heavily on the floor. Her breath whooshed from her lungs violently as he settled his weight on her. She snarled as she struggled to take control, her nails biting into his flesh. She broke skin, and they both shuddered deeply as he ground down, the fabric of his jeans burning across her already sensitive clit. She moaned, throwing her head back. "Fuck! Please don't stop. Is that what you want me to do? I'll fucking beg. For you, I'll fucking beg."

"You can beg all you want, little she-wolf. It won't change what I plan on doing to you," Rhekr whispered as his kisses against her neck turned rough.

She moaned, arching into it. "Fine, then I won't beg, but I will make you work for it."

To demonstrate her words, she bucked her hips suddenly, rolling and intending to get the upper hand. His weight shifted and Sasha managed to lunge away before he landed once more on top of her. This time, he straddled her back, and she growled, realizing she had put herself in the worst possible position. Rhekr's laugh sounded sinister to her ears, and she struggled some more, to no avail. He grabbed the nape of her neck, holding her down, and leaned back slightly. The slap across her bare ass echoed through the room, and she panted into the floorboards. She struggled a little more, nails leaving claw marks, but she knew he could smell how turned on she was as he slapped her ass again. "I can smell your arousal, little she-wolf. Are you done fighting?"

"Never," Sasha snarled.

Rhekr groaned and leaned over. "Good."

She felt his weight shift, moving from her back to her upper thighs. Whimpering, she arched her ass into his crotch as the sound of his zipper reached her ears. It was her only warning before he thrust into her fully, filling her pussy so completely that she screamed. Her orgasm tore through her body, and Rhekr cursed.

"Fuck. Just like that, fucking strangle my cock with your sweet pussy."

Sasha whimpered again, her eyes rolling back as he ground his hips down and somehow slid in deeper. He released the nape of her neck to grip her hair, arching her head back. She howled in pleasure, raking her nails deeper into the wooden floor as he mercilessly pounded into her. A deep ache built slowly inside of her, a second orgasm incoming, and Sasha bit her lip. From this angle, Rhekr's cock was filling her up completely and rubbing her in just the right way. She whimpered again, her orgasm so close as Rhekr leaned over her, his lips on her neck, fangs and teeth pressing against the sensitive flesh.

"Please," she whispered, and Rhekr growled softly.

"Please what, my little she-wolf?"

"Sink your fangs into me," she panted as he slowed down his thrusts and ground into her.

Her flesh parted under his fangs between one breath and the next, pleasure and pain blending so seamlessly that she choked, barely able to breathe as her second orgasm rippled through her from head to toe. She screamed silently, her body shuddering under him. Darkness threatened her consciousness as she felt Rhekr still, his cock jerking inside of her. He groaned against her neck, fangs retracting, and kissed the spot gently, his tongue teasing the marks. She shuddered slightly, her body absolutely limp and exhausted, never having experienced an orgasm that intense before.

Rhekr let his body cover hers fully. She relished the weight, and the way he gently kissed her neck again. He threaded his hands through hers and she turned her head so he could capture her lips.

She groaned at the soft kiss, his tongue exploring her mouth tenderly, so in contrast with their rough fucking. She sucked in a deep breath and opened her eyes to fall into the deep green abyss of his. Her heart skipped a beat, the familiar agony filling it once again, infiltrating her senses, and she pulled away.

"I... I need to uh... shower," Sasha stammered. To her relief, Rhekr didn't say a word. Only let her shake his hands from her and scoot out from underneath him as she all but ran away once more. The slamming of the bathroom door echoed through the screaming confusion of her mind as she rubbed at her chest and the bruised and broken heart within it.

Chapter Eleven

SASHA

COOL WATER TRAILED DOWN her body as Sasha leaned her head against the small, tiled shower. She had done it again. Fucked Rhekr, received another mind-blowing orgasm and utter bliss, then immediately ran away. Her fingers traced over her neck, where she had asked him to bite her. She didn't know what had come over her in that moment, but this felt much more intimate than just having sex. With a sigh, Sasha turned the shower off and closed her eyes, listening to her surroundings. She really didn't want to walk out and just find him waiting for her. What would they even say to each other? The way he had kissed her, looked at her after. It made her heart clench.

And that was not something she wanted to deal with at the moment. But eventually, she would have to leave this bathroom. Better to get it over with sooner rather than later.

Sasha steeled her spine and grabbed her dress, flinging it over her still wet body before going to the door. Per her senses, no one was moving about, and when she opened the door, her senses proved correct.

Where had that damn vampire gone?

A splash from outside drew her attention, and she padded over to the small window over the even smaller sink. Darkness had encroached, but the moon shone brightly through the Cyprus trees, and along with her night vision, she could clearly see Rhekr down on the ground. He was bent over, hands wading through the calf-high water he was standing in.

"What in the world?" Sasha muttered before turning around and heading to the door. She didn't try to be quiet as she took the stairs two at a time. She rounded the little cabin, hard ground turning to water within seconds. Wrapping up the length of her dress, she tied it in a knot at her thigh as she made her way over to Rhekr.

"Have you ever gone bayou fishing by moonlight before?" Rhekr murmured, still looking down instead of at her.

"Bayou fishing?" she asked, sure she had misheard the vampire.

His hands moved suddenly and Rhekr straightened, a snake in hand, and to Sasha's surprise, she squealed before reaching out and smacking Rhekr across the back of his head. "The fuck! You startled me."

Rhekr chuckled softly before putting his catch back into the water, and they both watched as the snake glided away. "Would you like to try?"

Sasha sighed and closed her eyes, letting the smells and sounds of the bayou skip across her senses. It was peaceful, quiet from anything human made. The only other person she could sense was Rhekr. When she opened her eyes again, he was looking at her. His eyes held a hint of sadness, longing, and age. Sasha nodded, her mask dropping slightly, allowing her mind to just still, if only for this moment. She could do this. It was better than talking about feelings, at least.

"Sure thing, ol' man. Teach me your bayou fishing ways."

Sasha stared up at the ceiling, the fan doing nothing but circulating the warm air. Her mind was a mess, and she was unable to sleep. She had fun tonight, and not in the 'booze, sex, and dancing' type of fun she usually did to drown out her feelings. No, she had fun in the more peaceful sense of the word.

They had laughed, water splashing around them as they lunged for the amphibians and fish living in the dark waters of the bayou. Her heart constricted a little as Rhekr's unfiltered laugh echoed through her mind. She knew earlier today she had feelings for the vampire, but the night's end cemented them in place. The way his laugh made her laugh, the way his smile made her smile. There was no going back, and she would have to figure out how to get past the festering pain in her heart to let him in. Because from the way he looked at her, the way he touched her, Sasha knew he felt the same way.

Though she wondered if he would hold back too. If he would be the one to pull away from her. He was essentially immortal, while she lived the span of a human life. Sasha closed her eyes and sighed. Just another damn thing to think about. Just one more heartache to be had.

The bed next to her creaked, and Rhekr's voice cut through the darkness. "If you are having trouble sleeping, I could suggest a few things."

Sasha snorted and turned to her side, facing the vampire. He wore a slight grin, a single fang peeking out. It was cute, and something Sasha wished she could see more of. There was so much about him that she didn't know, but she wanted to. "And what things would those be?" she whispered.

His soft chuckle sent warm shivers down her spine, and then her bed moved, scraping the foot across the floor to collide with his. Strong arms warped around her body, and Sasha took a deep breath, burying her face into his neck. He smelled of the bayou, but underneath, she caught hints of just him. His smell was something she could get used to, and Sasha buried herself deeper against him. "You unmasked your scent," she murmured against his neck. His pulse, slow and steady, picked up slightly as her teeth scraped against his skin.

"I wanted you to smell like me," he whispered back, and drew her deeper into his embrace.

They were fully on the one twin size bed now, their legs intertwined. Sasha was already starting to sweat from the heat of their bodies combined with the muggy night air, but she really didn't care. "Cuddling was not what I thought you were going to do with me, ol' man."

Rhekr took a deep breath. "Me neither, but feeling you in my arms reminded me of a time when I used to and I missed it. Thought you wouldn't mind."

Sasha felt tears threaten her eyes, thinking of the last time she was held like this. No, he was right. She really didn't mind. "Was it with the one you lost?"

"Yes, my mate. Over three hundred years ago."

She gripped Rhekr harder, a few tears escaping to slide down her face and onto his neck. Sasha knew anything she could say would be useless, having felt his exact pain before. Instead, she stayed silent and closed her eyes as their breathing deepened and sleep eventually overtook them both.

Chapter Twelve

RHEKR

"REMEMBER WHAT I SAID about Madam Marie?"

His little she-wolf stared at him, sunglasses covering her eyes, and she huffed. "Yes, yes. Play nice. She is more powerful than you."

"And you, little she-wolf. Don't underestimate her. There is nothing she doesn't know. She trades in secrets. Remember that."

Sasha sighed and looked away from him, watching the birds flying overhead.

They had left early, though not early enough in Rhekr's mind. Yet still, he was unable to release his hold on his little she-wolf this morning. Instead, enjoying their tangle of limbs. What he did worry about was how silent Sasha had been since last night, and he caught her looking at him with a haunted look on her face more than once in the last few hours.

He would have to ask what was on her mind once they safely made it from Madam Marie's territory and put these wannabe vampires to rest. In the meantime, though, he enjoyed the view, his gaze skimming over his little she-wolf's golden legs, all the way up to her plump ass encased in cut-off jean shorts. The tight tank top she was wearing left little to the imagination, and she wasn't wearing a bra or underwear under her choice of outfit. He would know, as he watched her dress this morning. Her toned arms were covered by the open button-down shirt he had been wearing yesterday, and he held his smile as his little she-wolf shifted slightly. He didn't miss how the collar of his shirt lifted as she shrugged her shoulder and how her breath deepened slightly.

He continued guiding their boat silently through the Cyprus trees, the water barely moving them at all. They were close, and Rhekr felt the sudden onslaught of magic rest heavy against his body. His little she-wolf stiffened and glanced at him.

Rhekr nodded and leaned forward, handing her a rope. "Tie off the boat on *that* tree." He pointed ahead to a tree which looked no different from the rest, but to a supernatural's sense was actually brimming with magic. He expected his little she-wolf to protest against the order, but she didn't, and instead quickly tied off the boat. Yes, something definitely plagued her mind. and Rhekr would get to the bottom of it, just as soon as they left this place.

Rhekr stood and held out his hand. "Do you trust me?"

To his surprise again, Sasha only arched a brow behind her glasses and placed her hand in his. She let him lift her to her feet before answering him. "I do."

Her words hit him like a sledgehammer to the heart. He knew his little she-wolf wasn't one to trust blindly, and to trust someone she knew for less than a week... he felt beyond honored. A little spark of hope rested within his chest at the possibilities this could open up. The possibility that she wouldn't outright refuse his presence after they dispatched these wannabe vampires from the bayou. But that was something to think about later.

For now, he pulled his little she-wolf closer and jumped off the boat.

Their feet landed on dry dirt, the scent of fresh cut grass assaulting his senses and his little she-wolf sucked in a sharp breath. "What the fuck?"

Rhekr glanced around them, finding the little cabin tucked inside a sun washed grove teaming with daisies and dandelions. It was a far cry from the bayou they had just stepped out of.

The buzzing of wings drew his attention as a dragonfly flew past them. His little she-wolf watched the dragonfly disappear into nothingness behind them, her face drawn tight as she released the hold on his hand and took off her sunglasses. "Okay... would you care to explain?"

He shrugged and started toward the cabin. Based on Madam Marie's mood at the moment, it would either take them hours or minutes to reach it. "Madam Marie is very old, and very powerful. She is of the fae, and this, my dear little she-wolf, is her territory. It is not an illusion. It is very much real."

"Riiight..." His little she-wolf paused, her eyes darting back and forth, before speaking again. "So, like... was that tree a portal to another country or something?"

"Yes and no. It is a portal, but where we walk is not another country. It is a pocket realm, held here by Madam Marie's magic. It is part of a world lost long ago."

His little she-wolf stilled, going silent, as the cabin, which seemed so far away only seconds ago, was now mere feet away. The door to the cabin flew open and Madam Marie stepped out, her long flowing white hair pulled up into a ponytail, showing off the pointed tips of her ears. Sunlight glinted off her mahogany skin, her arms tattooed in silver—the same swirling color from within the depths of her eyes. She wore the same outfit he had ever seen her in. Turn-of-the-century trousers and a button-down vest, no shirt underneath, and sans shoes, like always. She looked down her nose at them from the porch—not a hard thing when you stood around six foot five.

Sasha gaped at her before turning toward Rhekr. "She looks like she is twenty-five, tops!"

Madam Marie growled softly, showing off sharp teeth. "It took you two long enough. I've been waiting for days. Come in, come in. And thank you for the compliment, wolf."

She turned on her heel, going back into the cabin, and Rhekr reached out to stop his little she-wolf from following. "Don't let her looks fool you, Sasha. She is old, and the fae who maintain their youth do so by attaining it in unsavory ways. The moment you cross that threshold, a payment must be given just to leave, and I don't know what she will ask of you. Perhaps I should just go alone."

His little she-wolf glared at him through her glasses and shrugged off his hand. "You can't get rid of me that easily, ol' man. We came here together, and we are going in together."

From inside the cabin came a barking laugh, and with a sigh from him, they both crossed the threshold.

Inside, a low fire crackled as Madam Marie stood in the center of the den. She tapped her foot but didn't offer for them to sit. Which was quite odd for the fae woman, as she was, above all, polite in the old-fashioned sense.

"Let's get straight to the point." She stared off and glanced at Sasha. "The payment I will demand will be from you. I will tell you where the warlock who is making those abominations is, and you will stop him. Got it?"

Rhekr shook his head. "No. We will negotiate."

His little she-wolf growled, "Actually, yes. What is the payment?"

"Sasha," he growled, but both the women in the cabin ignored him.

"Tell me what festers in your heart, wolf. Tell me your story, show me your pain."

Rhekr stiffened as his little she-wolf inhaled a sharp breath. "My pain?"

"Sasha, you don't have to do this. We can find a different way. I'll make payment."

Madam Marie scoffed and threw her hand up in the air. "This is the fastest way. You knew I would be able to point you in the right direction. But if you walk away now, I will bargain with neither of you."

"I lost my mate," Sasha growled. "There, done, that is my pain. I lived through a loss I shouldn't have. Now tell us—"

"That is not your pain," Madam Marie hissed. "Tell me your pain. Feed it to me."

His little she-wolf's eyes widened, as if she finally realized what Madam Marie was asking. Rhekr shook his head slightly. "You don't need to do this. Not here, not now."

"Yes, I do," she whispered and stepped toward Madam Marie. "You want to feed from my pain, you want to feel how I felt? How it still haunts me?"

Madam Maire licked her lips and stepped forward as Sasha's scent changed. Pain laced with anger, shame, and lastly, guilt.

"It was my fault. It was all my fault because I couldn't protect my human mate. I couldn't protect him when my father ripped his head from his body in front of me. How I couldn't avenge my own mate and my brother had to take on the responsibility of killing our father, of taking over the pack when I should have. I grieve every day about what a failure I am, and I still can't pull myself out of the darkness. Every time I wake up, I think about how I failed as a mate and how I should have just given up and died right then and there. At least then, I wouldn't be such a burden anymore. And yet, here I am, still making my brother's life, the pack's life, miserable every time my demons take over."

Rhekr clenched his jaw and watched as a single tear burned a path down Sasha's face. He reached out to her, but she sidestepped him and instead glared at Madam Marie. "Is that what you wanted?"

Madam Marie licked her lips and purred, "That was excellent, my dear. I do love such old festering wounds like yours... and his, in fact."

She turned toward Rhekr and winked. "You two have much in common. Now, do step out while I have a conversation with dear Rhekr here."

He shook his head, ready to protest, but stopped as Sasha touched his shoulder gently. "Just get the information so we can leave this place. I'll be just outside."

Chapter Thirteen

SASHA

SASHA REACHED FOR THE doorknob, knowing she couldn't face looking behind her and seeing Madam Marie. She knew if she did, she would march right up to her and punch her in the face. Then they would never figure out where those twisted monsters were being made. But goddess, help her, she would be back to throttle the damn woman when this was all over.

Sasha flung the door open and stepped through, magic pulling and shoving at the same time, and she stumbled. Her bare feet hit cool stone instead of warm dirt and sun drenched grass. As she sucked in a deep breath, damp air and darkness coated her senses. Her ears rang, and she turned quickly as Rhekr roared her name right before the door slammed shut behind her.

Wrenching the door back open, Sasha was greeted with a janitorial closet. The ringing in her ears finally subsided, and she gently shut the door and turned. Her eyes instantly adjusted to the darkness. A long hallway stretched before her, interrupted only by cell doors, every few feet. Her ears picked up the steady beat of a heart, and Sasha took a deep breath. Inching forward slowly, she examined every step she took, glancing into every cell to make sure they were empty until she came upon the one with the heartbeat.

A young man, looking no older than twenty, stared blankly at the wall before him. Sasha sniffed the air, not sensing an ounce of magic. "Hey," she whispered, and the young man flinched slightly, but continued staring at the wall.

"Hey, shithead." She tried again, and this time, the young man blinked and turned his gaze to meet hers.

Eerie blue eyes swirling with gold flecks met hers, and Sasha stilled. Her flight-or-fight instincts kicked in. While she couldn't sense any magic, she knew this young man was something else. He narrowed his eyes at her, assessing, and Sasha did the same. When he went to turn back toward the wall again, Sasha growled, "Fine, I'll leave you be if you just tell me where in goddess named fuck I am."

"You smell like her," the young man hissed.

"Smell like who?"

The young man sighed and, finally, his rigid posture broke, his shoulders slumping and his chin hitting his chest. "You smell like her. Which means, you were sent by her. You can tell Madam Marie I will not be making a bargain. I can get out of this mess on my own."

Anger instantly filled her veins, warming her from the inside out. So this was another of Madam Maire's victims. Which meant he was on her team, hopefully. "The next time I see that bitch will be when I turn her into a punching bag."

The young man perked up a bit and turned to face her again. "Not a fan, I take it?"

"I only went because my..." She paused and shook her head. "I need to know where I am."

The young man blinked slowly. "Louisiana."

Sasha resisted the urge to roll her eyes. "I know that, but where?"

"New Orleans."

When he didn't say anything else, Sasha sighed. "Look, I'll be straight with you. If you know about Madam Marie, then you obviously know about magic. I am hunting something, someone and I need to know if that someone is here, okay?"

"Vampires," the young man whispered and went back to staring at the wall.

"Rhekr would disagree with calling them that, but yes. I'm hunting whomever is making them."

At the mention of Rhekr, the young man jumped off his bed quickly and was at the front of the cell door within seconds. Sasha took a step back, just out of reach, as he tried to grab her. He squashed his face against the bars and whisper-yelled at her, "Don't let Rhekr come. It is a trap. They need his venom to complete their experiments. That is what is missing..."

The young man trailed off, slumping against the bars until his frail body hit the ground.

Sasha kneeled slowly until she was eye level with him again. His stare was vacant once more, and she felt her heart break slightly. Reaching out, Sasha gently placed her hand on the young man's hand that was still clinging to the cell bar. He didn't register her touch, nor did he seem to hear her when she whispered.

"I'm not going to leave you here. Wherever here is... And I'm not going to let Madam Marie get to you, I promise."

A sudden click, the sound of mechanisms unlocking sounded from the end of the hallway, and Sasha quickly stood as a flood of magic rolled over her. In the doorway stood a figure, and Sasha growled. The sounds of whorls and beeps, along with a muffled scream every few seconds, filtered through behind the figure.

Lights lit up the cellblock, and Sasha winced, looking away to catch the gaze of the young man.

He was staring intently at her, a type of sadness etched in his face. He reached out to grip her hand, as if to comfort her, right before a tsunami of magic rolled through the cellblock and everything went dark.

Pain lanced through her head, her whole body on fire. It took more effort than not to open her eyes, and when she did, nausea rolled through her, and Sasha gagged. The stench of blood and putrid waste permeated her senses. The lights above her were blinding, but Sasha refused to close her eyes, somehow certain if she did, they would never open again. Finally, the pounding in her head subsided enough for her vision to clear, and her nausea settled slightly.

Her body still felt like she had been stretched across a spit and left to roast like a pig. She tried to move, only to find magic surrounding her, pressing her firmly onto the couch she was lying on. Every time she moved to sit up, the pressure would intensify, making her body burn even more.

A sigh echoed from her left, and the couch dipped near her feet. Only then did Sasha realize she was curled up in a fetal position. A hand reached out and patted her ankle. She growled, and a man tsked. "There, there. It won't be long now until that vampire comes to rescue you. And I'm sorry about the magic, but you are quite powerful, and I don't have a cell yet that would be able to keep you contained. Don't worry, though, I'll make sure little Hebert makes you a comfy one soon. In the meantime, enjoy the show."

Sasha's wolf struggled in her mind to take over, to attack and tear apart the magic that held her on this couch. Nausea built slowly again, this time for a totally other reason. Madam Marie had planned this somehow, and Rhekr was going to walk into a trap. For her.

Tears fell from her eyes as pain lanced through her heart. She couldn't lose another one. Not after she was just starting to heal. She would never recover from it. No... No, this was not happening. She was fucking strong, and she was going to make it out of here with Rhekr or die trying.

A commotion reached her ears just as the double doors on the other side of the room slammed open. Relief, followed by undeniable fear, flowed through her as Rhekr prowled into the room, coated from head to toe in blood. The man sitting on the couch stood and stepped in her peripheral. Sasha twitched her finger, trying to move her arm to reach out and grab him, to sink her nails into his flesh, but the burning sensation through her body became too much, and a sob escaped her.

Rhekr bellowed, his face turning savage, and he moved suddenly in front of them. The man laughed and snapped his fingers, a violent storm of magic tearing through the room. More tears streamed down her face as Sasha struggled to breathe until she forgot how to altogether. The warlock before her put his hand out, placing it on Rhekr's chest. She watched as her vampire, the man she loved, tried to fight against the magic as the warlock forced him to kneel.

A rage so primal it had to be from the moon goddess herself filled her veins, and Sasha sank into it until it was all she felt. All the pressure, the burning pain from the magic, disappeared as she pounced.

Time stopped as her hands found the warlock's neck and a sickening snap echoed throughout the room. Locking eyes with Rhekr, Sasha mouthed the words she never thought she would be able to say again as magic exploded around them.

Chapter Fourteen

RHEKR

MAGIC COILED AROUND HIS body, mixing with the very fabric of his being, holding him still in a way no one had been able to before. But he had felt this power before. The power this warlock was displaying wasn't his. No, it was a gift from Madam Marie and Rhekr cursed. He knew it was a trap, but he had to go after Sasha. He couldn't let his little she-wolf pay for his bad judgment. All he cared about right now was getting her out of harm's way, and then he would deal with this warlock and Madam Maire.

He had already dealt with all the monstrous wannabe vampires in the building, ripping off their heads and bathed in their blood before reaching the floor he could feel Sasha on. Her blood still coursed through his veins from the night before, and it was easy to use his magic to track her. Something Madam Marie had not anticipated.

Yet what he had not expected was Madam Marie sharing so much power with a no-named average warlock. He didn't know what their end game was, but as Rhekr locked eyes with Sasha, unable to move a muscle, he knew he was about to fail again. He was going to lose another love of his life, and this time he wouldn't recover from it. As the magic mounted, putting bone-shattering pressure on his body, the warlock reached out and touched him, forcing his knees to buckle. He wanted to say he was sorry, as his little she-wolf blinked slow and long before moving so suddenly, even Rhekr had trouble following her movements.

A sickening crunch rocketed through the silent room, and his eyes went wide as Sasha mouthed 'I love you' right before an explosion of magic ripped them away from each other.

He came to seconds later, ears ringing, and searched the blacked and smoking ruin of the room for his little she-wolf. He spotted her unruly mess of hair under an overturned table against the wall and crawled his way over to her. Pulling her into his lap, he held her face, tears streaming down his own as he rocked her. "Sasha, Sasha. Fucking open your eyes. Don't do this to me. I can't do this again. Please... Please."

He tried to clear the ringing from his ears, to no avail, and reached up to feel sticky wetness running from them. Blood coated his fingertips, and he dipped his head, sobbing until a presence filled the room, announcing someone was behind him.

Gripping Sasha's body tighter, he turned with a snarl to see a wide-eyed kid, not older than twenty and as scrawny as they come, staring at Sasha hanging limp in his arms. The kid blinked rapidly and Rhekr noticed his eyes.

The eyes of the fae.

Now everything made a little more sense. The warlock might have been working with Madam Marie, but he was getting his power from this kid. His hearing came back with a snap, making him grimace, and then all he could feel was his soul breaking as only two sets of hearts beat in the room. His and the kid.

"Save her," Rhekr's voice cracked. "Fucking save her. I will give you anything. Any deal, any bargain. Just bring her back."

The kid cocked his head and took a step forward. "Pretty wolf is dead?"

Rhekr slumped, realizing all too late that this kid was damaged goods. The vacant stare in his eyes was clear as day, but he still had to try.

"Please."

The kid shuffled forward, getting to his hands and knees, and Rhekr had to hold back a snarl as the kid touched Sasha's expressionless face. He turned to Rhekr with a smile and whispered, "It's still there. Don't worry, it's still there."

"What?"

The kid frowned and shook his head. "Her soul. It's still there."

Rhekr gripped Sasha tighter as hope ignited his own soul. "Do it. Do anything you need to do to bring her back."

The kid bit his lip, his eyes going strangely vacant again before he spoke. "Anything?"

Rhekr nodded. "Yes."

The kid giggled before grabbing Rhekr's arm. Pain lanced through him as he felt his life-force splitting in two. Rhekr sucked in a breath, trying to fill his lungs, even though it felt like he was drowning. A second later, another heartbeat filled the air, soft yet strong, as the boy fell to the side.

A small smile etched across his face as he closed his eyes and murmured, "The pretty wolf was nice to me. She doesn't like my mom. She told me she would save me."

Rhekr choked on the air as he filled his lungs, feeling light-headed as he pulled Sasha closer to him. He pressed his ear to her chest, lingering in the sweet sound of her heartbeat until the more sensible part of him took over. He had to get her out of here.

He needed to get her somewhere safe.

To recover.

He hoisted his little she-wolf in his arms and whispered into her hair, "I love you too, Sasha. Don't worry. I'll take care of you." Pulling away, he stepped over the unconscious kid before looking back with a sigh. Sasha would kill him if he left him here. He reached down and tucked the unconscious kid under his arm as well. "Don't worry, I'll take care of him too."

"Run that by me again," Hunter asked as he stared at Sasha, reaching out to take her hand.

Rhekr sat slumped in the most uncomfortable chair in the world, sweat beading down his forehead from the sweltering heat and humidity. The sounds of the bayou trickled in through the screen door of the cabin. Nancy's cabin, to be exact.

After almost losing the love of his life, Rhekr had brought Sasha and the young kid, whose name was Herbert, to the only place he could think of. The wolf pack welcomed all three of them with open arms. A day later, Sasha's brother and his mate, Lily, showed up at their doorstep.

Hunter rubbed his chest slightly, and Rhekr knew how he felt. The twins' bond went deep, and Hunter had felt it when Sasha had died. Rhekr rubbed at his own chest, feeling the bond that attached him to Sasha, just as deeply.

"Herbert, the young fae kid, he used my life-force to bring her back. I feel her too. We are bonded."

Hunter glared at him over the still unconscious state of his little she-wolf. "Bonded how? Like fated mates? Are you mates?"

Rhekr shook his head slightly. "No, no, we are not fated mates in the truest sense of the word, but believe me, I wouldn't trade Sasha for the world. I'm sticking by her for the rest of my life and hers."

Hunter leaned back, seeming satisfied by his answer.

The sudden twitch of Sasha's finger drew Rhekr's attention, and he leapt into the bed, cradling her in his lap within seconds as her eyes slowly blinked open.

"Hey, pretty little she-wolf," he whispered, his voice cracking.

His little she-wolf smiled up at him and reached out, cradling his face in the palm of her hand. "Long time no see, ol' man."

Chapter Fifteen

SASHA

A SMILE STRETCHED ACROSS Sasha's face as Rhekr melted into her hand, turning to kiss her palm. "I would ask if this is the afterlife, but I can hear you breathing, brother." Sasha laughed as she broke eye contact with her vampire to see the relieved look on her brother's face.

"Sasha... nice to know a stop at death's door didn't leave you changed," Hunter grumbled, but reached out to give her a hug.

Sasha chuckled and gave him a tight squeeze back. "I'm sorry I made you worry."

Hunter shook his head and broke the embrace, glancing at Rhekr before addressing her. "I'll always worry about you, but I think maybe a little less going forward. I'll leave you two to catch up."

Sasha didn't say anything until her brother stepped out of the cabin and shut the door. "Alright, ol' man. Tell me why I can feel you in my head and why I feel like I just got the best night's sleep in my life. Also, how am I alive?"

Rhekr settled in behind her, his arms still wrapped around her waist. She didn't mind it, though, and leaned back, getting comfortable as his heavyweight draped around her. Rhekr cleared his throat. "You died, Sasha."

"I figured as much. What did you do to get me back?"

"Begged."

She sighed and turned slightly to catch his mouth with hers, giving him a long overdue kiss. When they finally broke apart, they were both panting, and her body was screaming for her to mount him right then and there.

"You could, but there are ears at the door." Rhekr's voice slipped easily into her mind, and Sasha flinched slightly.

"That's... creepy."

Rhekr chuckled and nuzzled and nipped at her neck, drawing a satisfied growl from her. "Don't worry, you can do it back."

Sasha closed her eyes and concentrated on the feeling of Rhekr in her head. *"Can you hear me?"*

Goddess above, she sounded like a phone ad.

Rhekr snorted and answered in her mind. *"Yes, my little she-wolf. I can hear you. This is the side effect of bringing you back. Part of my life-force lives inside of you now and we are forever connected."*

"Does this mean we can just stare at each other in silence while still yelling at each other?"

Rhekr's laugh echoed through her mind before she could say anything else. "Wait," she echoed out loud. "Part of your life-force... What exactly does that mean?"

"It means we are connected. Forever now."

"Like... *forever* forever? Am I immortal!?" Sasha pushed away, looking at Rhekr with wide eyes.

He took a deep breath, and a sheepish smile spread across his face. "No, Sasha. I think it means I live as long as you do now."

"You think?"

This time, Rhekr shrugged. "All I know is Herbert bound us. Connected us. You don't have to stay with me, but..." He paused and grabbed her face, bringing her in for another kiss. "Sasha, I love you, and I couldn't bear the thought of losing you to death. I wouldn't survive it. Just knowing you're alive and hating me would be enough to get me through the rest of my life."

"Hate... hate?" Sasha stammered as she threw her arms around his neck and kissed him savagely. "I don't hate you. I don't think I ever could. Who is Herbert?"

"A fae kid. Madam Marie's kid, to be exact. I think you met him and promised him—"

"Oh, the young guy in the dungeon! The one with the eyes. Please tell me you took him somewhere safe."

Her words brought a smile to his face. "He saved you, Sasha. Of course I did. Pretty sure he is annoying Nancy and Lily at the moment."

She bit her lip before trying to squirm out of his arms, an idea blossoming in her mind.

"Trying to get away from me so soon, little she-wolf?"

Sasha scoffed. "My wolf is all pent up and needs to run." She paused, eyes hooding slightly, and she heard Rhekr's breath catch as her next words echoed through his mind. *"And you are going to chase me and catch me... if you can, ol' man."*

Rhekr's grip around her loosened immediately. *"Then I suggest you run, little she-wolf."*

Sasha bounced out of bed and sank into her magic. Seconds later, she shook her golden fur and sprinted out the door. A few startled yells greeted her, but her mind was only on one thing.

She leaped over the railing and into the swamp below before reaching dry land and ran with everything she had. Her lungs burned as she dodged trees, leaping over squishy sections of dirt and mud, taking her deeper and deeper into the bayou. She could feel Rhekr closing in on her and his mischievous laugh echoed through her mind just as shadows engulfed her and a pair of muscular arms encircled her from behind.

Her magic swirled over them both, and before she even hit the ground, she was human once more, Rhekr's heavy weight pushing her naked body into the soft ground. She groaned as he kissed her roughly, his cock already hard and pressing against her pussy. She wasn't sure when he decided to shed his clothes, but she was grateful as she lifted her hips and he thrust his cock into her with one long stroke. Her eyes rolled into the back of her head and a whine left her lips as Rhekr pulled out almost fully, only to thrust into her with even more force. Her hands curled in his hair as she felt her orgasm build and tear through her within seconds.

Fuck.

Rhekr knew exactly how she needed to be taken.

She scratched at his back, thrashing underneath him, and in the process, offered her neck to him. Feeling his hot breath over her pulse, she whined, "Fucking bite me."

As his mouth closed over her neck, fangs breaking her skin, the pain and pleasure exploded through her body as another orgasm caught her completely off guard.

Sasha screamed as her pussy clenched, and Rhekr stilled, his cock twitching inside of her. He slowly extracted his fangs and pushed her hair from her face, and she leaned in to lick her own blood off his lips. He groaned, and they sank into a brutal kiss before Sasha broke it off with a growl.

"I need you with me. I love you. And I can't think of any other person I would rather have annoy me for the rest of my life."

Sasha gasped as Rhekr ground against her slowly, his cock hard once more, and hitting her deep. He captured his lips with hers, snagging the bottom one with a fang before releasing it. "I love you too, Sasha. And I would be more than happy to annoy you for the rest of our lives."

Epilogue

RHEKR ~ FIVE MONTHS LATER

RHEKR GROANED AS HE gripped his little she-wolf's hips, watching his cock move in and out of her pussy. She was holding tight to the table he had her bent over. Her pussy clenched, pulsating over his cock as he drove his little she-wolf into her third orgasm. She whined his name, cursing him with a sigh as she slumped over the table. He came seconds later, and caressed her back with his fingertips, lingering on the red marks on her ass from when he spanked her earlier, which had led to this round of fucking.

His little she-wolf arched against his touch, and a satisfied grumble left her lips.

"What was that, little she-wolf?"

"I'm not paying for the damages this time," she answered in his mind, and he glanced around

their small room with a chuckle. It was thoroughly trashed, which was what usually happened. They weren't exactly gentle lovers, and that was one of things he loved so much about his little she-wolf.

He slid out from inside her and scooped her up in his arms, plopping them both onto the overturned bed of the rented motel room. She cuddled up to him and started running her hand through his hair until a buzzing sound permeated the room. They both sighed in unison, and Rhekr reached for their phone, putting it on speaker.

"Speak or we are hanging up."

"Really, that's how you answer the phone?" Nancy's voice trickled out, and his little she-wolf snorted.

"I mean... that's how I usually answer it." Sasha laughed before leaning in a placing a soft kiss on Rhekr's jaw.

"Right, well... returning your call. Spoke to your head witch, Gwen. All her leads have dried up. We got nothing about the whereabouts of Madam Marie. Hebert tried to help too, but..."

She went silent, and Rhekr gave Sasha a knowing glance. She frowned at him and took the phone from his hand. "Go ahead, tell us how his magic went astray this time."

Nancy chuckled. "I mean, I love that kid, but damn, his magic is really all over the place. We have talking alligators now."

"Come again?" Sasha laughed.

"You heard me, woman! The alligators speak now. They are demanding food, poetry, and for us to brush their teeth. Don't fucking ask again. Now... where are you two, and are you coming home yet?"

"Guatemala and no, not yet. We might have a lead. Was there anything else?" Rhekr answered this time.

"Naw, that was it. Miss you, Sasha! And I guess you too, vampire." The phone clicked off as Nancy hung up, and Rhekr tossed it to the side.

His little she-wolf narrowed her eyes. "We still have two hours before we need to meet with the pack down here and go hunting on that lead. What should we do until then?"

Smiling, he pushed his little she-wolf down on the bed, kissing her neck down to her breasts and skimming over her stomach before reaching her thighs. She immediately swung her legs over his shoulders, hands in his hair, and purred. "Alright, fang face. I guess we have time for you to go down on me."

Rhekr gripped her ass and pulled her pussy closer to his face and gave her a generous lick. His little she-wolf arched into his mouth as he flicked his tongue over her clit before sucking on it. *"Oh fuck,"* she whispered in his mind as she moaned out loud.

He focused solely on her clit with his mouth while pushing two fingers into her wet pussy. She groaned and ground down, riding his face and hand until she came within minutes. He chuckled as his she-wolf panted from her release. He rested his head on her hips, closing his eyes for a moment.

"Don't you go falling asleep on me, ol' man. We got a fae bitch to hunt down and destroy." His little she-wolf growled, but her hands held a different tone as she threaded them through his hair.

Rhekr chuckled. "Don't worry. I was just thinking."

"About what?"

"That I wasn't really living until I met you."

His little she-wolf stilled at his words before continuing to run her fingers through his hair. "Same, ol' man. You taught me how to love and live again. And if you decide to run off when you get bored, you will be the next powerful being I decide to destroy."

Rhekr laughed and shook his head, moving to scoop his little she-wolf and the love of his life into his arms. "Sorry to break it to you, my little she-wolf. You're stuck with me for life. I'll never get bored of you."

His little she-wolf laughed and grabbed his jaw, kissing him roughly. "I love you."

"I love you too," he whispered back before glancing at the watch on his wrist.

"You ready to go hunting?"

His little she-wolf growled, a feral grin spreading across her lips. "Always. As long as you are by my side." She held out her hand, and Rhekr did the same, twisting their pinkies together. The same thing they have been doing for the past five months every night. "Forever and always, by your side."

"Forever and always, by your side," Rhekr promised back before kissing his little she-wolf one more time.

The End